LOOKING FOR SMOKE

K.A. Cobell

Heartdrum
An Imprint of HarperCollinsPublishers

For my dad, the first storyteller I ever knew

Chapter 1

MARA RACETTE

Thursday, July 11, 7:15 p.m.

Something about the beat of the drum makes me stop feeling like such a fraud. Its steady pulse quiets all my doubts. Grounds me. My blood thrums through my limbs to my feet, telling me I belong. This land is mine too.

The pounding beat vibrates in my chest as I follow my parents into the circular dance arbor. We pass between crowded sections of bleachers and skirt behind the men sitting in a circle around their drum. Their cries make my throat dry and constrict, like it aches to sing in their rhythm. They pound the leather-bound sticks against the hide as one, the beat getting faster and their voices getting higher.

I weave behind a man filming on a tripod and take the stairs two at a time, slipping into a half-open row just as the older man at the drum, cowboy hat shadowing his face, whacks his stick harder and the others pause. A younger man in a flat-billed baseball cap sings alone, a wail sinking into his undulating voice, and then each of them hits the drum in sync again. Their voices rise to intertwine with his like a united battle cry.

Goose bumps rise on my skin as I settle into the bleacher bench and focus on the powwow dancers in the circle of turf, just past the drum groups. Women in beaded dresses with colorful shawls and men in buckskin regalia with feathered shoulder and back bustles dance to the beat. They have bells strapped around their legs and plumes of feathers in their hands. Some of their faces are painted in the old ways, with black and red, making them look fierce, powerful. Old women, little kids no older than four years, and everyone in between spin and sway to the drum song. Everyone feels the calling in their bones.

They all belong.

Beside me, Dad's head bobs to the beat. His black hair trembles over his shoulder with each movement until he pushes it behind his ear, a turquoise ring glinting on his thumb. Mom taps her foot on my other side, one leg slung over the other. Her blond hair is tucked in a bun at the back of her neck, just peeking out of the baseball cap she needs to protect her pale skin from the summer sun.

I sit still in the middle, trying to ease into my place between them. Like always.

The low sun beats down on us, lighting up the bits of dust easing through the arena on the slight breeze. It smells like dirt and horses and frying grease. It smells like Indian Days.

We've traveled here most years to attend our tribe's annual four-day celebration with thousands of other attendees, where we enjoy Native American traditions like powwow dancing and drumming, stick games, and horse relay races. I thought it would feel different this year, though. Now that we live here, I thought I'd feel less like a visitor. I'm sitting up here watching it all unfold just like before . . . one step removed. Maybe that's how it'll always be.

I slip my phone out of my pocket to take a picture of the expansive scenery in front of us and the mass of color and movement below us. The Rockies tower in the distance, smears of snow visible on some of the mountain range's jagged peaks, Glacier National Park hidden on their opposite side. The mostly treeless, low rolling plains sprawl out endlessly in every other direction, making the blue sky above this tiny town look massive.

Below us, hundreds of dance competitors are on the circular field for Grand Entry, grouped into the categories of dance they'll compete in during the powwows over the next few days. They bounce their way around the arbor, creating a rainbow spiral of color and texture, until their circle parts and the final beat thuds.

The Elder who led the dancers in for Grand Entry stands in the center of the arbor, garbed in his traditional regalia. His quillwork breastplate hangs still over his chest. There's a steadiness around him in the sudden quiet. He's flanked by Native war veterans holding national and tribal flags, and the head man and woman dancers. Higher even than the flags they hold is the eagle staff in the old man's hand.

The Elder raises the staff lined with eagle feathers, and we all stand as the drum group starts the Flag Song, honoring the colors and, more significantly, honoring the eagle staff—the first flags of this land.

I may still be figuring out how I fit in here, but I feel that pull, that reverence, watching the Elder honor the eagle feathers and our tribal Nation. Like those hanging feathers, I sway in time with the beat until the drummers stop and grip the sticks in their hands, catching their breath. My chest feels empty with the beat's sudden absence. Only the gentle jingling of the dancers' bells leaving the circular field matches the lingering buzz threading my skin.

The audience sits back down. "I'll get us some frybread," Mom says, touching my shoulder as she sidesteps past us. Dad squeezes her hand before she dips down the stairs with an easy smile. She knows she doesn't exactly belong here, but she doesn't mind. She's been part of this world longer than I have. She may not be Native herself, but she has Dad.

Dad swings his arm over my shoulders. "You should've learned." He nods toward the dancers gathering at the bottom of our section. I recognize a few of the girls from school. Their hair is tied back into sleek braids adorned with feathers and colorful ribbons. Intricate beadwork in striped patterns cascades over some of their shoulders and hangs in fringes down their backs.

The tallest of the group, Loren Arnoux, wears a sky-blue jingle dress. Rows of slender, cone-shaped, rolled tins line the entire skirt of the dress. One row loops around her chest and upper arms. A belt of rainbow beadwork and matching cuffs hanging on her wrists glimmer in the sun as she leaves the group. She's stunning. All their regalia is. Whether they've been passed down in their families or made only recently, each piece is painstakingly handcrafted. Every colored glass bead stitched with precision. Every piece of leather fringe cut just so.

"Maybe," I finally answer over the garbled conversations around us. Part of me wishes I did learn to dance . . . a bigger part of me wonders what other people would think. If I'd even be accepted out there. If it would be anything like the last few months at my new school, I'm glad I never learned.

Even now, the worst of the group, Samantha White Tail, watches my mom pass by, then glances my way with heavily lined eyes and a curled lip, hand sliding over her intricate regalia as if to remind me I'm not wearing any. I might be higher than her in the bleachers, but she's still looking down on me. She'd be sure to find a way to make me feel like more of an outsider if I were out there.

A mix of annoyance and anger curls my fingers into fists. She doesn't know anything about me.

She didn't bother to try.

I raise my fist to flip her the bird, but not before Dad notices the tense energy between us. His body goes still, as does my quarter of a bird. He opens his mouth to ask, but the emcee taps the microphone just in time.

I shrug off Samantha's rude stare as the murmuring dies down and relax into my seat like nothing happened.

Nothing Dad needs to know about at least.

The emcee's voice blares into the arbor. "Ladies and gentlemen, put your hands together one more time. Our first Grand Entry of this year's North American Indian Days . . . what an honor it is to be here!" The bleachers erupt with whistles and cheers. "Hoh man, you guys look good out there! And let me hear you holler for our host drum group, the Yellow Mountain Singers!"

The drummers raise their hands and nod to the cheering crowd before regripping their sticks.

"Thank you, thank you. And thank you to all of our wonderful dancers out there and all our concession businesses who came out. If you haven't grabbed yourself a frybread, you better do it before they close down all the stands later on, hey. I know I've had a few myself." The emcee laughs and adjusts his flat-billed cap.

"I know you competitors are ready to get out there and show us who the best dancers are, but we have something special happening here first." He clears his throat and bobs his head a few times. "The Arnoux family is going to do an Honor Song."

Even the visitors here must feel the air still.

"As most of you know, the Arnoux family has been through quite a lot the last couple of years. Rayanne 'Charging At Night' Arnoux went missing a few months ago." He pauses, his eyes moving over

5

the audience as he gives the moment the reverence it deserves. It happened just a few weeks after we moved here: Rayanne, Loren Arnoux's older sister, never showed up at school one day and hasn't been seen since. It didn't exactly help me settle in here. "Her disappearance is one we've felt deeply here in Browning. This is a terrible tragedy to strike the Blackfeet Nation, one that happens far too often, and we band together in prayer for our lost member.

"Rayanne was raised by her grandmother, Geraldine, and her grandfather, Dillon. Dillon Arnoux passed away close to two years ago, and even though Rayanne hasn't been brought home yet, the family would still like to honor Dillon here at the North American Indian Days, when so many of our Blackfeet tribal members have come out."

I find Loren Arnoux a few sections of bleachers away, near the emcee. She stands tall, her delicate chin tilted up, but her face is dark, her jingle dress still as stone.

The emcee pulls out a paper and smooths it across his jeans. "Dillon 'Weasel Moccasins' Arnoux was a very respected member of our community. He served six years on the tribal council and did a lot of great work helping the tribe develop ecotourism businesses on the reservation. He was a veteran who gave many years in service of this country. He is honored by his wife, Geraldine 'Good Shield Woman,' and his granddaughter, Loren 'Different Black Bird,' along with three brothers, many cousins, in-laws, nieces, and nephews."

The emcee nods to the group of drummers. They remove their hats. Their eyes dart between each other, a shadow passing over their circle, and the old man taps his stick against the hide. The group joins him like one mind, one body, gently pounding a soft beat.

"They ask for these people to please come forward for the give-away." He rattles off a list of names, but my mind is already sinking into the subtle beating of the drums. Until I hear *Racette*.

Dad grips my knee. "Mara Racette," he whispers. I forget how to move. Everyone in the bleachers has already stood for the Honor Song. Dad urges me to my feet and shoves me toward the stairs. I pass Mom on the way down, her hands full of greasy concessions and her mouth hanging open.

I slip to the bottom of the bleachers as Loren and her grandmother, swathed in a yellow shawl with long baby-blue fringe, enter the circular arena with their family members. I'm next to the emcee's table, hair damp against my neck, before I really even know what's happening.

BRODY CLARK
Thursday, July 11, 7:30 p.m.

Dad used to say all change comes with a warning first. He called it a sacred Blackfeet proverb—that's what he said about all the one-liners he pulled straight from his butt. He loved spewing that old Indian wisdom like a bad cough.

The thing is, he was wrong.

Maybe you can see change coming sometimes, like how he saw the warning signs that Mom was going to leave us. She got tired of helping Dad scrape by and split. Found a man with money and started a new family. She decided she wanted an entirely different life.

I didn't. Screw that.

A couple years after that, Dad had a heart attack and slunk dead in front of me. I was only twelve. There was no warning for that. No signs to see. Only me and my older brother, Jason, fighting against the ripple effects of it.

There was no warning that Loren Arnoux's sister was going to disappear and turn our whole friend group upside down.

You can't prepare for change. The best you can do is try like hell to get back to how things used to be.

Or as close to it as you can get.

My brother, Jason, turns off the emcee microphone and tucks it under his arm as the drum group increases their intensity and begins the Honor Song for the Arnouxs. Loren's grandma, Geraldine, leads the procession of dancers onto the circle of turf, gripping a framed picture of her late husband, who's holding both Loren and Rayanne on his lap in the old photo. The other Elders of the family, probably Dillon's siblings, dance alongside Geraldine, with Loren and other younger family members in a group behind. They step in time with the drums, moving slowly around the circle. Plumes bob. Bells jingle.

The audience in the circle of bleachers hardly moves after they stand to watch the procession. I shuffle past Jason and his co-announcer and stand in front of the emcee table to wait for the giveaway. I would've been surprised to hear Jason include my name on the give-away list if I hadn't read it over his shoulder a few minutes ago. I guess Loren still appreciates me even if she's been a recluse lately. Even if my dumb jokes don't make her laugh like they used to.

Even if I haven't exactly been there for her since her sister vanished.

Maybe that means we really could go back to how things were before all this. With a little more time. More patience.

Loren's best friend, Samantha White Tail, appears at my side. Even their friendship got all screwed up after Rayanne's disappearance. You can see it in the way Samantha stands tense. Face sunken.

Eyes hard. A choker of red, yellow, and blue patterned beadwork locks around her neck, matching several pieces in her regalia. A single feather sticks up from her beadwork headband, and two long braids hang down her chest. Her competition number card is pinned to her shawl, which she grips the edges of like she's holding on for dear life.

As the others who were called for the giveaway approach, I follow Samantha's gaze to the slow procession in the arena. The Arnouxs are dancing to honor the grandpa—but we're all thinking of Rayanne.

I didn't know Rayanne like I know her sister, Loren. I guess I knew her as much as you'd know anyone on the rez. Knew her enough to know she had a loud mouth, a weakness for studious-type kids, and a pretty face smooth as polished leather. Knew how much Loren loved her. Knew even Eli First Kill had an eye on her.

The drummers' voices bring me back to three years ago. To the giveaway I helped Jason organize for our dad. I was pretty broken then, but my brother picked me up. Taught me to understand Dad's journey. Life and death don't look much different, besides the social aspect of it. We still remember him. Carry his wisdom. We honored him, gave gifts in his name, just as Loren does now.

The procession returns to us. Loren gathers an armful of Pendleton wool blankets, and for a strange beat, I see her years into the future, walking toward me with freshly folded laundry, kids hanging on her legs with her same mud-brown hair. Smiling. Like she'd ever want that. Like I could ever have that. I blink the image away as her cousin scoops up some bright shawls behind her, fringe spewing from her arms.

Eli First Kill appears on the other side of Samantha, kid sister in tow, as usual. Without his dad, as usual. His eyes are barely wider than normal, only noticeable to a best friend and cousin like myself.

The new girl, Mara Racette, freezes at Eli First Kill's other side, light brown hair hanging bluntly above her shoulders. Her wide eyes are hard to miss, like a doe's in an open field the moment I raise my rifle and finger the trigger.

Yeah, First Kill was right about her. As he always is.

She doesn't belong here. Doesn't want to either.

Loren's cousin pulls an older, non-Native couple from the audience and gives them a shawl and a blanket to honor her grandpa. The couple is probably used to the idea that a person being honored should be *receiving* gifts. But it's the opposite for us—we give to others, even strangers, in their name.

Loren places a folded blanket into my arms, pulling my gaze from the couple. Her honey-brown eyes are rimmed with red, and black makeup smears at the corners. I give her a hug, patting the small of her back before she moves down the line and presses the last blanket into the new girl's arms. Loren puts a hand on her shoulder and leans in close, speaking words I'd never be able to hear even if the drummers weren't still singing.

Beats me why Loren wanted to include the new girl. I've never seen Loren speak to her unless she *had* to.

New-Girl-Mara secures the square of blanket to her chest like Loren might change her mind and snatch it back.

Maybe she should.

Next to me, Samantha White Tail is given a dark blue shawl, even more intricate than the one she already wears. She sets down a black backpack and pulls the shawl from her shoulders and unpins her competition number. Loren helps her repin it to the new shawl as tears spill over Samantha's cheeks.

Looks like she's crying about a lot more than the gift, but it's not like I'd know anything about that.

As Loren's cousins hand out small pieces of handmade jewelry to random people seated in the audience, I feel a collective intake of breath and follow the gazes from the bleachers beside us across the circle. Loren's grandma, Geraldine, leads in two white horses with red and blue beadwork plates on their faces. Eli First Kill's eyes dart between the line of people gripping gifts and back to the horses coming toward us.

The family members part, and Geraldine steps up to Eli. The drumming stops. "Where's your dad, Eli?"

The color leeches out of his face. "Gone on a work contract." His voice is barely audible as the row of us shifts to hear their exchange.

"Will you accept this gift—our finest horses—on his behalf? In honor of my Dillon?"

Nobody moves. The gift is massive. Humbling. It honors Loren's grandpa deeply.

Color seeps back into Eli's skin in red half-moons under his eyes. He nods once, and Geraldine places the leather reins into his hand and pats his shoulder twice.

"Your dad was there for me in a tough time and helped me in a way nobody else could."

Eli's jaw pulses before he says something else to her—probably something along the lines of, at least his dad was there for *somebody*.

Eli First Kill's dad works contracting gigs, but because there isn't much construction happening in a small town like Browning, he has to travel for work for days at a time. I don't know if it's better or worse when he *is* around. Eli never talks about it, but everyone knows his dad is a meth addict.

Eli wipes his eyes with the back of his hand and then eases his shoulders down, sinking back into his typical posture. Cocky. Un-ruffled. Owning the land beneath his feet. He has that way about him, Eli First Kill.

The air is dead around us. Only the horsetails swish.

Geraldine nods, and subtle jingling brings life back into the air as the family members leave the circle of the dance arbor, melding into groups of dancers waiting in front of the bleachers or slipping into the stands.

I follow Samantha White Tail toward the break in the bleachers, her old shawl twisting in her tight, white-knuckled grip. She looks like she's in a hurry to go teepee-creeping until the incoming Golden Age dancers block her path.

All of us from the giveaway are backed up, waiting for the dancers to move. I stare at the geometric beadwork stitched onto the carry loop of Samantha's backpack until Jason announces the dancers into the circle to the beat of another drum song. Just as we're moving, Jason hands the mic to the other announcer and steps away from the emcee table, blocking Samantha's path again. He gives Geraldine an upward nod. "I'm sure you want a picture of everyone," he says, "in his honor."

Geraldine nods. "Sure."

Jason puts a hand on Samantha's shoulder and ushers the group of us holding large gifts from the giveaway past the drummers and between the bleachers. Loren and Geraldine walk with Eli, fingering the horse's reins like it's painful to really let them go. I don't know what the First Kills will do with such fine horses, besides parade them in and out of Indian Days every year.

Eli's dad may just sell them for drug money.

We pass a tribal cop, Detective Youngbull, at the back of the bleachers on our way toward the concession tents. He's in his plain clothes, here to enjoy the powwow like everyone else, but he's got his chest puffed out with a cop's usual arrogance. Thinking he's all somethin'. It only got worse when he became a detective last year. Dry dirt shifts beneath our feet as Jason gives him an upward nod.

Samantha's gaze clings to Youngbull as she bites her lip, either because she's wary around law enforcement like a lot of us are or because she'd like to wrap him around her finger.

I'd put money on the second one.

I wonder what Detective Youngbull felt when we honored Dillon Arnoux—the grandpa of the girl he's failed to locate. Would ol' Dillon have given him even more hell than Geraldine? Does guilt weigh down his gut just hearing the name *Arnoux*?

Instead of going left to the many rows of crowded vendor tents, we hook a right toward a quiet area of trailers parked tight like a fresh pack of cigarettes. Jason finally says, "This'll work." Sweat shines on his forehead as he waves us into a group between two rows of horse trailers, the distant mountain range creating a jagged backdrop. We inch together, a group of Blackfeet, two horses, and a couple of light-haired, non-Native visitors who know nothing about who we honor. Or why.

Jason takes several pictures before he returns Geraldine's phone. Sweat drips down my back in the harsh sunlight. He catches my gaze for a beat and digs his fingers into my shoulder like only a big brother can before the large group breaks apart into separate conversations.

I head straight to the horses, rubbing my shoulder. "What did the First Kills ever do to deserve this?" I ask as I run my hand down one of the horse's necks.

"Psh." Eli's cheek splits into an angled smile. "Usually, we did *something*, and usually, we deserve a beating for it."

I pat the horse's sturdy back, suddenly hoping his dad will sell the horses to Jason and me. Even if he uses the money for drugs. "Ol' Geraldine must have you confused with some other First Kills."

Eli's brows waggle. "Better leave now before she realizes her mistake."

"No, Eli," his kid sister, Cherie, says, stubbornness laced into her high-pitched voice. Her crow-black hair is in perfect braids, and a shoe is untied. "We are *not* missing the intertribal dance. That's the only one I can do!"

"I know, I know," Eli says. He glances over the groups still mingling around us, pausing to catch Samantha's lingering gaze, then eyes the horse trailers. "We just need to get these horses settled somewhere."

Samantha peels her eyes from Eli and whispers to Loren, her talon-like nails digging into her arm, but Samantha turns her back the instant she sees me watching her. Of course. She's made it pretty clear she's not interested in me.

Loren whispers something and shrugs out of Samantha's grip. I only catch one word: "Later."

"They're beautiful," New-Girl-Mara says as she approaches us, blocking my view of Loren and Samantha. I guess she's done with her conversation with Geraldine and the random visitors. Probably trying to learn more about our culture just like them. Her eyes dart briefly to Eli and me, then to the horses as she rubs one of their soft noses.

"Do you ride?" Cherie asks.

Mara's full lips part into a hesitant smile. "It's been a while."

"My big brother and Little Bro do. They're doing Indian Relay Races tomorrow!"

"Little Bro?" Her eyes flick back up to me. Measuring. Judging. Why did Loren even want her here? She's never been a part of any of this. Never wanted to be.

"That's what everyone calls Brody," Eli says as he slaps a hand to my chest. "He was always following around big brother Jason, so little brother Brody became Little Bro. To *friends*."

My dad coined the nickname. I used to like it. Now it doesn't matter either way. It's stuck.

"And that's Eli First Kill," Cherie says, pointing directly at Eli's face. "And I'm just Cherie."

Mara rests her hand on the horse's neck. "And I'm just Mara."

"Are you doing the intertribal dance?" Cherie's eyes light up. "We can without regalia!"

I laugh and elbow Eli's arm before Mara can answer. "Yeah, she could rally up with the *other visitors*. Where she belongs."

The smile New-Girl-Mara had drops.

"Anyway." I clear my throat. "*We* have to get back to the arbor." I hope she doesn't miss the inflection.

We lead the horses between the trailers, kicking up enough dust to make Mara cough. Geraldine emerges with a couple of visitors from the opposite end of a trailer and heads toward the arbor and the crowds, still in deep teaching mode. Loren sidles up to Eli as we make our way down the main dirt path. "Take care of the horses," she says, a glint in her red-rimmed eyes. "Don't make us be Indian givers."

"That's very offensive," I deadpan.

Loren laughs, but it's not the deep, rolling sound I'm used to. It's still too flat. Too lifeless. I wish I could take that from her.

We pass Youngbull again at the break in the bleachers, the Golden Age category still dancing behind him. He trains his watchful gaze on Loren until we walk far enough that the concession trucks finally block his view.

I bet that guilt for being a total failure does eat him up inside.

Loren doesn't seem to notice his eyes on her. Or she's gotten good at ignoring it. "I don't know what to tell you, Eli First Kill," she says. "Your dad must've had some way with my grandma. I've never even seen them talk—"

Eli raises his palms. "I know less than you do, and I'd like to keep it that way."

Loren smiles again, but it doesn't reach her eyes. She squints as she walks, always trying to figure out the puzzle of Eli First Kill. He has a way of opening up just enough to keep you around and shutting back down to keep you wondering over him. He wasn't always like that.

The trick now is to let him be. Let him keep his secrets.

Works for me.

"I'll pass along the appreciation," he finally says. "Whether deserved or not."

Loren nods as we tie up the horses.

"And I'm so sorry they still haven't found Rayanne." Eli practically whispers it. Like saying it out loud is what makes her situation final. Or he's just protecting Cherie from hearing anything.

Loren somehow smiles and frowns at the same time. I pull her to my side, though my shirt sticks to the sweat on my skin.

"Yeah. Me too." She unfolds herself from my arm and makes a show of checking the competition number on her jingle dress. "It'll be weird dancing without Rayanne." Her voice is suddenly distant.

Monotone. So far from the Loren she used to be before all this crap. The Loren that used to make me cry laughing. The one I could picture filling up a row with kids together at powwow. She smooths the number again. I want to take her back to how things used to be, before Rayanne disappeared.

But I can't.

"That's the main reason I gifted her shawl to Samantha. So I could still feel her out there."

She doesn't have to say it—most of us know Rayanne is never going to be found. Tribal police have all but officially stated she's presumed dead.

Maybe that's why they don't seem too bothered about finding out what happened to her anymore.

They know she's already past saving.

I force a smile. "That's a nice idea. She's with you, though. In life or death, she's in your blood. She's always with you."

"Thanks." She glances up and down the dirt road, scanning the faces in the concession lines and crowd heading back into the bleachers. "Well, I should find Samantha. She said she'd do the intertribal dance with me."

"Good luck in the competition," Eli says as Cherie drags him toward a line of port-a-potties.

"I'll miss you out there," Loren calls after him. "You would've won this year."

He doesn't even glance back.

"Judge Connie 'Running Mouth' will miss you too," I yell. "And ol' Ron 'Sits With Crack.'" He doesn't turn but his head tips back in laughter at my new Indian nicknames for the judges.

Loren rolls her eyes in typical fashion but almost laughs.

I yank my shirt away from my damp chest, fanning myself. "You could win too."

She shrugs, but a smile tugs at her lips.

"Kill it out there."

A shadow slinks into her eyes, but she's gone before I realize what I've said.

Chapter 2

LOREN ARNOUX

Thursday, July 11, 8:00 p.m.

The back of my throat still burns. As much as I try to swallow it down, it stays there. Grandma adjusts my choker and hairpieces even though I'm about to go shake them out of place anyway. Behind her and my cousins, Jason raises the mic. "Powwow people, time for an inter-tribal dance! All are welcome. Get down there! Grab your neighbor, make 'em dance! We have a new drum group on the powwow circuit here, coming to us from Crow Agency . . . Return of the Buffalo! Make some noise for 'em!"

The drummers begin the song, and I hop onto the field, my jingle dress shaking in time. I see Mara through the jolting roaches of porcupine hair on the men's heads in front of me. She clutches the wool blanket in the bleachers and watches me. I give her an upward nod and bounce to the drumming, letting the beat and the jingling around me distract me from the clawing pain in my stomach. No matter what I give to that beast, it never leaves, not really. It's like a gaping pit, crumbling more pieces of me into it every day.

Sometimes I wonder if it will ever stop or if it'll eat away at me until there's nothing left to take.

My sister, Rayanne, won her age division for her fancy shawl danc-ing last year. She moved like a hot flame. She twirled and bounced like fire spreading across a decaying tree, her heat licking everything in its path. Her shawl flashed like the tips of flames in the dead of night. Like she couldn't be slowed and she knew it.

I desperately scan the crowded arena for Samantha. She said she'd be here—I made sure of it. I need to see that shawl. It may not move like flame anymore, but I'd settle for smoke.

A few dancers from every category dance to the intertribal song, as well as some casually dressed attendees, creating a sea of color and motion. I spring in time with the beat, hoping to see the flap of the dark blue shawl. Hoping for a tiny piece of Rayanne—my Ray Bear.

It's always been me and her. Today, we honored Grandpa, who I miss terribly, but my sister's absence in that arbor is the worst pain I've ever felt.

The drum is the only thing keeping my heart in check.

Amid the explosions of color is a splotch of eerie black. Eli First Kill stands at the base of the bleachers near the emcee, his black T-shirt clinging to his broad frame and folded arms. He claims he's done dancing. Even in the midst of the drumming, his face is cold, his body still as Chief Mountain.

Eli First Kill danced like an attacking mountain lion, feet barely touching the ground, chaotic but intentional. All taut muscle and powerful shocks rippling through his regalia. He posed to every beat-stop like he was making the music himself. Now he thinks he's over that. That it was nothing but a phase. The way his gaze clings to the quaking twin bustles in front of me makes me doubt it.

But then again, Eli First Kill has a way of making you doubt things.

After the song ends, I continue to scour through crowds of dancers leaving the arbor for Samantha. They meld into the bleachers, scatter to the lines of tents. Why wasn't she here? Why would she ditch me when she knew I wanted her out there? I shouldn't be surprised after how she's acted the last three months.

People in my life have disappeared one by one. My dad split before I was even born. My mom lost herself a piece at a time to drugs until she up and left. Grandpa died. Then my sister vanished, and in the wake of it, I withdrew and disappeared into myself.

Sam *let* me. She didn't show up for me like a best friend should've. Hardly bothered to check in. Never asked how I was holding up.

She wasn't there. And she still isn't.

Hot anger pools in the back of my head. I don't know why I thought giving the shawl to Sam was a good idea after all this. Why I thought seeing her dancing in it would repair our strangled relationship and patch up my broken heart.

Sam was supposed to make me feel better, but now the anger coils around my neck.

MARA RACETTE
Thursday, July 11, 8:10 p.m.

I grip the blanket as Dad and Mom both lean in, waiting for me to say something. The heavy wool is making my legs sweat, but I can't put it down. I'm not sure what to make of all this . . . My thoughts are knotted. The triangle view I have of the crowded dance arbor between my parents' faces can't even distract me.

"What did she say?" Dad finally asks, swirling his giant cup of lemonade. "Why did they single you out to be in the giveaway?" There's a lilt of hope in his voice, and it makes me feel suddenly defensive.

"Nothing important." But I'm already shaking my head at my own lie. I just don't know what to make of it yet. I never told my parents the extent of my high school misery here—how some kids treat me like an outcast. I didn't exactly try very hard to make friends at first. I was bitter about being here and nervous about fitting in. But it seems like it wouldn't have made a difference anyway . . . they decided I was an outsider without even giving me a chance.

Dad thought for sure I'd fit right in because *he* always did. I guess the difference is, when you grow up here, you never have to prove you belong. You just do.

The last thing I wanted was for Mom and Dad to get worked up or try to do something about it. They feel guilty enough for up and moving us here with only three months of my junior year left. And Dad feels guilty enough about why.

It's not just his fault we're here, though. It's mine too.

Dad was only trying to help.

Still, I don't want them making a bigger deal about it all than they should, so I've kept my mouth shut.

And this time, I can handle it myself.

Mom leans back a hair and widens my view. Eli First Kill stands at the base of the circular bleachers, hands jammed into his jean pockets. His black hair sticks straight up on top and cascades down the back of his head to his neck, blending into his dark T-shirt. It's messy by design, just like every other part of him.

He stares at the dancers, some in regalia and some not, moving in a purposeful circle around the arena. Little Cherie bounces a few feet in front of him, emphasizing how wholly motionless he is. I don't know how I can sit here and admire that angled face with those proud cheekbones and that jawline that looks like it was carved straight out of mountain rock.

His personality and his tongue are as sharp as all those angles.

Seeing him with his little sister is the only time he's seemed like a warm person with actual feelings.

Loren bobs in front of us. She nods my way, then continues onward, her head on a constant swivel, until she sees Eli First Kill, but he doesn't return her gaze. His is lost somewhere between the end of his long nose and the lively dancers passing him by.

"Tell us," Mom says as she watches Loren slip in and out of the other dancers.

"Rayanne wanted Loren to be my friend or something." I hand her the blanket and stand. "I'm heading to the bathroom."

I don't need to tell them everything. I don't need to tell them that Rayanne apparently thought Loren and her friends were too cold to me when I moved in and that they shouldn't have treated me like such an outsider. Rayanne and I barely ever exchanged more than a hello, and now three months after she's disappeared . . . *her* words are the first ones to try to bring me in.

Sure, it almost brought tears to my eyes when Loren admitted it. I wanted to believe her when she placed the blanket into my arms and apologized, but it's too soon to tell.

I'll believe it if she honors her grandpa by doing more than just gifting me a blanket and uttering a few words.

I skirt down the stairs just as the drumming stops. Brody sits by his much older brother, Jason, and some other guy at the emcee table. He watches me walk by, slowly unscrewing his water bottle. His muted black hair is the same length as mine, ends dangling against his shoulders and framing his sweaty face. I have to shield my eyes as I round the corner onto the dirt path. The sun hangs low on the horizon, baking whatever moisture is left in the air.

I pull my heavy hair away from my neck, and my elbow collides with bone. I spin around to see Loren Arnoux cupping her chin. "Watch it!" she says through her teeth.

I rub my elbow as her eyes bore into me. "Sorry." I don't really know why I apologize. I was slowly walking, minding my own business.

She looks me up and down, waggling her jaw open and closed. "Why are you even here?"

I bite my tongue and nod my head. That answers that, I guess.

She rubs her chin and turns mid–eye roll, then stops dead in her tracks. Her arms drop to her sides, and she grips the long tins sewn onto her dress. When she turns back, her anger is already gone without a trace.

She fidgets with her beaded collar like it's actually choking her. "I'm sorry." Meaningless words again.

"Sure you are." I want to walk away. I don't need or want her fake apologies, even if it makes her feel better about her sister being gone. But I can't bring myself to.

Her eyes glint with suppressed tears, and she looks up at the dimming sky. "It's not even about you. I'm just so . . . angry. All the time."

Of course I know what she's referring to. "I'm sorry." This time when I say it, I do mean it.

"It's like if it doesn't lash out sometimes, it's going to choke me from the inside." She almost looks scared as she says it, and I can't help but feel bad for her. "But that's not your problem—I meant what I said to you. Sorry I snapped. I just can't find Samantha, and it's making me hate her right now."

"The one you gave the shawl to?" I ask like I don't remember who Samantha is . . . like I'm not the one who actually hates her.

She pats the corners of her eyes and inhales shakily. "That was my sister's shawl. I wanted to see it dancing again, but Sam didn't show up."

I nod and scan the path. "I'll help you look for her." We head into the rows of vendor and concession tents, scanning the groups of people milling around. We circle a pavilion of crowded picnic tables and turn around when we reach an Indian Days camping area full of teepees and RVs.

Loren subtly jingles with each step and grips her arms tight. "Sam wanted to talk to me right after the pictures, but I brushed her off and told her to wait until after the intertribal dance, like we planned. It seemed like something was wrong . . . I need to check on her."

I wait for her to say more, but her voice fades.

This isn't only about Samantha.

Loren hardly looks at the people. Her gaze filters through everyone's goods in the next row of tents. There are stands filled with turquoise jewelry, intricate dream catchers, and purses and bags with patterned beadwork.

The scent of smoked leather overpowers the dust in the air as we pass a tent with handcrafted moccasins. Some are short and plain, with a few beads near the ties. Others are tall, with panels of beadwork up the entire length of the calves.

That smoky smell reminds me of Grandma Racette. Before she died, she always sent a pair of baby moccasins to each grandchild, starting with my older cousins and ending with me. I pulled mine out a few years ago when I was showing my baby box to a friend, the leathery scent hovering around us. She gushed about them and said she wanted some just like it for her *Indian Halloween costume*.

That was the first time I realized my friends in Bozeman would never entirely understand me and my culture. They'd never feel that pride and deep respect for the traditions at my back and the real, present-day tribe I'm an actual citizen of.

But now being in Browning, surrounded by other Blackfeet, I still worry I'll never be understood or accepted.

Grandma Racette got sick and died before she could teach me to bead or make quillwork. If she were still here, maybe I'd be out there dancing with her instead of sitting in the bleachers. Maybe I wouldn't feel so separate.

Loren runs her hands over the moccasins displayed in the front. "I just wish we knew where she was, you know?"

Samantha can't have gone far. "She's around here somewhere."

"No." She sniffs. "Not Sam."

Rayanne. I follow Loren back onto the main path toward the dance arbor. "Are they still looking for her?"

She digs her fingers into her temples. "Not hard enough."

Eli First Kill strolls through the break in the bleachers, Cherie tagging along behind him. I have the immediate urge to make a bee-line in the opposite direction, but he falls in stride on the other side of Loren.

"You're missing the tiny-tots fancy dancing," he says. "You could learn a thing or two."

Loren smiles, reining in her earlier emotions. I'd never guess she only just had tears in her eyes.

"Where are you heading?" He doesn't even spare me a glance.

Loren stops. Would she notice if I kept going? But I don't. She scans the path again. "We're looking for Sam. She wanted to talk to me."

Eli nods toward the arbor bleachers. "I think I saw her shoveling in another Indian taco during the grass dance."

26

Loren smacks him on the side of his arm, making his lips crank into a smile. "I'm serious."

"She was serious too. Serious about that frybread."

Loren rolls her eyes, fighting a grin.

"Jokes. She has a little brother, enit? Maybe she's watching him from the stands."

Loren takes off toward the arbor bleachers, leaving Eli, Cherie, and me scrambling to catch up. Eli finally glances down at me as we fall into stride next to each other, a question—or a coming insult—pulling at his angled brows. We pause in the opening between stands of bleachers.

The two of them peer across the arbor of dancers, and sure enough, they find her brother jerking passionately in his miniature regalia. Two feathers bob on his head as he ducks and bounces.

Loren scans the bleachers and groans. "I see her family. She's not there."

"What's going on?" Brody asks as he scoots out from behind the emcee table.

Eli shoves his hands in his pockets. "Loren's looking for Samantha."

Brody glances back at his brother and the other announcer before stopping next to Loren, shoulder brushing hers. Loren's slightly taller than him, even in her thin moccasins. "Did she take your sister's shawl and leave before you could change your mind?"

Loren squints and shakes her head.

"I told First Kill to do the same thing," he says with a lopsided smile. "Get your gifts and get out. I've had to fight a few visitors off my Pendleton already." He throws a thumb back toward the blanket folded on top of a pile of stuff on Jason's table.

Our old physics teacher walks by and gives me a hearty wave, ribbons fluttering gently against her shirt. I nod politely and then scan the bleachers for my parents without thinking. Mom still holds my blanket, staring at me, but Dad isn't with her. I shift my weight so my back is to her. I don't even know why I'm still here. It's not like any of them are talking to me.

Cherie leans against the side of the bleachers and kicks her toe against a brown patch of grass. I wonder if she thinks the same thing. Something in my chest wriggles, like if I stay here another instant, they'll remind me this isn't any of my business.

"I'll keep my eye out, Loren." I turn to leave, but she snatches my arm, almost instinctually. Her face is emotionless as she watches someone approach.

It's a middle-aged woman adorned in a breathtaking purple shawl. Her mouth is set in a tense line. "Have any of you seen Samantha?"

Chapter 3

BRODY CLARK

Thursday, July 11, 8:40 p.m.

The wild look in her eyes has my hair standing on end. Samantha's mom hasn't seen her daughter since the giveaway and she's not answering her phone. She's trying not to worry, but why wouldn't she? When this whole town has been wondering what happened to Rayanne Arnoux.

"She's gotta be around here somewhere," I say. What I don't say is that Samantha likes to get around. We all know it. I wouldn't be shocked to see her with Detective Youngbull, batting her eyelashes. Asking if he's packing heat.

First Kill grabs Cherie's hand and pulls her along as we follow Loren and Samantha's mom out of the arbor. Mara strides next to me, and I can't think of a reason to tell her to leave.

At least not one funny enough to cut through the group's combined tension.

Youngbull is still standing at the back of the bleachers, so I bet Samantha is with some city Indian from the drum circuit right now.

Loren takes us to the deserted trailers and halts. "Right here." We stand in the same place we did two hours ago, a smaller group and without the horses.

"This is where we took the picture," I confirm. Samantha's mom nods and looks around. The rows of vendor tents down the way are less crowded, and the rows of horse trailers next to us are now smothered in dusk shadows.

Mara spins in a slow circle.

I run my hand through my hair, trying not to laugh through the tense awkwardness like I usually would. "I didn't see where she went after that. Maybe out for a snag, yeah?"

First Kill punches my arm, wiping the smile off my face before Samantha's mom can see it, but the corner of his mouth jolts. He'd be the one to know something about Samantha's tendencies anyway. Not me. She's always interested in anyone *but* me.

Her loss.

Loren marches deeper into the row of horse trailers, and without a word, we all follow. Something tells me I should stop her, like there's something else we should be doing instead. But I don't.

Samantha's mom walks shoulder to shoulder with Loren as they scan between horse trailers. I wanna yell Samantha's name. Isn't that what you should do when you're looking for someone? But her own mother is deathly silent, so I try to be too.

She's gotta be off with some guy. Don't they realize that?

"This is silly," I finally say, but it comes out as a question.

We turn a corner, and Samantha's mom runs her hands along a trailer, her fingers thrumming against every hole in the metal. "Maybe," she says. "But she missed her Fancy Shawl Dance category."

We round another corner, and Loren stops cold. A trailer's door hangs ajar. The shadows inside are darker than the blue-tinged dusk light.

30

Samantha's mom steps forward. Isn't this when we holler at her to stop? Loren's only a beat behind her.

My gut drops, like it did when Mom threw her bags into the back of her truck. Like the moment Dad clutched his chest, knees buckling. It's like my body knew before my head did that things were about to change for good. Like something was happening I couldn't walk back from.

Like when I saw Loren's blank face the day after Rayanne disappeared and suddenly our friend group splintered apart like a tree struck by lightning.

Samantha's mom heaves open the door. The black shadows retreat farther into the cave of the trailer as the door swings on its hinges, and the bruising light illuminates geometrical beadwork in the shapes of flowers.

My ears flood with water, like I've jumped into a freezing lake. I'm distantly aware that someone is screaming, but my eyes are glued to the beadwork flowers made of white and yellow trapezoids.

How long did it take to hand stitch each bead on the legs of those moccasins? How much money did it cost? I follow the beadwork up to the slash of blue fabric across the metal flooring, and the scream finally cuts into my muted thoughts.

It's bloodcurdling, and everything hits at once.

Loren stumbles backward, her lips peeling back into a horrifying, gaping shape. Samantha's mom scrambles up the step, shaking the lifeless legs attached to the magnificently beaded moccasins.

First Kill yanks Cherie's face into his stomach, shielding her. Mara rips her hands from her mouth and barrels after Samantha's mom.

"Does she have a pulse?" Her quick movements bring my mind back to full speed.

I fumble my phone out. "I'll call 911."

LOREN ARNOUX
Thursday, July 11, 8:45 p.m.

I keep screaming until my legs quake. The pit in my stomach crumbles, hollowing out my entire body, and I sink to the earth. I dig my fingers into the shifting dirt, breaking nails. I gasp for air as Mara holds two fingers to Sam's splotchy, strangled neck, and of everyone here, she has to look at *me*.

Mara's light eyes are black in the falling darkness. She subtly shakes her head and scrambles out of the horse trailer. Her hands tremble as she teepees them over her mouth.

Sam's mom heaves her daughter's head up and pulls it into her chest. Even in the dimming light, the tears streaking down her cheeks are bright. The dark blue shawl sprawls out behind Sam's body, no fire in it now. No smoke. It's nearly black against the metal trailer floor, the colorful fringes like fingers reaching for something—or someone.

Sam's eyes are half-open, but they don't look right. They're empty.

Someone pulls me off the ground as a crowd quickly gathers, their frantic murmuring floating around us like thick dust. Arms wrap around my body. I don't know whose. I don't care.

Sam's dad shoves through the crowd with her aunts, a trail of her little brothers behind them. The horror buckles through his face, contorting his features and unleashing a broken groan that makes me sob. The aunts scoop up the kids and shuffle backward, mouths gaping open.

A siren filters through the panicked conversations. Just as the last bits of light are slinking past the horizon, red and blue lights splinter through the trailers. The flashing police lights cast shifting shadows over everyone's faces, making them all look guilty of *something*.

I push out of the arms holding me up and hobble to the adjacent horse trailer. I press my back against it as the dark faces around me nervously glance at each other. Anyone could've done this. The metal digs into my skin as my breath hitches.

Somebody here hurt Sam.

A tribal police officer kneels over Sam while another forces her wailing parents away from the trailer and pulls yellow tape around the immediate area. Two more officers show up and corral us on either side. An ambulance carefully rolls up the dirt road at the end of the row. No lights. No hurry.

She's already long gone.

Eli First Kill shuffles over, Cherie in his arms now. He presses next to me, his shoulder hot against mine. Cherie's breath whimpers in and out over his neck. He absently combs through his sister's hair as he stares at the tribal police snapping photos of my best friend and placing her phone into a plastic bag.

Brody leans against the trailer next to Eli, and eventually, Mara sidles up next to me. It could be hours or minutes before paramedics gently transfer Sam to a gurney and roll her toward the quiet ambulance. We can't go anywhere, so we have to watch.

The men pull the dark blue shawl out at her sides and wrap it over her body. It looks like a cocoon, just what it's meant to symbolize, but Sam will never create butterfly wings with the fabric.

She will never be free of this.

Mara's knuckles brush mine, and I grab her wrist as the men slide Sam into the open door and step in after her. The door closes with a final *thunk*, and part of me hovers over the ambulance as it drives away. Another piece of me is dead and gone.

An owl hoots somewhere in the darkness, and I know I shouldn't have given Sam Ray Bear's shawl. The harbinger of death hoots again.

That's some bad medicine.

We're ushered back into the dance arbor, but most everyone else is gone. All of our families wait in the bleachers. More tribal cops are there, notebooks in hand, questioning the few remaining people, including Sam's family. The drum groups are gone. Dance regalia is off.

Nerves vibrate through my chest as they sit me down with Eli First Kill and Cherie, Brody and Jason, Mara, Grandma, and the two visitors who were pulled into the giveaway and took pictures with us.

Grandma laces her fingers in mine.

Detective Jeremy Youngbull steps in front of us and motions someone over from a group of tribal cops. A man wearing a button-up shirt and tie walks over with his chin held too high. "Thanks, Jeremy." He sticks his hands into his slacks pockets. "My name is Kurt Staccona. I'm a special agent with the FBI. It seems like you in this giveaway group are the last ones to see Samantha alive."

Brody's leg shakes next to mine. On his other side, Jason leans onto his knees and runs a hand through his hair. At the end of our bench, Eli sits, arms around Cherie, staring straight ahead. His face isn't worried or scared. It's not even concerned—he's completely emotionless.

Mara chews her lip on the other side of Grandma, and just past her, the visitors wring their hands. No doubt they're regretting coming here at all. Wondering how they got roped into this giveaway and what it will do to their vacation plans.

"We want to question all of you," Kurt Staccona continues, "just to get a timeline of what happened after you all took your pictures."

"Hey now," the visiting man says. "I never spoke to that girl. I don't even remember what she looks like." Staccona raises his hand to cut him off, but he keeps talking. "We have no business being here. We're not even from here. We just want to get back to the KOA. We'll give the gifts back."

The woman with him rests a hand on his shaking knee.

"Like I said," Staccona says, "we just want to get a timeline of the night."

The visitor's face pales to almost translucent, and then it hits me. There were only a few minutes between the photos Sam posed for and the intertribal dance she was supposed to do with me. "You think one of us did this?" I ask. "That we turned on one of our own?"

Staccona ignores me and pulls out a notebook, but Youngbull meets my gaze, his chin jutting out from a face smooth with arrogance. They don't have to answer. It's obvious.

It's too quiet as Youngbull shifts on his feet. Of course one of us would turn on our own. One of us already did, and I know that better than anyone.

It's likely Ray Bear knew whoever took her. It's why there was no evidence found of a struggle, nobody to witness anything unusual.

Ray Bear started her day getting ready for school, and somewhere along the way, somebody she knew turned on her.

Fear settles heavy in my core, whispering that I should watch my back.

"You kids are welcome to have a guardian present when we talk to you." Staccona signals another officer over.

Eli First Kill stands. "I have to get my sister home." He strides toward the break in the bleachers.

"We'll need to question you," Youngbull says. It comes out like a command, but Eli only half turns.

Staccona clicks his pen and watches.

Youngbull stares him down. "I stood at that break in the bleachers working security all night. You all are the only ones I saw head to the area of the crime scene."

"Am I under arrest?" Eli asks as he hoists Cherie higher up on his broad frame. When the men are silent, he disappears through the bleachers. The brush of his footsteps through the dirt fades. I want to follow him, to escape this whole thing. Sam's half-lidded eyes are burned into my mind, and I just want to go sob under a rock somewhere.

I imagine myself running after him, but the image halts. What's he running from? And if they really think one of us did it, why do I assume I can still trust him after this?

The second officer pulls Mara to the side, her folks trailing them to another section of bleachers. Despite Jason's whispered assurances, Brody's leg still bounces next to mine, vibrating the whole bench.

This can't be happening.

Chapter 4

MARA RACETTE

Thursday, July 11, 11:00 p.m.

The officers finally head out, leaving us feeling rattled and uncertain after our interviews. The visiting couple booked it out of here after their questioning. Now, only my family, Loren and Geraldine, and Brody and Jason shuffle over the dirt, heading for our cars. Smoke smears the air, and faint voices drift in on the night breeze from the camps. The tops of all the teepees look like a serrated edge against the dark sky.

That's where we'd be if it were a few years ago, back before Grandma got sick. She was the planner, the one who could get Dad's older sister and her kids to make the drive from Oregon. She could convince Dad's brother to haul his family from Georgia, even after his kids were spread out at different colleges. She was always bringing us together. But now she's gone and its harder for everyone to make it work. Nobody pushes for it like she did.

Families must be over there sitting in circles inside their teepees like we did, telling Napi stories over their fires or playing pranks on their weekend camping neighbors. Kids are probably scampering around each other's teepees, peeping underneath the canvas as their parents scold them.

I wonder if word has spread yet. Would anyone take down their camps and go back home if they knew a killer was in our midst?

"It's heartbreaking," my mom says, shattering our silence.

Geraldine puts her arm around Loren, brushing against her jingles. "You have no idea."

I try to remember when I last saw Samantha, but just like when I was with the officers, she seems to fade away from the scene after the photo. I can't place her talking to anyone. I listened to Geraldine explaining the significance of the giveaway ceremony to the two visitors, but my gaze kept drifting to the horses.

Jason was explaining how he cleans and takes care of his own Pendleton blankets, and then they started to talk about the drum groups. Brody and Eli were petting the horses, and Eli seemed different with his little sister there. So I walked over.

I don't know where Samantha went. I don't know who she talked to. But it couldn't have been someone from our group. After they walked off, without Samantha, I went back to the arbor. A few minutes later, everyone else trickled back in.

Nobody was gone for long enough to kill her . . . were they?

"They'll find out who did it," I say. I wish my voice sounded more confident.

Brody and Jason look at me with arched brows, shadows hanging in their eyes. Past them, Loren shakes her head.

Geraldine fixes her gaze on me. "They won't."

The force in her words slows all of our strides until we stop.

Geraldine glances between all of us. "They didn't find Rayanne or who took her. Probably never will."

I swallow. "But . . . but the FBI is involved this time."

"No." Her expression is hard, but it's also lined with resignation. Her chin trembles as she shakes her head. "You know what they say."

There's a lull in the echo of sounds from the camp. Nobody moves. A cloud creeps over the crescent moon, blocking what little light we have, and all eyes seem to fall on me as I jerkily shake my head. I *don't* know what they say.

Geraldine wraps her shawl tighter around her body, and her voice slips out, emotionless. "If you want to get away with murder, do it on an Indian reservation."

The heat leaves my face. It slips down my neck and pools in my stomach, leaving an eerie chill in its wake. The clouds part again, and the moonlight hangs on Geraldine's features. The truth is heavy in her dark eyes . . . the truth she's been living. Suffering through.

These girls are going missing, dying, and nobody is getting justice for any of them.

Chapter 5

LOREN ARNOUX

Thursday, July 11, 11:30 p.m.

The rumbling of Grandma's truck is almost deafening, in a good way. It makes a nest of sound I can get lost in and helps numb the pain—for now. The feathered dream catcher hanging from the rearview mirror sways as she turns out of the nearby neighborhood where she'd parked. I hold my hands in front of the vents, warming them after the long, silent walk from the arbor.

The skin at the base of my skull is buzzing like it holds a beehive of incoherent thoughts. They're dormant now, but there's no telling when they'll burst out in violent chaos.

We dip in and out of pools of streetlight until we pull out of town, where only our headlights cut into the dark night over this empty road. The moonlight gives the slight hill crests in the plains beside us a faint glow, almost like we're riding black ocean waves.

After a few minutes of silence and nothing but prairie grass and rotting fence posts whizzing by, Grandma runs a hand through her messy braid. The twists are barely hanging on after the night we've had.

"I hate that I even have to ask," she says

My cheeks yank into a grimace. "So don't."

"I have to!"

"You have to, Grandma? You have to ask if I killed my friend?"

My heart is still broken, my throat constantly burning from being a hair away from tears, but sometimes I'm angry instead, like now. It grinds out in my voice.

She glances at me and clutches the fabric over her chest. "You were the *last* one to see her. And if I'm going to *hell* and back to defend you, yes, I need to ask first. That's standard procedure."

Hot anger blooms in my limbs and explodes before I can stop it. I swing forward and swipe at the dream catcher dangling from the mirror, twisting my fingers into the leather strands like claws. Beads pop off it and soar through the air and skitter across the dashboard. A single feather flutters through the air streaming out of the vent and lands on the vein bulging in my arm as I squeeze the torn leather straps still caught in my fist. "No. I did *not* strangle my best friend." I scream it, but it tangles in my raw throat and brings tears to my eyes.

She doesn't yell back. "I know." Her voice cracks and the new wrinkles around her mouth deepen. All the stress of the last few months is finally making her *look* like a grandma. The rest of her damaged dream catcher falls from the mirror into the empty cup holder with a dull thud. "I just had to hear you say it. And you listen here, I'd gladly go to hell to defend and protect you."

I know why she has to ask—why she worries about me. She's seen how my fuse has gotten shorter and shorter these past few months. Rage blinks in and out when I should be sad, sparking in my muscles and making me break things. I open my hand, letting the destroyed leather strands roll off my fingers to my feet and trying to make the shame from my temper roll with them.

We fall into silence as she massages between her collarbones, a steady motion I've grown used to. It's her way of keeping the tears at bay. "We're starting all over," she whispers.

Tears leak down my face, my hot rage fading with them. It's like I'm melding into the seat, slipping away from this moment. This place. We've already done this. We answered the questions, defended ourselves. I've already carried this guilt of being the last person. The last witness. Already wondered if there was anything I could've done in the final moments to change what happened.

The familiar regret is threading into my thoughts.

We've already lost someone we love and have the bleeding hearts to prove it, and we're still searching for closure.

We seem to be the only people who are.

And now Sam . . .

"It isn't right." Grandma chokes on a sob, her composure finally breaking.

The numb feeling slips away all at once and an aching grief pours into all my empty spaces.

Sam was murdered.

My best friend—the one I laughed most with and told all my secrets to. The heads to my tails. I can hardly breathe through the tears. How could someone do this? I catch Grandma's weepy gaze and see the question we don't want to ask. What if something like that happened to Ray Bear? Wondering what happened to her, what could *still* be happening, flattens my insides. The not knowing is the most agonizing thing.

It's painful to imagine—it's almost worse to hope.

We crest a low rolling hill and the headlights blare against Eli First Kill's bright white horses. Grandma slows down as we pass them trotting on the side of the road. He rides bareback, one arm clutching Cherie in front of him, the other holding the lead rope attached to the second horse trailing behind.

Little Cherie's face is wrinkled in misery as she bobs up and down. Eli's turns up at the starlit sky, and all his harsh angles are softened.

Grandma speeds up after we pass, and I watch them in the side mirror until they're just a speck of white. Where was his usual scowl? What right does he have to look so carefree on a night like this? The misery in my own chest is thick and dark, like I could claw it out and poison someone with it.

I hang my dress in my closet, the rolled tins glinting with the pink-hued light from my nightstand. I set my beadwork pieces on my dresser over piles of jewelry and perfume bottles. The crackle of the TV slips through the thin walls as Grandma settles in on the living room couch for the night. She stopped sleeping in her room at the end of the hall after Ray Bear disappeared. Maybe so she wouldn't have to pass by her door every night and think about how the room was empty. Maybe because she can't handle the silence as she tries to sleep.

I can't either. That's when the loneliness hits hardest. When it feels like a weighted blanket, but not in a good way. It's too heavy. It settles on my chest like a boulder.

Ray Bear's disappearance left a void in my life that I'm not sure can ever be refilled. It's not like any other relationship could come close. She was protective when she needed to be, despite being only one year older, but was my best sidekick the rest of the time. She taught me about boys and how to stick up for myself. She alone knew the pain I felt when our mom left again. When we realized she wasn't ever coming back—when we realized we weren't enough to make her come back.

Ray Bear was *good*. Better than me. The last conversation I had with her in this very room was when she told me she saw me ignore

Mara Racette in the school hallway. I put up my walls and only half listened to her rambling about how trivial and stupid we were being and how there were real problems much bigger than us out there. She said Grandpa would be ashamed of me for shunning the new girl in my grade. I told her to shut the hell up.

That was the night before she disappeared.

She was right. Now Ray Bear is gone, and nothing else matters anymore. Who cares if Mara grew up here or not? Who cares if she acts like one of us or not? If she thinks she's better than us or not? All I know is including Mara in the giveaway was the best way I could honor Grandpa *and* my sister.

Ray Bear was the only one who knew me as well as I know myself—maybe better.

How am I supposed to ever fill the gaping hole in my heart that's shaped like my big sister? Sam could've come the closest if she didn't pull away from me after everything happened and if she wasn't . . .

Dead.

I thought we'd have time.

I hated that Sam wasn't here for me as much as she should've been. I hated the distance that grew between us like dry rot. But I knew we'd work it out eventually. I'd patch myself up and we'd pick our way back to normal.

If we'd have known that time would be throttled to nothing . . .

Maybe we'd both have done things differently.

Maybe when she wanted to talk at the powwow, I would've listened.

I lean onto the dresser, gripping its edges, nausea swelling. I should've listened to her. My nails are chipped and caked with dirt from when I collapsed to the ground in front of her body. She'd cuss something ugly about my nails being in this state, waving her intricately polished ones in my face. Everything she did was artistic, including her zigzagging nail designs.

I scratch at the dirt under my nails, trying to go back. Wishing I could undo the night—the last three months. She needed me and I wasn't there. She was alone. I dig at the dirt with shaking fingers until I can't see it through the blur of tears.

Did I do this to Sam?

I gave her Ray Bear's shawl. I wanted to, for selfish reasons. I brought her into the giveaway. Is that what started it? The shawl? Or is it something even simpler—me? The two girls who were closest to me are gone.

Somewhere in my memories, the owl hoots again.

I yank Ray Bear's sweatshirt out of my closet, the one I borrowed months ago and never had the chance to give back, and pull it on. I switch off the light and crawl into my unmade bed, desperately trying to remember every detail of my final moments with Sam, torturing myself with everything I should've done—just like I've done with Ray Bear every night since she vanished.

ELI FIRST KILL
Thursday, July 11, 11:45 p.m.

I slow the horses down as we turn onto our long, gravel driveway, the slash of their hoofs cutting through the quiet night air. The deep blue above us, spattered with stars, drips into black at the horizon. The expansive fields past us are sunken in such deep darkness that the outlines of our small gray house and separate shop are barely visible at the end of the long drive.

No porch lights greet us. No dimly lit windows. Just an empty house, alone in a field of black. I slide off the horse, legs burning from riding bareback so long, and pull Cherie off. She immediately slumps onto the front step. It has to be almost midnight by now, way past her bedtime.

I lead the horses through the rickety paddock gate behind our shop before carrying Cherie to the couch and returning with pots full of water for the horses.

I unhook their beaded faceplates and run my hands down their sides as they drink. Somewhere under the pain of my burning muscles are too many emotions to track. This night has ripped me up and down. I feel like the woman from the internet video, the biker who went viral for getting too close to a buffalo.

The mighty buffalo charged her, hooked his horn into her belt loop, and thrashed her back and forth. She soared with him, completely at his mercy. She could've easily died. And maybe she thought she would until his force made her body fly out of her own pants and tumble to the ground. The buffalo stood victorious and proud, with a pair of jeans dangling from his deadly horn.

As much as I want to be the charging buffalo, the force of nature protecting his own, I'm not. I'm that woman, standing here petrified and pants-less, cheeks in the wind, a moment away from running for my life.

I've been thrashed, from devastated to deeply honored and humbled, to horrified, to angry, to scared out of my mind. It's too much.

I slip back into the house and lock the door behind me before switching on the battery-operated lantern on the counter. Cherie slumps over on the couch, her chest heaving with sleeping breath. I untie her shoes and carry her down the hall to her bedroom.

I lay her down and tuck her in, horse smell and all, and squat next to her bed. Her hand is tiny in mine. Fragile. "I know it doesn't seem like it," I whisper, "but things are gonna be okay." At least money-wise they will be, after selling those horses.

She pulls her hand away and tucks it under her neck, mumbling through her half sleep. "Do we get to keep the horses?"

I smile and push her hair back. I feel bad selling the horses that were just given to Dad, but not as bad as I feel when we don't have any money for groceries. And it's not like I can get a job when I'm the one watching Cherie all the time. "Maybe one. But no promises." I duck out of her room, leaving the door cracked before she can think to ask anything else.

Before she can ask about Samantha.

I sink onto the couch with a dry packet of Top Ramen, and my phone pings.

Brody: All good?

He's gotta be wondering why I hightailed it out of the arbor.

The yellow light from the lantern casts the room in a sickly glow. Shadows flicker across a bookshelf of CD cases and unread books. The TV in front of me reflects the depressing room, the only image it has shown for weeks. I take a bite of the dry noodles, but they turn to sludge in my mouth. I chuck the packet across the coffee table, and broken chunks splay out, skittering to a halt across the surface.

All good? It's not. And hasn't been for a long time now.

I click my phone screen off without replying.

I should check on Loren, see how she's holding up. But then she'll ask about me, and I don't wanna lie to her.

My thoughts are creeping, like nameless predators, toward Saman-tha. Toward the scene we walked into, to her so obviously empty eyes. I run my hands down my face. I can't go there. I can't think about her yet.

Loren's face sinks into my mind. The question in her eyes as I ignored the cops and left the arbor. I know I looked guilty leaving. Of course I did. But what else was I supposed to do? Leaving was worth the risk.

I'd do it again.

I need to be the buffalo, looking out for my own. Looking out for Cherie.

No matter the cost.

Chapter 6

UNKNOWN

Friday, July 12, 7:00 a.m.

A palm hovered over the fresh coffee, hot steam biting its skin. The worst part was waiting to see how it would all turn out. *It probably won't make a difference. How could it?* Earbuds went in, shutting out the background noise. Not many people even knew about the podcast, and it would probably stay that way.

A ring dug into the tender skin of a thumb as it pressed the stream button.

INTO THE AIR
EPISODE 113

[INTO THE AIR *THEME*]

TEDDY HOLLAND: Good morning from Big Sky country! It's a sunny 68 degrees here in Bozeman, with a high of 88 predicted, so it seems summer has finally struck us with a vengeance. I don't know about you, but it has me itching for huckleberry season to start. In fact, I polished off the last of my homemade huckleberry ice cream stockpile in a protein shake this beautiful morning.

And hey, for all of you dedicated podcast subscribers out there, stick around to the end of today's episode for a chance to win tickets to this month's Big Sky Country State Fair. We've got the hookups.

This is Teddy Holland, and you're listening to *Into the Air*. I've got Tara Foster here with me in the studio, recording before she heads out on her whitewater-rafting trip later today. She wanted to be here for today's episode because we have something different planned for all you listeners.

TARA FOSTER: That's right. We're starting a new limited series of episodes that will run for the next four weeks. We'll still be delving into our usual true crime, unsolved murder cases, but we wanted to bring awareness to a huge problem. One that, I admit, I wasn't even aware of.

TEDDY HOLLAND: We're talking about Missing and Murdered Indigenous Women, or MMIW. This is a recent movement for a devastatingly old problem. Let me hit you with some data here from the latest update from the NCAI Policy Research Center. More than four in five American Indian or Alaska Native women have experienced violence in their lifetime. Four out of five! More than half have experienced sexual violence. Almost half have been stalked in their lifetime. The murder rate of these Indigenous women is almost three times that of white women and as much as ten times the national average rate. Ten times! Here in Montana, Native Americans are four times more likely to go missing than non-Natives. They comprise over 25 percent of the cases while only being 6.6 percent of the population.

TARA FOSTER: The numbers are truly staggering, but we don't hear enough about it. And sadly, the exact number of missing or murdered

Indigenous people can't even be tallied because so many of them go unreported and just don't receive the investigations they deserve. The MMIW movement is trying to raise awareness of this issue so that the victims get the attention they deserve and so these Indigenous people might have the resources they need to support grieving families long term and prevent more harm coming to their women and girls.

TEDDY HOLLAND: There are truly so many cases that it was sadly easy to fill a four-week segment on *Into the Air*. I mean, in Montana alone, there are twelve American Indian tribes and seven reservations, all of which have seen these kinds of tragedies.

Today we're going to look into the still-active case of a missing young woman named Rayanne Arnoux. She's a member of the Blackfeet Nation and disappeared without a trace just three months ago from Browning, a small, rural town on the Blackfeet Reservation, which is nestled alongside Glacier National Park. We spoke with her grandmother, Geraldine Arnoux, about all that has happened.

GERALDINE ARNOUX [PHONE]: Rayanne has always been a good girl. She's my Ray Bear—that's what we call her. Ever since she was tiny, she was just so warm and so focused on other people's feelings. It was always easy for her to make friends and she has a lot of them. She's also a very talented cross-country runner. She's an amazing student. Anything she puts her mind to, she'll do it. Somehow. She had big plans to go to MSU after graduating and had already gotten her acceptance. I told her she should be a nurse like me, but she wanted to take it farther. She wants to be a doctor. She . . . she had so much going for her.

[SCHOOL BELL RINGING]

GERALDINE ARNOUX [PHONE]: It wasn't like Ray Bear to miss school. When the school secretary called me at work that day, I just knew something wasn't right. It wasn't like her at all.

TEDDY HOLLAND: Her younger sister, Loren, was the last person to see Rayanne that day before school. Loren needed to use their car to leave early to finish a project, while Rayanne stayed behind to wait for the bus.

GERALDINE ARNOUX [PHONE]: She never made it to school. I drove straight home, and she wasn't there either. She was just . . . gone.

UNNAMED HIGH SCHOOL TEACHER [PHONE]: As soon as we heard she was reported missing, us teachers knew what must have happened. You have to have hope . . . but we knew. These Natives who go missing rarely get found.

TEDDY HOLLAND: Tribal police didn't act on Geraldine's claim that her granddaughter was missing until a couple days later. They said she still might turn up. She was young. Perhaps she was just having a skip day. Her phone wasn't at the house, so they assumed she had it. They assumed she was fine.

GERALDINE ARNOUX [PHONE]: She wasn't answering her phone. I wanted the officers to try to locate her phone, but the new detective in charge didn't take me seriously. He said half the kids that go missing just run off and come back on their own, but I knew Ray Bear wouldn't do that. By the time he was willing to act on it, the phone was off. It went straight to voicemail after that.

TEDDY HOLLAND [PHONE]: What have you pieced together?

GERALDINE ARNOUX [PHONE]: We assume she must've gotten picked up by someone while she was waiting for the bus. The bus driver claimed nobody was waiting at her stop, so she was already gone. She wouldn't have been late for pickup.

TEDDY HOLLAND: There was no sign of a struggle found in the Arnoux home. No valuables missing. No signs of any altercation near the bus stop. Rayanne simply vanished without a single witness. Blackfeet Law Enforcement doesn't have any leads to speak of.

DETECTIVE YOUNGBULL [PHONE]: I really shouldn't discuss an active investigation. I can tell you we are continuing to organize search parties, collect tips from the community, and so forth. We want to find her too, and we're doing everything we can.

GERALDINE ARNOUX [PHONE]: The tribal police aren't doing anything. The detective eventually sent out search parties centered around our house and the bus stop. That didn't turn up anything because, of course, someone had to have picked her up in a vehicle. Not to mention the big April snowstorm that rolled in the next day. It covered anything we could've found.

TEDDY HOLLAND [PHONE]: It was certainly an unusually long and severe winter, even for Montana.

GERALDINE ARNOUX [PHONE]: The timing couldn't have been worse, but we still got out and searched. That support only lasted a couple weeks. When all the snow was finally melted, the Two Feather Project donated money and volunteers to help us organize more searches in more areas, but nothing ever turned up.

Tribal police think that because her phone hasn't been turned on since then, and three months have passed with no sign of her . . . it's likely Ray Bear probably won't be found alive.

TEDDY HOLLAND: It certainly doesn't look good. If the police had immediately issued an alert, if they had traced Rayanne's phone the minute Geraldine asked, if they had canvassed the road in every direction, maybe the outcome would have been different. If they had spread the word for everyone who traveled Duck Lake Road that morning to share any details they remembered, maybe someone somewhere would have seen something significant.

GERALDINE ARNOUX [PHONE]: I know what's likely, the police made it pretty clear, but a small part of me will always hope my Ray Bear will come back to us. Until we find her body, I refuse to give up my last shred of hope for her. Until then, I'll fight for justice. I'll fight for all the other sisters out there, taken from their tribes and their families.

TEDDY HOLLAND [PHONE]: You're fighting for Missing and Murdered Indigenous Women.

GERALDINE ARNOUX [PHONE]: We don't want any more stolen sisters. We want our voices heard. Where's the outrage? Where's the media representation? You know, we're a very powerful and resilient people. We can pull ourselves through anything, but we shouldn't have to.

TARA FOSTER: We hear you, Geraldine. We stand with the missing and murdered. After the break, we'll hear more from Geraldine and discuss all the resources available to learn more about these issues and what you can do now.

[INTO THE AIR *THEME*]

AD: Bozeman Hot Springs is reopening after a complete—

Trembling fingers found the pause button and swiped out of the app.

"It certainly doesn't look good . . ."

A fist clenched the earbuds and shoved them into a deep pocket. *Only time will tell.*

Chapter 7

MARA RACETTE

Friday, July 12, 7:30 a.m.

The squares of cereal slowly bulge into unrecognizable shapes. The milk turns tan before I've even touched the spoon. Mom skirts by and pours herself a cup of coffee on the other side of the kitchen island. Her gaze drifts behind me to the TV in the open family room. It's muted, but I know what she's watching for. . . . She's waiting to see if there's any word on the main news about Samantha being murdered last night.

"Turn it up." I don't know what she thinks she's sheltering me from. It couldn't be any worse than being there. Seeing it live.

Worry creases her forehead, but she taps the remote anyway and the anchor's matter-of-fact voice saunters into the room. Metal digs into my skin as I grip the spoon, waiting. He and another anchor drone through each of the segments like a slow-drip faucet until they pass control over to the weather forecaster.

They didn't even mention Samantha.

Rayanne didn't get any coverage, but I thought it was because she was only missing. Because she could've been a runaway. But Samantha—she was murdered. She was strangled in cold blood . . . and they didn't even say her name.

If we still lived in Bozeman, I'd never even know.

I drop the sweaty spoon and dig my fists into my eyelids, letting Samantha's eyes haunt me. They lurk in my mind, hovering just below the surface. The second I close my eyes, I see them. I push the bowl of sloshing mush away. I barely even knew her, but seeing her that way rips me up inside.

Dad squeezes my shoulder, making me jump. "You want to talk about it?"

I was right there. Why was it Samantha? How close was it to being me? I close my eyes, but her face instantly appears.

I don't want to live here.

I don't want to live on the rez where I've come face-to-face with the reality that these things just happen. Where it seems like we'll have to swallow the murders and try not to hope too hard for prosecutions. I wish we'd never left Bozeman, where I was never forced to think about the violence outside my door, but we didn't have much of a choice.

If I'd just kept my mouth shut, we wouldn't be in this situation. Our lives wouldn't have been uprooted.

Maybe I'd be dealing with the move better if it didn't happen so suddenly.

He pats my shoulder and sets his empty coffee mug down. "We'll need to talk about it sometime."

What's there to talk about? I don't think there's anything he could possibly say to make it better. She's gone, and those other kids have to be hurting a lot more than I am. Those kids were actually friends with her. . . . I didn't even like her. But even so, I'd rather picture her scowling at me when I raise my hand in class or calling me *loose braids* with an ugly smirk. Instead, I only see her lifeless in that trailer.

I shrug out of his grip. "I'm going on a drive."

Mom's at the door before I am. "Don't stop anywhere, okay? You shouldn't be alone right now after . . ."

I can barely mumble in agreement as I yank on my shoes and grab my keys from the hook by the door. I don't have time to change out of my leggings and hoodie. I need space. For some reason, it feels like the walls will crumble around me if I don't get out of here and into some fresh air.

I scramble into my dented white sedan and roll down the windows as I back out of the driveway. Barefoot kids are already outside in their square patches of dusty-green grass, chasing each other through their front yards, catching grasshoppers, jumping off rickety fences. I roll through our tight neighborhood of one-story homes, wondering where their parents are. Don't they remember people can be taken in an instant? Killed in a moment?

I crank the wheel back and forth until I can tear out of our neighborhood and speed past another. Finally, I hang a left onto Duck Lake Road, away from the tiny town. I accelerate, letting the wind rush through the car. My drawstrings wallop against my chest and my hair tangles into knots.

I pass a spread-out neighborhood, empty land stretching farther between everything the longer I drive. I eventually pass the turn-off to the Arnouxs' long road with squares of horse pastures behind small homes. I pass *the* bus stop. Finally, I ease my foot off the gas when there are only open fields along the road, spotted with cows and horses, old barns, and houses at the ends of long dirt driveways. Muted green meshes with tan across the land until it meets the dark foothills below the mountain range, all encompassed by the pale blue of the morning sky.

The prairie fields are already drying out from the summer heat and lack of rain. There's talk about wildfires, but hopefully it's just talk. The dull brown overpowers any green that was once sprawling across the landscape, sucking the life out of it.

Maybe it *should* burn.

After what happened along this road . . . after someone could pick up Rayanne and do something so horrible, maybe this whole area should be cleansed.

I used to love visiting here. Dad would take us on winding back roads in the forested foothills, tree branches scratching at our car windows, to all his old fishing spots. We'd make our own fire in the cool evenings and roast our catch, watching embers flicker toward the Big Sky.

Now it feels like the fire is spreading in my memories, like its heat is getting too close to my skin. I need to leave this place before I get burned.

I roll up my window when I'm finally breathing easier. There's still a lump in my throat, but maybe that will never leave. Maybe that's the piece of last night I'll always carry with me.

I ease off the gas even more as a figure materializes in the distance. A man walks with his hands resting on top of his black hair, elbows splayed out like a cross. His shirt is a drip of deep red in the nearly colorless scenery. His hands fall to his sides as I approach, and in only an instant, his face morphs from a stranger's to Eli First Kill's, and then he's gone, already a slash of color in my rearview mirror.

I chew my lip as I glance in the mirror again. I wonder what kind of grief he's going through this morning. He was there. I'll probably regret it, but I flip a U-turn and slowly catch back up to him. My car inches along parallel to him on the shoulder as I roll down all the windows. His tanned forehead shines with sweat, and it soaks into the V of his chest.

He glances up and down the road, then crosses it to meet me. He leans against the door, brows scrunched.

"Need a ride?"

His long fingers tap the inside of the door. "Not from you, Mara Racette."

"Why?" It comes out more forcefully than I mean it to. I guess it's a loaded question. Why now and why the last four months? I don't know why growing up somewhere else is enough reason to shut me out. I wasn't part of anything here, when they all were, but that doesn't mean I don't deserve to be part of it *now*.

His eyes meet mine and squint just slightly. His hair doesn't look so dark in the glaring sun. It's practically glowing. Finally, he pulls open the door.

As soon as he's buckled, I pull back onto the road, keeping the windows open. "Where to?"

"Near the dance arbor."

The image of the police standing in front of us in the arbor worms into my mind. I nod and readjust my death grip on the wheel.

Eli slouches into the seat, a picture of calm despite the sweat soaking his shirt.

"That's a long way to run."

He wipes his face with his sleeve. "No different than cross-country training."

I've never been alone with Eli before. I don't think I've been alone with anyone since I moved here. Unless you count a lab partner in the back of a science classroom. I glance sideways to find him staring at me, a hand slowly running along his sharp jaw.

I'm suddenly conscious of the tangles of hair resting along my shoulders and the pants I slept in.

"You really shouldn't pick people up."

"What?" I yank my sweatshirt away from the lump still settled into my throat.

"I'm serious. This is pretty stupid of you."

"I don't—"

He laughs dryly. "And on *this* road of all roads?"

"Oh." I regrip the steering wheel. "Well, I know you, sort of."

"That's plumb stupid. Don't pick anyone else up. Even if you know them. You hardly know *me*. Would you bet your life that I'm not the one who picked up Rayanne? Or the one who killed Samantha?"

I take my eyes off the road long enough to meet his dark gaze. A vertical scar gleams just above the slant of his brow.

I focus back on the road and the groups of one-story homes coming into view, fear pricking up my arms. I'd never even considered that. It didn't cross my mind for a second that someone our own age could be hurting these girls.

"You were with your kid sister." I shrug, like that should clear it up. Like I'm not second-guessing my decision to let him in this car.

"Doesn't matter. Someone could be an older brother—a father, even. A gentleman. A teenager. Your next-door neighbor. Your classmate." His gaze slides down my torso and rests on my fingers tapping against my seat. "Anyone can look like they have it all together and still have that poison in their mind. All they need is a moment to let it out."

I think of Dad and the moment he let something out I'd never seen before . . . the reason we're here in Browning, instead of back home in Bozeman.

Eli First Kill is right.

Maybe we all have a little bit of poison in us.

He sinks back into his chair with a gravelly sigh. "Ever heard of the Canadian Highway of Tears?"

I wet my lips. "No."

"Look it up. And never pull over for anyone again." He rests his arm on the center console before looking back at me, eyebrows raised.

I nod. "You're right."

We roll back into the small town in silence, slowing down alongside a barbed fence with plastic grocery bags tangled in its metal to let a pack of dogs cross the road. We pass a few storefronts, the geometric designs painted across the Blackfeet Trading Post, and a busier-than-usual Teeple's grocery before turning toward the powwow grounds. I glance at the clock on the dash. I would've expected more people to be walking up the dirt roads to the arbor. "What's going on?" I ask.

"No powwow today." He directs me toward a faded gray truck in a gravel lot. "The rodeo is still going on, but after last night, they canceled everything at the arbor today."

I park next to the truck. One *a* is missing from the *Tacoma*. "Makes sense."

"Thanks for the ride," he says as he throws open the door. "Let it be the last." He looks pointedly at me.

"Where are you going?" I don't know why I ask. I guess I can't help but wonder what the other kids are doing today and how they're dealing with what happened. What do you even do after something like this?

He rests a hand against the doorframe as he pulls a lanyard of keys from his shorts pocket. "Cherie and I rode the horses home last night. Have to get the truck home now."

I look past him at the gray Tacoma, dirt clinging to its wheel wells, a crack spidering across a corner of the windshield. I smile despite the awkwardness. I still can't believe what an incredible gift the horses were. The smile falls quickly as I remember what happened next.

He knocks on the roof of the car. "Watch the Indian Relay Races today if you need a pick-me-up."

The relays are wild, with the riders jumping off one horse and leaping onto the next as they whiz around the track. Someone always ends up dragged or left behind by their horse.

Eli's smile cuts into one cheek, then drops. "Or don't." He slams the door and disappears around his truck.

His nail marks are still pressed into the smooth console, but the material rises back into place by the time Eli's truck rumbles away, erasing all evidence he was even here.

BRODY CLARK
Friday, July 12, 10:30 a.m.

"We're gonna have to talk about it sometime," Jason says as he turns into the dirt parking lot by the racing arena. The truck lolls down a row of parked trucks and horse trailers before we can pull into a spot at the end. Thick dust hangs in the air as he shuts off the engine. The eagle feather swinging from the mirror on a leather string slowly comes to a halt.

I run my hands down my pant legs. "Not today." I don't want to talk about it. I don't even want to think about it. I need to focus on getting the horses ready for today's relay race.

He knows that. He's been hounding me about it for weeks. How I better not mess it up this year now that we have a real chance at winning that cash in the championship heat.

I don't want to think about the mess outside the track. When we're in there, it'll be just like old times.

Back in the day, First Kill and I used to take the horses out and pretend we were in the Indian Relay, jumping on and off the horses, barreling into the dirt real rugged like. I became the great Blackfeet stuntman starring in the next Old West film.

Jason told us to stop screwing around and do it for real. He was the first one to take us seriously. If we win, I bet it'll feel like that first day he took us to a real track, like the future was ours for the taking. That was long before he got all distant. Bitter. Like his resentment of being stuck here with me instead of off living his life is slowly building up.

Like he'd rather be anywhere else.

We'll win our first heat today. Easy. Then if we win in the championship on Sunday, maybe it'll finally feel like things are back to normal for a minute.

And that five-thousand-dollar purse won't hurt either.

Jason pulls his cap off and combs through his slick hair. "The police haven't even begun the investigation, Little Bro. They're gonna talk to all of us a lot more. I'm just saying, it might be easier to talk to me before you have to really get into with them."

I unbuckle the seat belt.

"I'm sure it wasn't easy, being there when they found—"

I throw open the door. "I said not today."

I shove down the feeling that creeps into my stomach anytime Samantha slips into my thoughts. Or when Loren's gut-wrenching scream loops in the back of my mind like a bad case of tinnitus.

64

Doesn't matter if we talk or not. Samantha's dead.

Everything's changing faster than I can keep up with, one thing after the next. Rayanne's disappearance was the first rock breaking loose in a landslide.

Jason shuts up and we meet at the back of the trailer to coax the horses out: Running Pretty, with his near-black coat; Double Stride, a solid matte of deep brown; and Fox, with a coat that's more red than brown. Jason pulls a bucket of paint out of the truck the same moment Eli saunters up, Cherie skipping behind him.

I clear my scratchy throat. "She's not allowed down there, you know." I get tired of him dragging her around us, but it's not like I can say that. She's a cousin too. However distant. And he doesn't exactly have a choice in the matter.

"Loren said she'd take her."

Jason pats the back of the truck. "Come here, kid." Cherie skips over, and Jason lifts her into the bed. He offers her his fist, and she pounds it with a cheeky grin. "Use your eagle eyes to make sure Little Bro isn't messing up the paint."

Eli chimes in. "Bro, maybe you should use Cherie's old finger-paints instead. Better suited for you."

I scoff as he tosses me a brush.

We each take a horse and paint bright red onto their back quarters in preparation for the race. I make jagged lines down Fox's sides and carefully dot paint down his back legs. He paces anxiously, pulling against his reins.

He must taste the dirt in the air, like me, and hear the faint conversations coming from the bleachers. My fingers prickle in anticipation. Eli makes three thick slashes down Running Pretty's thighs, like gouges from a giant mountain lion. He drops his brush back into the bucket and relaces his shoes.

"Think we can win it this time?" Jason asks. Double Stride has stripes of red paint around each leg and across his breast.

"If your mugger over here doesn't let the horse loose again." Eli stands and slaps my back. He forgets how much skill I need to catch the thoroughbred he comes blazing in with.

"That wasn't my fault, First Kill, and you know it."

Jason tilts his head, mouth slit open in an annoying smirk. "This guy. I don't know . . . kid?" He looks at Cherie, perched above us.

"Definitely Little Bro's fault." She cackles and jumps into Eli's arms. "But you won't mess up this time."

"He better not." A smile still stretches across Jason's face, but the look he gives me is clear. I can't let him down. Again. Being a mugger is harder than his job, though. As the exchange holder, Jason has to hold the fresh horse for Eli to jump onto.

"I wonder how many people even came out today," Jason says as he leads the way to the racing arena. "You know, after . . ."

"More than you'd expect," Eli says.

We fall into silence as we head through the gate. In front of the dirt track, the bleachers are crowded. People sit in tight groups on the benches or lean against the railings above the track. Jason leaves to check us in, nodding to friends in the stands along the way.

Eli lifts Cherie over the barrier to Loren's waiting arms. "Thanks again."

"Sure." There are bags under Loren's eyes, and her skin is unnaturally pale, but she still came out. After everything. "Hey, are you guys going to the parade tomorrow?"

"Of course." I shake the prerace jitters out of my hands. "I never miss a chance to fight over that candy."

Loren almost smiles. "Good. Me and my cousins are gonna be in front." She gently sets Cherie down. "We're dancing for MMIW and getting donations for the Two Feather Project."

The weight behind her words is clear. The same weight she carries for the girls she'll be dancing for.

Eli stills beside me. "We won't miss it."

"Cool." She nods toward the track. "Good luck. This year for sure."

Eli's gaze clings to Cherie as they take their seats before he focuses back on our group of horses.

I double-check all the snaps and buckles on the horse bridles. "Pretty wild night, enit?"

Eli runs his hands along Fox's neck, avoiding my eyes. "That's one way to describe it." His gaze flits past me to Cherie, drink in hand, and he shakes his head. "She was *right* there."

I don't know if he's talking about Samantha or Cherie.

"Did you see where she went?" I peer sideways at him, looping Running Pretty's reins around the metal fence. "Samantha." I remember Samantha watching him in those last moments. And how bitter I used to feel that she didn't watch me like that.

He finally meets my gaze. "No." He forcefully pats Fox's shoulder. "I was just looking at the horses and keeping Cherie out of their way."

I nod. "Me either. Seems like nobody did."

"Yeah. She was just . . . gone." He blows out a raspy sigh. "Like smoke in rain."

Maybe it was the killer who was gone like smoke. One minute he was hovering, thick and palpable. Then the next, with a little rain or wind, his fading tendrils completely disappeared.

Into the air without a trace.

LOREN ARNOUX
Friday, July 12, 11:30 a.m.

I hug Cherie tighter when Eli First Kill glances our way from the track. He didn't look worried last night, but he does now. I feel my own worries tightly stitched across the skin of my chest. With the powwow canceled today, Grandma thought it would be good to get out and watch the Indian Relay heats. To distract ourselves some-how—if that's even possible. She plops onto the bench next to us, ice rattling in two giant cups of lemonade.

She hands one to Cherie, whose eyes bulge open wide. "Sorry, Loren," she says with a lopsided smile. "Little First Kill gets yours."

Cherie grabs the drink only after I've laughed.

I lean in toward Grandma. "The podcast turned out good. Don't you think?"

She folds her arms and gently shakes her drink. "It's a start."

Grandma wasn't sure if she should talk to Teddy on the pod-cast. The lady from the Two Feather Project, Charmaine Momberg, thought it would be a good idea to get the word out. Grandma acted like they wouldn't be any real help, but it made me wonder if she'd already given up hope.

At least there's still something to hope for.

When Charmaine's sister, Noni Two Feather, went missing on the Crow reservation, they found her body within a couple days with a needle at her side. Overdose. But even when the evidence wasn't adding up and the family thought there was foul play, the police shut them down. Called it a clear accidental overdose.

Never mind the fact that Noni had been working with the feds to give up information on dealers in the area. And drug dealers are quick to turn on rats—everybody knows that. That world is ruthless. The feds should've been the ones protecting her. Instead, they rolled with the obvious explanation and said she went back to her old ways and OD'd.

Case closed.

Charmaine started the Two Feather Project to give other MMIW families more help than hers had. And to raise awareness in the media, like with the podcast.

"Do you think Teddy or Charmaine have heard about Sam?" If Cherie weren't on my lap, I could keel over my knees and sink to the floor from the pain of it all.

Grandma rolls her shoulders back and watches the first heat of horses pacing behind the start line, already kicking up a heavy cloud of dust. "I'll have to call and see."

It kills me that we have to wonder if anyone has heard of Sam's death by now. If word has spread past our reservation. If anyone else out there cares.

I scan the crowded bleachers. I recognize a lot of faces. My third grade teacher. My middle school basketball coach. Some of Grandpa's cousins. My classmates and their families. Lewis, the fastest checkout clerk from the grocery store. Even Mom's old high school friends. I know these people. It should be safe here, but it doesn't feel like it anymore.

It could've been me at the powwow. I was next to Sam during the photos. Why her? Did she stumble into the killer after that, or was she chosen? That day Ray Bear was taken . . . what if she went to school early and I waited for the bus? Would I be gone instead? I should be. Most days Ray Bear went to school early to study, and I was the one waiting for the bus. The only day it switched was the day she disappeared.

And worse—I could've stopped both girls from getting hurt. I know I could've. I was the reason each of them was alone. Sam, Brody, and I were supposed to finish a group physics project the night before Ray Bear disappeared, but when Brody bailed . . . I made us wait. We could've done it without him, but I didn't want him getting out of the work. I changed our plans like a brat and left Ray Bear alone that morning.

Sam wanted to talk after the giveaway photos. I told her we would later. I left her alone on that dirt road.

If I had stayed with each of them, none of this would've happened.

Now Ray Bear isn't here to share a tray of nachos while we watch Brody and Eli, me eating all the crispiest ones and her rooting around for the soggy, smothered ones.

Sam won't be at the next Grand Entry mumbling irreverent jokes under her breath while we wait, always talking louder than she meant to and sending us into a laughing fit.

Anticipation gurgles through my stomach as the relay teams with their second and third horses each take their places along the edge of the track, but it's not about the relay. It's the wriggling thought that these tragedies are only the beginning. I don't know if my heart can take any more.

Cherie sucks on the straw, puckering her lips. The same thought claws into my mind from last night, the one that tells me it's the girls close to me who become victims. That I'm the biggest link between them. Cherie shouldn't be around me.

My aunties, uncles, and cousins finally file in and fill the empty spaces around us, but it only makes my anxiety worse.

Nobody should be around me.

The starting flag swings down and the riders launch the horses forward. Eli's shirt is already a blur as he rockets past us.

The tingling in my blood tells me if nobody is punished for any of this, and soon, it's never going to stop.

Chapter 8

MARA RACETTE
Friday, July 12, 3:30 p.m.

My heel bumps a half-emptied box every time I lunge backward. My bedroom wouldn't be so cramped if I'd forced myself to finish unpacking the last couple moving boxes already. But if I do, that means it's really it. I'm stuck here. I pause the fitness app and toss my resistance band into the top box with all my other exercise equipment. It's not like any of it gets much use lately anyway.

Like right now, I never really feel like working out. And it's not like I have to be prepared for the summer job I had lined up anymore. That got ripped away too.

My chest tightens, and not because of the half-hearted exercise.

I yank the blinds open and collapse onto the square of light pouring onto my bed. It's too hot outside to sit in the sun, but the sunlight and blue sky are the only things cheering me up. I swipe out of the fitness app, open SnapShare, and scroll through my old friends' posts. My eyes burn seeing all the things they're doing this summer. Without me. Group dinners at MacKenzie River Pizza. Tubing on the Madison. Hanging around MSU's campus to get hit on by college guys.

I'm lost here. I can't do any of the things I used to do, even if I wanted to. I toss the phone against the tufted comforter and stare at a lone cloud drifting through the sky framed by the window.

I wish I could tell one of my friends what happened to Samantha, but what would they even say? Only Linzee has checked in on me after the move anyway. Everyone else isn't sure how to act. And I'm too bitter to be the one to reach out.

My phone pings as if on command. A text from Linzee lights up the lock screen: **Reid is hooking up with Molly like nothing happened. Can you believe that?! She didn't tell me of course. I had to find out through . . .**

The rest of the message won't fit into the preview. Something deep in my gut churns. This is exactly the kind of update I *don't* want. And the only kind she seems to give me these days.

After we left, Linzee tried so hard to prove that everything was fine between us. That my family moving, and why, didn't affect our friendship. But everything wasn't fine, and I don't care about whatever drama is happening with Reid and that old group, especially now.

Some people's sisters are disappearing, and their best friends are getting strangled to death. All my old problems seem pretty minuscule compared to that.

I open my phone but ignore the message. I type *Loren Arnoux* into the search box on SnapShare. It only takes a minute to find her, and her profile isn't private. Most of the photos are with her group of friends. They're sitting around bonfires, hiking in Glacier, posing in their colorful regalia. My breath hitches on a photo of her and Rayanne with a birthday cake. They look a lot alike.

I open the most recent photo of Loren and some girls in hoodies outside the high school. It's back from April 9. From *that* morning. She hasn't posted since the day Rayanne disappeared.

Samantha is tagged. I go to her profile. She posted here and there up until she . . . until yesterday. She and all the same friends are in most of them but without Loren. Loren is only in yesterday's, posing in her jingle dress with half a smile.

I don't know anything about these girls, but it seems like Loren hasn't even been hanging out with her friends anymore. Like after Rayanne disappeared, she removed herself, and her friends carried on without her. Who does she spend her time with?

I go back to Loren's page, and my thumb hovers over the *Follow* button. If she's dealing with all of this alone, maybe she could use someone to talk to. I know I could. And maybe she's open to being friends now, like Rayanne wanted her to. Like she claimed at the give-away. She may not log into SnapShare anymore, but I push the button anyway.

I toss the phone down and watch another cloud low on the horizon. It's dark and moving upward instead of sideways. I roll off the bed and press my forehead to the window.

Smoke.

I open my door just as Dad emerges from his room at the end of the hall, phone pressed to his ear. "Has the director set up a shelter for evacuees?" His voice is tight. "We can use the tribal offices. Yeah, we'll have to door-to-door it." He shoves his shoes on at the front door. "Uh-huh. See you there."

Outside the window, the smoke is billowing at the horizon, already wider than it was in my room. "Is it close?" I ask.

Mom passes me and hands Dad his wallet and keys.

"It's up near Duck Lake, but the winds are moving it eastward across the land fast. I need to head over and help divide resources."

"Are we okay here?" I ask.

"It's still plenty far north but keep Thunder Radio on for updates." He rests his hand on the doorknob. "I'll be helping some of the ranchers up there run their livestock in."

"Be safe!" Mom calls as he strides to his truck.

The thick mass of smoke still billows, but its edges are getting hazy as it spreads out. It's kind of pretty, in a horrifying way. I'm sure it wouldn't be if our home was one of the ones in the danger zone. If the police were knocking on our door to tell us to evacuate immediately.

My phone pings and displays a SnapShare notification. Loren followed me back.

Mom rubs the back of her neck as Dad disappears around the corner, and I remember how I wished the whole area would burn. I shouldn't have thought something like that. Shame heats my insides.

I was just scared.

ELI FIRST KILL
Friday, July 12, 6:30 p.m.

I can taste the smoke almost as easily as I can at a bonfire night at Brody's ranch. I can't imagine how thick it is up north. Cherie perches on the porch railing, in her own world, running her fingers through the mane of one of the white horses, which she renamed Marshmallow. I lead the other horse toward the gravel drive that Jason is just now pulling into, his trailer rocking behind him.

We made a deal before we left the racetrack today. I'll sell him one of the gifted horses for a bargain if he lets them both board at the ranch for a while. Cherie gets to keep Marshmallow, and we get a nice wad of cash. Win-win. Jason probably wouldn't be so generous with anyone else, but his dad and my grandma were cousins, which counts for something, I guess. And with all the times I brought Cherie with me to his ranch over the years to hang out with Brody or to practice relay transitions instead of leaving her home with Dad . . . I'm sure he guessed why. Just like everyone else.

He probably feels sorry for us. I can catch the pity in his face sometimes.

At least he keeps his mouth shut about it. Our business is our business.

Guilt drips in the back of my mind. The horses were gifts to Dad in honor of Loren and Rayanne's grandpa, but we need the money.

Jason makes a bumpy loop in our dead grass and halts in front of the house. I meet him at the back of the trailer as he lifts the door's latch. The metal door swings open, sending Samantha's slackened face slicing into my vision. I shake my head to break up the haunting image.

Jason doesn't seem to notice my strained breathing. I hand the reins to him before sitting on the stairs and sliding my shaking fingers along my jeans. I push Samantha out of my mind. "We're looking pretty good for the Relay Championship, don't you think?" I ask as Jason emerges from the back.

"That team from the Crow Nation might have a shot, but we can win it." He tousles Cherie's messy hair with a smile before untying Marshmallow's reins.

Like the Crow team, we won our first heat easily and had time to sit pretty watching the smoke roll out. When the rest of the heats were finished, the announcer told everyone they better get home or see to their affairs at the campgrounds. This fire might be a nasty one.

The smoke is billowing over the tan, dusty plains, and I can practically see the wind shaping it. Jason presses a thick stack of bills into my hand and claps my shoulder. "What was his name?" he asks, gesturing to the now-occupied horse trailer.

"Rayanne named him Storm Runner." It's a cool name, I have to admit. And it reminds me of her cross-country races last year when she'd come blazing in, long strides and set jaw. She had a hell of a kick that nobody could ever match. I'd never change that name after everything that happened. That's Rayanne's mark.

Geraldine had named our horse Big Easy, but when Cherie lit up thinking about renaming him Marshmallow, how could I deny her?

"Oh, he's not a Storm Runner." Jason adjusts his hat. "We'll change that."

That really chaps my hide, but I grip the wad of cash and keep my mouth shut.

"Anyway, come visit them whenever you want. Say hi to your old man for me." He winks at Cherie and climbs back into the truck.

As soon as he shrinks down the drive and turns onto Duck Lake Road, I count the bills. I'm still hoping to get the championship winnings, but this will last us awhile. Cherie hops off the railing and pops her hip out. "Are you gonna give that to Dad?" She trails me into the dark house, where I shove the bills into Grandma's old cookie jar.

"Nope. I'm in charge of our finances, and that's all you need to know."

"Are we at least gonna get our lights back on?"

I lean against the counter. "Hopefully soon. Wanna head to the grocery store? You can get any treat you want."

Her eyes peel open wide, and she tears out of the house before I've pulled out a few bills.

I have no idea why Geraldine would give Dad those horses. There's no way in hell he actually deserved them. But Cherie, she deserves them. And now we can get something more to eat besides commodity cheese and powdered eggs.

We barrel down the drive, gas needle hovering over empty, rattling engine desperate for more oil. "We just need to stop at the gas station." Cherie sighs dramatically, but it's cut off by sirens. Two police cruisers speed past, their lights flashing. I catch Detective Youngbull's face in the first one, and I think he catches mine. They're heading north, to the fire.

Cherie presses her nose to the window. "Do you think everyone's okay?"

I regrip the steering wheel. "Yeah. They just need to help, I think."

Cherie sinks lower into her seat and hugs herself.

I pull onto the road. "I changed my mind, sis. *Two* treats."

Chapter 9

LOREN ARNOUX
Friday, July 12, 8:30 p.m.

I plant myself in front of the dining room window and kick my heels up on the sill. Smoke engulfs the entire horizon. With the sun setting, it looks like cotton candy. The tops of the billows are a navy blue that curls down into purple and pinks, and at the center, against the black horizon, is a blazing orange. This is worse than the occasional prairie fires we get that surge low across the land, carried by the wind. This is different.

Grandma leans onto the sink in the open kitchen, drumming her nails against the porcelain. She grew up closer to Duck Lake, near forested Saint Mary. Maybe she's thinking about that old property. If its trees will be burned to black toothpicks. "I worry about little Cherie First Kill," she finally says.

I pull my feet down. "Why?"

"Their dad's always off working. No mom, just that troublesome brother. She's so scrawny. You think she eats enough?"

"He's not that troublesome." Eli's rough around the edges, but I've never seen him be mean to Cherie. Not once. "I thought you liked him."

"I did. But after he stopped coming around here . . . he has that way about him now."

I don't say anything, but I know what she means. He's different. He changed about the same time I saw his dad hanging outside the bars again or sleeping in his truck in the middle of the afternoon. What I don't get is why Eli thought he was better off acting like it wasn't happening. Why he thought he had to strap on a hard exterior, even to me. When he knows I *get it*. And now, when I haven't seen his dad like that in months, Eli's still behind his rough walls.

"I worry about her, that's all." Grandma fidgets with the dish towel. "You think their dad's doing okay?"

"Seems like you'd know better than me." She could've given those horses to any of her friends who helped her after Grandpa died. To Grandpa's best buddy. "Why'd you gift him those horses?"

She folds her arms. "He helped me when nobody else really could."

"That's what you said to Eli. What do you mean by it?"

"After your mom left, I was angry. I couldn't understand why she'd leave you girls or where I went wrong with her. Eli's dad was clean then, and he took the time to help me understand it wasn't like that. He said that, to her, it wasn't about us at all. He said addiction rearranges all your priorities without your permission."

My own resentment burns on. I still don't understand it, but Ray Bear seemed to. "Ray Bear used to say something like that too."

"She did. Ray Bear hated how the drugs changed your mom." Her voice comes out soft around Ray Bear's name. "She always told me your mom didn't mean to be a bad mother—the drugs made her be that way. I knew all that already, but hearing it from Eli's dad—from somebody who'd been trapped on that side of it, who'd fought his way out, that helped. I haven't talked to him since he fell back in, but now that he's been climbing out again, I thought the horses would help him remember. I hope he's doing okay again."

I hope so too. "He seems to have a lot of work. Must be doing something right if he keeps getting jobs."

She leans onto the counter. "You don't think he ever got Eli into drugs, do you?"

"Nah. Eli was always so pissed at his dad, he refused to do anything like him. Even when he's clean Eli hates him." I guess he's the opposite of Ray Bear in that way. He hates the person; Ray Bear hates the drugs.

"That takes time, yeah?" Grandma runs a hand through her long hair, black with grays speckled in. "Maybe we should have Cherie over here sometime, show her all your old toys."

My heartbeat picks up. I don't need her coming around here and being at risk of getting hurt. Whoever hangs around me is bound to end up missing or dead.

"I don't think that's necessary. Cherie seems fine to me. Happy, even." I turn back to the window, where several police cruisers surge down the road, lights flashing.

"I guess I'm just feeling protective." She walks across the room and sinks into the dining chair next to mine. "I have this feeling in my chest that won't leave me alone—if I let my guard down, something's going to happen to *you* too."

I feel that same anxiety, that same rope around my lungs. It gets tighter every day. "Maybe she just left, Grandma." My voice is weak. It's a line I've said a handful of times, and I believe it less every time. We both know Ray Bear wouldn't have left. And after Sam . . . well, everything is sinking in a little deeper.

Hope is getting thinner. Harder to catch in my searching fingers.

"Maybe that FBI agent will find out something about Samantha."

I nod, but I haven't forgotten Grandma's words that night. The likelihood they actually find evidence that leads to any real suspects is low. There were too many people there, and nobody saw anything.

Or if anybody did see something, they're not saying so.

She watches me, her thin eyebrows casting worry into her eyes. She looks at me like that a lot lately.

Like she can see I have less and less to hang on to.

I stare at the rolling smoke until she rises from the chair and heads into the living room. She fiddles with the radio on the bookshelf, below the buffalo hide. It hangs down the entire length of the wall, the end disappearing below the top shelf. Grandpa shot that buffalo a few years before he passed away. He said it was the biggest bull he'd ever seen, and he told anyone who'd listen. He wasn't really the bragging type, but I think he was desperate to talk about anything besides Mom leaving us again.

For the next year, I swear we didn't have a single meal without buffalo meat in it. Stew, burgers, Indian tacos, even buffalo steak with our breakfast eggs.

Mounted on the other wall is a four-point mule deer. Grandma wouldn't let him keep any more taxidermy in the house, but now that he's gone, she refuses to take it down. That and his own grandpa's hunting rifle stay untouched. The gun rests on a custom stand behind the radio. It's a useless antique and maybe worth something, but probably not.

They were his treasures, so now they're Grandma's treasures.

Maybe someday we'll do that with Ray Bear's things. We'd frame her college acceptance letter on the wall. Sew her running T-shirts into a quilt. I swallow back the pang of coming tears and let the words run through my mind again. *Maybe she just left.*

Static crackles out of the speakers, then a voice I recognize from

Thunder Radio. "The fire is contained on the southern edge, but the Blackfeet Homeland Security director is urging everyone in Zone 2 to have an evacuation plan in place and belongings packed up in case the winds shift. Resources are pouring in from counties all over to get this thing fully contained as soon as possible."

A booming knock on the door makes Grandma and me both jump. She flicks off the radio and strides across the entryway, her hair swaying across her back. When she opens the door, two tribal cops are the last people I expect to see.

Her arms drop to her sides, and the door slowly swings the rest of the way open. "There's no way we have to evacuate. The radio just said—"

Jeremy Youngbull raises his palm. "That's not it."

There's a long pause that makes me inch closer to the entryway. Youngbull's gaze flicks from me back to Grandma. The other officer stands motionless, staring between us. Hope flickers in my gut. Did they find out something about Sam? Do they have a suspect?

But they wouldn't come to my house to tell me that. There's only one thing that could bring them to our door.

"We found her," Youngbull says. His smoker's voice is unusually gentle.

Grandma's hand flies to her chest. Her fingers dig into her shirt, wrinkling the fabric.

"We found Rayanne's body."

I'm suddenly behind Grandma, wrapping my arms around her chest as we sink to the floor. I stare at Youngbull from my knees, like he's my only lifeline, like whatever words he speaks next are the only thing I can cling to.

He squats down to our level. "Some men drove their trucks into the evacuation zone to round up cattle. They were driving through fields and saw something strange. It was . . . it was her. We'll need an official confirmation, but she had on all the jewelry you described. Not the jacket. And no bag or phone." He swallows and clasps his hands. "We have her. And now that this is a murder investigation, Kurt Staccona with the FBI will take over the case."

I blink away the blur of tears.

"Sorry it's not better news. I know we warned you this could be the case, but to know it as fact . . . I'm just so sorry."

Grandma breaks out of my grip and stands, yanking me up with her. She drags her hand across the tears on her cheeks. "What else do you know?"

Youngbull stands and shares a look with the other officer. "Staccona will get you up to speed."

"C'mon, Jeremy. I went to grade school with your folks. I went to their wedding, for crying out loud. You know how we've been suffering." Her tone sharpens, chiseling the dead air. "Tell me what you know."

He chews the inside of his puckered cheek. "We can't know for sure, but Staccona thinks they're connected. Rayanne and Samantha."

Dread settles into my stomach, hot and thick. "He thinks the same person killed them?"

Youngbull pulls at his collar. "It's likely."

I already felt that in my bones, but now it has to be true. Somebody did this to the two girls closest to me. And there's no telling if he's done.

"How?" Grandma asks, a rasp in her voice.

"There'll need to be an autopsy, but it looks the same as Samantha."

He runs a meaty hand up and down his arm. "Looks like she was manually strangled."

A whimper catches in my throat, and I grip the door to keep myself standing. The image of Sam's lifeless face melts from memory to imagination. It pools on Ray Bear's face, lying in bone-dry field grass, smoke drifting overhead.

"Staccona will be in touch with you soon. I just wanted you to have some time to process the news first." He nods at the other officer, and they turn in sync and walk to their car parked on the street.

I stand there, gripping the open door as they drive away. My arm trembles as they disappear from view. Smoke eases into the house, and the neighbors on the property across from us stare, probably with a mix of curiosity and dread. Finally, Grandma pulls me away and shuts the door. She leans her forehead against the wood and locks the dead bolt. "At least we know now," she whispers.

I run to my room, slamming the door so violently my jewelry falls off the nails on the shaking wall.

The last string of fraying hope shreds. It unravels in my chest like bits of tinder, ready to be engulfed by the heat spewing from my shaking limbs.

She's gone. She's dead.

Fire rages in the gaping pit she left in my stomach. It crackles and chars my insides. Twists and mangles my ribs. My fury is burning under my skin, desperate to get out. Desperate to spread.

I scream and swing my arms, unleashing it. Everything on top of my dresser tumbles across the room. A perfume bottle shatters against the wall. I kick my chair over with a bang. I send loose plastic hangers flying off the closet rail like shrapnel. One gets caught around my arm. I yank it off and wrap my sweaty palms around it.

Nobody found Ray Bear until it was too late.

Nobody protected Sam.

I snap the hanger in half and throw the plastic pieces at the wall.

The scream fizzles out in my aching throat, and finally the tears come.

Chapter 10

UNKNOWN

Saturday, July 13, 10:45 a.m.

Fingers drummed on the laminate desk, then flipped open a manila folder. Leading the parade would certainly be a statement. A good one. Sure the volume knob was pointing low, the radio was switched on. Most people were already at the parade. Few would want to miss it. Static filtered from the speaker until the sound sharpened with a little tuning.

THUNDER RADIO-107.5 FM

[THE HALLUCI NATION'S STADIUM POWWOW]

DJ EASY PLUME: What's up, Thunder Radio listeners? That was Stadium Powwow, and this is your host, DJ Easy Plume. I'm here counting down to the live updates of the annual North American Indian Days Parade. Things got a little shaky last night here in Blackfeet Country with that fire, but the parade is on and coming at you in less than fifteen minutes.

First up, we have some fire updates. Thanks to our neighboring counties who rushed to give us aid, from Polson to Great Falls, the fire is nearly 100 percent contained. We have the Blackfeet Homeland Security Director Pete Three Strikes on the phone to speak on it. Here he is, folks.

PETE THREE STRIKES [PHONE]: Thanks for having me on, Easy. I just wanted to publicly acknowledge our brothers and sisters who were out fighting those flames. The winds wanted to create a real tragedy for us out there, but everyone banded together, and it was really something to see.

I want to express thanks to the fire chiefs and departments from all our neighboring counties; they came with much-needed equipment at a moment's notice, and you can bet we'll do the same if they ever find themselves in a similar situation. Also, thanks to the BIA Roads Department, who did a lot of pushing dirt to help corral this thing.

The teamwork and leadership were top-notch. We've come out very fortunate thanks to that.

DJ EASY PLUME: That's really something, enit. Hey, thanks, Pete. I hope you get a break long enough to enjoy the rest of Indian Days. Take care.

All right, relatives. I want to take a moment to address the tragedy that happened here in Browning two nights ago, when Samantha White Tail was killed. She was only seventeen, with a full life ahead of her. Our whole tribe is grieving her loss. Her family would like her to be remembered as a bright light and warm spirit, full of creativity, passion, and joy. She was a kind older sister, a selfless daughter, and an empathetic friend.

Our thoughts, prayers, and support are with the White Tails during this difficult time.

There's only a few moments now until the parade is set to start, and I'd like to dedicate this next song to Samantha. Rest easy.

[FAWN WOOD'S "REMEMBER ME"]

DJ EASY PLUME: We're back again, live here at the parade start. I've been told there's been a change in the lineup. We have Loren Arnoux, sister of the missing Rayanne Arnoux, leading the parade out. Listen.

[DRUM SONG BEGINS]

DJ EASY PLUME: I have literal chills, folks. Loren and four Arnoux cousins are all rezzed out in their jingle dresses and leading the parade. They are making quite a statement here. They have red hand-prints painted across their mouths, which is the symbol of the #MMIW movement. These women are strong and doing their part to raise awareness of the disgusting rate at which Indigenous women and girls go missing or are murdered.

They're dancing for our stolen sisters.

They're also collecting donations for the Two Feather Project. Charmaine Momberg, Noni Two Feather's big sister, created this organization to support victims of domestic and sexual violence and to provide resources to the families of missing and murdered Indigenous people. They're doing amazing work, so get those dollars flowing in.

The Two Feather Project is also raffling off one of Samantha's original canvas paintings. She was a gifted artist with talent beyond her years. She called this painting *Shawls in Sunset*. Enter to win on the Two Feather Project website—all proceeds go to the White Tails.

I personally knew Samantha White Tail and I ran cross-country with

Rayanne Arnoux my senior year, and I know they would both be proud to see this from these young women here in the parade. It's a show of solidarity and resilience—a powerful one.

Wow—

A cough sounded down the hall, and the radio switched off. The heaviness stuck, even though the sound was gone. Loren would never let this go. She'd always be hungry for answers. She'd start digging.

And she wasn't the only one.

Chapter 11

BRODY CLARK
Sunday, July 14, 9:50 a.m.

I roll out of bed and ease the blinds open. The ranch is hazy. The sun is a yellow orb past the smoke. It's almost like we're closed inside it. Trapped here. Uneasiness spreads through me. I hate not seeing the land sprawling for miles to the mountains at the horizon. It's making me claustrophobic.

I blame Jason for that.

Back in the day, when the family still went on camping trips together, Jason stuffed me in the bottom of my sleeping bag and sat on the end one too many times. I thought it was funny at first, until that panic started in my chest and barreled into my limbs, taking all my breath with it. He wouldn't get off until I was ready to break my nails clawing at the zipper line.

I don't remember if he stopped doing that because he finally grew out of the joke or if it was because I got a new sleeping bag with a double zipper. Or maybe it only stopped because Mom left us for Mr. Moneybags, and we never went camping again.

I was young. He was an angst-filled teen. It was his job to torment me or whatever. He changed, though, after he went off to college and Dad died. He deferred the rest of his schooling so he could come home and raise me and take over the ranch. He knew I wouldn't want to be stuck with Mom and her second family.

He did that for me, and now he's the only person who hasn't left me.

We've been doing just fine, the two of us, but if he's bitter for the years he missed out on, I don't blame him.

I'll always owe him for that.

I pull on my Wranglers and sit on the edge of the bed in front of the window. The smoke will settle here until the wind picks back up. Luckily, in the night, it finally calmed enough that the wildfire fighters were able to get it totally contained. I should be glad the air is dead, but I wish it would blow away now.

I stumble out of my bedroom to the back mudroom. Jason's work boots are already gone. I tug mine on and head out the back door to the horse barn. When I stroll in, Jason sets his shovel against the wall, already finished mucking the horse stalls. "You know, this is *your* job, lazybones. If you don't start pulling your weight around here, I'm gonna make you go work somewhere else."

I grunt, which makes my throat burn in the smoky air. He wouldn't. He knows I'll probably work here till I die. Just like Dad.

"Mom called. Says she's gonna be at the championship today."

"I'd rather she wasn't."

"Same." He carries a set of brushes to the two new horses' stalls. "She wants the bragging rights when her sons win the Indian Relay, enit? Even though she hardly sees us." He brushes across Storm Runner's back. He's always been even more bitter than I am about Mom leaving us, and that's saying something. He was older, with twice the childhood memories with her, so the betrayal was deeper. "Even though she has *new* sons now. Isn't that right, Lightning?"

"Lightning? Seriously, Jase?"

"Better than Storm Runner. This horse needs a new beginning—like Marshmallow got."

"Hell no, it's not. Lightning is on the same tier as the name Marshmallow. A seven-year-old girl would name him that. Storm Runner is rugged."

He turns, face suddenly serious. "We're not keeping the name he got from Rayanne." He grips the brush until it creaks. "Like we need that kind of reminder all the time. That's bad medicine."

I scoff. "'Kay, then."

But he's right.

"Make yourself useful and go pull the trailer around. We'll load the horses before setting up the bonfire area."

I stride out of the barn, back into the haze. I don't need a reminder of Rayanne all the time. Or Samantha. Honestly, this claustrophobic smoke is the only thing that's muted Loren's scream in my head from when we found Samantha's body.

And the guilt that prods my gut about Rayanne isn't going anywhere.

Obviously, I didn't hurt Rayanne, but I have enough to feel bad about. Enough to keep me awake at night. Not that it compares to what Loren is going through. That keeps me awake at night too. I want to be there for her like before, but I don't know how. Or if she would let me. She pushed everyone away after her sister disappeared, especially Samantha. Whether she meant to or not.

I hop into the truck, where the clock on the dash tells me I slept in until well past nine. Jason's already filled up a new bucket of red paint for the horses and put it in the bed of the truck and even had time to make a run to the store to buy plenty of cases of beer for tonight.

Hopefully, we win. It'll be embarrassing to have so many people here if we don't.

MARA RACETTE
Sunday, July 14, 10:00 a.m.

The faint smell of burning wood still lingers in the house. I imagine that's why Dad keeps holding his coffee mug right below his nose instead of setting it on the coffee table. The steam must burn his nostrils, but he doesn't seem to care. His eyes have a glassy look to them as he stares at Grandma Racette's sunset teepee painting on the wall above the fireplace. He's stuck inside his head.

I get it.

I could paint a picture of the scene of Samantha's death. . . . It's sunken into my vision, like a black-and-white image taped to a sunny window. I could trace every detail of it. It glows like a flickering candle at night. Sits in the background of my vision during the day.

I never thought I'd see something like that. Never imagined I'd find a body, especially not one murdered in cold blood.

I've never had such a close-up view of how awful the world can be.

It has to be just as bad for Dad, if not worse. He and another guy from the tribal offices found Rayanne. Three months later than everyone hoped. Three months' worth of more gruesome details to pulse behind his eyelids.

I pour my full bowl of cereal down the disposal and ease onto the other end of the couch. I'm not sure Dad even notices me here. I flick on the news and mute it, reading the captions just like Mom. They're talking about the fire and how it's mostly controlled now. Not a word about Rayanne.

At least this time there's a reason for it. The police don't want to divulge anything about the flurry of investigating they're *hopefully* doing now. Word will probably spread soon, though, almost as quickly as that wildfire.

I open SnapShare and go to Loren's page. Part of me wants to message her, but I don't want to get in her business if she doesn't want it. I wonder if she'll go to the powwow today. If it were me, I couldn't. I wouldn't want to see anyone, let alone dance in front of everyone.

Mom strides into the room and turns the TV off. She rests a hand on Dad's shoulder, pulling him out of that faraway place. "What do you think about today?" she asks. "Your cousin Leni said he'd save us a spot."

He runs his fingers through his stringy hair. Maybe he's the one who's making the house still smell like smoke. He didn't shower after he came home. He didn't do much of anything.

She squeezes his shoulder. "Maybe it would be good to get out?"

He takes a gulp of his coffee and nods. "I'll hop in the shower."

He dumps the rest of his coffee into the sink and then disappears down the hall, leaving Mom standing in the middle of the living room with hands on her hips.

I roll the hem of my shirt between my fingers. "He's taking it pretty hard?"

She meticulously straightens the frames in the gallery wall of family photos. "Both of you have been through an ordeal."

"It's nothing compared to what Samantha's family and the Arnouxs are dealing with." I sink further into the couch.

"I know. Doesn't make it any less hard for you two, though."

"It's too bad we moved here at all." It's hard to keep the bitterness out of my tone, because of everything we've been through, but also because of everything I left behind. I'd still be hanging out with my friends this summer if things didn't fall apart. We'd be watching movies every night. Going to concerts on the weekends. Hiking.

I wouldn't have had to give up the summer internship opportunity of a lifetime . . . one high schoolers probably never get. Mom knows how much that hurt—it was her friend who swung it for me, after all. I would've been helping the athletic trainers for MSU's football team. Seeing if sports medicine or physical therapy is something I want to pursue. I've half-heartedly looked for a job here . . . but there's not much open and nothing will compare to what I almost had. It would've looked amazing on college applications too.

Instead, I'm here, figuring out how I'm supposed to deal with all this.

I can tell Mom's thinking the same thing, but she's too supportive of Dad to admit it out loud. Or maybe she blames me for this too. I'm too committed to acting like everything has been fine for me here to press it further.

She adjusts the embroidered pillows next to me and then busies herself with the morning dishes, letting the moment pass.

Ever since the move, there's been a wall up between my parents and me, but after we found Samantha, it feels even thicker. Like I physically can't speak to them about it. I kept too much from them before Samantha died, and now, it wouldn't do them any good to know. It would only make things worse, like last time.

The conflicted feelings gnarled around my chest are complicated. I feel like grieving the tragic loss of Samantha, but the bitterness and hate I felt toward her didn't die with her. They're still laced in, bringing a smear of guilt too. Maybe being around Loren or the other kids who actually liked her would help me unwind the mess.

I open my phone to the picture of Loren and Rayanne. I don't know what it's like to have a sister, much less lose one, but I bet it feels like a piece of yourself has been hacked off. I can't imagine how much she's hurting.

I open a direct message to her. **My dad told me what they found. I'm here if you want to talk about it. I'm also here if you don't.**

I send it. Then I also shoot her my phone number.

She has plenty of people she could talk to about it—she's not like me. She had a bunch of cousins our age at the powwow. Aunts and uncles. Dad's siblings and my first cousins all live across the country and all my extended cousins are either way older or way younger. I fall awkwardly alone in the middle, and we never stuck around long enough during Indian Days trips for me to get too comfortable with anyone anyway.

Loren is surrounded by family here, but maybe she'll take me up on the offer to talk. Maybe we could also talk about Samantha.

Something happened to me the night we found her, and probably to Loren, Brody, and Eli too. Something that has me closed off and rattled, and I think they're the only ones who'd get it. They shut me out for so long, but after this trauma . . . we're stuck in something together. Whether we like it or not.

The dance arbor is even more crowded than it was on the first powwow night, despite what happened with Samantha. I could be imagining it, but it seems like fewer people exit the bleachers alone. The women go in groups and fewer kids run off by themselves.

Everyone is tenser. And they should be . . . there was a killer here that night. Who's to say the same one isn't here now?

I know I'm not walking out of these bleachers alone.

The sky is still hazy. It gives the blue a sickly twinge of yellow and the towering mountains at the horizon look shadowed. Dad clasps his fingers tightly together next to me. I wonder if anyone else knows Rayanne was found yet. The FBI and tribal police must be working hard to keep it confidential for now.

There's a different emcee today. A long, black braid hangs underneath his tan cowboy hat. When he taps the microphone, part of me expects him to announce the news to the crowd, but he only announces the Grand Entry. The drum circle starts their song, but the beat doesn't ground me this time.

My heart pumps out wriggling anxiety with each beat of the drum, like every whack of the sticks is signaling another second gone by. Another second when killers walk free. When families live in fear.

Today, when the singers wail, my eyes burn. I don't know if they're putting their own pain into the song or if they're pulling mine out. I scan the dancers bobbing around the circle. Sure enough, Loren came.

She dances near the center of the circle. The tin jingles on her dress bounce up and down in perfect time with the drummers. She doesn't move from her place, and the rest of the dancers make a slow circle around her. Her head is tipped back, and her cheeks shine.

The jingle dress dance is one of healing. The sound of the rolled tins and the steps of the women wearing them are a prayer in themselves. I hope she feels the power in it now. I hope it brings some kind of healing into her heart. She's going to need it.

We all are.

Her whole posture is different today. She's not dancing to win.

She's dancing to feel something. She's dancing for Rayanne.

I pull my gaze from her, like I shouldn't be watching something so personal. Instead, I glimpse Kurt Staccona entering the arbor. He slips past people gathered at the emcee table and stands a few feet back with his hands clasped in front of his belt. It pulls on his suit jacket and shows the bulge where his gun is secured underneath it.

He nods at two uniformed tribal officers across the arbor, carefully weaving to the base of our section of bleachers. I recognize one of them from that night we were questioned about the photographs with Samantha. From the night she died.

Did something else happen? Or are they just here for safety reasons? I should feel comforted knowing they're here watching, but I don't. My stomach stitches like I'm running through a side-ache.

Kurt Staccona climbs a few steps up the bleachers and leans close to a man. He gestures to the man to follow him. I recognize him as the bus driver who should've picked up Rayanne. Did they find something on him?

One of the police officers gestures for Geraldine to retrieve Loren from the dance turf. Something is definitely happening, but I don't have much time to wonder what, as the other officer appears at the end of our row and asks my family to follow him.

I don't know if it's all in my head, but it feels like the entire audience watches us descend the stairs.

Chapter 12

ELI FIRST KILL
Sunday, July 14, 1:00 p.m.

The crowded bleachers stand tall over the mostly flat land. Even with some smoke still hovering, it's packed here. The haziness makes the sky look tan over the track, like we're already hot in the middle of a race, blazing forward, dust engulfing us. It's not a Big Sky anymore—it's closing in on us.

We group the horses at the railing with Jason and his buddy, Tom, who agreed to be our back holder this year. All four of us stand in the dirt, donning our matching red silk ribbon shirts, shifting as nervously as the horses do. Yellow, turquoise, and orange ribbons cascade down our backs in a triangle shape.

I wanted T-shirts printed with eagle feathers crossing on the backs, but Jason wanted to look more traditional, and he had no problem shelling out the money to have them made. He was right; we do look slick.

Adrenaline pumps into my limbs as the announcer begins introductions. "Eagle Express, from the Shoshone-Bannock Tribes at box one. Running Wild, from the Crow Tribe at box two. Storm Relay, from the Lakota Tribe at box three. Rascon Relay, from the Colville Confederation at box four. And our very own War Brothers, from the Blackfeet Nation at box five."

The bleachers erupt in cheers as Jason, Brody, and Tom lead our second and third horses to our transition spot. Back in the starting area, dust kicks up around Running Pretty's feet, and I strain against the reins to keep him from taking off before we're ready. The man with the orange starting flag takes his place behind the line. Nerves curl up my neck, quieting everything else surrounding us, erasing the stress always hovering over me. Here, the race is all that matters.

The reins dig into my palms as Running Pretty pulls against them. The horse from the Crow Tribe turns in a quick circle and bumps into Running Pretty, jerking me to the side. I pull him into another spin before he bumps the horse on our right. I can't help but smile, even as another horse kicks dirt into my face.

This is that good kind of chaos.

I dig my thighs into Running Pretty's bare sides as the man behind the line holds his arm steady, the orange flag flitting in the breeze. Dark dust sprays around us, floating in front of the flag as he slowly raises it.

"Race!" the man yells as he swings the flag down. I kick Running Pretty, launching him forward. The crowd screams behind us as Running Pretty strides to the front of the pack, his mane whipping against my chest. I lean into his stride, making my body one with his.

The Crow horse sidles up next to us, his air making the hairs on my leg stand up. The rider is so close I can see the threads in his maroon vest and the sweat beading on his forehead. Our horses jostle against each other for most of the lap. I inch ahead as we come out of the last turn.

The bleachers loom ahead, full of people on their feet screaming. I slow Running Pretty a touch and steer him toward Little Bro, who jumps up and down with his arms raised at the edge of the track. I steady myself and focus my gaze on Fox. Jason turns him in a tight circle just past Brody.

I leap off the horse, sending him careening to Little Bro. Then I take two massive strides toward Fox, jaw set, and leap. I throw my arms around Fox's neck and get a leg over his back just as Jason smacks him on the rump. He soars down the track as I heave the rest of my body onto his back and grip the reins.

"Sko, Fox!" I steal a glance backward. The Crow rider is a stride behind us. My shirt flaps violently in the wind, and my eyes blur from the speed. I take the bend tight, bumping into the Crow horse again. The Lakota horse is pushing him from the other side.

"Go, Fox," I yell, mouth dry.

The black Lakota horse surges ahead halfway through the curve and cuts to the inside, disrupting Fox's stride. The crow rider sidles up with us, the trail of dust from the Lakota horse's hooves soaring into both our faces. I suck in air through my teeth and hardly slow Fox down as we charge toward Brody. His eyes are wide in panic as he sinks into a ready position.

I jump off Fox, and my knees buckle from the rapid impact into the shifting dirt. I barrel forward too quickly, arms windmilling, and fall into a roll, terrified I've lost it all. I manage to spring straight back up into a stride and vault onto Double Stride.

My knee slams into his side and jolts with pain, for both of us. He rockets forward before I'm secure. I cling to his neck, my face slamming into his shoulder with every stride. Through the stream of dust pouring out of my hair, I glimpse Little Bro behind me, face down in the dirt, getting dragged by Fox's reins. Jason throws his arms around Fox's neck, halting him and saving us a disqualification.

The Crow rider surges past them, and I finally get enough leverage to heave all the way onto Double Stride just as we pass the Lakota rider. His feet are dragging in the dirt as he clings to the reins, fighting to stay on his frantic new horse. A cloud of dust follows them as the gray horse flings the rider off the reins.

The rider tumbles into the dirt and rolls under the inner barrier, just missing the deadly hooves of the Crow horse as he strides into place next to me. The riderless horse bobs in front of us, dutifully continuing the race but getting in our way.

The Crow horse bumps into us and inches to catch up with the loose horse ahead. I let him have the lead and steer Double Stride to the very inside of the track, my leg only inches from the metal barrier as we lean into the curve. "Sko, brother!"

My mouth is dry as bone, my limbs tight with adrenaline. We're only feet behind the Crow rider, who's trying to maneuver past the loose horse. As we near the end of the straightaway, he steers his horse around the outside of the loose one.

I lean lower, smacking Double Stride's shoulder. "Yah!" His infamous stride lengthens, and we squeeze between the loose horse and the barrier right into the curve. My skin burns against the barrier before the riderless horse makes way and bumps into the Crow rider on the other side. The wind bites my face as we launch out of the curve. "Sko!"

On the straightaway, Double Stride soars. I scream at him to run, knuckles white over the reins. The Crow rider is only a couple of strides behind us, but I know we have it. Brody and Jason jump up and down at the fence, their fists raised in the air as Double Stride blazes toward the finish line.

The crowd is a mass of waving arms and screams. I spot Cherie as I'm crossing the finish line, her little face bright with joy. A real smile pries its way onto my face. For once, we probably look like normal kids, no cares in the world, no problems at our backs. Warmth rolls through my relaxing muscles as I career past the crowd.

I forgot you could smile so hard it hurts your face. After feeling robbed last year when our horse got loose, winning means even more this year. And that five-thousand-dollar prize money is gonna make things at home easier, even after it's split four ways.

While the relay emcee announces the third and second place teams, I search for Cherie in the bleachers in front of us, but find Detective Youngbull standing like a vulture behind her. He's not cheering or clapping. He's not even smiling.

Cherie bounces next to her friend from school and the friend's family, oblivious to Youngbull's ominous presence behind her. He's not here to help anyone. He's got a look in his eye like he's wondering whose life he can screw up next.

His eyes meet mine, as do those of the three cops next to him, as I hoist Cherie over the railing to join my team in the winner's circle, along with Brody's mom's family and Tom's family.

I force myself to hold my smile as somebody snaps a picture of us. The announcer hands Jason a fat envelope of cash and shakes his hand. Little Bro claps at my side.

The announcer yanks my arm into the air. "Eli First Kill, everyone! The warrior who carried War Brothers to victory! Showing everyone exactly what great horsemen the Blackfeet are!" He releases my hand and claps me on the shoulder. "Let's hear it for War Brothers, your Indian Relay champions, one more time, ay!"

I should be shaking off the cops' stares and waving to my fans in the bleachers.

We've finally won it all, but the surge in my pulse is for everything I'm probably about to lose.

When the other family members head back into the stands, I set Cherie on Double Stride's back and help lead the horses to Jason's trailer. I glance back toward the stands to make sure the cops aren't following us.

Maybe they'll leave us alone after all.

"You had me nervous on that last one," Tom says as we get to the gravel lot. "I wasn't sure you'd stay on!"

"I knew he'd stay on, but Little Bro almost let Fox slip again." Jason throws his head back and laughs. "He was all ready for that mud Slip 'N Slide."

I only caught a glimpse of Brody being dragged through the dirt on his stomach, but I imagine the full sight was epic.

Brody scoffs. "I wouldn't have if First Kill didn't send him in so hot. He was practically at full speed!"

We were, and I remember his look of terror. "Did you drop on purpose? Was that the only way to hide that you plumb pissed your pants?"

Brody shakes his head. "This guy . . ."

"It's okay, Little Bro." Jason slaps his back. "I'll get the garden hose out and get some nice mud going for you tonight at the forty-niner, yeah? It'll be the main event."

"Maybe he'll even get some girls to mud wrestle with you. It'll be the most action you've got all year, ays." My lips relax into a smile at his expense.

Jason cackles.

"That's not true and you know it, First Kill." Brody raises a steady finger, all serious except the glint in his eyes. "But I wouldn't refuse such an idea."

I lean in toward Jason. "The girls would."

Jason's eyebrows yank up. "Ays! You bet they would."

Brody shakes his head and laughs. "Whatever." He disappears with Running Pretty into the trailer. "You're one to talk, anyway, on babysitting duty all the time."

I pull Cherie off Fox at that exact moment. He's mostly right, but he doesn't need to know that. "Jason's always babysitting you too, and we both do fine. Enit, Jason?"

Tom and Jason laugh as Brody emerges from the trailer rolling his eyes. He opens his mouth, ready with his comeback, then freezes. Two tribal cops approach.

Lies write themselves in my mind, one for each step they take toward us.

Cherie is feeling sick, and I have to get her home.

I promised our dad I would get us home in time for dinner.

I need to get the cash to the bank before it closes.

I need to go ice my swollen knee.

They're on the tip of my tongue until Jason steps forward with a crooked smile and extends his hand. Youngbull shakes it, matching his grin. "Nicely done," Youngbull says. "That was quite a race."

Jason shrugs. "It was a team effort, but the horses are the true stars. Were you watching Fox?"

"Oh yeah." Youngbull folds his arms, nails digging into his sleeve. "He runs just like Stella. Almost a mirror image, yeah?"

Jason looks at me and nods toward Youngbull. "Jeremy and I were buddies in high school. Played ball together. One of my dad's horses had two foals. He let me have them, and I sold one to Jeremy on a good deal. Fox and Stella."

I nod and square my shoulders as Youngbull's gaze lands on me. It's not a friendly one. I'm sure mine isn't either.

Jason takes off his flat-billed hat and runs a hand through his sweaty hair. "Gettin' paid to watch the relays, huh . . . must be nice."

The cops laugh.

"What are you wasting time over here for?" Jason glances at Brody again, who finally steps out of the trailer and pulls Fox from me.

Youngbull's smile fades. "There's been some developments with Samantha's case. We need to ask everyone more questions."

Brody and Jason share a look as Brody pops back out of the trailer.

"I already told you everything I remember," Brody says. "Which isn't much." He disappears back in with Double Stride.

"We're still gonna need you to come down to the station." Youngbull rests his hands on his thick belt, next to his pistol and radio. "You too, Eli." He's posturing like a predator.

I grip Cherie's shoulder and open my mouth to spew one of my lies.

"It's in your best interest to come in, kid. The more you avoid it, the more it's going to look like you have something to hide." Obviously, that's already his assumption.

I don't want to drag Cherie to the station, but I can't have them digging into our business if I keep refusing. The last thing we need is them sniffing around our house. "Fine." I grab Cherie's hand and step sideways.

She digs her tiny foot into the dirt. "We didn't do anything wrong." Her voice cracks.

"Quiet, Cherie. They don't need to talk to you. Just me."

"We'll drive you." Youngbull's voice slips out casual, but I know it's calculated. He wants us stuck there as long as he needs, waiting for a ride back.

"Nah. Cherie's got a booster." It's the easiest excuse.

I steal a glance back at Brody as I lead Cherie to my truck. He rakes a hand down his face, probably worried about how much this'll cut into his prep time for the forty-niner at his ranch.

I never wanted to be caught dead bringing Cherie around a bunch of tribal cops, but I want them showing up at our house even less.

I have plenty of things to hide, but doesn't everyone?

Chapter 13

LOREN ARNOUX
Sunday, July 14, 3:00 p.m.

I drum my nails on the laminate table, pinkie to thumb, thumb to pinkie, and back again. The sound echoes harshly in the sparse room. An empty chair sits across from me. It's not quite as cold looking as the interrogation rooms in the movies, but it's basically the same. Grandma puts her hand over my fingers, halting their clacking.

I'm lucky I got to take off my regalia before they whisked us to the station. I'd be sweating in here. "Why'd they have to stick us in here like criminals?"

"I'm sure they're just keeping everything official. As they should." She fans her shirt away from her chest.

Finally, the door swings open, and Kurt Staccona walks in with two bottles of water, condensation sticking to the plastic. "Sorry about the wait." He sets the bottles in front of us and slides the chair out with a grating squeak. He rests an ankle over his knee and folds his hands over his lap, like he's done this a hundred times.

"Do you have any leads?" Grandma asks as she unscrews the cap.

"Not yet. We're gathering information right now. It's looking more and more like Rayanne's and Samantha's cases are connected. Both girls were manually strangled. . . ."

Grandma stops mid-drink and puts the bottle back down.

"This will be hard to hear." He pauses for a second. "They each have a nearly identical fracture line in their hyoid bone and evidence of trauma on the back of their heads. It's the same MO."

I close my eyes and squeeze the water bottle, letting its cold surface bite at my palm.

"I know this is the last thing you want to be doing," he says, "but we need to go over everything that happened with Rayanne that morning. We need every bit of information we can get as we fit it into what we can gather from the crime scene and piece it together with Samantha's case."

My stomach churns painfully. I can't stop imagining Ray Bear cast into a field, a halo of brown hair tangled into the grass around her. Were her eyes open like Sam's? Or closed like she was stuck in a permanent sleep?

Or did she still even have any . . . I blink rapidly, trying to wipe away the image.

"As you know, the scene is three months old. We may not get enough evidence to point to the murderer, but we're doing our best. Anything will help. Let's start at the beginning."

I glance between him and Grandma, head pounding. We've already done this. "Can't you just listen to the recordings?"

He slides his foot back to the floor and leans his elbows onto the table. "I'm on the case now, Loren, and it'll be most helpful if you start at the beginning. Why did you need to go to school early?"

I try to shove the emotions down while Grandma gives me a reassuring nod. "We had a project due that morning."

He spreads his palm out on the table, sinking into a fake casual posture. "Who's we?"

"Me, Brody Clark, and Samantha. We had a physics model we

110

should've worked on earlier, but it didn't happen. We had to meet in the library early to finish before first period."

"And did you?"

"Barely. It was still wet with glue when we handed it in."

"When do you think you left that morning? And when did you get to school?"

My leg bounces under the table. "We were supposed to meet at seven, when the library opened, and I was there waiting for a few minutes. So maybe 6:55. So I probably left around 6:45."

"Same question for you, Geraldine." His gaze follows Grandma's hand as it runs up and down her arm. He knows all this. He's just gauging our reactions.

"I started my twelve-hour nursing shift at the hospital at six o'clock. I heard Loren's alarm through the walls right as I was heading out the door at 5:45. They already checked the hospital computer clock-in records."

"Did Rayanne act differently at all that morning?"

"I only saw her for a few minutes before I left. I don't remember if I even said goodbye." Something pricks in my throat, making my voice crack. I was still mad at her from the night before.

"What about in the days leading up to her disappearance? Was she acting different or talking about anyone new?"

Grandma and I both shake our heads. She was normal.

"Any chance she was getting into drugs?"

Grandma's arms tense. "No. She wasn't like that."

His eyebrow arches. "You can't always tell at first. Sometimes those drug dealers roll through town, and the pretty girls get their stuff for free."

Of course this fed would go there. It's what everyone always assumes, isn't it? Like Ray Bear and other victims brought this on themselves. It makes me sick.

"Most of these cases revolve around drugs."

Grandma purses her lips. "No. Not this one."

I let the bitterness at his accusation sink into my voice. "She saw drugs wreck our mom. She'd never touch them. Never." It's hard to forget the way Mom aged at light speed and how we seemed to blink in and out of existence to her. She'd go days without noticing us.

"Okay. Tell me about your morning at school. How were things going between you, Brody, and Samantha?"

I go over the question again after his abrupt change. Youngbull never asked me more about my morning at school. Ray Bear was nowhere near us, and Staccona knows that. "Fine . . . why?"

"You all went to first period together? To turn in the project?"

"Yes. What does that have to do with Rayanne?"

Grandma leans forward. "Are you trying to imply something here?"

He ignores her and continues. "At what point did your grandma tell you Rayanne was missing?"

I stare at the chipped corner of the table, trying to keep the emotion out of my voice. "Not until I drove home after school." She should've told me sooner. I would've left and helped look for her. I don't know if it would've made a difference, but now I'm stuck wondering. I always will.

"Were Rayanne and Samantha friends?" He doesn't give any hint of what's running through his mind.

"Kind of. Sometimes Rayanne would hang with us when Samantha would come to the house. Sometimes we'd be at the same parties." I open and close my mouth, instantly regretting bringing up parties.

He continues before I can. "Did they ever have relationships with the same guy?"

I hug myself tighter. "I don't . . . I don't think so. Rayanne never really dated anyone." She did have a thing for Eli during their cross-country season, but nothing ever came of it. I told her she shouldn't go there. I said he was too much of a player, but mostly I didn't want her ruining our friendships. She definitely didn't date him, and she wasn't one to casually snag either.

But I don't tell him any of that. You can trust cops to always make something out of nothing, and Eli doesn't need that.

He shrugs one shoulder. "That you know of."

"She would've told me."

He barrels on. "Did they do any of the same extracurricular activities? Have anything in common at all?"

They both fancy shawl danced, but not really together. They went to the same school but were a grade apart. Ray Bear was a gifted, straight-A student, dreaming of going to college, then med school. Sam struggled in school but was an artistic genius, always creating something beautiful out of nothing. They both did track, but not the same events. Didn't even like the same music. They were basically only ever together outside of school activities with me.

What else did they have in common? Me.

They were both close to *me*.

BRODY CLARK
Sunday, July 14, 3:30 p.m.

Jason shifts the truck into park and glances in the rearview mirror. The police cruiser slowly pulls around us and stops as the cop steps out of the passenger side. Youngbull gives him a nod then drives through the lot into the employee parking area. The man struts toward the station's front entrance all cocky and self-assured like. He doesn't even glance at the rez dog sprawled out on the asphalt, head resting on the curb like it's a feather pillow.

Cops always have me on edge. Not because I'm doing anything wrong but because they have power. You never know what people are going to do with it. "You think he'd notice if we left?" I say, trying to break the tension. The man immediately turns and stares into my window. Uptight. Impatient.

Jason runs his fingers through his hair before unbuckling. "No sweat, Little Bro. You've got nothing to hide."

"I doubt they care about that."

His door pops open. "Pull yourself together. Just tell them everything you saw. They only want our help. We're not suspects." He hops out of the truck and shoves his hat back on.

"Not yet, at least," I mutter. I don't think it would take much to make any of us from the giveaway into suspects. We were the last ones to see Samantha alive, and we were all in the same general area as the crime scene.

And now that fed is sniffing around. I bet he cares more about closing cases than solving them.

I slip out of the car, wishing for a minute that Dad was walking in with me instead of Jason. He'd have made like he had a real sacred pep talk coming, only to spit out something like, *Gird up those Rocky Mountain oysters. Blackfeet don't get scared.*

A load of crap.

Somehow it would've helped, though.

We pass a long-legged, white-haired guy and a short lady—the non-Native visitors who were part of the giveaway. He's red-faced and grumbling something about wasting his time, sending the rez dog scampering out of his path. They're probably wishing they had stayed wherever they came from.

Youngbull meets us in the lobby and leads us through a room of cubicles and down a hallway of closed doors. "How're your folks?" Jason asks. He's a picture of cool, despite being led into a room with a plate on the door that says *Interrogation Room 2*.

"They're good. It was a pretty close call with the fire, though. It was on its way to their land before the wind changed." He gestures for us to sit in the two chairs behind an ugly table.

Jason pulls his chair out and sinks into it, legs spread out like he's in a living room catching up with an old friend. "I'm sure that was a relief. I forgot they lived up that way."

I plunk into the chair, easing into a relaxed position like him.

"Sure was." Youngbull pulls a mini notepad from his front pocket and slips a pen out of the binding. "Listen, I know we already went through everything at the dance arbor. We just need to clarify a few things for the feds. It's no big deal." His pen waves in his hand as he speaks.

"Of course, big-shot Detective," Jason says. "It's good Staccona is taking it seriously."

Youngbull clicks his pen. "Brody. Did you see much of Samantha before the Arnoux giveaway?"

I rub my palms together and think. "I saw her in a group with Loren right before, didn't look like she was talking much. I'm not sure where she went after that. I didn't see her again until she was standing next to me for the giveaway."

"Did she look like anything was bothering her?"

"She teared up when Loren gave her that shawl. Besides that, I didn't notice anything." I leave out the part where she was probably checking out Youngbull as we walked past. Don't need to stroke that ego.

"Then, Jason, you escorted the group to take a picture. Is that right?"

"Right. I had some time during the dance and figured Geraldine would want one. We found an aisle that was just big enough. It was a little too bright for a good photo, but what can you do?"

"What next?"

We're silent for a few beats. I remember what Jason said in the car. Just tell him everything I saw. "After the photo, everyone kind of split into groups," I say, "but I didn't notice who went where. I walked straight for Eli First Kill and the horses. I wanted to see if they really were all that fine."

Youngbull holds his pen over the notebook but doesn't write anything. Just waits.

"That Mara girl came over, and Eli's kid sister was running her mouth about something to her, I don't remember what. Then Loren, Eli, and I walked with the horses back down the main path. I didn't see where Samantha went."

"Eli and Loren will be able to confirm you were with them until the moment you found Samantha?"

"Well, no. We walked away together, but then Eli went off with Cherie to the port-a-potties, and Loren went into the arbor. But right after that, I went and sat with Jason at the table. I was there till we went looking."

Youngbull nods and shifts his gaze to Jason. "What happened with you after the photos?"

"After the pictures, I gave the phone back to Geraldine. We were just chewing the fat for a second. Then she pulled those visitors over to explain the significance of their gifts, but I had to get back to the emcee table before it was time to announce the next dance category. I didn't see Samantha talking to anyone, and I didn't see her on my way back to the arbor."

Youngbull slides his thumb across his jaw. "Right. Did you walk back with anyone?"

"No," Jason says. "I'm curious, why does it seem like the focus is only on the photo group when there was a whole powwow full of people?"

"I was working with security that night. Me and some other guys were able to eliminate a lot of people through our observations, as well as a home video we obtained that accounted for about half of the arbor. And I didn't witness anyone else besides your group going into the deserted trailer area." He shrugs casually, like he's not the one who placed us directly into the suspect pool.

"Gotcha." Jason realizes it too and stares him down for an uncomfortable few seconds.

I run my hand up my arm, and Youngbull tracks its movement. "Brody," he says slowly before looking me dead in the eye. "What about the morning of Tuesday, April 9? What were you doing then?"

I blink a few times. "A Tuesday . . . probably in school?"

"The day Rayanne Arnoux went missing, you were in school?"

My heart pounds like a drum. "I thought this was about Samantha."

Jason gently sets his palm on the table, drawing Youngbull's gaze. "I'm sorry, what's going on now?"

Youngbull looks back at me. "The morning Rayanne disappeared, you were in school?"

"Yes. I was with Loren finishing a project before school, and then we turned it in first period."

"Multiple people could confirm that?"

I steal a glance at Jason, who stares at me with brows slightly raised. "Yeah. Loren and Samantha were with me the whole time."

That he writes in his notebook. He underlines Samantha's name before resting his hand over the page. I force myself not to look at Jason again. "What is this about?"

"Jason, where were you that morning?"

"Oh. Um, I would've been at work. At the auto repair shop. I work half days Monday through Friday, and I haven't missed a day in . . . I don't know how long. A long time."

"Does the owner keep a record of clock-in times?"

He shakes his head slowly. "I don't think so, but he keeps a detailed record of whatever we're working on that day and how long it takes. For billing purposes."

"Carlson Auto Repair, right?"

Jason nods as Youngbull writes it in his notebook. "What's this about?"

Youngbull ignores him. "Brody, could you describe your relationship with Rayanne?"

Jason moves his palm across the table and stops it in front of me. "Don't answer that, Little Bro. What's this about, Jeremy? I thought you just wanted to clarify a few things."

Youngbull folds his arms, the little notebook digging into the fabric of his sleeve. "That's what I'm doing."

"Really? Because it's starting to feel an awful lot like we're suspects. Like we should have a lawyer here."

He blinks once. "You can get a lawyer if you'd like."

Jason sucks his teeth, a clear sign he's getting frustrated. I know it well. "And why are you asking us about Rayanne?"

They stare at each other, and my mouth goes dry. Loren's scream drips into the back of my mind, and guilt roots into my gut. I just thought I'd have to talk about what I saw at the dance arbor. I didn't want to talk about Loren's missing sister and how if we had just finished the project the night before, she'd probably still be here.

It's wild how one small choice can domino like that.

Finally, Youngbull speaks. "We found Rayanne's body."

My jaw cranks open. Jason freezes beside me. She's been gone all this time. Loren's family has been desperately searching for her. And now, after Samantha dies, they finally find her.

"That's awful," Jason says, voice tight, "but what does that have to do with *us*?"

"Maybe nothing." Youngbull's voice is smooth, but his eyes are hard. "That's what we're trying to find out."

"You know me, Jeremy." Jason leans forward. "You know the skeletons in my closet. It's nothing like *this*."

"What do you mean?" I ask before a hard look from Jason shuts me up.

Youngbull doesn't even blink. "Knowing the skeletons in your closet is exactly why I'm asking."

What kind of skeletons does Youngbull know about that I don't?

Jason's open palm pulls into a fist. "Fine. We're done here." He stands, and so does Youngbull. He's already to the door before I clamber out of the chair after him. "Let us know if you find any dirt on us. You might be looking for a while."

Youngbull puts his arm on the doorframe before I can pass through it. "If you don't talk to me, the fed will get you to talk to him.

Samantha's and Rayanne's cases are connected now. There's going to be a lot more digging." He glances at Jason. "And I can't protect you from that."

He drops his arm, letting me pass, and I don't glance back until we're out the front door and at the truck. Youngbull stands behind the glass doors. Watching. Sizing us up. Outside, Loren and Geraldine sit on a bench in front of the windows, crying. If we were anywhere else, I'd say hi. All I can do is raise my hand before slipping into the truck.

At least now Loren knows Rayanne is gone. She's not lost or suffering somewhere. She's not in pain.

There has to be some peace in that.

Chapter 14

MARA RACETTE

Sunday, July 14, 3:45 p.m.

Agent Staccona must be roasting in his long-sleeve dress shirt, though he doesn't look it. This interrogation room is too warm and cramped with all four of us in here. It's stressing me out and I don't even have anything to hide. Mom, Dad, and I are just giving our accounts to help Staccona make sense of a tragic situation . . . that's all this is.

I don't feel nervous talking to him exactly, but this whole situation has me scared. I could easily become the next victim in a tragedy like this. I'm not that different from Rayanne. Or Samantha, as much as she wanted me to think I was.

Just because I wasn't raised here doesn't mean I don't share the same vulnerabilities.

I can't get a read on Dad's emotions beside me as he stares at the table between us and Agent Staccona.

"This is all really helpful, Mara," Staccona says, carefully placing a pen on his closed notebook. "It may not seem like it, but every detail helps us create a fuller picture."

He asked all the same questions they already asked me in the dance arbor on the night Samantha was killed, but this time he included questions about the day Rayanne went missing too. I guess because they have her body now.

"But," Staccona continues, "there's another part of the picture we'd like to fill in." He crosses one ankle over his knee and gently rests his fingertips on the table. His gaze flicks from me to Dad.

"Why did you guys move here in March? Why not wait until after Mara finished her school year?"

The room suddenly feels even hotter. Why does that matter? Words tumble though my head as I try to formulate an answer before my parents can.

Mom jumps in. "MJ has been wanting to come back to Browning for a long time. This is his home."

Dad lets out a slow, quiet breath and glances past me to Mom before focusing on Staccona. "I'm sure you're already aware."

I sink lower in my chair, feeling just as small as I did when I ruined things.

Staccona opens his mouth and pauses for a split second. "Yes, but I'd like your explanation."

I want to disappear. I was stupid. And weak. I put Dad in a bad situation.

"I had to resign from my job at Fish and Wildlife in Bozeman," Dad says. "I had a disagreement with the director."

"About?" Staccona asks. But his unchanged tone makes it clear he knows exactly what about.

Dad's reddened face still sits in my mind, with a vein bulging in his forehead and spittle flying out of his mouth. It was like a match falling toward gasoline. I'd never seen that side of him, the one he keeps wrapped up tight in a button-down shirt.

Dad's voice is calm. "His son was disrespecting my daughter."

~

"You don't need to worry." Mom rubs her hand across my shoulders, making the uneven plastic chair wobble. We've been waiting in the lobby since Agent Staccona booted Mom and me out of the interrogation room to talk to Dad alone. I'm not sure how long they can talk about him stumbling upon a body. It's not like he was alone . . . another man who works at the tribal offices was out there with his truck when he found her. "They're just doing their jobs. I'm sure things changed a lot after they found Rayanne." She sighs. "That poor girl."

It seems like she's already shrugged off the concern that came up with Staccona's questions into our move. I can't. The embarrassment and resentment still linger in my core, on top of the fear of what else they're asking Dad.

Mom's hand pauses on my shoulder. "That agent doesn't have anything to twist, right? Kids here haven't tried anything like . . . before?"

"No. Nothing like that." It's true enough, and all she needs to know. All I'll let myself tell her. My knees bounce, shaking the chair. "Why did they have to separate us three?"

"They just need Dad's account of the discovery officially recorded. And Agent Staccona knows you don't need to hear the details about *that*." I hug myself to hide a shudder. Her hand falls, and her gaze gets lost somewhere on the crumbling bulletin board beside us. Maybe she already heard the details.

Jason and Brody stride into the lobby. Detective Youngbull trails behind them and waits at the front door, watching them exit and get into their truck. The horse trailer is still attached, and I see bits and pieces of them through the holes across its side. I haven't heard if their team won the Indian Relay. I didn't even get to hear who won the dance competitions.

Brody waves at someone outside before they pull out, maybe Loren or Eli. I still haven't gotten to talk to them about anything. "I'm going to get some air."

I slip out the door. The air is even hotter than it was in the interrogation room. Loren and Geraldine sit on a bench under the shade of the building. Their eyes are puffy and red-rimmed, and I instantly regret coming out here. The last thing I want to do is bother them. . . . They don't need anyone else getting in their business.

I turn to go back inside, but Loren sees me before I can disappear. "I thought I might see you here." She smiles ruefully.

"We're seeing a lot of each other lately. Unfortunately." I fold my arms. "I mean, that's not—"

"I know what you mean." She scoots on the bench and waves me over. "Sorry you got roped into all this too. That's my fault." It's partially true. If she hadn't included me in the giveaway, maybe I wouldn't be anywhere near this now . . . but Dad may have still been the one to find Rayanne.

I perch on the edge of the bench and cross my legs. "You don't have to be sorry." I glance between her and Geraldine. "*I'm* sorry. I can't imagine what you're going through."

Loren sinks farther into the bench, and the smile disappears.

Geraldine nods. "And at least we know now." She pulls out a tissue to wipe new tears. "The not knowing broke us every day."

Down the dusty road beside us, two groups of rez dogs growl and yap at each other, filling our silence. One lunges, and after a two-second tussle, they all take off down a side street lined with duplexes.

Loren taps her scuffed Vans against the worn asphalt until the barking fades away. "I got your message. Thanks. There's a forty-niner tonight at Brody's. It's sucky timing, but they always throw one for the younger crowd during Indian Days. It's tradition. You should come."

I'm surprised she's going to a party, after seeing how absent Loren has been from her friends' SnapShare posts. And after the last few days we've had. "You're going?"

She glances at Geraldine and nods. "Grandma thinks I need to be around friends more."

"You do." Geraldine folds her arms and sniffs. "As long as you stick with a group. No going off alone. And no being stupid."

A week ago, I would've passed immediately. But now . . . maybe Loren and I could actually be friends. It's hard to know how genuine she's being, but something's pulling me toward her. I don't know if it's the trauma of finding Samantha together or wanting to help her during her hard time or what. "Maybe," I say, "but I don't know where he lives."

"I can pick you up."

"Just be alert and careful. And behave." Geraldine glances at her watch. "Let's go, Loren. We have to get dinner to the White Tails before my night shift."

Loren stands. "I'll swing by in a few hours."

ELI FIRST KILL
Sunday, July 14, 4:00 p.m.

Cherie's chip bag crinkles as she swings her legs in the chair next to me. She glances at me between mouthfuls. She knows a little of what's going on, but not everything. And I'd like to keep it that way. I'm not sure how to play this yet.

The door swings open to reveal Kurt Staccona. I glimpse Mara Racette's dad, red-faced as he walks out of view. Staccona watches him a beat before stepping through the open door. His brown hair is parted in an uptight kind of way, but he strides in and sinks into the chair with a relaxed posture. Or so he wants me to think.

I stick my hands in my pockets. "Are you allowed to question me without a parent here?"

He pulls an ankle onto his knee. "Is one coming?"

I shake my head. "My dad isn't getting home until late tomorrow from his work trip."

"You're free to leave whenever you need to. We aren't keeping you here. We just need your help." He emphasizes the last word like that's what I'm really doing here. I'm not stupid, but hopefully he doesn't know that.

"What do you want me to say?"

"You left the dance arbor before we could ask about your whereabouts that night. Was there a reason you split?"

"I'm on babysitting duty when my dad has work contracts. I didn't want to keep Cherie up all night."

He cocks his head. "That's it?"

I stare into his eyes, unblinking. "Yup."

"Your dad had to be gone the weekend of Indian Days of all weekends, huh? That's too bad."

"Yup."

"Why? Wouldn't he want to be here for your tribe's biggest celebration?"

My hands start to sweat. "You ever have to work a case on Christmas? Your kid's birthday?"

He doesn't answer.

126

"He needs the money whenever he can get it."

"So where did you go after the photos that day?"

"I walked with Brody and Loren down toward the camps to tie up the horses. Cherie didn't wanna miss the intertribal dance."

"Is that right, Cherie?"

My muscles tighten. "You're not talking to her. Just me."

Cherie nods anyway, mouth full of chips.

"It sounds like there was a point in time when you separated from Brody and Loren. You had a few minutes alone." There's a shift in his tone.

"I wasn't alone. I was with Cherie."

"You took her to the port-a-potties, correct?" I nod, but he's already barreling on. "Does your sister need your help inside for some reason, or did you send her in alone?"

I bite my tongue as his tone gets even harsher. Somehow both answers seem equally damning.

"I do it by myself!" Cherie interjects.

He nods, and a corner of his lips perks up. "So that's, what, a couple minutes you were alone, then?"

Bitter frustration sparks into my limbs, making it harder to sit still. "It was only a minute, and I was waiting right outside. I wouldn't ditch my kid sister. I know what kind of people are out there."

"What are you referring to? Do you personally know anyone who would do her harm?"

"No." I feel him backing me into a corner, trying to get a reaction.

"Can you describe your relationship with Samantha?"

I dig my fingernails into my palms. "Nonexistent."

"I don't know about that. We pulled up some text history between you two from Samantha's phone. She sure texted you a lot, with no response. Did she give you a reason to ignore her so fervently?"

I force myself to swallow.

"Did she make you angry?"

"I think we're done here. I didn't see where Samantha went. I don't have any other information for you." I stand up, half expecting him to force me to stay.

He doesn't move. He just asks, "Can I see your hands?"

My fists clench harder in my pockets. "Why?" I back toward the door. He still doesn't make a move. I slip my hand out and yank the door open, disappearing on the other side with Cherie on my tail before he can say another word.

I pull her down the long hallway, desperate to get out of this building. I don't know if I made it better or worse. I do know he's not done with me yet. It makes me want to gag. I shove the front door open and step into a wall of hot summer air.

I've fallen into a situation that's only gonna make everything worse. I can feel it. The mistakes I made when I thought I was helping. The line I've been walking on is shifting in the wind. Cherie's hand is like a dead weight in mine. The empty house waiting for us is drawing me in like a fish on a line. It doesn't matter where I want to go, what I want to do. I'm always getting pulled back there. I have responsibilities I didn't ask for, a dad who I hate, a sister who deserves better.

I love Cherie more than anything, but sometimes taking care of her feels like walking up an icy hill. I trudge up, making strides until I'm breathless, until my legs are aching. And when I look around, I haven't moved an inch. I'm walking in place on the ice.

She's the most important thing in my life. But she's also an anchor. Sometimes that's good. Necessary. Other times it drowns me.

I start the engine and glance at her in the back seat in her booster. I wasn't going to Brody's tonight, but if I don't break free just for a night, this pressure in my chest might kill me.

Or worse, topple this flimsy house of cards I've built for us.

Chapter 15

LOREN ARNOUX
Sunday, July 14, 5:15 p.m.

White paint is peeling off the wood handrail. Its curled edges scratch at my palm under my tight grip. If it weren't for the pack of dogs barking, I'd hear the dry, footlong grass rustling against the sides of the double-wide trailer as we mount the steps to Sam's front door. Crumbling dirt barely hangs on to the textured bottoms of kids' boots strewn across the sagging porch.

Grandma doesn't have to knock with all the White Tails' dogs announcing our arrival. I wish they'd shut up so I'd have a minute to get myself together. I'm breaking into a sweat being here. I don't know how I'm supposed to face her parents when I might've been able to stop all this—when all I feel is regret.

Sam's mom appears with a cup of dog food. "Shut up already!" she yells, tossing the brown kibble onto the grass. The dogs swarm it. "Come on in."

"Hey, Cubbie," Grandma says, her voice pricked with sadness.

Sam's mom tosses the cup into a bucket and holds the door open for us. I almost smile at the familiar pattern. Sam did the same thing to shut the dogs up whenever I came over.

But she's not here.

And I can feel her absence inside this house, like its own person. It stands between each of us, whispering about the things we've lost. It sits on her dad's slumped shoulders. Musses her mom's usually smooth hair.

Her dad nods a hello from behind the plaid living room couch, his fingers digging into the worn fabric. I can picture Sam sitting below him, sinking into the dip between cushions, clunky hand-me-down laptop humming on her legs. I can almost hear the clacking of her quick fingers as she chatted with guys or pulled up a funny video.

I tear my gaze from her old spot to the desk beside the couch. Underneath scattered papers and wads of envelopes, a corner of the ancient laptop pokes out. My fingers twitch with the urge to grab it. Maybe there's something on it that would help us figure out what happened.

"She was worried about you, you know." I jump at Sam's dad's whispered words. Grandma and Sam's mom murmur quietly in the kitchen as they lay out all the homemade food we brought.

Tears streak his cheeks. He rakes a hand down his face, his nails chewed down to the beds. He always had a steadiness about him, but now, his eyes are full of unease. Like he's been wrong about everything.

It didn't seem like Sam was worried about me, but I should've been more worried about her. I was too wrapped up in my own problems to see hers. My blood thrums with regret. I could've stopped this. All of it.

Her dad's face sinks into a trembling grimace and it's shredding the little bit of composure I came in here with. I can't watch this.

I should've been there.

The words swirl through my head, tangling like fishing line. Sam wanted to talk to me after the giveaway photos. I said no. I told her to wait. It's my fault she was alone.

I can't think straight. I can't breathe.

I should've been there.

I make a break for it, running out the door and back into the car without taking a single breath. When I'm locked inside, I scream. I sob. I soak my sleeves with tears. Bruise my palms on the dashboard.

When Grandma slides into the driver's seat twenty minutes later, I'm empty. And for once, she's angrier than I am.

She wraps her hands around the steering wheel, muscles tense. "I'm worried about them. Her dad's taking it really hard, like he's the one who failed her. He can't work much. And they were barely making ends meet before all this." She looks like she could yank the steering wheel right off.

Sam stressed about money when her dad put everything into starting up their small hardware store. She worked the counter to help out when he couldn't afford to hire anyone. Who will do it now?

I stare out the window at the lone tree in the small yard. A Big Wheels trike hangs from the sturdiest branch by two ropes. A perfect rez swing. Do Sam's littlest brothers even understand what's happening? "Has the Two Feather Project contacted them yet?"

"Yeah. Charmaine's got them a donation to help in the meantime. And she's setting up some counseling services for them."

"Good."

Grandma starts the car. "She'll do it for you too."

Talking about how I feel isn't going to change what happened. It's not going to make things right for Ray Bear. Or Sam.

It's not going to bring any answers.

That's the only thing I need. Answers.

"No." It's easier for both of us if I lie. "I'll be fine."

I perch on the edge of the couch, key ring spinning on my finger. The buffalo robe on the wall hovers over me like a dark shadow. The antique rifle on the shelf in front of it glints in the near-sunset light creeping through the windows, almost like the towering shadow itself is gripping it. Hunting something. I shudder and tuck my fists into Ray Bear's hoodie pocket, squeezing my keys tight enough that they feel like shards of glass in my palm.

My face is still hot and swollen after crying in front of the White Tails' house. I don't wanna go to the party—not without Ray Bear and Sam.

Not after everything that's happened.

They should be climbing into the car with me. Sam already a little drunk and singing made-up words to songs too loud. Ray Bear would be wearing this sweatshirt, rolling her eyes at Sam but smiling any-way. At the party, Sam would've gone after the rez ball kids, the ones who thought they were somethin'. I'd have drifted to Brody to laugh at kids being idiots and guess who'd start the first fight. Ray Bear would've had her eye on things. We wouldn't stay all together at the party, but we'd make sure to leave together. Safe.

That's what we thought, at least.

I don't think I'll ever feel safe again. Not with Sam and Ray Bear's killer still out there.

I need answers. I'll never feel okay without them.

Youngbull certainly hasn't found any. That fed probably won't either, as much as he likes to act like he will. My insides squeeze and grind.

Somebody has to figure this out.

Kurt Staccona's voice slips into my thoughts. *Any chance she was getting into drugs?*

I stare at the buffalo robe on the wall, shaking my head. Ray Bear wouldn't have. Not after that stuff took our mom away. We were just little kids when she split the first time. I dug out an old photo album and started scribbling across Mom's face. Ray Bear yanked it out of my hand and yelled at me. She said it wasn't Mom's fault. It was the drugs. The *drugs* stole our mom. Ruined our family.

Ray Bear wouldn't have made the same mistake.

Staccona *has* to ask stuff like that.

I chuck my keys at the floor and head straight for her room. Some tribal officers already combed through it when she went missing, but I never have.

I pause at the door, steeling myself, and turn the knob. The door swings open with a whining creak. It looks the same as it always did. Bed made, schoolbooks lined up neatly on her small shelf, shoes and running spikes in rows on the floor of her open closet. Her cross-country race bibs are taped across her wall in a perfect grid. A hint of vanilla hangs in the air.

I drop into her desk chair before I can talk myself out of it and pore through her old notebooks and schoolbooks. I rummage through her junk drawer. Dig through the pockets of her clothes, clawing at lint and fabric. Dump out her jewelry bin. Lift her mattress from the box spring.

I turn the whole place upside down until tears prick at my eyes. There's nothing helpful here. Only pieces of the Ray Bear I knew— the pieces that didn't see this coming either.

Her room's a mess now. Her belongings are splayed out like

roadkill, just like our lives in the wake of her disappearance. I scramble out the door, slamming it behind me. I rest my clammy forehead against the wood and pound my fist against it, shaking its old hinges. I *knew* Ray Bear. I did. Why are Staccona's questions making me doubt that?

My phone buzzes violently on the kitchen counter, making me jump away from her door.

I shake out my arms and head back into the golden light at the front of the house, the phone still ricocheting against the laminate. When I pick it up and turn it over, my sister's name blares across the screen.

Rayanne Arnoux is calling me.

Chapter 16

ELI FIRST KILL

Sunday, July 14, 8:00 p.m.

After my best attempt at spaghetti, which Cherie informed me didn't taste half as good as a can of cold SpaghettiOs, I get her cleaned up and into bed. Her pajamas are last year's size. The shirt comes halfway down her stomach, but at least it'll keep her cool while the house is still full of hot summer air.

She looks as tired as I feel. There's a dull ache in my knee from my bad relay transition and that bone-tired feeling everywhere else. The kind that's more than physical. I'd feel more relieved about the championship prize money if I didn't also feel Staccona hovering behind me like hot breath on my neck.

It makes me want to bag this whole idea, but I need a break.

The lantern fills Cherie's room with subtly pulsing yellow light. Books and little toys are strewn across her bookshelf, which Grandpa made for her with his bare hands.

She pulls her stuffed moose under her chin and watches me straighten her faded pink quilt. "Why do we have to eat fake spaghetti now?"

I laugh and sink to my knees next to her, my elbows creaking the mattress. "SpaghettiOs are fake, Cherie. They're terrible for us."

"I don't like real spaghetti, even if it's good for me."

"You'll get used to it." Hopefully, we'll get the power back on soon too. I ruffle her hair until she swats my hand away.

"Maybe you're just bad at cooking."

"Hoh, don't insult your Elder or you'll be on cleanup duties next time." I give her a fake glare and pull my phone out of my pocket, which is half-charged from keeping it plugged in during our car drives today. I wave it in front of Cherie's face. "Do you remember how to use this?"

Her eyes light up. "911 if something happens to you. And Sling Shotters when I'm bored." She reaches for it.

I pull it to my chest. "That's right. Do you remember how to find Brody? What letters his name has?"

She rolls her eyes, too smart for her own good. "B-R-O-D-Y. Or L-I-T-T—"

"Just Brody. Listen . . ." I spin the phone in my fingers. I could be making a terrible mistake. But she's safe here. Much safer than she'd be sleeping in the truck parked near people who are drunk or high. I'll lock the doors behind me. "I'm going to Brody's for a little while you sleep."

"You're leaving?"

"Yeah. But you keep my phone—not to play Sling Shotters. To call Brody if anything happens and you need me. I'll be near him, so if you need me, you use my phone to call him. Got it?"

"So I'm babysitting myself?"

"That's right. You're big enough now. But you have to promise to only use the phone if you need me. Don't waste the battery. Just leave it on your dresser. Okay?"

She nods, a smile exposing her dimples. "You got it."

I grab the lantern and back out of her room. "Night, little sis."

By the time I've double-checked all the window locks, Cherie is snoring gently in her room. I pull on a black hoodie and jeans and slip out the front door, turning the handle twice to make sure it's locked. She'll be fine.

I hop into my truck, and even though my gut twists at the thought of really leaving Cherie here, I already feel more relaxed.

The number of times I've actually been alone in the last few months . . . I don't want to count. I turn the radio on, roll down the windows, and cruise past town and out to Brody's ranch, which is set out of the way and on a lot of land. Everyone likes forty-ninin' there almost as much as going to Cutbank Creek river parties. And his cows are far off enough that you can't smell their stink. Much.

Dozens of cars are already parked in the field grass alongside his long driveway. Most I recognize. Some are probably out-of-town folks here for Indian Days. I pull my hood up against the quickly cooling night air and walk toward the orange glow past Brody's house. It smells like summer camping, like Grandpa is sitting next to me whittling a willow stick, ready to spear through a hot dog.

Two separate bonfires are lit with an assortment of logs and stumps around each one. Teenagers and twentysomethings fill them and dot the surrounding area in groups, but they're not holding roasting sticks, just beer cans. A few couples make out as they perch on top of the metal fence enclosing the horse pasture. Even more people showed up than Brody thought.

Brody spots me coming and digs into one of the open coolers on the back of his deck. "First Kill, you made it!" He raises his hands, a can of beer in each, and struts over. He's clearly already downed a few. It makes a few heads turn at my approach.

He shoves a can into my hand. "This mean dear ol' Dad is back?"

I glance around as he pulls me toward the nearest fire. "What?"

"Your little shadow isn't with you. She with Dad?"

"Oh. Yeah. Last-minute surprise." I don't need anyone knowing a seven-year-old is home alone. "Hey, what time is it? I forgot my phone."

He clumsily pulls out his phone to check. I get a good enough look to notice there aren't any missed calls. Good. We drop onto a log, and Brody takes a hearty swig. "There are two hot girls here from Great Falls. They watched the relay." He juts a thumb over to the next fire. "I told them they could meet you." His brows waggle.

Maybe that's what I need, but as Brody leers at them and sloshes the poison in his can, I'm not so sure. He glances down at mine, and I quickly pop it open to bump cans. As he chugs the rest of his, he doesn't notice I don't touch mine.

Chapter 17

LOREN ARNOUX

Sunday, July 14, 8:40 p.m.

My fingers move in slow motion as I force my thumb to swipe to answer the call.

I press the phone to my ear, but I'm too panicked to speak. I shuffle toward the mostly abandoned landline phone on the kitchen wall, ready to call the police if I need to.

The words finally tear out of my mouth. "Who is this?"

The voice on the other end is deep and uncertain. "Hey, sorry. I found this phone and this number was one of the emergency contacts in the lock screen?"

My other hand wraps around the phone on the wall. "You found it?"

"Me and some buddies were heading to a motel in Saint Mary. We had an exploding soda situation and had to pull over to clean up." He laughs awkwardly. "We saw the phone a little ways off the road, kinda under a big rock, and grabbed it."

"What road?"

"Uh. Duck Road? Or something."

I stare out the window above the kitchen sink—down the very same road. "Are you still there?"

"Nah. The phone was dead. We've been driving for a bit, but we got it charging and turned it on. We didn't think it would actually work! When it did, we thought we'd try to find the owner."

I pull the other phone off its receiver, the dull dial tone blipping into the room.

"You do know the owner, right?"

He could be telling the truth. The enthusiasm in his voice and the way he pauses—waiting for some gratitude—make it sound legit. Or he could be the person who took Ray Bear. I should tell the tribal police right away and have them pick it up. Question the guy.

But the sudden urge to see her phone with my own eyes, to hold a piece of her . . .

To see for myself if she was hiding anything from me before the police tell me what it was. Or take the phone and never tell me anything at all.

"Yes." I hang up the landline phone with a decisive clack. "It has to be right now. Can you meet me at IHS . . . the Blackfeet Community Hospital?"

I tap the steering wheel, glancing at Mara's front door, thoughts racing.

Mara opens the passenger door with a creak and settles into the seat beside me. "Thanks for picking me up." She buckles her seat belt and then gets a look at my face. "Regretting it already?"

A laugh flits out my mouth. "Nah." I try to hold the smile, but it turns into a grimace.

"You all right? We don't have to go. I swear I won't be offended."

Of course I don't want to go to a party. But all I'm thinking about is that phone call . . . I roll the hem of Ray Bear's sweatshirt between my fingers and blow out a long sigh. I don't know the right play here.

"I was serious in that message." She tears her gaze from some long, dead grass shaking in the slight breeze and looks me in the eye. "If you ever want to talk about anything, you can. I feel pretty messed up after Samantha, and I didn't even like her. I can't imagine how you're feeling right now. . . ."

None of my friends asked if I wanted to talk about Ray Bear's disappearance. They acted like they didn't want to bother me. Sam acted like she was terrified of upsetting me, so much that she actively avoided me. Now this girl, who I've been nothing but cold to, is offering. Maybe I wouldn't have withdrawn so far if my own friends had done that.

"I'm here in any way you need. That's all I'm saying."

I nod at the sincerity in her voice. She may regret the permission she doesn't realize she's giving me.

Resolve floods me. This is reckless. And I shouldn't involve her. But the doubt that maybe I didn't know my sister is creeping into my head like mold. And the fear that this Staccona guy will be able to tell a story based on whatever they find in her phone without us having a chance to see first feels even worse.

I put the car into drive. "Okay, then. You're gonna regret offering."

She squints at me as I flip around and head toward the hospital, but it's too late to back out now. I tell her about the call on the way.

Twilight makes the plains behind the hospital look like a cold desert. The mountains looming at the horizon are a blue as deep as overripe serviceberries, with a smudge of their purple-pink juices bleeding up into the darkening sky. Grandma wouldn't approve of this.

A black SUV pulls into a spot at the front corner of the lot and a short, blond guy who looks like he kisses his biceps climbs out, tapping the top of his door with impatient fingers.

Mara sinks into her seat, barely peering over the dashboard. "This is a bad idea."

It is. But I can't dwell on that now.

"He might not have shown up if I told him everything. I didn't want to spook him."

"Or . . ." She throws her hands up in the SUV's direction. "*He* could be the one who hurt your sister." She whisper-shouts, even though the windows are closed. "Just call the police. Don't talk to him. Wait until Youngbull comes."

I shift in my seat, staring her down. "You'd understand if it were your family member ripped away. You'd want to see it for yourself first."

She avoids my gaze, instead keeping her eye on the waiting car.

"They're not figuring anything out. But if I could just see if she kept anything from me . . . maybe *I* could. *I* knew her best." I try to keep the traces of the rage-fueled fire in my chest from sparking.

"But what if he's the guy? He could throw you in his car and—" She can't even finish the thought. "What then?"

I open and close my mouth. I don't know *what then*. I just know I'll never stop wondering if I don't look myself. "I'm doing this with or without you."

I don't tell her I'm scared. I don't tell her that I picked her up first just in case something happens to me. It doesn't matter much anyway, because my anger overshadows my fear by a long shot.

She growls out a sigh. "Fine. But call the police first so we know they're on their way. And so you don't look as sketchy."

She's right. I call the tribal police station to let them know what happened and then move quickly. The feeling of sand rapidly slipping

143

through my fingers is heavy as I slide back into gear and roll through the rows. I pull into the spot beside him.

Mara groans. "There's like three other dudes in there. Loren . . ."

Time's already ticking. "Too late." I step out of the car.

"Loren?"

I nod.

I glance at the faint shine of other pairs of eyes behind his car's partially tinted windows as he reaches into his cup holder and then stalks around his car toward me, too slowly. He cradles a beat-up iPhone in a pastel-pink case.

My breath hitches. How many times did I see that case as Ray Bear took pictures of me, making ugly faces so my real smile would come out? As I watched her laugh under her breath and scroll her feed. As she used its calculator, feverishly hunched over her homework like a beautiful nerd. As she texted me from across the room when Grandma was mad at us.

He places it into my outstretched hand. It's a cold, hard weight. A piece of her we've been missing. I put in Ray Bear's birthday for the passcode, and then our faces light up the screen. I suck in a gasp of air that turns to sludge in my throat.

I haven't been able to see Ray Bear since they found her. And I may never get to. But seeing her recovered phone is almost like holding her hand and getting a last moment with her.

The guy is close enough to see the background image. "Are you sisters?" His reflection is in the corner of the screen, hovering. Too close. I glance at Mara inside the car, gripping the door handle.

The guy swings his arm in my peripheral, sending white-hot panic through my body.

I jolt against the car, adrenaline thrumming into my limbs, a thousand scenarios running through my head that all end with my head cracking on the asphalt and his fingers digging into my throat— only to see the guy's hand combing through his hair now frozen in place and his eyes peeled wide.

"Sorry . . ." He glances at the other people in his car, awkwardly raising his palms. "I'll head out now. . . ."

"No." I push off my car and square my shoulders. I shove the panic out of my voice even though adrenaline is still blazing through my body. "You can't go yet."

His mouth hangs half-open like he's waiting for the punch line.

I nod to the outline of a phone in his pocket. "Google *Rayanne missing in Browning*."

His face blanches, and he fumbles out his phone. "What are you talking about?"

I hug the phone to my chest as hot tears pour over my cheeks.

Another guy opens the back door of the car and pokes his head out. "All good?"

Mara finally emerges, her eyes darting between each of us.

"That's *Rayanne's* phone?" the first guy asks, looking up from what must be a local article on her disappearance.

The second guy approaches and reads over his shoulder. "Seriously? Shouldn't we be giving that to the police?"

Mara takes over, explaining that they're on the way. Telling them what the last three months have been like. Giving me time.

I shove the mess of feelings down and check the road for any cop cars. I act like I'm staring at our picture and dive in, forcing myself to see as much as I can while Mara distracts them. To see if there's any hint at what happened. To see if there's any chance Ray Bear *did* hide something from me.

Youngbull already looked into her calls with the phone company and said it didn't turn up anything suspicious, so I don't waste time there. I check her recent text messages and email. Scan her recent photos. Scroll through her contacts for names I don't recognize.

The blond guy paces as Mara keeps talking.

Nothing jumps out as out of the ordinary.

I cradle the phone with my shaking hands, subtly using my thumb to open her SnapShare DMs, Staccona's voice in my head asking if she was dating anyone. She didn't really message any guys on it.

Except Eli First Kill.

I scroll through the few messages. There are some from during the cross-country season related to practices and meets, sprinkled with a few linked posts of funny memes and reels. But then they stop for months. Until out of nowhere, Ray Bear wrote, **I miss you. Please stop being such a stranger.** On April 8—the day before she went missing.

But Eli never replied, which sounds about right.

It doesn't automatically mean something. I already knew they got close during the season, and I knew it didn't go anywhere after that. That's exactly what their DMs show.

Isn't it?

I press the phone to my chest. Maybe there isn't anything else on here that shows a glimpse into why she vanished.

"I'm sorry," the guy says. He looks past Mara. "I swear, we just found it." He stares at the phone in my hands. "Holy crap. We didn't see anything else. Shouldn't you— Shouldn't I . . . I don't want to get in trouble." He reaches for her phone but pauses as tears pour down my cheeks.

"She just wants to feel close to her sister while we wait," Mara says, stepping between us again. "Because you know what this probably means . . ." She says it to distract them, but it still jerks my heart. Because we both know her body was already found. That this isn't a missing persons case anymore.

The public doesn't know yet.

Mara whispers to them now, making them lean in close. I catch Sam's name.

I stare at the screen one last time, ready to hand it over, but I bring up Safari in a last-ditch effort. There's only one tab open to a search engine. I tap the search bar, and a drop-down list appears.

Her previous searches punch me in the gut.

Meth cost per ounce

Fentanyl

How much does one fentanyl pill go for?

The guy runs a hand through his hair, glancing over his shoulder. I stare at the list. It doesn't mean anything. Grandma and I would've been able to tell.

I'm certain of it.

I knew my sister.

I glance at the guys and frantically tap the X's next to each of the searches, erasing them. I knew her.

I swipe out of all the apps I opened and press the phone to my forehead before the guy's nerves bring him directly in front of me. I place the phone back into his outstretched hand.

He wraps his long fingers around it. "Were you messing with anything?"

I blink. "No. I just wanted to hold it before they take it."

"Okay." He scans the road, shifting on his feet. "Hopefully this helps you find her."

I clench my teeth, swallowing the truth. I don't know if anyone else is allowed to know yet. I lean against my car, numbness spreading into my limbs. I don't let myself wonder if I just screwed everything up. A cop car finally appears on the road and turns into the lot. I knew both of those girls as well as I know myself. They had nothing to do with drugs. I'm desperate to find a reason for their deaths, but that can't be it.

Chapter 18

MARA RACETTE
Sunday, July 14, 9:45 p.m.

Loren cuts the engine in front of Brody's ranch house. The headlights shine across the rows of parked cars, tires sunken into dry grass and tracks of mud. Silhouettes move together inside one of the cars, and she instantly flips the lights off to send them back into darkness. The property behind the house is faintly lit with moonlight, and even in its shades of black I can tell it sprawls on for miles, weaving in and out of veins of trees.

She's been quiet since we left the hospital parking lot, letting the tribal police take all the necessary steps with the phone and the guys who found it. I wasn't so sure Loren was thinking clearly tonight, but when her grandma popped out of the building in the middle of her nursing shift to hear what was happening, the officers didn't let her see the phone, just like Loren guessed. And boy did that piss her off.

They didn't care. They slipped it into a plastic bag and that was that.

Even though Loren stressed me out of my mind . . . she was right. But was it worth it?

She tucks her hands under her thighs, staring at the braid of sweetgrass on her dash.

"So did you find anything . . . noteworthy?"

She opens her mouth then snaps it shut. "Wasn't it weird that Eli First Kill left the dance arbor during questioning?"

I lean onto the console. "You think he knows something?"

"I plan to find out."

"Tonight?"

She shrugs. "Might as well."

"I mean, it did look like he had something to hide. But I gave him a ride the next day, and he was rudely adamant that I should never pick anyone up for a ride. For my own safety."

"That's a good way to describe him. Rudely adamant." She opens her visor mirror and dabs at her smudged eyeliner. "Sounds just like him, doing something kind of chivalrous but being rude about it so you're not sure if it's nice or not."

"Are you two pretty close?"

"Kinda. We were when we were young. Then he changed a couple of years ago. Got cocky and dismissive. Sometimes I still see the same guy. Other times I doubt he cares about anything."

I picture him securing Cherie to his chest after the powwow. "Except his sister."

She flips the mirror shut. "Hopefully."

"Why do you think he changed?"

"His dad got back into meth." She pulls her key out of the ignition and presses it between her fingers. "I don't know why it was different between us that time, though. He knew me and Ray Bear already went through that. He knows he doesn't have to act for us."

I guess that explains why Loren and Rayanne were raised by their grandparents.

"But you didn't answer. Did you see something about Eli on Rayanne's phone?"

She loops her wristlet of keys over her hand, turning to me with sudden energy. "Not exactly. But we're breaking into his truck." She jumps out of the car, leaving me scrambling out after her.

"What's that supposed to mean?" And why *we*?

She weaves through parked cars, giving the car with the couple hooking up inside a wide berth, then ducks behind a black truck with massive tires at the end of a row.

I crouch behind her. "You're joking, right?" But I know she's not.

She peers around the truck's bumper. A grove of young cottonwoods and a tangle of undergrowth swallow the property to our left.

"Haven't we been reckless enough for one night?"

She rolls her shoulders back and strolls up a couple rows, stopping at Eli's faded gray Tacoma. I guess that's her answer.

I follow her and peek into the slightly open window. "What do you think you're going to find in there?"

"Hopefully nothing. Give me a boost."

There's no stopping her. I wave a mosquito out of my face and clasp my fingers together. She steps into my hands and squeezes her arm down the small gap of the open window, fingers inching toward the manual lock.

It clicks.

I guess we're not technically *breaking* in.

She hops down and slips into the driver seat, yellow light from the ceiling pouring over her.

"Just hurry." I don't know Eli well enough to know what he'd do if he caught us. I scan the rows of cars as muffled shouting carries over on the cool breeze. Dark shadows flit across the orange firelight glowing in the far row of cars.

Loren shuffles through the contents inside the console, gum

wrappers spilling out. A Flamin' Hot Cheetos bag crinkles in the cup holder.

A car door slams somewhere close. I duck, stomach dropping like an anchor. "Hurry up!"

Loren cusses under her breath and opens the glove compartment, fingers shaking now as she flips through papers inside.

The more frantic she gets, the more paranoid I am someone will catch us. Or maybe it's the other way around.

I step onto the back tire to check the truck bed. Nothing but bits of dry grass and a crushed pop can. I open the back door and see Cherie's pink booster seat. This is pointless.

Loren shoves a small stack of papers back into the glove compartment. "Nothing but expired car insurance."

"Let's just go."

She slams the glove compartment shut, making me flinch.

I close the back door as softly as I can and grip the edge of the open driver's door. "C'mon." Footsteps brush against the prairie grass a couple rows up. Maybe less. "Loren."

She sprawls across the center console and reaches into the cup holders on the passenger side.

Through the tinted glass of the window, a figure in a hoodie steps out from between two cars, heading right toward us. He's tall, his gait stalking.

I grab the back of Loren's shirt and yank her off the console and out the door, sending her stumbling backward, crunching into the nearby undergrowth.

I shove the door closed, dashing around the back of the truck and behind the next car, Loren on my heels.

With the faint glow of the fires at his back and his hood on, the guy's face is completely shadowed. He slowly looks over the cars in front of him. "You dirtbags stealin' stuff?"

I hold my breath.

Loren laughs, making the figure jump, his hooded face whipping in our direction.

I jab my elbow into her arm, but she doesn't shut up. "It's not Eli," she mumbles. She'd recognize his voice better than me. "But I think he's high on something." She sinks lower, barely peering over the car, and goes eerily still.

The guy's twitchy and nervous, scanning the cars from behind his hood. He's not in his right mind, and I can't help but imagine that shrouded face hovering over me, air halting in my strangled throat. He shoves a plastic bag of something white into his pocket and breaks into a run past the car we crouch behind.

Loren stands and leans her elbows onto the car.

I rest my forehead on its cool surface. "You know, this is *not* the night I was expecting." My parents would be pissed about all this. It was hard enough to convince them to let me hang out with Loren and a "big group" when a killer is still on the loose.

We've been asking for trouble.

She straightens up.

"And apparently it was all for nothing too."

"Maybe. These were in the cup holder." She opens her palm to reveal a box of matches and a hair tie. "These are the kind of hair ties Ray Bear and I use." There's a question in her voice.

"Probably Cherie too."

She nods like that's what she expected me to say. Something is flickering in her eyes, and it's not the unsteady light.

"What did you see on that phone?"

She loops the hair tie around the box of matches and spins it. "Eli and Ray Bear may have had a thing last fall, but I couldn't tell for sure."

"She wouldn't have told you?" It seems like the kind of thing sisters would talk about.

She sucks her teeth. "I thought she would've. But the day before she went missing, she DMed Eli that she missed him and to not be such a stranger. So now I'm not sure."

It could be something. Or it could be nothing. "Even if they did have a thing, is that really enough to suspect Eli? That doesn't really mean anything."

"It's not like I have much else to go on. And isn't it usually the husband or the boyfriend who's guilty?" Anger flares in her voice.

Loren may not know Eli as well as she thought.

And I don't know either of them at all.

She chucks the items under a car. "If he's hiding something, I'm gonna find out."

BRODY CLARK
Sunday, July 14, 10:00 p.m.

I zip off my jacket and toss it into the mudroom before heading back onto the deck. The blue-black night sky is clear. Teenagers crowd the yard. The fires are inviting. We won the Indian Relay. I already feel light enough to forget what I was so worried about. The police interrogations are annoying, but that's it.

I don't know why I ever let them freak me out.

I grab another beer and strut across the grass to First Kill and the two smokin' hot girls. I drop onto the log and put an arm around one of the girls, who's named Carly. Or Camry. Or Carmel. Something. "Don't tell me First Kill is boring you with a play-by-play of the race again." I say it like I'm not the one who's been recapping it for anyone who will listen. Or even pretend to listen.

Eli clenches his can with two hands. "Nah, man. We were talking about your epic mudslide again."

"Yeah? I'll show you an epic mudslide. Turn around and check your underwear."

Callie throws her head back and laughs into my ear. I don't know if it's the alcohol, but I'm pretty sure this girl is into me. I pull her in tighter and smell her bonfire hair.

I'm almost certain we're about to leave the fire and head to my room until Loren and Mara meld into a group standing across the fire from us. Loren's hair is wavy from wearing braids all day. Her dark eyes are black in the shifting light.

Again, I don't know if it's the alcohol, but she's looking at me with a rage like she's jealous. And I like that. Carmen intertwines her fingers with mine at her shoulder. I gesture across the fire. "Ladies, this is Loren Arnoux." I'm not sure what Mara Racette is doing here, but I'm feeling easygoing enough to include her. "And Mara."

The girl bobs her head. "Camry." She gasps. "Oh, Loren. I didn't recognize you without your regalia. I keep hoping they find your sister." Her eyes dart between all of us. "And I'm real sorry about Samantha. Wasn't she a friend?"

Loren's eyes bore into me and then Eli. "Yes. She was."

Camry drops my hand and leans forward. "Do they know who did it yet?"

We all shake our heads, and we all take turns watching each other shake our heads. Like we're answering a question we've been afraid to ask each other.

"I tried to help the police." Camry's voice is quieter now, so we all lean in. "I saw Samantha earlier that day in the concession line. That tall, old white guy was behind her, and I was behind him."

I shift on the log. "The visitor they pulled into the giveaway?"

Loren leans even farther, so close the fire's heat must be biting her skin. Eli does too. Waiting.

"And?" Mara asks.

"Well, that's pretty much it," she says. She talks quickly as everyone leans back again. "But he was all distracted like. The lady with him was trying to talk to him, but he was just really staring at Samantha. It was *strange*."

Loren cocks her head, mulling it over.

"Are you sure he wasn't staring at the menu?" Mara asks.

A flicker of a smile pulls First Kill's cheek.

Camry stiffens next to me. "I felt weird about it. Take it or leave it."

Again, I don't know if it's the alcohol, but I usually know a good idea when I hear one. A hum in my veins is confirming this one. "It's actually very fishy," I say, drawing the group's gazes. It makes more sense the longer I think about it. "That night, he told the police he'd never seen Samantha before, and apparently, he was staring at her in line just a little earlier?" I shake my finger. "That doesn't add up."

Loren nods subtly before looking at Eli. "And what do you think, Eli First Kill?" Her gaze is hard. Or is she coming onto him? I can't tell. Now I'm the one feeling jealous.

Eli carefully sets his can on the ground. "I think we should leave the speculation to the professionals."

156

Loren and Mara share a long look, and I feel like I'm missing something.

I don't like that.

Loren folds her arms. "Is that why you left that night? To let the professionals speculate?"

He glances at the two girls between us.

"That's what you said when Ray Bear went missing, too. That the police would find her." Loren's cheeks twitch. "How'd that work out?"

First Kill nods in slow motion. "I'm not doing this right now."

"Yeah? Or ever, huh?" She laughs bitterly. "Cherie's not here. What's your excuse now?"

He squeezes his fingers until his knuckles crack. "My excuse is, I don't owe anyone anything."

"Wow." Loren shifts her gaze back to me, and not in that good way.

I scoot an inch away from Camry.

"That's it. I'm pulling *that* card. My sister is gone, and you two are gonna talk to me about it. Now."

First Kill and I don't move. Neither do the stunned girls between us.

"Get up!"

Her yell brings me to my feet and draws a lot of looks from the groups around the property. Jason stands on the back porch holding a glass bottle. Watching us. Evaluating.

"Be back soon," I say to the girls.

Finally, Eli stands and falls into stride with me as we follow Loren and Mara across the grass and onto the dirt tire tracks that lead to the back of the horse barn.

She halts at the backside, where the firelight doesn't reach us, and leans against the wall, arms folded. Seething. A dim yellow light is mounted above our heads. The shadows etched across her face make her look harsh, and when she pulls her sweatshirt's hood on, it's almost impossible to see her expression. It sends uncomfortable swirls into my gut.

I should've called her after we found Samantha, but I couldn't make myself do it. I figured I'd only make things worse. And I never know what to say.

"So what's up?" I ask, swinging my arms to ease the tension.

Eli scowls.

"I thought we should talk about the elephant in the room," Loren says.

I don't want to. It's easier to pretend things are still fine. "Who, First Kill? He's put on a few pounds since cross-country season ended, but I wouldn't go so far as to call him that."

Loren's head cocks slightly to the left, and I know she's rolling her eyes. It's her signature look—at least when I start throwing out my stupid jokes. "I'm serious."

Eli shoves his hands into his pockets. "What do you want us to say?" They stare each other down for a beat. "Go around in a circle and cross our hearts that we didn't strangle Samantha?"

Loren goes completely still. "Why not?"

Eli's scoff turns into a laugh, and I join in.

I tap my elbow into Eli's arm. "Should we pinkie promise too?"

He looks at me soberly, like I crossed a line I should've known was there.

"Cut it out," Loren says. "You're seriously joking about it when she's not even in the grave yet?"

My smile drops. "It's the alcohol." She knows it's not. That's just me. It used to amuse her.

Not anymore.

"We wanna know who we can trust." Mara only looks at me for a second, and then her gaze rests on First Kill. He doesn't shrink under it, but he doesn't challenge her either.

"The police questioned you today, right?" Loren asks.

We both nod.

"Do you know why?"

I wish I had another beer in my hand. Eli glances at me. I nod. He shakes his head.

Loren's voice softens. "They found Ray Bear's body."

Eli takes an automatic step back.

Chapter 19
MARA RACETTE
Sunday, July 14, 10:45 p.m.

Eli's face is pale, even in the dim light. I can't tell if he's shocked or terrified . . . maybe a bit of both? Brody clearly already knew Rayanne was found, so the police must've told him in his interrogation. Does that make him more suspicious or less?

I don't know these guys well enough to gauge much from their reactions, but I watch closely, trying anyway.

Eli rakes a slightly shaky hand across his face. "What do they know?"

Loren leans against the rough wood of the barn, hands shoved in her hoodie pocket. "They think she and Sam were killed by the same person. So all of us who were last with Sam—"

"Are now suspects for Rayanne too," Eli finishes.

"Right. So I need you guys to talk to me. I want to believe it wasn't any of you who hurt my sister, but you need to prove it."

"Well, I know you're singling me out." Eli sees exactly what's going on. "You and Brody had your project. Wasn't Mara in that class too?"

I nod. Not that they'd actually remember if I was there that day or not. I'm sure I don't sit in their memories like they sit in mine.

Brody's lips curl into another unsteady smile. "Hey, Samantha was always pretty rank to New-Girl-Mara. You think she decided to get some revenge?"

He says it like I'm not standing right here in this circle of shifting feet. His smile fades when Eli and Loren ignore him. He knows it's a weak joke and an even weaker theory, but at least he's half admitting Samantha was cold and mean . . . always reminding me I was an outsider. But what about him? He'd make anyone laugh at my expense. If I was going to get revenge on anyone, he'd be right up there with Samantha.

"I don't know how to prove it to you," Eli says, frustration sharpening his tone. "I'm not a killer. That's all I can say."

Loren pushes off the barn, stepping closer to Eli. "But you had a thing with Ray Bear, didn't you?" It doesn't come out of her mouth like a question, more like an accusation.

Eli shifts backward, moving just outside the circle of the bulb's dim light. "So what?"

Loren goes still. She was right; her sister kept it from her. Eli kept it from her.

Brody is stunned into silence for once, and even the voices from the fires hit a lull.

Loren grabs handfuls of Eli's sweatshirt. She yanks him down to her level so fast his hair gets whiplash. "What did you do to her?"

Eli's expression is surprisingly blank. . . . I couldn't read it even if I'd known him for years like everyone else. He pries her shaking fists off. "Nothing. If you don't trust me, don't trust me. I don't care." He turns on his heel.

"So that's it, then?" Loren calls out, a growl frying her voice.

He casts a glance back before he disappears around the corner of the barn. A bit of panic shines in his eyes. Because he can't *prove* he's innocent or because he's not . . . we'll see.

Loren turns her gaze on Brody. "Did you know about him and Ray Bear?" Some of her fire is sputtering out, but there's still heat in her tone.

Brody puts his palms up. "Hey, I knew he had a thing for her . . . but I didn't know they were bumpin' uglies." He backs up slowly onto the dirt treads and retreats around the corner just like Eli.

By the time Loren and I walk back to the fire, she's breathing slower, Brody is stumbling into his house with that girl he was with, and Eli is nowhere in sight. The other girl is sitting with some different guys on the fence, so not off somewhere with Eli.

"I hate him sometimes." I assume Loren is talking about Eli until I see her staring at Brody's back door.

"Do you . . . *like* him?"

"Not like that—I just can't believe he can turn around and do that." She points a shaking finger at the door.

I'm usually not one to make waves, but Brody pisses me off. "So go stop him."

"Nah."

"Why not? Make him talk to you. If he's really that drunk, maybe he'll tell you what you need to know."

She pulls her hood off, firelight flickering in her focused eyes.

"He obviously likes you. If you walked in there, he wouldn't even mind."

"He likes any girl who breathes."

Not me. "He's different with you. Seems like he genuinely cares about you."

She twirls her hood's drawstring. "You'll be okay out here?"

"It won't be the most stressful part of my night."

She covers her mouth and laughs. "My bad."

I shift closer to the fire, letting it warm me. "Just do it now, before it's awkward for everyone."

"Right. Okay." She jogs across the grass and weaves between the teenagers standing in front of the deck. After she disappears through the back door, I count to twenty, and then the girl Brody was with storms out onto the deck . . . just like I thought she might.

I retreat from the fire and perch on the fence, away from any people. It's enough that I'm here. I don't need any small talk with kids I don't know at all. Goose bumps rise on my skin, and I hug myself against the cool night. The scent of the bonfire smoke hovering here erases the scent from the wildfire. In the still air I can almost forget the fire and how Rayanne was found because of it. Almost.

Eli appears across the yard, slipping from between a row of parked cars. I only recognize him by his strut and all-black palette. Hood up, hands buried in his pockets. Alone. I don't know why he's still here, but he probably wonders that about me too.

As if on cue, he looks toward me. After a slight pause, he changes course and heads my way. I grip the fence a little tighter. I'm alone now. Would anyone around the fires notice if Eli dragged me off somewhere? Would I be able to stop him?

"Where's Loren?" His rude tone still surprises me. Does he do it on purpose, or is his voice naturally abrasive?

"She's inside with Brody."

His eyebrows furrow so quick and deep, I almost laugh.

"She wanted to talk to him."

"That probably wasn't a good idea. He's pretty wasted." He pushes his hood off, releasing his disheveled hair. "I mean, whatever, she's a big girl."

I look over Eli's shoulder at a group laughing by the fire. Jason pokes at the fire with a big stick. "They're just talking."

Eli leans a shoulder against the fence, a little too close to my legs. "What are you still doing here?"

I feel instantly defensive. "What's that supposed to mean? Am I less deserving to be here than any of these kids?" I wave my arm at the crowd in front of us.

The corner of his mouth perks up for a half second. "I just meant, you're alone. You're at a party alone, not talking to anyone. So why are you still here?"

He's got a point. "One: Loren is my ride. Two: I could say the same thing to you. You look miserable."

His arms tense. "I'm not."

"You're not fooling me. Why not just leave? Or are you wasted too?"

He sucks his teeth as he looks me in the eye for a few seconds too long. "*You* leave."

I should've expected him to say something like that . . . but my jaw still drops. He struts back toward the fire and plops into an old camping chair directly facing me. A few kids from our school fill in the gaps in the circle around the fire as soon as he's joined it.

Smoke mars his face as it eases into the air between us. He pulls his hands behind his head and stares me down. Claiming his territory like an alpha rez dog.

Screw him.

I drum my fingers along the fence and stare at the back door. I told Loren I'd be fine, but the chill seeping into my bones coupled with the icy stares Eli keeps throwing my way make my silent, vision-inducing bedroom seem preferable to this now.

And Eli's not the only one staring.

Jason takes a drag from something on the back porch, an orange ember glowing dimly. I can't see his face under the bill of his hat, but he's looking my way. Until two scantily dressed sophomores round the corner of the house, drawing his attention.

Another kid I don't recognize watches me too. Probably an out-of-towner, but maybe he assumes the same thing about me. He's nursing a glass bottle and has had teens filtering over to him all night. Quick, hushed conversations. Money changing hands. He's dealing something.

The shifty guy by the cars probably bought drugs from him.

I don't like his eyes on me.

I glance at the back door again, then at Eli. He raises his chin, as if he's proving that I'm the miserable one now, not him. He eases farther into his chair, challenging me. Waiting to see how long before I crack and dip out of here. It makes me want to buckle down, but the stares coming from the out-of-towner at the other fire push me off the fence.

I head toward the barn to find some peace away from the stares. Eli wins again.

I wish Loren would hurry up.

I pass under the dim light at the back of the barn. Eli's shocked face paling underneath it flashes into my mind. A face like that says he thought they'd never find Rayanne's body—maybe because he's the one who hid it.

Or maybe he's hardened enough that he just figured, like most everyone else, that she was gone and nobody would see a trace of her ever again.

I slip into the barn, the smell of horses and fresh hay already calming me.

Maybe all his face said was that he'd never given up hope she'd be found alive. He had a thing with her; maybe he's been holding in some silent pain this whole time.

One of the horses sticks his head over his stall gate at the sound of my approach. I pet his sleek, white neck, just like I did after the giveaway.

I don't know how I even ended up here . . . how suddenly I became Loren's sidekick in tracking down her sister's killer. This was not what I envisioned when I told her I was here for her.

Does she honestly think one of her own friends could be capable of murdering her sister?

I rest my palm on the horse's nose, drawing in his warmth.

The door behind me creaks open wider. I spin as a shadowed person steps into the barn. The yellow light illuminating the doorway behind him only casts his figure into near blackness. I sift through the images of who I remember seeing around the fires, trying to match the shape.

He shifts just enough that the dim light skates across his features. "Don't feel like hangin' at the party?" he coos. He's the one who's been watching me.

I grip the cool metal of the horse's gate. "I just needed a minute."

His half-lit smile sends fear prickling over my shoulders. "I could give you a few."

I scan the dark walls. "No thanks." I take a slow step back, sliding my fingers on the rough wood.

Samantha pours into my head. Alone and cornered. Is this how it started? I step back again, the smell of hay and horse and dirt the only thing between me and him. Were these Samantha's last smells in that horse trailer? Did she know what was coming? My throat is tight like fingers are wrapping around it, squeezing harder with each beat of my heart.

He takes a step forward, his unsteady eyes raking over me. "I saw you checking me out. You wanna snag."

"No." My pulse thrums into my fingertips as I slide them along the next stall's gate, not daring to take my eyes off him. There has to be some kind of sharp tool in here. Something to defend myself with. I take another step back, and my hand collides with a shovel hanging on the rough wood wall. I casually grip the handle.

He tugs at his shirt as he takes another step. "I saw you . . ."

Someone else steps into the dim light. "She said no." For once, Eli's rude tone is a relief.

The guy turns, wobbling. "Get outta here, First Kill. I'm not doing anything different from you sleeping around the rez."

"Psh. Only when they want it."

The guy turns back to me, his voice thick. "How do you know she doesn't?"

"Sterling, she couldn't act like she wanted you if I *paid* her to."

He scowls. "What'd you say to me?"

"I said . . . you couldn't get a girl to want you if you took a course on it at the Blackfeet Community College. Aaays." A smile flits onto Eli's face as he gives the guy, Sterling, a shove.

Sterling stumbles past me, clenching his fists. "You lookin' for a fight, First Kill?"

I skirt through the doorway, putting Eli between us.

Eli holds his arms out. "Skoden."

Sterling holds his fists up but doesn't come any closer. It looks like his head is still spinning from the shove. And the booze.

"Let's. Go. Then." Eli slows his words, daring the guy to come at him. When he doesn't, Eli turns to me and points his lips back toward the bonfires.

Sterling looks a lot smaller and drunker now that Eli's told him off. I could've taken him with that shovel, right? My skin is hot, my muscles still tense from the thought of putting up a fight.

And I would've.

When I pause under the yellow light, Eli grabs my arm. I tug against him, keeping my eyes on Sterling. "*I* could take an acting course at the community college, and I still wouldn't be able to fake it," I shout.

Eli pulls me a few more steps from the doorway, hissing out a laugh.

The anger at what that guy wanted to do to me is sizzling through my blood. I could've stopped him. I could've swung that shovel. "The acting professor couldn't even fake it, you fugly son of—"

Eli puts his free hand over my mouth and guides me around the corner of the barn, his chest rumbling with laughter. "Easy, easy. Don't aggravate him even more."

I pull his hand off my face and tug my arm out of his grip. He doesn't try to stop me. He looks over his shoulder, grinning.

I tell myself I could've stopped him, trying to shut out the small what if. *What if I couldn't have?* Would I have ended up like Samantha and Rayanne? Is that where this was going? Or was he just a hammered idiot who really thought I was checking him out? I didn't have to find out—because of Eli.

"Who was that?" I ask as we stride back toward the bonfires.

"Sterling Yellow Wolf. Dropped out of school last year." He glances over his shoulder again. "You okay?"

"Yeah. For a second I thought I was going to end up like—"

"Oh." He stops in his tracks. "No—he's not . . . He gets like that when he's plumb wasted. Thinks he's all somethin'."

I glance back, making sure he's not following us. "You don't think he's the one who hurt Samantha?"

"I doubt it. They were cousins. He's an idiot but they were always tight." He starts walking again. "Probably why he's wicked drunk, if you ask me."

The fact that he gets like that when he's drunk isn't any comfort to me. That's not an excuse. If anything, it only makes me wonder what else he's capable of. Especially if he's a drug dealer too. Eli's probably known him most of his life . . . it makes sense he's not going to suddenly imagine him as a killer. But the way he cornered me in that barn—that's more telling than years of acquaintance.

We stop at the same spot on the fence where I was sitting before. I hop onto it, and surprisingly, Eli does the same.

"You don't have to stay here. I said I'm fine." I'm not sure that's entirely true, though. The adrenaline is fading, leaving my muscles prickling like they do after intense interval training. It has me feeling on edge. There's no way I'm wandering off alone again. I should've known better, and I'm sure Eli is thinking the same thing.

"You know, that was—"

"*Plumb stupid.*" I say it even louder than he does, thinking about what he said when I gave him a ride. "Yeah. I know."

"See, now you're catchin' on." He flashes a smile of approval and a few uncomfortable seconds tick by. "Were you just trying to say hi to Marshmallow?"

"What?"

He laughs. "That's what Cherie named one of the giveaway horses. We're boarding him here."

"Marshmallow?" I can't help but smile. "Very . . . majestic."

He nods sagely. "Real sacred too."

I scratch my neck and glance back at the barn. "Seriously, though, I'm fine. You can go."

"It's all good. I don't feel like talking to them anyway." He jerks his head toward the group he was hanging around before.

"Well, I know I'm the last person you want to talk to. Just go home."

I hate the way I stare at the crease in his cheek when he smiles again. He leans onto his knees. "I guess I don't really want to be home right now."

I get that. Not that I have the same kind of problem with my parents that he has. It's just when I'm alone . . . I think about everything. Like the terrifying way Samantha was hurt. And how nobody has any idea who did it. The thoughts circle round and round, keeping me awake. Maybe it's the same for Eli.

It must be a thousand times worse for Loren. She's dealing with the crushing grief and the deep anger that nobody was able to fix it. Nobody protected her sister and best friend. It's no wonder she was dragging me around in her no-baked plans tonight.

The need for answers must burn hot and constant beneath all the other emotions. There's no way to know just how much she'd risk to get them.

I shiver against the night air as our silence stretches on. The temperature is dropping quickly.

Eli clears his throat. "I'd offer you a ride home, but I don't think I can after what I said when you let me out of your car."

"Technically, you said that was the last time *I* could give *you* a ride. Not the other way around."

He puts his hands back on the fence, fingers brushing mine. "Same concept."

"Guess I'll have to wait for Loren. If I'm lucky, Brody will pass out soon, and she'll have to leave, right?" My teeth chatter against the final *T*.

He glances at the goose bumps on my arm and bounces his leg on the bottom rail. "If I can't give you a ride, I can at least barge in and tell her you're waiting. I need something from Brody's phone anyway." He hops down and struts across the grass before turning back. He glances over his shoulder at the group around the fire, then pulls his hoodie off in one smooth motion. He tosses it at me without a word, then heads for the house.

Chapter 20

ELI FIRST KILL

Sunday, July 14, 11:30 p.m.

I'm not sure what I'm expecting to find in the house. I just need to make sure Cherie hasn't been calling Brody's phone. I put my ear to his door. Silence. I knock quietly, but nobody answers. I test the knob and push it open.

Little Bro is passed out, mouth gaping, legs hanging off the mattress like he fell backward midconversation. It wouldn't be the first time. Loren's curled up at the end of the bed, the tracks of tears on her cheeks shining. Guilt rips into my chest. I haven't been there for her. But what else can I do? I have my own problems to worry about.

The outline of Brody's phone is obvious in his jeans pocket. I slip it out, knowing he sleeps like a rock when he's drunk. There aren't any notifications on the screen, but I unlock it just to be sure. Brody's always had the same stupid passcode, 1111. He calls himself an open book. As if he's ever read one.

No missed calls. I set the phone on his desk.

I should wake up Loren, but she looks like she used to. I haven't seen her face so peaceful since before everything went down. She looks so much like Rayanne it kills me.

I can't believe they finally found her body.

Hearing that hit so hard I had to go sit in my truck for a sec so they wouldn't see how much it affected me. I shake off the grief creeping back up and slip outside into the cold. Mara Racette's still alone on the fence, wearing my sweatshirt. At least nobody's bothering her.

Her light brown hair swings against her shoulders as she turns at my approach. Orange light from the dying fires makes her face look warm when usually she's cold and closed off. Probably because of me.

I shove my hands into my jeans pockets and lean against the fence. "Bad news."

"What happened?"

"Nothing. They're asleep. Looked like Loren had been crying a lot."

She leans onto her knees and groans. "So you didn't get what you needed either?"

"I did. Brody's idiot passcode is 1111." I smack a mosquito away. "I wasn't about to wake her up, but you could. Or . . . I could give you a ride. The *last* last time."

She fidgets with the drawstrings of my sweatshirt like it's as much hers as mine. "Loren's suspicious of you."

Of course she is. Especially now. Isn't everyone? She watches a group of kids weave through the cars to leave. It's getting less crowded here. I look past her to the barn. I wonder if Sterling is still in there. Her eyes are wary as she scans the rest of the people and lands on Jason tossing another log onto one of the fires. When she looks back at me, clearly waiting for my response, she seems to soften.

"Are *you*?" I ask.

She's staring right at me. I hardly know this girl, and it should feel awkward, but it doesn't. "I haven't decided." She juts a thumb backward. Toward the barn. "That helps."

Stopping a ringy drunk from taking advantage of somebody makes me less suspicious. Noted.

She keeps looking at me, and for some reason, I want her to keep talking. The fact that she hasn't already decided my guilt when I've been so evasive makes me want to convince her I'm innocent.

I hop onto the fence and sit next to her. "Ask me whatever you want."

She squints. She doesn't think I'll actually answer. And now I know I'll have to.

"Are you affected at all? After finding Samantha?" She digs her nails into the cuffs of my sweatshirt. *She* clearly is.

I don't want to admit something that probably makes me look weak, but I do anyway. "Yes."

"You don't really show it."

I look at the dimmest fire, now barely more than glowing charcoal. "I can't afford to."

She doesn't ask me why, and I'm glad for it because part of me might actually want to tell her. Instead, she says, "I hated her guts, you know. But I'd never—" She shakes her head. "I'd *never* wish that on anyone. Whenever I'm alone, I can't stop myself from picturing the way we found her."

I nod. "So that's why you came tonight?"

She waits for a group of girls to pass by us. "Partly. Mostly I just wanna help Loren. But it's nice being around you guys who . . . get it. You were there."

I scratch my neck and force myself to keep talking, because she's voicing something I didn't know I was feeling too. Besides asking if I saw where Samantha went, Brody and I haven't spoken a word about it. "I keep picturing Samantha too, and it makes me feel sick. But then it always switches, and I see Loren's terrified face. . . . She's been through too much. It's all changed her, and that kills me."

She nods slowly. "What about Rayanne? You really dated her?"

My palms squeak against the metal fence. I shouldn't answer. I should bail like I did when Loren started digging where she shouldn't. But I let myself voice a piece of it. "For a little while, last year. Feels like forever ago."

"Doesn't it hurt?"

The grief I let out in the truck threatens to leak out again, but I swallow it down. That's another thing I can't afford to show. "We were over a long time ago, but yeah. More than I'd like to admit." Even to myself.

We fall into silence until she asks what I thought she would. "So why'd you leave the arbor that night?"

I watch a slew of drunks shove each other around, figuring out how I'm supposed to answer that. Somebody howls from across the yard. A truck engine rumbles to life. "Everything I do, I do for Cherie. That's the honest truth. I left for her." That's all I'll let myself say. And all that matters.

Surprisingly, she doesn't push it. "You didn't do it?"

"I promise I had nothing to do with either of their deaths." We're only a foot apart, and the moonlight is faint, but she's seeing me more clearly than anyone has in a while. I raise my pinkie, drawing a smile from her.

She hooks my pinkie with hers. Her skin is warm against mine.

"I swear I'd never hurt anyone like that." I don't expect her to believe me. I wouldn't. You can't trust anyone in this bass-ackwards world, no matter what they swear on. But it feels good to think for a second she might.

She drops her hand. "Maybe you can give me a ride now."

Half of me eases into the trust she's almost offering. The other half sees the bit of hesitance there as she glances at Brody's back door again. Maybe she'll only take my ride because it's better than the alternative—waiting around for Sterling to find her again.

For some reason . . . I just need one person to believe I didn't do it. Just one. "How about this? Take out your phone."

She pulls it out and unlocks it.

I hold out my hand, and she gives it to me. I add myself to her contacts. "Go wake up Loren. Text me when you're home safe." I hand the phone back. "And then try to believe me. If I was the sicko doing all this, I could easily do it tonight. It's not me."

She slides off the fence and shoves the phone into her back pocket. "Okay." She moves to pull off my sweatshirt.

"Nah. You can give it back later." I walk through the smoke toward my truck but stop and make sure she's heading into the house. I saw the fire in her eyes as she gripped the mucking shovel. Maybe Mara Racette isn't as helpless as I thought she was. If I hadn't seen Sterling follow her to the barn, she probably would've messed him up good. At least in the state he was in.

But . . . that doesn't mean I'd like him to try again.

Chapter 21

LOREN ARNOUX
Monday, July 15, 12:20 a.m.

The bonfires are only piles of smoldering orange wood. They send gentle crackles into the crisp night air. I walk across the deck, every board creaking under my weight. It's dead out here—not a person in sight. Beer cans litter the grass. I'm surprised there isn't anyone passed out or asleep somewhere on the ground.

I step into the parched grass to head for my car, but I walk straight. I try to force my body to turn, my chest heaving and my muscles throbbing. I can't stop. I keep walking toward the hot coals.

The warmth wafts up to my face, and then my knees give out. I fall forward, heat singeing my skin until I'm splayed out across the orange coals. Finally, my body responds, and I roll out of the fire across the dry grass, shirt in flames, until I hit her.

My sister lies next to me.

I breathe out her name. "Ray Bear."

Her clothes are brown and wrinkled, but she smiles. Her dark eyes are like pits in the night. Flames crackle behind her, climbing trees and creating a wall around us. I look over my shoulder at Brody's house. It's falling into itself, smoke pouring out of the roof.

When I look back at Ray Bear, her skin is sliding off her bones.

She grabs my shoulder, desperation curling her fingers, and shakes me. The jolting motion makes her hair fall out in clumps. I scream, trying to break out of her grip.

I shake her arm off and clamber backward. Hot coals and dry grass crunch under my burning palms.

She's crumbling away in front of my eyes.

I'm still scrambling backward when I collide with something.

Ash floats around me as I skid across the ground over a pair of legs. It settles around us as I inch toward her head. Mara Racette stares back at me, motionless. Red blooms across the skin of her throat, and it seizes as she struggles to breathe.

"Make it stop," she whispers, just before her throat collapses in on itself.

I sit up in Brody's room, sweat clinging to my shirt. I blink until the figure standing over me sharpens into Mara's face.

Make it stop.

"You fell asleep," she whispers.

My throat tightens, almost like hers did. Like the invisible hands have slipped through the darkness and found me instead.

"Sorry," I whisper. Brody snores from the middle of the bed, his legs hanging off the edge.

Mara's posture relaxes, but my whole body stiffens in warning. That's some bad medicine.

I never thought I'd be one of the superstitious Blackfeet, but the prickling under my skin is laced with paranoia. Back in the day, if a member of a war party had a bad dream, they'd turn back.

They wouldn't ignore that bad medicine.

Make it stop. I shake my head, trying to dispel the words still echoing through it.

Mara needs to stay the hell away from me. I thought we could be friends like Ray Bear wanted, maybe even do more digging together, but this is an omen I can't ignore.

I slide off the end of the bed without a word, and we slink out of Brody's room to find Jason smoking a cigarette in the living room. I'm too embarrassed to wave. This isn't even a walk of shame, but it feels like one.

We pass Sterling Yellow Wolf at the back sliding door, one cheek red and swollen, but he doesn't acknowledge us. Or he's too drunk to even notice us.

Mara stares over her shoulder at him and grips my arm as we shuffle down the deck's steps. "What happened in there?"

Make it stop.

I didn't go into Brody's room with a plan. Mara was right, though; he happily kicked the girl out for me. He thought I was coming onto him, and I let him think that for a second. Then I slapped him.

I made him talk about that morning. When we turned in the project. I told him how everyone stopped asking how I was doing. I told him how it feels to find out your sister is dead. I vomited my emotions until we were both crying.

Yeah, Brody Clark cried. His drunk mess probably won't remember most of it, but that's okay. I will.

Then he passed out. I didn't mean to fall asleep. After he started snoring, I only closed my burning, swollen eyes for a second.

"Nothing." It's all I say until I drop her off at her house. She can think what she wants. All I know is that we can't be friends.

Or else she might end up dead.

I can't go home. Not yet. Not when Eli First Kill's revelation about dating Ray Bear is needling through my thoughts. Fog slowly climbs up the car window beside me before Eli First Kill finally slides into the passenger seat. It only took three calls and a text to get him out of his house. Grandma told me not be alone with anyone. But she also told me not to be stupid, and we're well past that.

"You here to accuse me of something again?" There's less poison in his voice than earlier.

I cut to the chase. "What happened with you and Ray Bear? I saw messages between you two. I know she missed you. Why were you avoiding her?"

He stares straight ahead at his truck—the one I broke into just a few hours ago.

"Did she do something to piss you off?" I know he's not all steel. "Please tell me, or I'm gonna assume she did something to really upset you. Enough to make you—"

"She was too good for me."

I clutch my seat belt. "She said that?"

He almost laughs. "No. *I* did. I knew it. She knew it." He glances at me. "You'd agree."

I let him choose his next words.

"She was going places. Getting ready to head out into the world. I'm never going to leave. I've gotta watch over Cherie. Clean up my dad's messes." He practically hisses the last part. "She was a big plans person. I'm not." He taps his leg. "So I broke things off late last year. No use dragging her down and distracting her from her big dreams."

"So it wasn't just casual, it was real."

"Guess so." Emotions flit into his face, too fast to place. "For a minute."

"Why didn't she tell me?" It hurts worse than I expected.

"She didn't want to upset you. She knew you wouldn't have liked it."

I told her not to go there . . . but would I really have been mad? If Ray Bear was happy, I'd like to think I would've gotten over it. "How'd she take you ending it?"

"Don't know." Something like guilt filters through his features.

"Eli." Impatience flares in my voice, but I rein it back in. "C'mon."

"She didn't appreciate me making the decision for her." His shoulder twitches. "But it was the right one."

I hate that I can't even remember if Ray Bear seemed off anytime last year. I wish she would've told me. What else was she hiding from me to spare my feelings?

Why was she searching for stuff about drugs? Why was she looking for the price of meth and fentanyl? Eli stares at his dark house in silence and I wonder how bad things must've gotten here in the last couple of years that made him change. He built new walls for some reason. Maybe Ray Bear saw why.

"Will you be honest with me . . . was Ray Bear around your dad much?"

He schools his features tight again, replacing his emotionless mask. "No."

"You don't think she ever got . . . drugs from him or anything?"

His brows twist. "No."

"Could you ask him? Just to check—"

"She'd never— Why are you asking that?"

It sounds even more ridiculous after saying it out loud. "Just something Staccona asked about. Stupid."

"Plumb stupid." The poison spills back into his voice.

The doubts still itch through me, but at least I'm not the only one who's shocked to imagine Ray Bear of all people getting into drugs. As for everything else he's said, I don't know how much to trust. It's hard to believe Ray Bear never would've told me about him. Paranoia that something bad happened between them worms its way around my head, but underneath that I still worry about him and his family.

He looks past his truck to the big shop. Its metal framing reflects glints of the moonlight. He's probably shutting back down to the guy who *doesn't owe anyone anything*. I'm lucky he's already said this much.

I keep pressing anyway. "I haven't seen your dad hanging around town for a while. He's been working a lot?"

He slides his fingers to the door handle. He doesn't pull it yet, but he doesn't answer either.

It's probably a good thing. Maybe he's keeping himself good busy. "Does that mean he's doing okay?"

He pops the door open, and I notice his knuckles are red and swollen. "Just stay out of it."

Chapter 22

UNKNOWN

Monday, July 15, 7:00 a.m.

Heavy eyes, aching head. This one would hit harder. The information about Rayanne was out there now, all public knowledge, but if they hadn't connected the dots by now, they probably never would. Phone brightness turned all the way down in the dark room, the stream button was pressed.

INTO THE AIR
EPISODE 114

[INTO THE AIR THEME]

TEDDY HOLLAND: Happy Monday, Big Sky Country! I hope your weekend was good enough to carry you through another long week. It certainly gets harder as the summer goes on, especially here in beautiful Bozeman, Montana. You can't *not* be an outdoors person when you live here. We've got a lot of good stuff coming up, and just like last time, if you stick around to the end of today's podcast, you'll have a chance to win two tickets to the Big Sky Country State Fair. You do not want to miss that.

This is Teddy Holland, and you're listening to *Into the Air*. If you missed our last episode, we're changing things up for the next four weeks. We're dedicating the next month of *Into the Air* to the Missing and Murdered Indigenous Women movement. MMIW for short.

We shared some statistics with you last episode, which you can find on our website, along with plenty of links to good resources you can check out. Before we get into the next MMIW case today, I first want to touch on *why*.

Why are the rates of violence against Native Americans and Alaska Natives so much higher than those against the rest of the population? I have a guest with me here in the studio, Charmaine Momberg. She's on the American Indian Council at MSU and is a founder of the Two Feather Project, and she's here to answer just that.

So, Charmaine. Why is this happening?

CHARMAINE MOMBERG: Thanks for having me, Teddy. I appreciate what you're doing here. I listened to your last episode, and it sounds like that tribal policeman would probably tell you that it has a lot to do with drugs. Alcohol. Poverty. Bad parenting. And there is definitely a lot of that. The pipeline of vulnerability comes into play. But it's more than that.

TEDDY HOLLAND: And those things happen within every race. Every population.

CHARMAINE MOMBERG: Exactly. It's such a complex issue. There's a lack of vital resources, for one. There's often a lack of coordination and communication between intergovernmental agencies and conflicting jurisdictions with tribal, state, and federal entities.

It's made it difficult to keep accurate data on all the missing women, let alone find them. There are definitely systemic issues at the root of this widespread problem, which I'll get deeper into, but the worst part is—hardly anyone even knows about what's going on.

Mainstream news outlets don't help. They're not spreading awareness like you see for other cases. The hordes of internet sleuths aren't diving into the MMIW cases and rallying around those victims like they do for so many others. We don't see the same viral crowdfunding pages being shared. Media makes a huge difference.

TEDDY HOLLAND: Absolutely. As you heard last week, Geraldine Arnoux also touched on this huge media problem.

[BUZZING]

TEDDY HOLLAND: This is . . . this is strange. Geraldine is actually calling me right now. Do you mind if I take it, Charmaine? Let's keep recording.

CHARMAINE MOMBERG: Sure, go ahead.

TEDDY HOLLAND [PHONE]: Geraldine, how's it going?

GERALDINE ARNOUX [PHONE]: Hey, Teddy. I just . . . I thought you should know . . . something happened.

[CRYING]
[SHUFFLING]

CHARMAINE MOMBERG [WHISPERING]: Stop recording.

[STATIC]

[RECORDING ENDS]

[SOUNDBITE OF WIND]

TEDDY HOLLAND: Listeners . . . that was a tough phone call. For all of us. I stopped recording out of respect to Geraldine, but started again when she was ready to record statements for *Into the Air*. You know, I had every MMIW episode planned, and most of my material worked out, but as Geraldine said at the beginning of that call, something happened. We'll get back into my discussion with Charmaine later in today's episode. For now, let's return to the Arnoux case.

On Friday, we talked about Rayanne Arnoux, a high school senior from the Blackfeet Reservation who disappeared without a trace. We heard from her grandmother and Blackfeet Law Enforcement, who had no leads, but a lot happened over the weekend.

The Blackfeet Tribe hosted the North American Indian Days in Browning. This annual powwow goes on for several days with contest dancing, rodeos, sporting events, you name it. Thousands of people attend, including other Indian Nations and non-Native visitors.

[SLOW DRUMBEAT]

TEDDY HOLLAND: It was on Thursday, the first night of the powwow, when another girl from the Blackfeet Reservation was killed. She was found on the campgrounds, mere yards away from busy sales tents and crowds.

As you can imagine, it rattled an already traumatized community.

Then, a wildfire erupted across the tribal lands and led to a heartbreaking discovery.

[SOUNDBITE OF CRACKLING FIRE]

TEDDY HOLLAND: Men who were aiding in clearing out the fire's path stumbled upon Rayanne's body. It had been nearly three months since she went missing.

GERALDINE ARNOUX [PHONE]: I haven't seen her. They haven't allowed me to. But they told me the April snowstorm that dumped a few feet on us starting the day after her disappearance helped preserve her body a lot longer than usual. Hopefully, that'll make a difference in the case.

TEDDY HOLLAND [PHONE]: I'm so sorry to hear about your granddaughter. I was really hoping for better news for you.

GERALDINE ARNOUX [PHONE]: Thank you. At least we know now, and maybe we'll have enough to get justice for her. And for Samantha. Now that it's clear a crime was committed, Ray Bear's case has been turned over to the FBI, like Samantha's. It should've been done a long time ago.

TEDDY HOLLAND [PHONE]: Has the FBI been able to tell you anything at all?

GERALDINE ARNOUX [PHONE]: The most they can tell me so far is that the cases look similar. The girls . . . were killed in the same way. The working theory is that the same person strangled both of them.

[SNIFFLING, BLOWING NOSE]

TEDDY HOLLAND [PHONE]: That had to be hard to hear.

GERALDINE ARNOUX [PHONE]: Oh yeah. But that, combined with the similarities between the girls, has the cases connected. It's possible the FBI will be able to make something out of it all now, but I'm trying not to hold my breath.

TEDDY HOLLAND [PHONE]: You don't trust them to get it done?

GERALDINE ARNOUX [PHONE]: A new agent's on the case. Another non-Native rolling through to get his hardship assignment over with. Three years dealing with the rez and he gets to choose his cushy new assignment after. He doesn't actually care about us, but is he any good at his job? Only time will tell.

[SOUNDBITE OF EERIE WIND]

TEDDY HOLLAND: Geraldine never stopped looking for Rayanne or holding out hope that she'd be found alive. I can't imagine the sadness and disappointment she's feeling now. Unfortunately, her situation isn't unique.

This episode's MMIW case started last year when a fourteen-year-old girl went missing from the Crow Reservation. She was last seen with her court-appointed guardian—

Face hidden under a pillow, eyes pulsed with heat. A finger trembled as it held the pause button. *They've got nothing.* They liked to act like they had things under control, but they didn't. It was becoming clearer. They'd never figure it out.

Chapter 23

BRODY CLARK
Monday, July 15, 1:00 p.m.

When Loren stormed into my room last night, I had a few things on my mind, but the last thing I was expecting to feel afterward was guilt. I guess I should have because it's always hanging over my head lately. I keep going over all the things I should've done differently for her.

That's not going away anytime soon.

The thing is, I've never been good at being there for anybody. I'd rather make 'em laugh. It's always worked on First Kill. But when Loren didn't feel much like laughing and I didn't know how to help with the fears about her sister . . . I dipped out. And she finally called me on it.

I knew she was struggling, but I only thought about myself.

I've had it bad for Loren for a while, but now all I can think about is how I've never been good for her. And I'm part of the reason she's been such a wreck.

In a weird way, last night felt like old times, before things got jacked up. Grief was ripping her up, but it felt like she was coming out of her isolation, like she actually wanted my help. She was opening back up.

I've gotta keep her from disappearing again.

I drag a trash bag across the grass, collecting the last few beer cans scattered around the fence. Some drunk buttheads even chucked theirs into the horse pasture. The sun makes my head pound, and I'm already sweating. At least the smoke isn't hovering anymore.

Jason's royal-blue truck turns up the driveway and eases to a stop in front of the house. He hops out with fast food in hand. "Did you seriously just wake up?"

"What's it to you?" My own voice grates in my head like sandpaper.

He sucks the straw of his drink and tosses me a grease-soiled bag. "So you and Loren, huh? You think that's the smartest thing right now?"

"We're not—that's not what it was."

"That Staccona guy is going to keep looking into us, I can guarantee you that. I can't imagine Geraldine is going to be happy about you and Loren with all this still going on."

"Just drop it. I said nothing happened."

"Man, you're pissy, enit. I'm just saying. You don't want to give Geraldine any more reasons to not like you."

I dig into the bag. "What do you mean any *more*?"

"Word on the moccasin telegraph is you're not as likable as you think you are, Little Bro."

I peel open a hamburger wrapper and freeze midbite as a patrol car turns up our driveway. I toss the burger into the bag full of beer cans and shove it into the garbage bin just as Youngbull and Kurt Staccona step out of the car looking like cocky SOBs.

"What can I do you for?" Jason asks.

Youngbull scans the yard and points his lips toward the black remnants of our fires. "I'm sure you weren't burning fires during stage two restrictions."

Jason waves a hand. "It was ceremonial, enit. Is that why you're here?"

Staccona holds up a pristine piece of paper. "We have a warrant to search your vehicle and cell phone."

For the first time since this whole mess started, Jason looks surprised. "Why?" He snatches the paper out of Staccona's hand.

I grip my phone tighter in my pocket.

"We have enough probable cause to search your truck. We have witnesses placing a truck matching yours in the area Rayanne disappeared from on that morning. And after checking your employer's records, you didn't begin working on a car that morning until 8:15. Fifteen minutes past opening."

That's it? That's enough to slap him with a warrant?

Jason crumples the paper as he folds his arms. "That's ridiculous. I always need some time to get everything together and figure out what the car needs before starting. Do you even know how many rigs like mine there are around here?"

"Matching the model and royal-blue color? Four in the entire county."

Jason paces as Staccona and Youngbull pull on latex gloves next to his truck. "There's another one on the rez. I've seen it."

Staccona nods. "Two are registered in the area, including yours. If you would, please." He motions toward the truck.

Jason heaves out a breath. "Fine. I have nothing to hide." He hands over his phone and glares at Youngbull as he uses the fob to unlock the truck.

I try to catch Jason's gaze, but he won't take his eyes off the men as they pore over the truck. They dust for fingerprints. Go through the trash in his glove box. Pull out the floor mats.

It's violating. They might as well pull our pants down and inspect our underwear for skids while they're at it.

Staccona points to a dent in the passenger-side door. "What's this from?"

"Little Bro here opened the door into a bollard at Town Pump."

My cheeks heat, but the fed doesn't say anything else. He just takes out a swab and runs it all over the dent.

This isn't going to help Loren stay open with me. She's going to snap back closed faster than a spring-loaded trap.

It feels like hours before the men finally leave.

"What did I tell you?" Jason asks. "Staccona is going to be on our balls." He says it like there's some kind of vendetta against us.

Or him.

It's not just his ol' buddy Jeremy Youngbull getting into our business anymore. It's somebody who doesn't give a piss about us.

"Should we be worried?" I ask.

He grips my shoulder. "No. But we're going to need a lawyer."

MARA RACETTE
Monday, July 15, 2:00 p.m.

A lawyer . . . the thought makes my stomach churn the same way it does after an intense workout. The kind where you know you pushed way harder than you should've. I stand motionless in the bathroom, letting the water run over my hands. Why should we need one? We haven't done anything suspicious. The only thing that brought us into this mess was me receiving a gift in the giveaway. If I hadn't gotten one, I'm sure Agent Staccona would care less that Dad is the one who found Rayanne's body.

Wouldn't he?

I shut off the water and let the drips slide off my hands onto the faucet knobs. Mom said the lawyer is just to make sure we're all treated fairly. That we're all heard. That's not what it feels like, though.

It feels like we're in a bad spot, and I don't like it.

The doorbell rings. I grip the hand towel hard enough to make my knuckles ache. For some reason, it makes me want to talk to Eli First Kill of all people. Is his dad making him talk to a lawyer too? Does he have bags under his eyes from struggling to fall asleep between all the nightmares?

I pull out my phone and open our messages from last night.

Me: Home safe and sound.

Eli: 👍

I thought it would end there until another vibration ripped me from almost-sleep a while later.

Eli: Do you believe me?

I stared at the moonlight glowing around the edges of my curtains, wondering why my gut told me to trust him. He's definitely hiding something, but that doesn't necessarily make him guilty of anything.

Eli: It's okay if you don't.

Me: I think so.

Eli: 🤘

Eli: That's the closest emoji to a pinkie promise I could find.

Me: 🤘

I half smile until a knock rattles the loose knob on the door. I shove my phone back in my pocket and emerge to be introduced to the lawyer waiting in the living room.

"Mara, hi. Jon Miller." He's a barrel-chested thirtysomething-year-old. A blue tie hangs down a pin-striped dress shirt. He shakes my hand and smiles, strictly professionally, like he must in a courtroom, and then sits at the end of our kitchen table with an open laptop.

I sink into a chair and fold my hands in my lap.

He launches into the same kinds of questions the police have asked me—twice now—but he doesn't make me feel like he's trying to trap me like they did. He seems to like all my answers, which makes me feel a little better.

"I already told your dad this on the phone last night, but I just wanted to make some things clear with you too," he says afterward. "First and foremost, don't let the tribal police or Agent Staccona question you without your parents and me present."

I nod.

"Second, try not to worry. The fact that they're interested in you teenagers, of all the people who attended the powwow, tells me they have *very* little to go off of right now. Yes, Detective Youngbull says he didn't witness anyone else enter that area *from the arbor*. Anyone could've gone into the area from the opposite side. It means nothing. It would never hold up in court. Simply being one of the last few people to see Samantha White Tail alive is not suspicious. It's just the place they have to start.

"Your school attendance records show you were in class the day Rayanne went missing, so they have nothing on you there either." He pivots toward Dad. "Same for you, MJ, with the events leading up to you discovering Rayanne's remains. You weren't alone; you were helping clear livestock in the exact area designated to you by the fire chief; you immediately called the police. They have nothing on you."

Dad nods, and Mom squeezes his shoulder.

"And you weren't even part of the giveaway. You were in the stands with your wife when everything happened with Samantha."

"Aren't there any videos to sort through?" Dad asks. "I saw at least one person filming at the powwow. That could show who never left the arbor."

"Actually, there is." He casually raises a palm. "But the camera angle doesn't capture your family or the main break in the bleachers. The authorities used it to rule out quite a lot of people from the opposite side of the arbor who never left their seats. Samantha's whole family and the owners of the trailer she was found in are all clear."

I shudder at the thought of Samantha's cousin: drunk, stumbling Sterling. I wonder if he was one of the family members cleared. But if I ask, that'll only lead to more questions. Mom and Dad don't need to hear about what happened in that barn . . . or imagine what *could've* happened. I handled it.

It's frustrating to think we could've avoided all this if we simply chose different seats on the opposite side of the arbor.

The lawyer clasps his hands. "Try not to worry. At this point, they're grasping at straws. My job will be to make sure they don't twist any of them."

I want to believe him . . . he makes it sound so simple. But Dad's face is deathly tense, and it doesn't sit right with me. When Jon Miller walks out of our house, I'm left wondering two things.

How easy would it be for the tribal police or Kurt Staccona to twist something about us?

And if they really are grasping at straws here, how is the real killer ever going to be found?

Chapter 24
LOREN ARNOUX
Monday, July 15, 6:20 p.m.

I set my phone on the kitchen table and spin it in a slow circle while chewing my fingernails. They're nubs at this point. I used to shape them with Grandma's old emery board and paint them a new color every few days—Ray Bear doing my right hand. Now I'm lucky if I don't make them bleed.

It's too quiet in this house.

Grandma stands in front of the stove, still in her work scrubs, stirring a giant pot of something. The scent of garlic and onion fills the air. It almost tricks me into thinking things are normal. That I'll look up and Ray Bear will be across the table with a textbook. I'd ask her where she keeps her old junior year physics homework so I can copy her answers, knowing full well she'd never tell me. She'd chew her pen cap and say I'm distracting her.

But she's not here.

Grandma digs into the fridge. Now that Staccona finally gave the go-ahead for her to tell our relatives about Ray Bear being found, they're all on their way for a late dinner. It'll be nice to see them but painful to talk about it all.

Grandma's hardly said a word about it—that's how I know she's mad. When the frustration at the lack of progress turns to anger, she usually keeps a lid on it. She's been mostly silent since coming home from work. She must've been expecting they'd find something on Ray Bear's phone by now, but I don't want to ask what's on her mind because it would make me sick to pretend I didn't get a look at the phone first. That I'm keeping things from her. I'm already on the verge of tears. I have been since last night.

Mara made me think maybe I *could* talk about what happened. And that maybe I should.

There was something therapeutic about telling Brody all the feelings shredding my insides. So therapeutic that when he asked if he could stop by for a minute, I said yes. I haven't had a friend over since before. I thought maybe Mara could be that friend . . . but that dream has to mean something.

As good as it felt talking to Brody before, I want to back out now. I've always been the social loudmouth. The one laughing the loudest at the parties. Now it's a fight just to make myself smile at someone, let alone carry on a conversation.

The doorbell rings, making Grandma jump.

"It's just Brody." I pry myself out of the chair to let him in.

"Hey." He's still wearing the same clothes from yesterday. The smell of campfire clings to him as he slides past me. He looks like he's still hungover.

I lead him to the living room, and he collapses onto the easy chair. He slumps low enough on its arm that the barrel of Grandpa's old gun, mounted on the shelf behind him, looks like it's pressing right into his temple.

The steady beat of Grandma chopping something in the kitchen pulses into the room.

"You're looking rough."

He flashes a grin. "It's called being ruggedly handsome."

"Did the party continue all day today or what?"

He pulls off his white hat and rakes back his too-shiny black hair. "I wish." He slumps onto his elbow, cap perched on his chest. "The cops searched Jason's truck."

The chopping in the kitchen halts. "Really?"

He presses his knuckles into his eyes. "It's a load of crap, Loren. Somebody claims they saw a blue truck somewhere on Duck Lake Road that morning. That's it."

I don't say anything. Jason's blue Ram is pretty memorable.

He pushes off the arm and rests his elbows onto his knees. "I'm telling you . . . there's no way." His eyes plead with mine. "He couldn't have . . . done all that . . . and still started work at eight a.m. I just need you to know that."

Still, I don't say anything. I focus on the scuffed plastic of my turquoise phone case.

"He was still home when I left for our project that morning. There's no way he could drive all the way out here to your neighborhood, all the way north on Duck Lake Road where they found her, and still get to work on time. It's—it's impossible."

He's got a point. Brody is southwest of town. We're north. Ray Bear was found . . . much more north. But still. "I don't know what you want me to say. I'll just leave it to that fed to figure out."

The chopping resumes.

He shoves his hat back on and adjusts it. "He's my brother. I just needed you to hear me."

"Okay."

He stands up and forces a smile. "Anyway, I'll leave you to it."

I follow him to the front door, caught off guard by how soon he's already leaving. I knew it would be quick, but that's really all he came to say? He didn't want to talk about anything from last night?

He opens the door and pauses when he's halfway through it, knuckles white on the knob. "They didn't find anything, by the way. And our lawyer said Jason doesn't have anything to worry about. So just remember what I said."

I've got nothing to say to that, so he slips into the dusty air without another word. He doesn't wave as he pulls out of the driveway and disappears down the road.

I jump as Grandma suddenly appears in the doorway to the kitchen, holding up a chopping knife. "You shouldn't be talking to him about stuff like that. It's a conflict of interest."

I turn the dead bolt.

She waves the knife. "I'm serious. Youngbull's already having a hard enough time scraping together an investigation. Don't let a punk kid like Brody go messing it up."

I don't think he's trying to mess it up, but I do think he'd do anything for his brother. I'd do the same for Ray Bear. Would he still defend Jason if he knew he was guilty, though? That I don't know. Everybody's line falls somewhere different.

I don't think I'll ever be myself again if the investigators don't solve this. I can't let that happen. I'll stumble between depression and fear and rage until I don't even know who I am anymore. I'd rather die trying to find the killer myself than let that happen.

Chapter 25

ELI FIRST KILL

Monday, July 15, 8:00 p.m.

Cherie's opening her mouth as wide as she can to prove she brushed her molars when the doorbell rings. My stomach drops into my butt and nearly pulls me into a heap on the bathroom tile.

Cherie's eyes open almost as wide as her minty mouth. "Is it Dad?"

"No. He wouldn't be ringing the doorbell." I creep to the end of the hall to peer through the dark living room to the front windows, barely lit with fading dusk light. I can't tell what kind of car is out there. "Wait in your room, Cherie."

I point back down the hall until she stomps into her room at the end. Only the cops would show up unannounced. Brody always texts first, and everyone else knows I'm not interested in seeing them.

I snag the lantern from the bathroom counter and set it on the living room coffee table before I steel myself at the door. Everything could be about to fall apart.

I open the door.

"Mara Racette." I can't help but smile with relief, but I drop it as quick as I can.

She raises her chin. "Eli First Kill."

Adrenaline is still snaking through me as I pull the door open. I'm so glad it's not the cops that I let Mara step inside before thinking better of it. She steps onto the entry tile and waits for me to close the door behind us.

I stand awkwardly beside her, seeing the small, square living room through her eyes. The lantern doesn't even light the corners of the room. The walls pulse with its yellow glow, making the whole place look eerie. The doorway to the kitchen behind us is near-black. Shadows hang heavy around the framed photos on the wall in front of us, which haven't been updated in years. Mine is still from eighth grade. Cherie is just a toddler in hers. Dust clings to their edges and a spiderweb dangles from the ceiling above them. Probably looks a lot different than her house.

After she scans the room, she faces me. She's wearing a jean jacket over some sort of concert T-shirt. It matches the light blue of her scuff-free Converse. "Sorry, Loren told me where you live."

Of course she would. "What are you doing here?" My voice comes out harsher than I mean it to.

Her lips press into a thin line as I see the answer to my own question. My sweatshirt is folded in her arms. She hands it over.

"Oh. Thanks." I tuck it under my arm and shift on my feet.

"I washed it."

"You didn't have to do that."

She looks at the front door behind me just as Cherie pokes her head into the hall. I should open the door and invite her to leave. I should. But as I think about the quiet hours ahead after Cherie goes to sleep, I don't want to. All I do is stare at my phone or listen to music until my brain finally shuts off and I can sleep a few hours.

Mara takes a step for the door. "Well, anyway . . ."

"Hang on. I'm just getting my sister to bed. Do you want to wait until I'm done?" I gesture to the couch. "We could hang."

"Where's your dad?" The concern in her voice tells me even *she* has heard the rumors about him.

"He's heading back from a job. It'll still be a few hours."

She grips the edges of her jacket. "Okay. Sure."

I motion for her to follow me into the living room and grab the lantern. "Sit anywhere. Sorry"—I hold the lantern up—"it's . . . part of Cherie's routine. I'll bring it back in a minute." It's not like I'm going to tell her we had to shut off the electricity because the past due balance got out of control.

The lantern creates a tunnel of light as I pass into the hallway and then expands into Cherie's room. She frantically yanks the covers over her legs, like I couldn't possibly have seen her peeking in the hall, and plasters on her most innocent smile.

I set the lantern on her dresser and kneel in front of her bed. "Time to sleep, little sis."

"I need a Napi story, Eli."

I'm eager to get out of here with Mara waiting in the living room. "Not tonight."

"Please? I need one. I miss Daddy."

I put my hand on her cheek to keep her from saying anything else. "Okay." I settle against the wall next to the door, facing Cherie. Grandpa used to tell us Napi stories over campfires or when we couldn't sleep. Even Dad would tell us some every now and then, but they were never as good as Grandpa's versions.

It hurts to know Cherie won't remember his versions of Napi, the Old Man trickster who helped shape the world us Blackfeet lived in, so I make mine as close as I can to his.

"One cold night, when Napi was walking through the forest, he heard some chittering. He crept toward the sound and found many squirrels playing in hot ashes. Some squirrels would lie in the ashes while the other squirrels buried them. When the squirrels couldn't take the heat anymore, they would yell, and the others would uncover them right away.

"After tricky Napi watched them take turns, he came out of the trees and asked if he could play with them. The squirrels said yes but told him he'd have to wait for his turn. Napi said he didn't want to wait too long, so he better bury them all at once to save time. The squirrels thought that was a very smart idea."

Cherie snickers into her hands.

"So all the squirrels lay down, and Napi covered them with hot ashes. Some of them started getting too hot, so they called out, 'Let us outta here!' But Napi covered them with *more* ashes. And more ashes, until he couldn't hear their calls anymore. That trickster Napi roasted them until they were cooked enough to be his dinner!

"Then he laid them all on a scaffold of willow branches to cool and fell asleep while he waited. But when he was fast asleep, a sneaky bobcat came and ate all his squirrels!"

Cherie laughs with satisfaction.

"When he woke up, Napi was so mad at Bobcat, he pulled his ears so hard they stretched out and ripped off half his tail. And that's how Napi created the lynx from a thieving bobcat."

Cherie smacks her forehead. "That Napi is so dramatic."

"Enit." I stand up and grab the lantern. "They don't call him a troublemaker for nothing."

Her smile slowly fades. I couldn't care less that Dad isn't here tonight, but Cherie's not old enough to see only the bad in him. She doesn't get that things are better when he's gone. I guess that means I've been good at shielding her from the worst parts of his addiction. Or at least good *enough*.

"Chin up. Night, little sis."

She waves and tucks her hands under her pillow. I back out of the door and pull it closed to a crack. I almost drop the lantern when I see Mara sitting on the floor behind me. I put my hand on the wall to steady myself. "What—"

"Sorry." She shoots to her feet. "It was so dark in there." She points a thumb backward. "And quiet." I get it. If she hates sitting alone in her own house, of course it has to be worse in someone else's. And the sun has probably fully set by now.

I laugh the shock out of my chest. "If you wanted a bedtime story too, you just had to ask. Tuck-ins aren't free though." I lead her back into the living room and sit on one end of the couch. I set the lantern on the coffee table in the middle of some of Cherie's hair stuff. She doesn't ask why I keep it on instead of turning on the ceiling lights. Maybe she checked the light switches when I was gone. I shouldn't care.

She sits on the other end of the couch and faces me with her legs crisscrossed. "My dad used to tell me Napi stories too."

"Are you even Blackfeet if you don't get told Napi stories?"

She smiles. "Or have a feather or something hanging in your car?"

"Or have a broke-down car in your yard?"

She laughs gently. "I don't."

"I don't either—at the moment." I smile and tap the scuffed-up, white bottom of my Vans.

"I *am* Blackfeet, you know." She folds her arms. "Everyone likes to act like I'm not because I didn't grow up on the rez. But I am."

I swallow back a pang of guilt. "Nah, you're one of those Pretendians."

She's silent for a second. "You're serious?"

My lips quirk into a smile. "So then, what's your Indian name?"

Her posture stiffens. "Never got one. What's yours?"

"Mad Bear."

She covers her mouth as a burst of laughter spills out. "Sorry. It's just fitting."

I try not to smile. "My grandpa pulled it from our family line."

"Did he speak Blackfeet?"

I nod. "I was too stubborn to learn before he died." I kick off my shoes and mirror her position on the couch, crisscrossed facing her. We fall into silence, both looking somewhere at the couch between us. Samantha flashes into my mind. I see her as she was the last time she sat on this couch—asking too many questions.

"I meant it, you know," she finally says. "I believe you."

Warmth rises in my chest.

"I don't know who could've done it, though. Maybe Brody?"

The warmth gives way to crackling, like blackened firewood. "Why?"

"There's no way it was Loren or Geraldine. I know it wasn't me. And I believe you." She chews her lip, and I find myself watching too closely. "Brody and Jason were in the last group with Samantha, and I have no reason to trust either of them."

"I do." I've known them both my whole life. "We're cousins."

Her head cocks. "You are?"

"Somehow. My grandma and his mom were . . . second cousins? So we're . . ."

She squints, attempting to math out the relation before giving up. "Something."

I clear my throat. "I think the proper and official term is cuzzes."

"Right, of course." She flashes a smile. "Well, even though he's your *cuz*, I dunno about Jason. He was at that party full of teenagers just watching. Checking girls out."

"He stays to make sure nobody is doing anything too bad on his property. Or riding one of his horses off into the sunset. Keeps his eye out."

"He sure didn't seem to mind when that sicko followed me into the barn."

My mind automatically retraces my steps after Sterling. I clamp down on the anger churning through my gut. "He probably didn't see."

"I think he did. And I still think Sterling could have that violent side to him. He showed that loud and clear."

I grip the back of the couch. She could be right about him. I thought he and Samantha were close, but people change. "I guess so. But what about the visitor? Tall guy with grasshopper legs?"

She drums her fingers on her leg. "Oh yeah. I'd believe it for Samantha during Indian Days, but why would he be visiting back when Rayanne went missing? You know . . . if they really were both killed by the same person."

"Maybe they weren't." I shift to kick my feet up on the coffee table, nearly bumping the lantern. "I doubt the cops know that for certain."

"Well, then I'd still say Brody could be a suspect for Samantha's death even though he couldn't be for Rayanne's."

"He wouldn't hurt them. Wouldn't even have a motive to." My feet create massive shadows on the walls as I shift them in the light.

"He didn't have any sort of *relationship* with either of them?" Her eyes squint just slightly.

It's not like that's a smoking gun. Having a history with both of them wouldn't mean anything. But Little Bro doesn't anyway. "No. He doesn't usually have a problem getting girls, but neither of them gave him the time of day, no matter how hard he tried."

"Well, *that* could mean something. Maybe he was bitter about that."

I shake my head. It sounds worse than it is. I think they both knew deep down that Brody has always had a soft spot for Loren. They didn't want to get mixed up in that. "It wasn't Little Bro. I know him."

She cocks her head. "I know him too, and he's terrible. He made the last few months miserable for me. Even more than you did." She looks around the room like she just realized where she is and is wondering why she's still here. "With his rude jokes and snide remarks about how I'm an outsider. Always making me feel less than, like I wasn't even deserving of walking the same halls. You never told him to stop. You all are the reason I feel like I don't belong here."

The subtle lantern light makes her hair glow warm. Her eyes are shadowed as she glances at me, and the truth is, she does belong here. She's one of us. If she doesn't feel it, of course some of that is my fault.

I'm a loner because I want to be. She is because we made her. I made her.

"Little Bro isn't so bad. He has his faults. Believe me, I know. That's part of why—" I put my feet back on the floor and run my hand down my jeans leg. "He's rude and entitled. I know."

She leans onto her knees. "Why what?"

I grab Cherie's hairbrush from the coffee table and start wrapping a handful of spilled hair ties around its handle. "Nothing."

"Hey. Last night you said I could ask you anything. Did that have an expiration date?" Her voice is steady. "Remember how I'm trusting you? You could do the same."

For some reason, I want to.

"You seemed so quiet and shy when you moved here. Like a fawn." Everyone was whispering about the new girl with the big green-gold eyes. She didn't say much, just watched everyone. She has a striking face, but there was something childish about her at the beginning. I couldn't figure it out then, but I think I'm starting to.

She rolls one of her shoelaces between her fingers, watching me with those eyes.

"Bro . . . had his sights set on you." I snap a hair tie on the brush. "And like I said, he's entitled and manipulates people into giving him what he wants; most of the time they can't even tell. He was gonna get you to give him whatever he wanted, then drop you. He saw you as an easy target."

And I saw her as weak.

She pinches the shoelace between her nails, expressionless, waiting.

"I didn't want him screwing with you, so I figured I'd talk him out of it. Make him think he shouldn't be interested in somebody like you. Somebody so different from us." The words taste sour and wrong coming out of my mouth. "I thought I was helping."

She laughs dryly. "You just assumed I was incapable of handling myself? Because I didn't walk into school my first day with my mouth running?"

I toss the brush back onto the table. I saw her like a little kid. I saw her like I see Cherie. But the vibe she carried with her wasn't childish. She just wasn't hardened yet. Life hadn't roughed her up too much. That's rarer to find in kids on the rez.

"I'm not some doormat."

I remember the resolve in her eyes as she wrapped her fingers around the shovel. I hadn't seen that before.

"I only tried to turn Little Bro from you. Then Samantha jumped in and said you were quiet because you thought you were better than us rez kids. Richer. Smarter. She got everyone thinking you were a stuck-up snob before I knew what was happening." It probably speaks more to Samantha's own insecurities, but I don't say so.

"Wow."

"I didn't mean for the whole group to catch on and escalate. Honest."

She shakes her head. "Yeah right. You know the kind of power you hold."

I twist on the couch, one arm slung over the back of it. "I just didn't want Little Bro using and abusing you."

She stares at me for a long moment. She should be looking at me with fury now that she knows I started everything and didn't stop it when it got out of hand, but she's not. "You're just like my dad."

That's the last thing I was expecting her to say. "What now?"

She nods slowly, like something's clicking into place. "You assumed I wasn't capable of standing up for myself—of having an actual backbone. And you didn't even give me the chance to fight my own battle."

I open my mouth to protest, but I guess she's right. "I thought—"

"You thought you were helping. Just like my dad." Her tone instantly sharpens. "Why does everyone assume I can't handle myself?"

There are a few beats of silence as I'm left playing catch-up with her sudden change in emotions.

Her skin flushes with dull red. "Just—forget it." We're getting deeper than she meant to.

"What did your dad do?"

"Nothing." She crosses her arms. "It was my fault anyway."

I doubt that. "What did he do?"

She holds my gaze, indecision playing at her twitching brows, then lets out a slow breath. "There was this guy at my old school—Reid. Total douchebag. He tried really hard to make me think he liked me. We hung out a couple times. I knew he was a player, but . . ." She shrugs. "I usually give people the benefit of the doubt."

That was her first mistake.

"My parents and I went to this food-truck roundup thing where there were tables scattered around and people everywhere. I saw Reid sitting on a curb with his friend and overheard him talking about me."

I know what's coming next by the way she can't look me in the eye.

"He told his friend he was just trying to add a Native American girl to his body count."

My face scrunches into a scowl. "Dick."

"Yeah."

If she's comparing her dad to me in the slightest, I already know where this is heading. Because I know what I would do. Just hearing about it now is bringing heat to my face.

"I was pissed—"

"You should've been."

"But I shouldn't have let it get to me. I cry when I'm mad and I went and told my mom what he said . . ." Her cheeks flush with embarrassment. "She told my dad and—I should've kept my mouth shut."

"What did he do?"

She watches the pulsing lantern, eyes glazing over. "He lost it. He stormed over and shoved Reid up against a brick wall. Hard. Told him to stay away from me and threatened to mess up his face or something like that. His head got all scraped up."

Good.

Mara lets loose a grumbling sigh. "Reid's dad was my dad's boss. Of course Reid squealed. I was humiliated by the whole thing and most of my friends all bought into the guy's story of it all being a big misunderstanding. My dad had to resign or be fired."

"That guy deserved it. I would've decked him."

She raises her brows. "I know. Just like an overprotective dad."

"I'd prefer *dangerous uncle*."

She shakes her head, biting back a smile.

"I'm all jokes, but that wasn't your fault. He's the one who lost his temper. Not you."

"Maybe."

"Sorry you had to deal with the fallout of his actions."

She scoops one of Cherie's loose hair ties off the coffee table and spins it on her fingers. "Seems petty after everything that's happened here."

I know she's talking about Rayanne and Samantha, but my mind is stuck on the jerk who wanted to use Mara and the friends who didn't have her back. And then it slips to the kids here, me included, who didn't treat her right. We assumed she didn't know what things have been like for the rest of us growing up here, and she didn't. But that wasn't her fault either.

Just because our experiences have been different doesn't mean we can't understand each other. I should tell her that, but she changes the subject before I can.

"So . . ." She stretches the hair tie so wide I think it might snap apart. "If you would concoct an entire stupid plan just to keep Brody from pursuing me, why do you even like him?"

I throw my head back and laugh. She's awfully direct. "I told you—"

"He's not just your cuz, he's your best friend. Why? Say three good things about him."

I suck my teeth. "He's funny." I know there's more, but I draw a blank. "He's on my relay team." I try my best not to smile but fail.

Her scoff turns into a laugh. "Seriously, answer me honestly why he's your best friend."

He's the evil I know, but how do I explain that? From the early years we'd spend nearly every day together running around his ranch, joking one second and punching each other the next. Hunting trips where he'd always pretend he saw game before I did and take my shot, missing most of the time. Shoving each other into creeks as soon as our fishing lines finally got a tug, all for the laughs.

"I know him. I know all the bad parts about him. It's easy to be friends with someone you know will never surprise you."

"So when he's a douchebag . . ."

"I expected him to be. There's comfort in that." Maybe he's not the nicest guy to everyone, but a lot of it's for show. And he makes us laugh. He's stuck around all these years, even when lately, I'm always looking after Cherie, cleaning up Dad's messes, keeping our house in order. He knows I deal with crap and doesn't push me when I disappear. "We grew up together." That's the best way I can sum it up.

"Maybe you're right about him," she says. "I'm not sure I can trust him, but it's more likely Sterling or the tourist guy in the giveaway did it. We should look into that visitor more."

"As long as you don't think it's me, suspect whoever you want." I smile, but the heaviness of the whole situation weighs it back down.

She taps her phone to check the time. "Anyway, I should go. My parents don't know I'm here. They're all worried about my *safety*."

We stand up in sync, and I trace her steps to the front door.

"They should be." I open the door and rest my hand on the knob. "Thanks for bringing the sweatshirt back," I say as she's halfway through the opening.

She pauses, only inches of space between us. "No problem." She wants to say more; I can see it in the way her lips part, but she doesn't. And now I'm staring at her lips. "Bye." She shoves Cherie's hair tie into my hand and strides down the steps.

I'm already dreading being alone.

"Oh." She pauses at her car door. "If you didn't already, you should get a lawyer. Me and my dad got one. He'll be there if we're ever questioned again or whatever."

I lean against the doorframe as I process her words. I'm not sure why she assumes I could afford one. Or that my dad would care enough to hire one even if we could. And this is the first I've heard of anyone who wasn't involved in the giveaway being questioned. "Why does your dad need one?"

"He found Rayanne's body. I guess Staccona really laid into him about it." She pulls open the door. "Anyway, see you around."

"Text me when you're home safe."

She nods and dips into her car. I wonder if she ever told her parents how we made her feel like an outsider here. If her overprotective dad knew how mean Samantha was. What he might have done if he had.

They moved to town right before this all started, he found the body when nobody else could, he lawyered up.

Everyone has a little poison deep down somewhere. Even the people you trust.

I close the door and lock it but peer through the blinds until her rear lights disappear onto Duck Lake Road.

Chapter 26

BRODY CLARK
Tuesday, July 16, 1:20 p.m.

I turn up the volume on the TV, but even over the machine-gun fire, I can still hear Jason and the lawyer through the walls of my bedroom. He didn't want me sitting out there listening when I didn't need to. He wants to keep me out of it as much as he can. I think he can feel I'm more stressed about all this than he is.

I need to be more like him. Even keeled. Assured. I don't know how he stays so cool about it.

I doubt any of the other kids' rigs have been searched.

At least the cattle ranch is doing well enough that he can actually afford a lawyer. A good one at that. There's no way we could've afforded one in the past. The hollow feeling of opening a mostly empty fridge and the ghostly pressure against my toes from squeezing into too-tight shoes edge into my thoughts. From the hard days after Mom left and Dad wanted us to keep up with school instead of helping him more. Pushing Jason to go to college. Sacrificing.

I hope we really can afford all this and Jason isn't just throwing us into deep debt.

Some nasally preteen yells into my PlayStation headset. "Come on, EagleRib! Pull your frickin' weight!"

The respawn countdown ticks on the screen over my dead body, and the other team takes the lead.

"Whatever, CALLofDOODIE. Don't get your Pampers in a bunch." I try to concentrate on the Battle Shock team match, but my legs are restless. My mind is on the hum of conversation outside the door.

When I die again, the hum stops. I pull off the headset and listen, but they're silent. Then the crunch of tires on our gravel driveway sends chills dripping down my core, like slow water on Glacier's weeping walls.

I shut off the PlayStation and crack open the blinds. Kurt Staccona and Jeremy Youngbull are sauntering to the front door like they own the place. The bastards are even wearing sunglasses.

Beads of sweat form on my forehead as I stride down the hall. Jason's lawyer positions himself at the end of the entryway and nods. The black braid down his back is just as long as the bolo-tie hanging down his buttoned chest.

Jason opens the door. "Have something else to search?"

Staccona looks between the men.

"Dalton Gaudreau," Youngbull says. "Good to see you."

Dalton extends his hand to Staccona. "I'm the Clarks' lawyer. What's your business with my client?"

Staccona glances at me, the shadow in the corner of the room, before answering the lawyer. "We have some more questions for Jason."

I press farther into the corner as they argue back and forth the reasons why Jason should or shouldn't agree to the questioning. Ultimately, they decide to go into the station, as a show of having nothing to hide. Dalton Gaudreau will make sure they're not trying anything funny with Jason.

It doesn't make me feel much better.

But at least it's him and not me. I'd probably say something stupid. Something they'd try to turn on me. Something they'd twist all wrong.

But I never hurt Rayanne. Or Samantha. I'd swear it on Dad's grave.

I'm still worried about what Staccona will find. Youngbull basically gave Jason a warning—that fed will dig into anything, even whatever skeletons Jason thinks are in the past.

After the men head back to their car, Jason draws me out of the dark corner. "You don't have to worry. Dalton is going to make sure I'm heard. That's what we're paying him the big bucks for." He shifts his body so he's blocking Dalton's view of me and leans closer. "Got it?" What he's really telling me is to stop acting scared. I'm making him look bad.

I swallow. "I'm not worried."

He smiles for a beat. Always the big brother seeing right through me. "Man up and do something to stay busy. Don't stay here and spiral." He points a finger to my chest until I respond.

"Yeah. See ya."

He shoves his hat on, more forcefully than necessary, and leaves me alone in the house, minutes away from spiraling.

A distraction, that's what I need. I grab a fishing pole and tackle box and hop into my white truck. It's only a half-hour drive to Lower Two Medicine Lake. There's nothing like fishing in the lands of our ancestors.

That's as good a distraction as you can get.

I load up my rap playlist and speed off the ranch toward the looming mountain range—the Backbone of the World. With the jagged peaks in front of me and the low hills whizzing by beside me,

I can almost forget that Jason is probably a murder suspect.

Almost.

I can even see She Who Waits Mountain. A big rock sits somewhere up there, looking like a person standing watch, like an Indian woman waiting for her husband to come back from a war party.

That never would've been Mom. She'd be long gone, everyone else be damned.

The closer I get to the mountains, the greener the landscape gets and the denser the trees become. When I finally cross the Two Medicine River and pass through East Glacier, I pull off to get a milkshake at Glacier Treats.

The red tables scattered across the asphalt are full of people holding stacked ice cream cones or slurping at their straws. Most of them look like sunburned tourists. I get in line in front of the small cabin-like building and stare at the list of flavors from the shade of the surrounding pine and fir trees, trying not to imagine Jason back in the interrogation room.

I jump at the sound of my own name.

"Little Bro? Is that you?" A guy from the closest table stands up, squinting at me.

He's got a wrinkled brown face under his white cowboy hat and a belt buckle that's much too large for anyone's good. I recognize him, but I can't pin from where.

He strides over, hand outstretched. "Bugs Schmidt. Been a while, enit."

I shake his hand and move up in line.

"You remember me? I was your old man's butcher for years. Jason's too. Man, musta been about three years since I seen you. I'm good with faces." He half smiles and glances back at some kids who must be his grandsons.

"That's right. Good seeing you." I move up in line again, but he keeps talking.

"I've been calling Jason, but he ain't picking up. You'd think he owes me money or something, ays." He hangs out his tongue and laughs.

I can't quite joke back when the real reason Jason isn't picking up is because Staccona still has his phone. Searching it. I'm about to come up with an excuse, but my eyes catch on somebody over his shoulder.

The visitor from the giveaway photos.

He's at the farthest table, stuffing his face with an almost-empty cone. Jason is sweating in a hot interrogation room, with a lawyer, and this guy is out enjoying the sun. Why isn't the fed pulling him in? Is he so squeaky clean?

Bugs keeps talking, shifting on his feet, blocking my view of the guy. "I haven't heard from your brother in a long time. I'm trying to figure out if he's found himself another butcher."

I move up in line, peering around Bugs. Trying to see who the long-legged guy is sitting with.

"Did he?" Bugs's voice buzzes around me like a horsefly.

The visitor takes a massive bite out of the cone.

"I dunno." Jason's the one who runs the ranch, not me. He doesn't include me in the business side of things.

"Will you tell him to call me? If he's taking his cattle to somebody else, I'd like to know why. And I'd like the chance to get his business back, enit. I've got a long history working with your ranch. That should count for somethin'."

The visitor watches a family with a teenage daughter walk by on the street as he shoves the last bite of cone into his mouth, and I decide right then to follow him.

If he's hiding something, I'll find out.

That Camry girl from the party said she saw him watching Samantha at the powwow. That alone should be enough to make him suspicious. I'll find something to confirm it.

"Yeah, okay," I say to Bugs, but I'm watching the guy stand up and wipe his mouth with a napkin.

"Next!" somebody calls from the order window.

I glance from the window to Bugs to the visitor tossing his napkin into a bear-safe garbage can. "Never mind," I say to the girl in the window. I brush past Bugs with half a wave and jog to my truck before I can change my mind.

I guess I'm not fishing after all.

Instead, I follow the visitor in his blue four-door all the way back to his campground, only a few minutes' drive from Glacier Treats. I ease through the rows of RVs and tents until I see which number his motor home is parked in, then I park at the campground office.

I dig my phone out of my pocket and text First Kill to double-check my memory.

Where did Rayanne used to work on weekends?

I don't expect him to respond anytime soon.

After glancing up the road the visitor's parked on, I hop out and head to the campground office. I pass by a massive sign reminding guests not to start fires while wildfire danger is at Extreme, and a bell dings when I pull open the door.

The cabin-style building is full of tacky gifts and a see-through ice cream freezer. I pass by Glacier National Park T-shirts and sweatshirts hanging on the walls and turn through aisles of key chains and moose-themed kitchenware.

A middle-aged woman with sparse brown hair like a bird's nest comes out of a room behind the counter at the same time I step in front of it. There's a pleather-bound book on one end of the counter. Bingo.

"What can I do for you?"

I tap the counter, brushing the edge of the book. "I wanted to extend my stay."

"What's the name on the reservation?"

Shoot. "You know, I can't remember if my auntie made it or my dad. It's spot number seventeen."

She shakes the mouse of the chunky computer on a shelf next to the counter. "Seventeen. Stern. How many days did you want to add?"

"Just one."

"That'll be twenty dollars."

I glance at the guest book. The woman stares at me expectantly. "Hang on." I snag the least obnoxious souvenir sweatshirt and hand it to her. "This too."

"69.99." Ouch.

I hand her a wad of bills and set the bulky sweatshirt over the guest book while she counts them and sticks them into the cash register. She tears off the receipt and holds it out between two fingers, like a cigarette.

I shove it into my pocket and then scoop the sweatshirt and book into my arms and turn on my heel, all in one smooth motion. I stride straight out the door and into my truck parked around the corner.

This is probably a long shot, but it's worth it to check. I open the book to the scrawl-filled pages and scan the guest signatures filling the lines in pen and pencil for the last week. On Wednesday, the day before the start of Indian Days, Andrew Stern signed his name when he checked in.

I stare at his signature, committing every loop and curve to memory, and flip the pages back to April.

Wouldn't that be something if I found his name in here sometime before the day of Rayanne's disappearance too?

It would be pretty damning.

My phone buzzes with a text from Eli.

Glacier treats in east glacier. Y?

I sink to a stop in Eli's gravel driveway, his porch to my right. His big shop straight ahead. His gray beater truck is here. His dad's isn't. The sun is blazing low over the mountains, making the tan fields look pink. I'm still slashing through the gravel when Eli opens the door and leans against the porch banister.

"Lemme see it."

I called Eli on the drive home from the campground and told him what I found in the guest book. I couldn't wait.

I pull the book out from under my arm and toss it to him. He scans the ink-filled pages in the middle to find Andrew Stern's signature for his current campground stay, then opens to the page where I placed the ribbon bookmark.

To the day before Rayanne went missing, inside the guest book for the campground, which is near the place Rayanne worked on most weekends since the last summer.

"Holy!" He leans into the book, his nose practically touching the page. Right where Andrew Stern is signed in as a guest, on April 8. "We've gotta get this to the cops."

I snatch it out of his hands. "Do you actually trust them? Youngbull has beef with Jason, and Staccona doesn't give a damn about any of us. He just wants to get through his hardship assignment and get off the rez. He'd throw any of us under the bus in a second."

"This is huge, Bro."

"But it isn't. Yet. It's not actual proof of anything except he likes to come around Glacier. And maybe he saw Rayanne down the road at Glacier Treats. We need more." I need more.

"Like what?"

"We need to tail him."

He blows air out of his lips and laughs. "Good one."

"I'm serious. We're driving to that campground tomorrow, and we're gonna follow him until we catch him doing something."

He shakes his head but doesn't say anything.

"*Then* we'll take it to the cops."

"Fine, but I guarantee we're not gonna catch him doing anything. And Loren and Mara are coming too."

Good. The more, the better. Especially Loren. If I can prove to her that Jason didn't have any part in this, maybe we'll finally get the cops off our backs and find some semblance of *normal* again.

And then I can stop worrying that Staccona is going to unearth something about Jason's past. Something he hasn't even told *me*.

"Sounds good, then." I tuck the book under my arm and crunch through the gravel. "Hey, I thought your dad was already home."

Eli folds his arms. "He got back again late last night, but he had a day job over in Kalispell today. Good money."

I bite my tongue. Daddy First Kill works like a dog for that money. Then spends it all on his drugs.

It's sad, really, but at least Eli's dad is alive.

Mine's not.

Chapter 27

MARA RACETTE

Wednesday, July 17, 6:30 a.m.

I change my shirt three times, even pulling some options from one of the last unpacked boxes. I don't know why. I guess I'm not sure what the recommended attire is for stalking someone. It has nothing to do with seeing Eli . . . at least that's what I tell myself.

My parents only agreed to my plans to head into Glacier when I promised our group would stay in public places and stick together. That'll be true enough. Probably. I volunteered to drive in the group message last night, and after Brody and Loren agreed, I got the reaction I wanted.

Eli texted me privately.

Eli: I know what you're doing.

Me: 😒

Eli: You're a little sneak, Mara Racette.

Me: Guess you'll have to let me give you a ride now.

Eli: Well played.

After I pick up Loren, we head to Eli's house in silence. So much for being friends, I guess. Maybe she just needed a sidekick in her amateur sleuthing the other night. I'm glad they included me today, though, because ever since Eli brought it up, I've been wondering about this visitor guy.

Another truck is in Eli's driveway now, next to his gray Tacoma. Bits of orange rust peek out of the edges of the wheel wells where the brown paint is chipping away. I guess his dad is home again. I didn't need to be a part of the tight-knit groups of Browning High School to hear the rumors about Eli's dad. Meth is a huge problem on the reservation.

I'm sure he's not the only kid dealing with that in their family.

Maybe his dad is getting it under control if he's working so much. I hope he is, for Eli's and Cherie's sakes.

Eli emerges from the house wearing the black hoodie I returned to him. His hair peeks out of the front of the hood as he collapses into the back seat and grunts a hello.

"Good morning to you too," Loren says.

He grunts again.

We get Brody next, who struts halfway to the car with a piece of dry meat hanging out of his mouth before jogging back into his house. He reappears in the doorway, tugging on his signature gray-and-black acid-washed sweatshirt with a giant yellow Guns N' Roses cross on the chest, and slides into the car with his jerky breath. He's even less conversational than Eli. It's not until we pass through East Glacier twenty minutes later that they perk up. Brody directs me to the visitors' campground. It's just after seven thirty when we roll past the main office.

"Park there," Brody says as he points to a spot by a horseshoe game area. I roll the windows down and turn off the engine. Lodgepole pine trees tower around the perimeter of the campground and stand in patches throughout the RV rows.

The outside air has a chill to it, but it's faint enough to know it's going to get hot today. Birdsong and the smell of pine ease into the car from the surrounding trees. A few campers putter around their sites, starting their morning fires or carrying their totes to the bathroom buildings.

"Which RV belongs to gangly legs?" Eli asks.

Brody points to a motorhome a few slots down the row in front of us. A pale blue four-door is parked behind it.

"What's his name again?" Loren asks. She fidgets with her appliqué earring. Circles of colored glass beads surround a black feather. I don't know if I've ever seen her without the pair on.

"Andrew Stern," the boys say in unison.

Silence creeps around us until my stomach rumbles. "We should've brought donuts for this stakeout."

Loren digs into her purse. "I have Life Savers. They're donut shaped."

I take one and pop it into my mouth. It almost feels like we're hanging out . . . as friends.

"There," Brody whispers.

Stern's camper door opens, and a woman emerges, duffel bag slung over her shoulder. She's the same woman from the giveaway. Probably his wife. We sink low in our seats as she walks toward us and turns down the narrow road, heading to the bathroom building.

A few moments later, Stern comes out. He opens a storage compartment on the side of the motor home and pulls out a folding hammock. I tap my nails on the steering wheel. "So what if he never leaves? Are we going to sit here all day?"

Loren rests her head against the window. "This is a waste of time."

"C'mon, guys." Brody leans in from the back and rests an elbow on the center console. "Our patience will pay off." He bounces his leg, hardly noticing it makes the whole car shake.

"I doubt it," Loren says.

Brody elbows her shoulder. "You heard the girl at the party. Stern was watching Samantha in some type of way."

"I also heard her say the cops didn't take that seriously." Loren sinks in the seat and rests her feet on the dashboard. "Maybe they *would* if we took them the guest book."

Brody leans back into his seat and runs a hand through his shoulder-length hair. "We will. We just need a little more first. Enough that Staccona could never ignore it."

Loren doesn't say anything. I catch Eli's gaze in the rearview mirror. "We'll give it two hours," he says. "Then we're out of here, yeah?"

The three of them argue over how long we'll stay creeping while the man sets up his hammock. He disappears into the camper for a few minutes and emerges with breakfast sandwiches on two paper plates.

At the same moment, his wife appears at the end of the road in a change of clothes and a towel over her shoulder. They have their routine down pat.

Someone else's stomach rumbles from the back seat as we creepily watch the couple eat their sandwiches, and then the woman grabs a book from inside the motorhome and stretches out in the hammock.

"You've gotta be kidding me," Eli grumbles.

I can't help but laugh. "They're not going anywhere anytime soon."

Brody leans onto the console again and then back into his seat. "Two hours. Give it two hours."

I pull out my phone. It's already 8:10.

"I'll even go get some snacks from the main office. Powdered Donettes just for you, Mara." He's so desperate to stay, *he's* even acting like I'm part of the group now. It makes me like him even less.

I sit up straighter. "Look." Stern leans down and kisses the woman, keys in hand. They share a few words we can't hear, then he stoops into his little car and turns on the engine.

We sink in our seats as he drives past the car, but he doesn't even look our way. "Go, go, go," Brody whispers. I turn the key and trail him, with some distance, out of the campground.

I half hope Stern is taking a drive to Glacier and up Going to the Sun Road. If he doesn't do a single shady thing today, which he probably won't, at least those cliff-side views would make this worth it. Whenever we'd visit in the summers, we'd find a viewpoint to pull off on and Dad would break out his binoculars. We'd scan the mountainside across the canyon or the valley below us for wildlife. Bears, moose, white-tailed deer. We even saw a mountain lion near his aunt's cabin in Saint Mary one year.

It's no wonder our ancestors called this place home. Every crevice of Glacier is breathtaking.

Stern doesn't drive up Looking Glass toward the Saint Mary entrance, though. Instead, he makes a sudden turn into the parking lot for the Glacier Park Lodge. A perfectly manicured, grassy hill descends from the lodge, with paths lined with flower beds.

A plain white teepee sits in the middle of the grass, out of place against the massive log lodge towering behind it. I bet tourists love to take photos inside it.

I turn into a parking spot.

"What's he doing here?" Eli asks, leaning to see where Stern ended up.

Loren unbuckles her seat belt. "Probably meeting someone for breakfast?"

"He already had breakfast." Brody pops open his door. "We gotta follow him."

"Yeah right," Loren says. "He'll recognize me. Probably you guys too."

Eli puts his hood on. "Not anymore, enit."

Brody closes his door and glances at me and down at my sweatshirt, which also has a hood. Loren's only in a shirt, and Brody's sweatshirt is hoodless.

"Fine." I pull my hood on and slip out my door after Eli. We cross the lodge road and slink into a patch of trees between our spot and Stern's.

Stern walks across the deep, green grass, straightening his lumberjack button-down. His jeans are too short for his long legs, making him look even taller. I'm about to dash out of the trees after him until he halts outside the teepee.

He leans against a support pole and pulls out his phone. He types something into it, then watches as a man and a teenage girl cross the parking lot and ascend the grassy hill toward him. "Oh, I forgot my phone," the girl says. Her voice is clear in the still morning air. "Meet you in there," the man says. He tosses her a ring of keys and continues past Stern toward the lodge, while the girl dips between parked cars, her black ponytail swinging.

Stern watches the man stride away, then turns on his heel toward the cars in a sudden rush.

The grounds are quiet. So quiet I can hear the dull click of the girl unlocking her car a few yards away from us.

Stern is making a beeline for the teenager, head bent into her car, searching for her phone. He's going right for her.

Eli dashes out of the trees into the parking lot. I'm only a stride behind him as we duck behind a sedan, eyes locked on the girl. Her back is to Stern, completely oblivious to his hurried approach.

"He's not . . ." My voice comes out a whisper.

Eli presses his palms to the car's hood, lines of muscle tensing across his arms. Stern glances over his shoulder toward the lodge her dad disappeared into, then focuses back on the girl in front of him. He's only feet from her when Eli springs out of his crouch.

How quickly could he grab the girl and wrap his hands around her neck? Is that how quickly it took to kill Samantha? A single moment clear of witnesses?

Eli's shoes grind across the pavement as he halts. Stern passes right by her. She jolts in surprise at his close proximity but carries on digging under her seat. Eli stands frozen on the pavement, palms hovering open at his sides as Stern unlocks his own door.

I glance back at my car as Eli crouches next to me again. Brody's forehead is pressed flat against his window, and Loren's fingers are digging into the hair on top of her head. At least we weren't the only ones who thought that was going to turn out differently.

Stern pulls out two glass bottles of purple soda, huckleberries plastered across their wrapping, and strides back to the grass and up the hill toward the lodge.

Eli jerks his head, and I follow him, waiting behind massive log columns at the entrance before slipping into the building a few moments after Stern. The door opens into an expansive room with cathedral ceilings. Full log columns rise up the length of the space and intersect the walkways of the second and third floors, bordering the main space, with their own log handrails.

Elaborate furniture with stained wood frames are grouped together across the space, and warm light emits from lanterns hanging on giant chandeliers.

We press against the wall underneath one of the second-story walkways, next to a gift shop entrance. Stern ambles across the room toward a woman sitting on a couch, her back to us. He leans over her, presses the soda into her hand, and kisses her.

LOREN ARNOUX
Wednesday July 17, 12:00 p.m.

I twist the thread hanging off the frays in my jeans while Mara, Eli, and I sit in the car outside of Eli's house. Andrew Stern, the white-haired visitor, is a sketchy one, all right. He's even cheating on his wife. But if he's killing people, we're not going to randomly catch him in the act. We need to do something with what we *do* know.

The dates in the guest book could mean something. If Brody turns it in, maybe the feds could get a warrant and prove that Andrew Stern was staying nearby at the time of each murder. Maybe they could check his bank history to see if he went to Glacier Treats on the days Ray Bear worked.

We don't have the means to find a deeper connection between Stern and Ray Bear—but *Staccona* could.

Brody was pissy when we dropped him off, but there's not much we can do about that. He's the one with the guest book, and he doesn't want to turn it in yet. He wants to make sure we have enough so Staccona takes the book seriously. It's true; he could brush it under the rug if it seems like too much of a stretch. And Brody would probably get in trouble for taking it.

"Brody's sure adamant about this." Mara digs her nails into the seat belt across her chest. "You think they're finding anything substantial on Jason?"

Eli sticks his arm out the open window. The knuckles that I noticed were swelling the other night now have only faint shades of bruising. "I just don't see it. He's a good guy." He's quick to defend Jason. Maybe too quick.

And what if it's Eli? As much as I want to, I haven't ruled him out either. He admitted he had a secret relationship with Ray Bear. It could've ended badly, even if he claims it didn't. The timing of her *I miss you* DM is definitely suspect.

"So who *could* you see doing it, then?" I ask. "Let's hear it."

He stares out the window at the old, rusty brown truck we're parked next to. Must be his dad's piece of work. A bird chirps from the roof of the shop. "I guess anybody." He heaves out a breath. "It could be anybody."

As soon as Mara puts the car in park in my driveway, I shove open the door before she can say anything else. Before she can ask about hanging out again. I don't even thank her for driving.

She needs to stay far away from me. I'm the only one who's gonna figure this out.

I don't look back to see her face. I don't need to add more guilt to the things I'm already dealing with. The anger that I can't seem to get closer to figuring this out is already curling all my muscles, making them ache to release the tension before they snap.

I throw open the front door and hurl my purse onto the cabinet in the entry, releasing my rage and panting through my teeth. The bowl of change barrels down with a crash, and coins scatter across the floor as the door bounces off the wall violently and back into my hip.

The rage halts when I see Youngbull sitting at our dining room table, legs sprawling across the floor beneath it. "Sorry." I drop to the floor, sweeping the coins into a pile and back into the bowl. Through the still-cracked-open door, I see his patrol car across the street. I didn't even notice it when Mara stopped the car.

I was stuck in my own head.

Grandma clutches her shirt and waves me over with her other hand. "Clumsy, this one." She forces out a laugh. "It's okay, Loren. Leave it."

I shut the door and tread lightly across the carpet, shame heating my cheeks and sucking away the remnants of my anger. "What's going on?"

"Jeremy's just filling me in on Rayanne's case." An ounce of frustration drips into Grandma's voice, like he really isn't filling her in on much. "They still haven't gleaned anything from her phone."

He doesn't say hello, just watches me.

Grandma rubs her hand back and forth across her collarbones. "Everything okay?"

Not at all. "Yeah. Sorry about that. Clumsy." I wave my hand toward the few coins I missed on the floor.

Youngbull taps his fingers on the table. "All good. Emotions certainly run high after tragedies like this." He pauses his tapping. "Lashing out is understandable. And normal. It only becomes a problem if you start to direct it at a person. Ever done that?"

I shake my head. What's he trying to say?

"People can snap, especially if there's a mental health issue. Anyone would understand that . . ."

"No . . . no, I'm just dealing with a lot." I don't like the path his mind is taking. I'd never hurt anyone—no matter how mad I am. I force steadiness into my voice and ease into the chair next to Grandma. "Do you have a suspect yet?"

Youngbull spreads his massive palm onto the table and watches me for a few uncomfortable moments. "We have persons of interest but no suspects. I want to be clear about that."

I nod.

"The bus driver gave us a tip. He was able to remember seeing one car driving near your neighborhood that morning. He was fairly positive it was a royal-blue Dodge Ram truck."

"Just like Jason's," Grandma says.

"Because he was also with the giveaway group before Samantha's murder, we wanted to look into him more. We searched his truck. We found another set of fingerprints, but we don't have them on file. We didn't find anything else. It was pretty squeaky clean. We've had him in for questioning, but we'll pull him in again."

"There's nobody else?" I squeeze my fingers until my knuckles pull white.

"We have a few potential leads that could give us more persons of interest, but for now, we're keeping those under wraps." The weight of his gaze makes it hard to breathe.

"What about that visitor guy from the giveaway?" I ask.

"We haven't ruled him out in Samantha's case, but he gave us an alibi for the date of Rayanne's abduction."

That's not what I was hoping to hear. "Doing what?"

"We can't share that type of thing, but his alibi has him in a completely different state."

That gives me pause.

That can't be right. That visitor is lying. I open my mouth to tell Youngbull about Andrew Stern's signature in the campground guest book, but Grandma doesn't know what I've been doing today. She thought I was finally getting out with friends in Glacier, not stalking a grown man.

Is that a crime?

Youngbull's tense voice cuts into my racing thoughts. "Your grandma told me Brody was harassing you about the case."

"He wasn't—"

"I strongly advise you don't speak about the case with anyone. I know he's your friend, but with his brother being a person of interest . . ."

It was hardly harassing, but I don't want to mess anything up. I nod. Today was stupid. I need to be smarter, for Ray Bear.

Grandma folds her arms. "You shouldn't be talking to Brody at all."

Youngbull puts his palms up, almost as big as baseball mitts. I have to shake away the image of beefy hands like that wrapping around my sister's throat. "Just keep everything confidential," he says. "If he tries talking about the case again, you call me. I'll let him know that's inappropriate."

I fold my arms, just like Grandma. "Fine."

I only have to talk to him one more time. Just to tell him the visitor lied about his alibi. That should be enough to convince Brody to take the guest book to Staccona now. Staccona won't be able to ignore that. And the visitor won't be able to lie his way out of it.

"That's all I have for you." Youngbull scoots his chair away from the table. "Unless you have any other questions."

"What about Eli First Kill?" Grandma asks.

The air in my lungs turns to solid ice. I search her profile, but she won't look at me. "We know him, Grandma."

"We know everyone on the rez. Doesn't mean I should trust any of them."

Youngbull rests his hands on his legs and watches me. "We did find a strange text history between him and Samantha, indicating some kind of strained relationship."

What's that supposed to mean? Sam never told me she had a thing with Eli, but she didn't exactly say a lot to me the last few months. Eli didn't either, for that matter. Maybe everyone was keeping secrets from me. Just like I didn't know Ray Bear had some kind of relationship with Eli last year. Maybe everyone is *still* keeping secrets from me.

"Rayanne also placed a two-minute call to Eli the day before she disappeared."

My stomach drops to the floor. "You told us you didn't find anything strange in her calls." I should've looked when I had the chance, but I believed it when he said they didn't find anything in her calls in the phone company's records. I should've known they were keeping things from us. I can't believe how stupid I was to skip her call history.

"It's not necessarily strange. Eli was at school the day Rayanne was abducted. Right, Loren?"

I can picture eight-year-old Eli sitting in my room. His family had just moved in with his grandparents while his dad tried to straighten himself out. Our addiction-riddled mom had just taken off for the second time.

He cried sometimes, but we acted like we didn't notice.

I feel loyal to that little boy. To the years we shared a silent struggle at school.

But I feel more loyal to my sister. To my flesh and blood.

"Yes," I say. "But everyone knew Eli had a screw-off first period."

Youngbull brings his hand to his puckered chin. He tries to ease into the movement casually, but I can tell he's never heard this before. "What does that mean?"

"Eli was a teacher's aide first period. He showed up late a lot, but the teacher didn't care as long as he finished everything she needed."

His whole body is still.

So is mine.

I don't want it to be Eli. I don't want to put him through anything he doesn't deserve, but if every lead isn't looked into, Ray Bear will never get any justice. None of us will.

Chapter 28

ELI FIRST KILL
Wednesday, July 17, 11:30 p.m.

When I've rolled over for the thousandth time, I give up. I unlock my phone and pause the music. I should feel better. Instead of glimpsing the cool blue moonlight at the edges of the blanket covering the window, I see the warm glow of the porch light. We got the power back on and stuffed the fridge full of groceries thanks to the money from selling Storm Runner. But I'm stuck on something . . . I should've said more to Mara Racette when she was here. I open our text messages. I close them. I want to tell her, but I don't. I want her to trust me, but she shouldn't.

She's gonna leave this place someday. She doesn't need me dragging her down.

But she believes me.

I open our text chain again.

Me: Mara Racette, are you still awake?

Mara: Unfortunately.

Me: Have you tried listening to music? Maybe that'll help.

Mara: I am, and it doesn't.

Me: What are you listening to?

Mara: Sam Smith. You?

Me: A random hard rock playlist

Mara: Well that's never going to help you sleep.

Me: 🤘

Me: I mean rock on this time, not pinkie promise.

A minute passes, and I swear it gets even quieter while I wait.

Me: Can I come see you?

Her typing bubble appears and disappears.

Me: Just for a little while?

Mara: Okay.

She's already sitting on her front porch step when I pull up to the curb. The light flickers above her, making the geometrical designs on the Pendleton blanket draped over her shoulders look like they're in motion. I slide out of my truck into the blackness of the night and shut the door as gently as I can.

The stars are white splatters across the deep navy-blue, endless sky. Big Sky Country at its finest. I pull my sweatshirt on, which still smells like Mara's detergent, and walk up the sidewalk toward her.

"I'd ask how it's going," Mara says as I sink onto the step next to her, "but it's almost midnight, and you're here. So it must not be great." One of the corners of her mouth perks up.

"I just realized I should've told you something."

She pulls the blanket tighter.

I stand up and lean onto the railing, but then it feels like I'm talking down to her, so I sit again, facing her as best as I can on the step. One of my knees touches hers.

"What?" The curves in her brows shift from curiosity to impatience.

"I didn't say sorry." I ignore the voice telling me to shut up. "When I told you about Little Bro and why I excluded you. I'm sorry for that."

"Oh."

"It was stupid to assume things about you and think you wouldn't already be on your guard. I was wrong about you, and I just wanted you to know I'm sorry."

She leans onto her knees under the blanket, bumping my leg. "What were you wrong about?"

I rest an elbow onto the top step. What wasn't I wrong about? "I thought you were shy and fragile."

"You said like a fawn." She shakes her head subtly.

"Yeah. Easy prey for the predators out here." I'm making it sound even worse. I dig my fingers into my knee. "Not that what anyone projects makes them into prey or not . . . I just mean—I was wrong. You have a quiet presence, but it's not the same as prey. You're like a hawk. A different kind of predator."

She smiles, and it makes me want to keep talking.

I bust out my wise Indigenous voice, looking into the distance. "You have a heavy presence. I feel it. You're quiet, but you're there, observing. Like a hawk surveying its land. You're good medicine."

She playfully bumps my knee. "I'm gonna take that as a compliment."

I drop the voice. "It is."

When she smiles again, I realize our faces are only a foot apart, and I find myself noticing the curves of her lips as her smile fades.

"If I'm a hawk, what are you?"

"We already established I'm *Mad Bear*."

She laughs. "No, you're not a bear. You're more like . . . a buffalo."

I bite my tongue to hide my surprise.

"Sometimes you're quiet too, but you have a *big* presence. Every-one knows if they cross you, you could end them. You seem calm, but your power is very apparent." She cocks her head and nods. "Just like a buffalo."

"You're not gonna understand why, but that's the most I've felt *seen* in my entire life." That's all I've tried to do. Keep out of trouble and take care of Cherie. Be the buffalo ready to defend her if anyone bothers us.

"Good." Her smile is bright in the moonlight, and I can't help but smile back.

"I thought you'd hate me. *I* would."

Her gaze drifts to the cracked sidewalk. "The thing is, I didn't expect to fit in with less than three months of school left." Her mouth presses into a grimace. "I knew I wouldn't have any friends for a while, and I didn't try that hard to make any. Everyone is so tight here. Most of you have known each other your whole lives. You've all got a bunch of family everywhere. I'm the odd one who doesn't. I knew I'd be thought of as this newcomer who hasn't been a part of . . . anything. What hurt was that I felt like my identity wasn't accepted. Like I couldn't just own it . . . I had to prove I deserved it or something."

"That's not what it was."

She barrels on. "It was like . . . I'm not full, so I don't count. I didn't grow up here, and my family isn't very traditional, so I must not know any of the culture. I haven't been *here* with you, so I'm not one of you."

I shake my head. "I'm not full either. That's not . . . I think everyone just thought you didn't *want* to be one of us. We didn't mean any of that."

"Well, I already worried about where I fit in with everything, so it just got worse moving here. I know who I am, but when I have to

241

prove it to someone else . . . it makes me doubt myself, I guess. I don't have all the same experiences as you guys, but being Blackfeet is still a huge part of my identity." She raises her chin when she looks at me. Still proud even when she's doubting herself. The faint light from the Big Sky makes her high cheekbones glow. She knows who she is; she just wanted us to know too.

"You're Blackfeet, Mara Racette. Nobody can take that from you."

She looks at the ground and smiles in slow motion. "I know."

"I *am* sorry."

She meets my gaze. "I forgive you."

I hold out my pinkie. "Promise?"

She drops the blanket to hook her pinkie around mine. "Promise."

Now our faces are only inches apart. I unhook my pinkie and run my fingertips down the smooth skin of her arm. She's frozen as she watches my thumb trace a slow circle on her forearm.

When she looks back at me, I lean in. Her gaze dips to my lips—

A grating creak rockets into the dead air. Mara jumps away from me, turning toward her dad holding the front screen door open. "The hell you doin'?" he says, squinting against the porch light directly above his head. He's in pajama pants with multicolored trout plastered across the fabric, and his hair is tussled on one side.

Mara and I stand in unison. She pulls the blanket tightly around her. "We were just talking."

He looks me up and down. "You shouldn't be out here alone at this hour. It's not safe. You know that." He jams his thumb backward. "Get in here." He steps to the side, waiting for Mara to pass through. His rough, just-woken-up voice is intimidating, even when paired with the cute pajama pants.

242

Mara steps through, a half smile hanging on those lips I was so close to kissing.

She doesn't seem concerned that her dad is drilling holes into me with his glare. I wonder what that overprotective dad would've done if he'd walked out a few seconds later.

"Get off my porch." He says it quieter, but the poison still sharpens his words.

My headlights illuminate another car in my driveway. The clock on the dash flips to 12:37 a.m. Rage and paranoia churn through my blood as my tires slash through the gravel and skid to a halt behind it.

My fingers twitch, ready to strangle whoever is snooping around our house or aching for my rifle's weight. I throw open the door, scanning the car in front of me.

I hiss out a breath when Little Bro steps out of the pickup and into the beam of light hitting his bumper. I should've recognized the back of his white truck, but my adrenaline was working faster than my brain was. Still is.

"What are you doing here?" There's venom in my tone, but that's the adrenaline talking.

He brushes his hair out of his eyes. "I need to talk to somebody."

I glance at the dark porch and quiet my voice. "You couldn't text first?"

"I was already driving, trying to clear my head. I'm freaking out, man. Jason says the FBI is trying to twist everything against him."

"Doesn't he have a lawyer?"

He shifts on his feet. "Yeah, but if they want to screw him, they're going to! The FBI just wants to slap a *case closed* on it. They'd sacrifice anyone to do it. I can't have them taking Jason away. My dad's

243

dead, my mom left me for her new family. Jason is the only person who hasn't left me."

There's real pain shredding his voice, so I don't tell him he's dead wrong. He's more messed up from his mom leaving him behind than he'd ever say out loud. But I never left him either. And his mom would take him in now if he needed it. He has some aunties in Heart Butte. He wouldn't have *nobody*. He's just spiraling. "So give them the guest book. If you don't trust Staccona, give it to Youngbull."

He spits out a breathy laugh. "I trust him even less."

Since when? "Wasn't Youngbull Jason's best buddy? You really think he'd screw him?"

He sputters and paces between the trucks. "You can't trust anyone. Who knows, maybe Youngbull's the one with something to hide. He's been everywhere. He was at the powwow working security. Samantha was eyeing him like maybe they were gettin' it in. Just like she eyed you. And pretty much everyone but me . . ." He shakes his head. "He's the one who put the suspicion on us in the first place. Youngbull's someone Rayanne would've thought to trust too."

He's desperate. Swinging and missing in every direction. I shut off the engine, plunging us into further darkness, and position myself in front of the steps. "I don't know what to tell you. Jason has a lawyer. At least trust *him*. That's what you're paying him for, enit?"

"You don't get it. You're lucky your dad was out of town for Indian Days. If the police were bringing him in for questioning all the time, then you'd get it."

I back up the porch steps. "Maybe." I shove down the thought that if I really were in that position, it wouldn't hurt if they took Dad away. It makes me feel guilty, but having him around can sometimes be worse than if he was locked up.

"Was your dad really out of town? You don't think he would've done anything while he was tweaking?"

"Hoh! Really, Little Bro?" He usually lays off about my dad.

He wipes his face. "Forget it." With that, he climbs back into his truck and cuts a circle through the wide, gravel driveway, passing the rusty brown truck and my gray Tacoma before disappearing into the night.

Chapter 29
MARA RACETTE
Thursday, July 18, 8:00 a.m.

For the first time since Samantha died, I fell asleep easier last night. Instead of her face slinking through my mind, it was Eli's. I kept replaying the moment his focused eyes and that scar ticked over his eyebrow leaned closer. Just thinking about how we almost kissed makes me smile . . .

Until I emerge from the hallway to find Dad sitting at the kitchen table, steaming coffee cup in hand. "What were you thinking last night?"

I freeze at his rough tone. "What do you mean?"

Dad shoves away from the table and stands. "What do I mean? You sitting alone with that kid in the middle of the night?"

I guess I should've been expecting a lecture, but his temper is simmering way too close to the surface for what actually happened. "It wasn't the middle of—"

"Mara." Mom strides into the room, taking her place next to Dad. "It's not safe right now. You know that. You shouldn't have—"

I dig in my heels. "I was sitting outside our front door. Talking."

The conflict shutters in and out of Mom's gaze, like she's weighing how much anger is warranted. "You should've told us. Something could've happened."

She has no idea how much I haven't told them. "Don't make a big deal out of it."

Dad steps toward me. His eyes are unsteady, like he hasn't slept right in days. "I see a decomposing teenage girl and I'm just supposed to *not* imagine it's you?"

I flinch at his sudden volume change.

"Somebody's killing girls just like you." He's yelling now. "And you go off with a guy I don't know or trust. You're not making a big *enough* deal out of it."

Mom puts her hand on his arm, wide eyes showing she's just as surprised as I am.

"You're sneaking around. Asking for trouble." Red creeps up his neck.

"You should've told us and brought him inside." For some reason Mom's measured voice irks me more than Dad's shouts.

Dad looks too much like he did the day he stormed after Reid. The day he lost complete control of his temper. Bitterness seeps out in my voice. "Why do you think I don't tell you?"

Dad's face suddenly slackens. He knows exactly why. He turns away and looks at his watch, but not before I catch the shame in his eyes.

I shouldn't have told Mom and Dad what I heard Reid say. I should've dealt with it myself. But Dad should've controlled himself. He's the one who went off the rails.

He's the one who snapped.

"I—I've gotta get going." Dad shoves his phone into his pocket and gathers his work bag and earbuds from the counter before slipping out the front door without another word.

Mom slumps against the counter in the awkward silence that follows. "He just wants to protect you."

I get it. I do. But I've seen that his protection isn't always helpful. She has too.

My phone vibrates with a notification.

Eli: So when can we finish talking?

I wanted to text him last night, but I wasn't sure if he was glad my dad cut us off. I glance at Mom, staring blankly at the counter, and text back.

Me: I didn't know we weren't finished.

Eli: Oh, we definitely have some unfinished business

Me: OH you meant "talking"

Me: Yeah, we can finish that anytime you like.

Eli: How about now? I'm making pancakes.

Maybe he's right. Maybe I *should* hate him after how he acted at school. And maybe Loren's right. Maybe we shouldn't trust him. Yeah, he was stupid. But if he was doing it for the right reasons . . . what's so wrong with giving him another chance?

"I'm going on a drive." I move like Dad and make a break for the door before Mom can try to convince me otherwise.

The second I turn onto Eli's driveway, I skid to a halt. There's a mass of cars at the end of it in front of his house. The garage door to the shop is open. Red and blue lights blink. Something terrible has happened again.

It must be Cherie this time, or could it be Eli? Did his addict dad hurt one of them?

As I sit and stare, leg tingling as I hold my foot against the brake, I realize there's no ambulance . . . no fire truck. The saliva in my mouth turns to gravel.

It tumbles into my stomach like a dead weight.

Kurt Staccona guides Eli out the front door, hands cuffed behind his back. His hair ricochets back and forth as he stumbles down the steps with Staccona's tugging.

He glances down the drive before he's shoved into the back of the police car, and he sees me. Face drained of color, eyes clinging to my gaze . . . I know he sees me.

The worst part about it is—he looks guilty as hell.

Chapter 30

LOREN ARNOUX

Brody's ranch is quiet—but not too quiet, like my house. While Grandma is at the hospital, the silence at home is crushing. Here, the air is just clear. Empty except for the brush of the dry prairie grass shifting in the breeze, carrying an earthy scent like overturned dirt and horses.

Brody shuffles out the front door before I've even shut the car door. That's how it is out here, away from town; you can hear anyone pulling up in your driveway. He fans his shirt away from his chest, the late morning sun already blazing. "What's up?"

"You haven't heard?" I lean against my car's hood. "They arrested Eli."

His mouth launches open. "What—Eli? Eli First Kill?"

That's about what my reaction was too after Youngbull updated Grandma and me at our dining room table this morning.

Brody trudges past my car and paces in the gravel. "I don't— Why Eli?"

"Youngbull found out about Eli's screw-off mornings at school." Thanks to *me*.

Brody closes his eyes and nods. It wasn't exactly a secret that

Eli would roll into Ms. Littlefield's classroom halfway through the period. It was just that nobody thought much of it.

"Then they got some kind of tip—he wouldn't say what—that made them go check out Eli's house this morning. They found a jacket in his car they think belonged to Ray Bear." Maybe I didn't search his truck well enough. Maybe it was stuck under the seats.

Brody pauses his pacing. "I don't . . . I didn't think—" He squats down and rests his head in his hands.

"I know." I thought I'd feel better now. They have an actual suspect. But the knots in my stomach don't feel right. I don't want to believe Eli would've hurt my sister.

Maybe in that two-minute phone call Youngbull mentioned, Ray Bear and Eli agreed to meet up in the morning. What else would they talk about for such a short time? Maybe they fought.

Brody stands up and resumes his trail across the gravel. "I would've thought his deadbeat dad was capable of something like that. But Eli—"

"Maybe it makes sense." I grip the back of my neck. "He had a secret relationship with Ray Bear. And Youngbull said he had a strange text history with Sam. I never knew anything about that."

He nods slowly. "They snagged once. Samantha wouldn't leave him alone about it."

He had a physical relationship with both of them and nobody ever told me.

Secrets. Acid crawls up my throat. "But . . . it's Eli."

Brody folds his arms, some of the earlier panic dripping away from his face. "I mean . . . if they found something . . ." He stops short as the muscles in his jaw pulse to a beat I can almost hear.

"But so did you. If you give them the guest book, they can look into it. It'll prove Stern lied about his alibi."

"It doesn't sound like they need it anymore." The muscles in his jaw go still.

I know he's right, but I keep pushing. "You dragged us after Stern to clear Jason's name. You wouldn't do the same for Eli First Kill?"

He leaves his line in the gravel and strides back toward the house. "Jason is my brother, Loren. You of all people should get that."

I open and close my mouth as I follow him.

He halts in front of his porch. "Why are you questioning it? Shouldn't you be happy they finally made an arrest?"

Of course he's right. I should be, but it's painful too. "Because it's Eli."

He leans against the porch railing, the old wood creaking. "I know."

My eyes burn against the dry air. "Just give them the guest book so it's not hanging in the back of our minds and we can be certain it's Eli."

He rakes his fingertips across his glistening forehead. "That book was a long shot anyway. It doesn't prove anything."

"It'll prove Stern lied to Staccona about his alibi. Just turn it in. Then we'll *really* know."

"Okay. Yeah. For First Kill." He can't meet my eye. He really does think it's useless, and it probably is, but I have to be sure.

He steps onto his porch without saying goodbye and digs his fingers into his long hair, making it look like soaring black wings. The door slams behind him. First his brother, then his best friend.

Now I know what he felt like before. To wonder deep down if he really knew Jason.

I thought I knew Eli. Thought I'd seen him in his hardest, worst moments. Maybe I have no idea what his worst could possibly be.

BRODY CLARK
Thursday, July 18, 6:00 p.m.

I shove my feet into the rocks at the lake's edge. The cold of Lower Saint Mary's crystal-clear water bites my skin. I grab a handful of the smooth, flat rocks and sort out the best skipping rocks. Now that the wildfire is burned out and they're just monitoring for hot spots, Mom wanted us to come up for dinner.

She claims she missed us.

Her little monsters squeal and shout from the wood raft floating several yards out. They look like toothpicks wearing their massive orange life jackets.

A yellow rope stretches across the water's surface, keeping them tied to a tree on shore. Half of me wants to go cut the rope so they drift away, finally letting us have some quiet.

I bet they'd float all the way to Thunderbird Island.

My stepdad emerges from the shed, fishing gear in hand. I stand and hurl my rocks across the surface of the water, watching them skip way past the rocking raft.

"Help me set up the night lines?" he asks. The sun glistening in his dirty-blond hair shows it's more than half-gray now. He opens his multitiered tackle box, ready to set up the poles overnight to bring in ling in the morning. It's like he ordered it from a fancy catalog. Looks a lot different than Dad's rusty case filled with a mishmash of his ol' standby lures.

He's got all the bells and whistles with that IHS doctor pay.

"Nah." I trudge across the shifting stone shore back to the cabin-style house.

Inside, Jason leans against the kitchen counter next to Mom, concern etched into her overly tired face.

Having a second family at her age does that.

"Anyway," Jason says as I close the door behind me, "they should get off my back now."

"I just can't believe it was Eli. He's such a good boy." Mom hasn't been around Eli for years but she's acting like she still knows him. She shakes her head until the beaded barrette starts slipping out of her black, stick-straight hair. Her gaze drifts to me like she wants to say more, but I look out the line of front windows framing the lake.

The water shines with a golden glow as the sun dips below the surrounding trees. The kids on the raft shove each other. Screaming. Stumbling. One falls off and gets the back of his life jacket caught on the corner of the raft.

"Seriously?" Mom strides past me and out the door.

Jason hops onto the counter, his feet swinging in the open air. "Feeling bad about Eli?"

My stomach clenches at his name, threatening to send up my dinner.

"I get it."

I scoff. "No, you don't. He's my best friend. First you, now him. I can't protect everyone."

"What are you talking about, Little Bro?"

I slide my hand along the countertop until it squeaks. Outside, Mom tugs on the yellow rope, hauling the kids closer to the shore. "I was looking into stuff to clear your name."

He shrugs. "I was too. I didn't find much. Though I did find it interesting that my top-choice lawyer was already taken by Mara and MJ Racette."

"Why?"

"I just didn't know why her dad would need one. He wasn't even in the giveaway group. What did you scrape together?"

"I tried to find dirt on that visitor guy. It wasn't working out, and I was starting to think you were screwed. And now . . . First Kill. I don't think I can fix that."

He leans across the space between us. "Hey. If they think he did it . . . there's no fixing that, Little Bro. And as terrible as it is, it's good they have somebody in custody now."

I grind my teeth to keep from gagging. First Kill has been my best friend since I can remember. We're more than distant cousins. We should know each other like we're brothers.

But we don't. And we're not.

Maybe we used to be, but every time something changes in our lives, we get pulled farther apart. I don't think there's anything I hate more than change.

We have so little control over what we're dealt in life.

"They have evidence linking him to Rayanne now. You can't involve yourself anymore." He lifts his palms, long fingers steady. He's so casual about it. Happy he's not a suspect anymore.

I'm relieved too, but it's mixed with sick disappointment. Guilt I didn't see this coming. Sadness for what we're losing. "I know he looks guilty. I just didn't want it to be Eli."

"You need to get over it. We're okay now. And we both know I didn't kill Rayanne." He raises his brows, waiting for me to agree.

I nod.

"With evidence Eli might have, let's just hope they leave us out of this whole mess now. And you keep yourself out of it too. First Kill's on his own."

He stares at me until Mom walks back in. He doesn't need to say any more for me to feel the heat behind his words. *Leave it alone.* Guilty or not, Eli has to figure out his own mess.

His dad sure as hell won't be much help.

"You two need to come around more," Mom says as she gathers plates from the table. "You haven't been here since my birthday in April. I worry about you."

"You never worry about us." Jason's lip curls in disgust. "Isn't that why I gave up college to take care of Little Bro, so you wouldn't have to?"

Mom's forehead wrinkles with hurt. "I didn't ask you to do th—"

"And you've got plenty keeping you busy." Jason pulls his truck keys out of his pocket. Right on cue, the three terrors run into the house, dripping lake water and snot.

"Are you still planning on going back?" Mom asks over the sudden chaos. "To college?"

Jason shoves open the door. "Don't need to."

"The ranch is doing well?"

"You don't need to worry about it. I'm taking care of us just fine. Better than Dad even." Dad worked a lot harder than Jason does, but somehow Jason turned things around. Maybe Dad's health was declining a lot longer than we knew about.

"Really?" The doubt in Mom's voice is obvious. She of all people would remember how we barely scraped by. It's why she left it, isn't it? She rearranged her priorities and bailed.

She decided Jason and I weren't worth it.

256

I never mattered to her.

"Yup," Jason answers, but we barely hear it over the kids whining about how cold they are. One of them falls off a chair and screams, diverting Mom's attention.

I can't get out of here fast enough.

Chapter 31

MARA RACETTE
Thursday, July 18, 6:00 p.m.

I loop my last resistance band onto the hooks I mounted on the wall over my new equipment shelf, now filled with kettle bells and free weights. The empty cardboard box sits flattened across the room. Only one box is left, half-full of books and framed pictures with old friends, but I can't bring myself to do any more. Yet.

I collapse back onto the bed and stare at the ceiling. Finding shapes in its texture is almost as good as finding them in the clouds, like I used to do on the trampoline in my old backyard. It's what I did when I was stressed out, but we had to leave that behind in the move. That was back when all I worried about was my calculus test or who was asking me to homecoming. Which friends were fighting. Which classes and extracurriculars would look best on college applications.

Back when I didn't have to wonder if the guy I'm crushing on is actually a killer.

I rub my eyes, but the image of Eli ducking into a police car is burned under my lids. It pulses hot, like the memory has been branded there.

It can't be true, though. . . . I've seen opposite sides to Eli, and I can't accept there's another side underneath him capable of that. Even if he's avoiding the police and keeping secrets, like his hidden relationship with Rayanne. He was at school the day Rayanne never showed up. He was with Cherie at the powwow. He's so protective of her, he never would've left her alone.

It doesn't make sense.

If he's the one who killed those girls, how am I ever going to trust anyone again? Why bother trying when people can lie so easily?

The doorbell twangs down the hall. I roll across my bed and peer out the blinds to find Jon Miller's car in the driveway. The lawyer.

I roll back and bury my face into the pillow. I just want to be done with this whole thing. It's grating into our lives in steady strokes, taking narrow pieces out of us one bit at a time.

At least it's better than what Loren has been dealing with. Someone tossed the grater aside and threw her and Geraldine's lives into a meat grinder.

And now Eli. I'm sure he's just hanging on by a thread. Everyone probably believes he did this. There's a thrumming in my bones telling me it's not true.

He's not the one who made this mess. He's been dragged into it like the rest of us . . . I'm almost certain.

I can't let someone get away with all this. I slip out of my room and creep down the hall.

"With the new developments, I really don't think you'll have to stress about it," the lawyer says. He's without a tie today, just a paisley button-down shirt with the sleeves rolled halfway up his forearms.

"That's quite a relief," Dad says, patting his palm against the arm of the couch. "I was getting pretty worried."

I step into the room. "About what?"

Dad grips his knee. "Oh, nothing. The authorities have their culprit."

I glance between Dad and Jon Miller. "Worried about what?"

Dad shares a look with Jon.

The lawyer clasps his hands together. "Someone was calling around recently, looking into your dad's work schedule for back in April. But that was before the police arrested the culprit today. I think that should stop anyone trying to bring your dad into this——"

"Before they arrested Eli." I dig my nails into my palms.

Dad licks his lips. "Right. It's a huge relief, my girl."

It can't be true. A panic I don't quite understand is surging through me. They've got it all wrong.

"This is why I was so upset you were alone with him," Dad says. "You can't trust anyone. Maybe now we'll finally get some peace here with him behind bars. Maybe the Arnouxs and the White Tails can have some closure."

I blink away the tears forming. I'm not relieved. Not yet.

Mom pipes in from the kitchen. "I know you were friends with that boy. That has to be a lot to process."

"He didn't do it."

All three of them stare at me. Jon's face is frozen in practiced neutrality, but Mom's pinches in sympathy—or maybe pity. Dad is barely containing his frustration.

I stand my ground. "It wasn't him."

Jon speaks, still holding his stone-still expression. "They found evidence in his truck—a jacket, I believe."

I throw my hands out. "And they just now found it? After all this time? Right after his meth-head dad comes home from a work trip?"

Mom's mouth pops open. Dad runs a hand through his hair. Jon doesn't move an inch.

"Awfully convenient, isn't it? I was in his truck a few days ago, and I didn't see any jacket."

Dad cocks his head. "When were you in his truck?"

When I broke into it. "Doesn't matter. Eli's behind bars, but I promise you, I don't feel any safer."

I storm out of the room before they can question me, tears leaking down my cheeks. My gut is telling me I'm right, just like it told me to trust Eli.

At what point do you know if your gut is just full of crap?

Chapter 32

ELI FIRST KILL
Friday, July 19, 8:00 a.m.

I knew the charade wouldn't last long. I hoped it would, and I tried like hell to keep it up as best as I could. Footsteps echo down the empty hall, somebody vomits a few cells over, a fluorescent light buzzes. I swing my legs off the paper-thin bed and rest my feet on the cold tile floor. There's an icy mass in my throat, sending sick drips down my insides, telling me everything is about to slip from my fingers.

Or maybe it's *been* slipping in slow motion since April.

I swallow past the pain. How am I gonna get out of this one? Either way, I'm gonna lose. Either way, I become the buffalo at the bottom of the buffalo jump. Dead, ready to be skinned and gutted, only good to the hunters who drove me over the cliff.

No good to Cherie.

The footsteps stop outside my cell. Youngbull opens the barred door with a ghostly creak. "Time to talk to Staccona."

He leads me down the hall and pushes me into an interrogation room almost identical to the one we talked in before, only Cherie isn't here. And he isn't offering me chips and drinks.

And my hands are cuffed.

Minutes pass. Sweat soaks into my shirt. Finally, Staccona comes in and struts to the chair across the table with a gotcha smile.

He casually pulls his ankle over his knee. "Today's the day to tell the truth, kid. You cooperate, things will be much easier for you. Honesty is going to make this all a lot less painful for everyone. Got it?"

It's gonna be painful all right, honesty or not. He doesn't offer me a public defender, and probably hopes I'm clueless enough not to ask for one. I don't need one, though. I already know the price I have to pay here.

I look him dead in the eye. "I'm innocent."

He sucks his teeth and nods. "We have Rayanne's jacket in the back of your truck. It has been confirmed to be hers."

Anger churns under my skin, but I tense my muscles to keep it from showing. "And I'm sure you tore up the house looking for anything else. Didn't find anything, did you?"

He spreads his fingers across the table's surface. "What we do have . . . is irrefutable." He won't admit there's nothing else. I already know there's nothing.

"Where's Cherie?"

He waves my question off. "Why Rayanne? Did you see her waiting on the road on your way to school?"

"Tell me where Cherie is, and then I'll tell you what you want to know."

"An officer took her to her school friend's house, just like you asked. He even wrote a note for your pops to see after that job."

A little tension drips out of my neck.

"Did you and Rayanne get into a fight?"

I run my thumb along the cold metal of the handcuffs. I'm already surging over the cliff's edge. What I say next will only speed the fall. It's imminent now.

"That's not even my truck." I raise my eyes to meet his. "Ask anyone. Nobody's ever seen me drive that."

"It was parked in *your* driveway."

"I don't drive that rust bucket. I drive the gray Tacoma, which I'm sure you searched as well and found no traces of Rayanne."

"Your fingerprints were all over the door handle and stick."

"Because two nights ago, I put it in neutral and rolled it out of the shop. That thing hasn't run in a year. You can check."

"If it doesn't work, why take it out?" He cocks his head. "Felt like getting her running again?"

"Because I'm trying to keep up appearances."

His eyes squint just slightly, giving up that he has no idea where I'm going with this. "That's enough, kid. We have Rayanne's jacket in your possession. We were tipped off that you usually showed up late to school in the mornings, though your attendance record doesn't reflect that. We have you near Samantha's murder scene. We have a record of you blatantly ignoring Samantha's constant texts. You and Rayanne talked on the phone the day before she was taken. What we'd like to know is why."

"What I'll tell you is—that old car hasn't been out of the shop in close to a year. It hasn't seen the light of day since before winter. Since well before April. Rayanne has never been near that car. And the one time I roll it out, magic evidence just happens to appear?"

"Big deal. You could've transferred it in there anytime."

"*I* didn't."

He chuckles a deep, grating sound. "Are you really trying to tell me you've been framed?"

"You're asking the wrong questions, man."

His smile drops. To his credit, he doesn't get angry. He actually thinks about it. "What appearances are you trying to keep?"

I give it another second.

"Why did you roll that car out?"

"I didn't kill those girls, Staccona, and I can prove it. Unfortunately, I'll really screw my family by doing that."

His foot shakes over his knee, showing his impatience. "Is that your dad's car? You said he had his own truck doing manual labor in Kalispell." Now he must be wondering if my dad is the culprit. If they should send a team out to grab him. "Did he have something to do with this?"

"The morning Rayanne disappeared, and every morning since the beginning of April, I was late to school because I had to get Cherie to the elementary school first. She was terrified of the bus." I plant both feet on the floor. "Check her attendance records. And check with her bus driver. She's never been on. Maybe the school even has a camera."

"Your dad could've taken her that day."

"No."

He clasps his hands over his lap, his foot still now. "What appearance are you keeping up?" Understanding is seeping in.

It's over. I force the words out. "Our dad left in the beginning of April. Never came back."

I've just sent the first stone crumbling from the wall I've carefully built around us, let loose the secret I've been sacrificing everything to keep, and he stays silent. Waiting.

"People have been asking a lot of questions lately. I rolled the truck out so it would look like he came home."

He's quiet for another beat. "You and your sister have been on your own since April?" More stones fall. Control is slipping from my death grip.

"Yes, but in all honesty, it's not much different now than when he *was* around." The difference will be people knowing about it. People who can decide I'm not capable of taking care of her. People who will rip us apart.

"He just took off . . . you haven't heard from him since?"

I swallow a bitter lump. "For all I know, he could be dead in a ditch somewhere."

He nods slowly.

I could've tried to say it was just one of those days I needed to drive her when my dad was working out of town, or maybe when he was high, but they would've figured it out soon enough. My dad would've needed to excuse the school tardies, and they would've tried to confirm with him. Or they'd have had social workers come sniffing around. It's over.

"Why hide it?"

Dread pours into my limbs. "At first, I thought he'd be back. Then when I knew he wasn't . . . I didn't want Cherie going into foster care. That system is garbage. I don't trust anyone else to keep her safe."

I've heard too many foster care stories firsthand. Siblings separated for years. Young girls abused in the worst ways.

"Well. Maybe he didn't go as far as you thought." His suspicion is creeping toward Dad.

"The way I see it, someone thought he was really home and wanted to frame him. It's easy to make the notorious drunk and drug addict look guilty, but he's long gone."

Staccona grips his ankle, his nails sinking into the fabric. He stares at me, stone-faced, calculating. "We'll talk soon." He stands and slips out the door.

I should feel relieved in the silence he leaves behind, but the room is closing in around me. I can't get enough air. All the lying, all the sacrifices to hold on to the illusion things at home were business as usual . . . all for nothing.

Somebody threw a cherry bomb into our facade.

And Cherie is the one who's going to pay for it.

Chapter 33

BRODY CLARK
Friday, July 19, 6:00 p.m.

My jaw aches from grinding. It's almost like the old days when First Kill and I would catch a ride with the upperclassmen to Lower Two Medicine Lake, fishing gear in hand.

We'd laugh so hard razzing each other to impress the guys, my whole mouth would start hurting in that good way. Once, a black bear stalked into the clearing, and we all clambered into the back of a truck and fishtailed out of there. Teeth clenched. Lungs tight.

My jaw muscles were sore the next day.

That's how it feels now, but with disappointment and worry. No laughs. Just dread. The past week has been never-ending dread.

Or longer than that, if I'm honest.

I lean back in my chair, TV screen holding on the PlayStation home screen. I find my stress ball between all the piles of video games on my desk and toss it straight up and catch it in my palm, the *BIA* showing perfectly on its top.

Someone from the Bureau of Indian Affairs came to the high school career fair last year, drumming up interest in their summer internships. I took a ball even though I had no interest. Not an ounce. I'll be set on this ranch. Just like Jason and everyone before us. I toss the ball again. I don't know who thought stress balls would be a good idea. They're good for nothing. Least of all *stress*.

I squish it in my palm. It's done nothing in the last week to calm me. I toss it again.

I went from one problem to the next. A brother to a *brother*.

Why First Kill?

I sit up and chuck the ball at the wall. A dull thump sounds, and the ball plops onto the floor, back into its perfect sphere. Pathetic.

It can't even give me the satisfaction of a good impact. Screw that.

I grab the PlayStation controller and raise my arm, ready to hurl it into the wall, when tires crunch through the gravel driveway.

I toss the controller into the chair and stride down the hall to the front door. It's not Jason. He's working in the cattle fields.

I shove open the door as a gray truck sinks to a halt behind Jason's Ram.

First Kill glares at me over the steering wheel.

My aching jaw yanks open.

They released him? I can't deny the relief snaking out of my chest. He wouldn't be out if they thought he was guilty. Right?

He shoves open his door with a creak and stomps through the rocks toward the porch.

"Who'd you have to bribe to get out?" I start, but the scowl on his face sucks the humor out of me. "I mean, I'm glad to see you, man. I was sick about it when I heard."

He stops in front of the steps below me, fists tight at his sides. "Yeah? Couldn't have been *that* sick."

I wet my lips.

"Not effing sick enough to turn in the guest book."

Oh. "I—"

"You had a whole day. I kept hoping you'd finally turn it in to give them someone to look at besides me. But you didn't."

What is everyone's deal with that guest book? "I didn't think it would help. I heard . . . I heard they had something big on you."

"You could've tried, dog face."

Ouch. "Don't *imiitāisskii* me, man."

He points a shaking finger at me. "You could've tried. But you didn't, so I had to lay down all my cards. I had to admit that my dead-beat dad is *gone*."

"What are you talking about?"

"My dad split in April, left us high and dry."

"I—I had no idea."

"Exactly. Nobody did. That's the point. It was my secret, but now it's out, and Cherie has to go into foster care. So screw you."

I open and close my mouth like a trout out of water. "It wouldn't have helped you."

He mounts the first stair, coming almost eye level to me. He's an inch lower, but his anger more than makes up the difference. "You would've done anything to clear Jason's name, but you didn't give a piss about mine."

I thought he was done for. I thought we'd never be friends again because he'd be locked up for the rest of his life. Now we'll never be friends because he thinks I left him in the lurch. Turned my back on him.

He's not gone. He's here in the flesh. I have to give him something, keep him with me. "I couldn't give it to them."

He shakes his head. "You *wouldn't*."

"Listen, First Kill. I messed up."

He takes the final step, looking down at me now. "Yeah. You did. They took Cherie from me, and I'll never forgive you for it. You and the dirty bastard who—"

"No." I flail my arms out. "I mean, I *really* shit in my medicine bag, man."

"What are you talking about?"

I run my clammy hand along my arm. He and Loren, so obsessed with that guest book. "I did something stupid. I . . . I was so worried about Jason, I messed with the guest book."

He steps back, head cocked. "How?"

I pause, listening for any sign of Jason. "I found a random entry for that week in April that was written in pencil. I erased it and faked Andrew Stern's signature in pen. I knew what it looked like from his real entry last week."

"You what?" His look is enough to have me regretting saying anything, but it's too late. It's done.

"Stupid, I know. I just wanted you to help me follow him so maybe we could really find something. I regret it, and I'll get in trouble if I get caught. That's why I never gave it to Staccona. Why I never can."

He rests his hand on the porch railing and squeezes his eyes shut. "That's insane, even for you."

"I know."

It was a rash decision, one of the dumbest things I've done. I guess I panic when it feels like things are falling apart. I've lost too much, had too many things toss me into a tumble dryer. My family has betrayed me. They've been ripped away. I've been left behind. Broken. I'm sick of it. Sick of losing everything I care about.

Now my instinct is to dig my heels in and fight to keep the few things I have left.

Even if it hurts me.

Air hisses through his teeth.

"Sorry you were expecting something from it. And sorry about Cherie."

He smacks the porch railing, making me wince. "I came over here ready to beat you, ay. Somebody should."

I shift my weight. "Skoden. Just lemme round up all my rez dogs first so it's a fair fight."

He cracks a smile, running his fingers over his right knuckles. They're flatter than they should be after his squirrelly years of fighting.

He's whacked me a few times over the years, but never all-out. Dad used to watch us scrapping in the yard and bestow another piece of his self-proclaimed Indigenous wisdom to keep us in check: *You can butt heads, just don't lock antlers.*

I'd hate to be on the receiving end of Eli's fist at full strength.

"Where are they taking her?"

"A family in town. You know, the social worker asked your mom. She said no." He pauses for a beat, watching me. "Said she didn't have enough to give right now."

"I coulda told you that." Mom couldn't step it up for her own son. Why would she for a little cousin?

"Yeah. Should've guessed."

"Cherie will be okay," I say. "They'll make sure of it. What about you? You don't have to go somewhere too?"

"Nah. The family taking Cherie only takes kids under nine. The social worker and Youngbull argued about what to do with me for a while. They knew I'd never stay anywhere they take me. And I'm eighteen in less than three months anyway, so I get to stay in my

272

house. The social worker will check in now and then."

"Good."

"I can't get Cherie back until I'm eighteen and prove I'm holding down a job, though."

"Sucks, man."

"Yup. Now I have to go say bye." He steps back down the steps and gives a sarcastic smile. "But at least I'm not in jail for murder anymore."

His violent steps in the gravel shoot pain through my head. "Hey. When did you say your dad left?"

He pauses with his hand on his truck door. "April. Sometime before Rayanne."

"Huh. Suspicious timing, enit?"

He pulls it open. "He's a good-for-nothing meth addict, not a killer. 'Sides, he was long gone before everything went down." He dips into the truck and flips around without a backward glance.

I don't know if the feds will see it that way.

LOREN ARNOUX
Friday, July 19, 6:00 p.m.

Sam's small house is too crowded. Every square foot of the open living area is taken up by people here to support her family. They shift along the kitchen table with a spread of food across it, perch on the arms of the couch with paper plates balanced on one hand, huddle in tight groups in the corners of the room. The air is heavy with the spice of chili and sweat. It's sour, like it's been passed through too many people before it gets to me.

The White Tails can't have a funeral for Sam yet because of the continuing investigation, but they wanted to put on a feed. They need the support. The community.

Grandma and Sam's mom are in the kitchen, surrounded by other women whispering and wiping tearstained cheeks as they prep more food. Sam's dad stands in a group of men behind the couch, including some of Grandpa's old friends. They swap fishing stories between bites, doing their best to distract him from the pain.

Even Jeremy Youngbull, dressed in a T-shirt and baseball hat, takes a turn, claiming he once reeled in a nine-pound kokanee.

I can't believe it's only been a week since Sam's murder. It feels like it's been a month. And these three months without Ray Bear feel like a year. Why is it that time flows slower when you're drowning?

And why is it that when Youngbull told us they had released Eli, all I felt was relief?

Maybe the selfish part of me didn't want to lose someone else close to me. Or maybe I just knew deep down he couldn't be the one.

But the relief is coupled with a sick worry. I don't know if we're ever going to find peace. Youngbull didn't sound too confident. The way he twisted his meaty hands together told me he's just as worried as we are.

Worried the killer's already dispersed like smoke, leaving the black, mangled charcoal for us to clean up.

They don't even know who could've put that jacket in the First Kills' old truck. Maybe Eli's dad knows more than we think.

I crumple my unused paper plate with shaking hands. Seeing everyone holding plates of food makes my gut feel hollow—but not because I'm hungry. Because this is all wrong. It makes me sick that this is even happening. That the living room my best friend and I laughed in has turned into a place to grieve her.

That dozens of people are in and around this house, and she's not one of them.

I slump against the living room window. Even more people sit on folding chairs in the yard, cans of pop in the grass at their feet. Sam's youngest brother sits alone on the Big Wheels swing behind them, gently swaying back and forth. His bare feet barely brush along the tips of the unkempt grass.

I bet he's wishing Sam were here to push him.

The emptiness in my core cracks like glass, and anger and sadness seep through the fissures, swirling and bubbling together like acid. My fingers shake, begging to move—to break something. The walls close in around me. The heavy air gets thicker.

I push off the window, desperate to get out, and then I see it on the desk beside the couch.

The corner of Sam's old laptop.

Chapter 34

ELI FIRST KILL

Friday, July 19, 6:00 p.m.

The faded blue duffel bag is way too big for Cherie. Filled with all her clothes and a few favorite toys, it drags behind her in dramatic lurches, catching on the front rug and then on the dusty porch mat too. Her little arms tense and strain, but she insisted—she can do it herself. So I let her.

It thuds down each porch step in time with my thumping heart.

Every step she takes tears at the rope that's always connected the two of us. The one I've been desperately hanging on to, ripping my palms to bloody shreds.

Cherie drops the strap once she's hauled the bag into the gravel, and the woman from Blackfeet Child and Family Services carries it to the trunk of her car.

Cherie sits on the bottom step, eyes welling with tears. "I don't wanna go."

I squat in front of her, eye to eye. "I don't want you to go either." I slide my tongue along my teeth, forcing my breath to slow. "But you have to. I can't—"

"You said Dad was coming back." Her little fist pounds against her knobby knee. "You said he was working hard."

She's looking at me like *I'm* the one who betrayed her. Like *I'm* the one who failed her. And maybe I did. After all that, I'm losing her anyway.

"I know. I didn't want you to be sad."

She won't look me in the eye.

I lied to her. I lied to everyone. And for what?

I don't regret much. I've done what I had to. Pushed everyone away, put up walls, put my sister before myself every time. I'd do it all again—except lie to her.

I showed her she can't always trust me, and that hurts almost as much as shipping her off to some other family.

She stares at her shoes, tears spilling over her cheeks. "Why did he leave me?"

I clench my teeth, fighting to keep my cool. I can't lose it in front of her. How do I explain this to a seven-year-old? She deserves so much more than she's ever gotten. I rest my elbows on my knees and pull her hands into mine. "He knew you'd be safe with me."

Wisps of hair hang out of her braid around her face. It's not as tight as the braids I do for her. Somebody else is going to do her braids, brush her hair. Will they make sure to hold it right so the tangles don't hurt? Will they be patient when she wiggles too much?

Will they keep her safe?

The woman's footsteps crunch through the gravel. My chest is splintering open, and time is spilling out of it.

It's been me and her. Nobody is going to take care of her like I have.

Cherie looks over my shoulder at the approaching woman and leans in until our noses touch. "Maybe Dad will come back," she whispers urgently. The drip of hope in her voice hits me like ice. "Maybe he'll come get me and bring me back home."

"No." I drop her hands and hold her face, brushing the whisps of hair back. "Listen to me, Cherie. If Dad ever comes to see you, do not go with him."

"Why?" The hope cracks.

The honest truth is—I don't trust him. I stopped a long time ago. I never told a soul, but the last few months before Dad left, he was in a bad way. He'd yell around at night, threatening to kill somebody who wasn't there, searching the house for something he could never find. The meth was making him paranoid.

Another honest truth—I was relieved when he left.

"Promise me, Cherie. If he comes, don't go with him. Only me."

"Okay," she whispers.

"And I promise *you*, I'll bring you home. As soon as I can, I'll bring you back here." I pull her into my arms and stand up, digging my cheek into her loose braid. My chest is crumbling as our last seconds run out. I did everything I could. I tried my hardest.

But it seems like for me, no matter how hard I try, I still get the short stick.

We both do.

The woman opens the back door of the sedan with a click and holds it open expectantly. "It's a good family, Eli. They've been doing this a long time."

I try to believe her. We went back and forth, weighing all the options. Brody's mom seemed best, but she said no. My auntie in Billings would've taken her, despite her mobility issues, but she's so far. Too far to visit. Mom's family across the state cut us off six years ago. Not a word since. And I couldn't bring myself to suggest Loren's grandma, with everything they've got going on.

This should be temporary, so in the end we went with a local

Blackfeet family. One she trusts. One that'll let me visit anytime.

"You be good, ay?" I squeeze Cherie one last time. "And you tell me if anything happens you don't like."

Cherie nods against my cheek, her tears smearing across my skin. I try to set her down, but she wraps her legs around my waist and clings to my neck.

"It's time to go." I can only whisper it, or my voice will crack and that'll be the end of holding it together.

She squeezes tighter. "No," she yells, disintegrating into sobs.

I try to pull her off, but her nails dig into my neck, breaking skin. Her wails ring in my ear. I'd take her and run if I could. But we have to do this the right way. It kills me, guts me like a field-dressed deer, but I have to peel her hands off me. "Please," I whisper, more to myself than to her, as she fights against it. Tears spill out of my eyes, mixing with Cherie's as she claws her fingers into my shirt and throws herself against me in sheer panic.

A sob escapes my tight throat as I heave her away from me, dodging her desperate reaching. Pushing her away from the only stable thing in her life.

This is the worst pain I've ever felt.

The woman wraps her arms around Cherie and pulls her toward the car. Away from me. Her eyes cling to me through the tears, and for a miserable second, I wonder if she'll ever forgive me for this. If she'll ever understand it.

I bite down on my tongue, still as the air between us. I blink away the blur of tears. "I'll see you soon. Promise."

My face is burning, my lungs seizing. It takes everything in me to stay upright and wave as the car makes a tight turn and rolls down the driveway.

The rope snaps. Cherie, the anchor who's been holding me in place, rips away from me. But there's no weight lifted. I'm loose and aimless. Alone and at the whims of the wind.

LOREN ARNOUX
Friday, July 19, 6:30 p.m.

The back of my neck itches, like everyone in the White Tails' house is watching me. Like they know what I'm about to do. There's a picture on the desk of Sam and her three younger brothers. I pick it up and run my fingers along the plastic frame, but the corner of the laptop presses into my stomach.

I shift the papers covering the laptop as I put the frame down to expose the charging light. It's still plugged in under all this clutter. I glance at Grandma in the kitchen, still talking with Sam's mom, then pluck the charging cord out of the port and slip the laptop under my arm.

Weaving around furniture and dodging new arrivals to the feed, I make my way to the hallway that leads to the bedrooms. The murmur of conversation fades as I slip into the bedroom Sam shared with her youngest brother and shut the door behind me.

It's quiet. The air is stale, like the brother must not be sleeping in here anymore either, but there's a hint of leather and something sweet. I flip on the light. A wool blanket hangs over the window on one wall. On another hangs a canvas painting of powwow dancers. Sam painted it last year, capturing the swing of the shawls and the bounce of the skirts perfectly in smooth neon colors. This painting is even more beautiful than the one her parents gave to the Two Feather Project to raffle off. I'm glad they kept this one. It's bright and dynamic—just like Sam was.

A half-finished beadwork earring rests between cups of colored glass beads on her small desk. A tiny braid of sweetgrass is layered between lines of beads in the earring. She was the most artistic person I knew. She had so much more to create. So much more to share.

It feels like I'm doing something wrong treading in here. Sneaking where I don't belong. Sitting in memories I don't deserve.

I perch on the edge of her bed and open the laptop. It takes several seconds for the screen to boot up.

Sam was probably the last person to touch this laptop. One of her cousins handed it down to her after he upgraded for work. It's ancient but still kicking. Sam's prized possession. She never let her brothers touch it.

"Sorry, Sam," I whisper when the twirling circle finally disappears. First things first, I open the iMessage app. The last updated conversation is with Eli First Kill. Youngbull mentioned their "strange" text history . . . now I'll see if for myself.

The day before her death, Sam texted him: **Can I ask u somethin?**

A few days before that: **r u entering this year?**

She sent him messages fairly regularly, with no response any time. Not a single one.

Can u talk?

Wyd?

Just let it go already

Hey

Wyd?

Is ur dad home?

Why is she asking about his dad?

I scroll backward through another month's worth of Sam reaching out to brick-wall Eli when the door swings open with a high-pitched creak.

Youngbull steps into the room.

He looks taller here in this tiny bedroom than he ever has in my house. Or around town. His head nearly touches the doorframe, and he towers over the bed beside him. My fingers are frozen on the laptop.

He closes the door with a click—I don't know if it's the latch catching or if he just turned the lock.

"What are you doing?" he asks.

My palm squeaks against the computer. "Nothing, I—"

He crosses the room in a single stride and pulls the computer off my lap with one massive hand. He glances at the screen and shakes his head. "What are you thinking?"

My suddenly empty hands shake with him looking down at me. He's too close. The sharp bite of his antiperspirant settles over me.

"Are you trying to do your own investigating?" His rough voice keeps me from answering. He closes the laptop and holds it at his side. "Stop."

I should keep my mouth shut. "Why?"

His free hand pulls into a fist. Fat tendons roll back and forth over his knuckles.

Dread oozes into my chest, slowing time to a crawl. He had his eye on us at the powwow. He would've seen where Sam was after the giveaway and where she went. If he pulled over near Ray Bear on her way to the bus stop that morning in April, she wouldn't have seen a reason to worry. Ray Bear and Sam would've trusted this guy until the second he wrapped his massive hands around their throats.

"Don't do this to yourself," he says. "You'll just make things harder for us."

Us? My gaze is locked on his tight fist.

"And get yourself hurt."

I meet his eye. Is that a warning? A threat?

I dig my fingers into my best friend's bedspread, heart pounding. Is his face the last face she saw?

A creak lurches into the room, making Youngbull turn with a start.

Grandma quickly glances between us from the doorway. "What's going on in here?"

I scramble across the room and stand beside her.

Youngbull raises the laptop with one hand. "Loren is snooping into Samantha's messages, trying to investigate."

Grandma doesn't say anything.

"This is serious," he says. "A killer is still out there—"

"You think we don't know that?" Grandma whispers harshly. She grips the doorknob and looks him up and down with disgust.

He sucks his teeth and looks back at me. "A killer is still at large. You need to leave the investigating to us. For your own safety."

Grandma pulls me through the door and down the hall, muttering under her breath all the way to the car.

I'm already buckled in when she slams her door shut. "Are you mad at me?"

She laughs dryly. "I'm pissed. But not at you."

A car pulls next to us, and Sam's great-grandparents get out, but they don't go inside the house—they head straight for her little brother on the swing, wrapping him up in their arms.

I glance at the wide-open front door, hands tingling with fading adrenaline. Was Youngbull going to hurt me if Grandma didn't barge in? Or was he really worried about my safety? Either way, he's right—purposely searching for a killer is stupid. But I can't stop.

Grandma pounds a fist against the steering wheel. "This guy. Who is he to talk about investigating? He hardly lifted a finger for Ray Bear. He didn't take her disappearance seriously. He and the rest of them shrugged it off and let Samantha die next. That's on them. *They* did this. Even if they miraculously find the guy, they already failed."

They did.

I did too. But I won't stop trying to figure out who did this. It's the only way I'll be able to live with the guilt of not preventing any of it.

Chapter 35

UNKNOWN

Friday, July 19, 8:00 p.m.

Lamplight caressed agitated fingers. *The idiots don't know what they're doing.* They'd be going in circles until the end of time. Knuckles cracked, then opened a search browser. *Let's start at the beginning.*

911 RECORDING, APRIL 9

DISPATCH: 911, what's your emergency?

911 CALLER: This is Geraldine Arnoux. My granddaughter Rayanne is missing.

DISPATCH: (typing) When's the last time you saw her?

911 CALLER: She didn't get to school. She was supposed to take the bus, but she never showed up.

DISPATCH: Is there anywhere else she would have gone?

911 CALLER: No. I know something's happened.

DISPATCH: What's your address?

911 CALLER: [redacted]

DISPATCH: (typing) You don't think she left by her own choice?

911 CALLER: No way. I know something's not right.

DISPATCH: You didn't see her this morning?

911 CALLER: I had to leave for work early. She was still asleep.

DISPATCH: Do you think she left during the night?

911 CALLER: I don't—she didn't leave. I need a tribal cop here. Something happened to Rayanne.

DISPATCH: (typing) Okay, I have a unit on its way. Let me just get some more information for them. Are any of her belongings gone?

911 CALLER: Her phone and her schoolbag aren't here.

DISPATCH: So she could've left. Is anything out of place? Any sign of a struggle?

911 CALLER: She didn't—no. No, everything looks normal—to me. I don't know. I need somebody here looking!

DISPATCH: Okay . . . (typing) . . . okay, just hang on a minute.

911 CALLER: Okay.

DISPATCH: I'm just speaking with the unit. So you didn't see her before you went to work. . . . At what point did you think something happened?

911 CALLER: Her school called to tell me she wasn't in her classes. She never skips. She's not like that.

DISPATCH: So she didn't make it to school—you went to your house after the call?

911 CALLER: I tried calling her phone, but she wasn't answering. I got a bad feeling about it, so I left work to check. She isn't at home. She wouldn't go anywhere else.

DISPATCH: So nobody has seen her since last night?

911 CALLER: My other granddaughter must've seen her this morning before school. She would've told me if she didn't. She had to go to school earlier.

DISPATCH: (typing) Okay. Have you checked with her?

911 CALLER: No—she would've told me.

DISPATCH: All right, well, the unit should be getting to [redacted] in just a minute. They'll talk with you about filing a missing person report.

911 CALLER: Something happened to her.

DISPATCH: It's only been a little while. Just hang tight for the police. I'm going to let you go now.

911 CALLER: I don't . . . Okay—

DISPATCH RECORDING, APRIL 9

DISPATCH: Unit 530 to [redacted]. Possible missing person.

DETECTIVE YOUNGBULL: Copy 530. Who?

DISPATCH: Rayanne Arnoux.

DETECTIVE YOUNGBULL: What's the code? What—

DISPATCH: Hang on, detective. (static) Code 1. No signs of struggle. Caller is sure something bad happened but can't point to any reasons why.

DETECTIVE YOUNGBULL: Ah. When was she last seen?

DISPATCH: This morning.

DETECTIVE YOUNGBULL: (inaudible) It's still morning! Code 1 it is. I'll get there when I get there.

DISPATCH: She'll want to file a missing person report.

DETECTIVE YOUNGBULL: 10-4.

The crackling words lingered in the air long after the recording stopped. *"I'll get there when I get there."* A terrible thing to have said. Even worse was all the words unspoken underneath it, but it's not like that counted as evidence.

LOREN ARNOUX

Friday, July 19, 9:00 p.m.

There's an unsteadiness in my body, like I haven't fully recovered from Jeremy Youngbull's scare. Pinpricks of nervous energy still curl over my skin. I can't erase the sick feeling that if he wanted to hurt me, I couldn't have stopped him. I wouldn't have stood a chance. I got the faintest hint at the helplessness Ray Bear and Sam must've felt in those first moments.

I grab Ray Bear's hoodie out of the dryer, bonfire scent now washed out of it, and pull it on. The warmth clinging to it does little to calm me. I retreat back down the hall, passing Ray Bear's silent room, and burrow into my bed.

I want to believe that Youngbull came into Sam's bedroom with good intentions, but I can't decide if he was threatening me or looking out for me. What else would've happened if Grandma didn't come in when she did?

Would he have laid me out, hands crushing my windpipe?

I might've been able to find something more useful in Sam's messages if he didn't follow me into her room. He messed up my chances.

I rub my eyes until blinking shapes twirl in the darkness under my lids. There's still one message chain I can look at. I open my phone and go to my text history with Sam. It's years old, full of pictures, late-night complaining, fights, laughs. I've never deleted this thread, and my storage breakdown proves it.

I mindlessly scroll backward, the gray and blue text boxes blurring across the screen. My thumb flicks all the messages past in a steady motion. I don't know why I bother. Reading through our old conversations will only hurt. It'll make me wish our young, dumb selves could've seen this coming.

I finally make it to the beginning, when I first got this ancient phone. Sam was always there for me. She cussed all wicked about my mom when I was mad she was gone but eased up the times I hoped she'd come back. The times I was sad.

She always texted back immediately in the days after Grandpa died, and always with a joke handy. I had some rough times, but Sam wasn't a stranger to that. She was a solid friend through it all.

So why was it different when Ray Bear disappeared?

Why did she pull back like she was afraid of me? Like I was so broken I'd be contagious? It doesn't make sense. She was a better friend than that, but I was too wrapped up in fear and sick with grief to remember it.

Maybe something else was going on.

Ray Bear would've helped me see that. She could always read people's emotions, but even more than that, she could always see the *why*. She was more perceptive and understanding than anyone.

Ray Bear was the *one* person who would've helped me figure out what was going on with Sam before it was too late. I couldn't see it on my own.

I'm not my best self without my sister.

I stop at the last conversation Sam and I had before Ray Bear disappeared. Before everything changed. It makes me sick to see the words. To know if I just got over myself Ray Bear would still be here.

Me: Brody's flaking out. Says his bro needs help with cattle.

Sam: Typical. We don't need him tho. I'm about to come over.

Me: Don't. I'm not letting that lazy pile off the hook again. He does this every time.

Sam: It's not a big deal. I still want to come. It'll be easier without him anyway.

Me: Too late. I just told him he has to meet us at the school tomorrow an hour early.

Sam: k . . . gotta see if I can get a ride.

Sam: u home w Ray?

Me: ya

Sam: Can I still come hang w u two?

I never replied. Ray Bear had been holed up in her room since getting home from track practice, then all of a sudden came into my room and jumped down my throat about Mara Racette. Talking about how immature we were being and how little it mattered compared to much bigger problems "out there." She didn't know how right she was.

She didn't usually get so riled up. Maybe she *was* on edge that night. And why did Sam want to hang out with both of us? She'd never cared if Ray Bear was around or not before.

I stare at the message, knowing I'm chasing ghosts. But if there was any way Ray Bear was getting into drugs . . . maybe Sam knew it. Maybe she retreated afterward because she had the same secrets. Maybe that's what she was going to admit after the giveaway. That they got mixed up with a rough crowd.

With the wrong people, girls can disappear for any reason.

One of Sam's texts to Eli was asking if his dad was home. She and Ray Bear both had a thing with Eli, which made me doubt him.

Maybe I should've been doubting his dad. Maybe he's still around and maybe he's worse than he's ever been.

I sink onto my pillow, squeezing my phone so tight the case creaks. There are too many maybes. Enough to stitch together and weave any story I like.

All maybes do is keep me awake at night, reminding me how little we actually know.

Chapter 36

MARA RACETTE
Friday, July 19, 11:00 p.m.

There are still gashes in the gravel. Miniature canyons of precarious rocks run the length of the driveway and collide with each other in tight turns and divots around the two trucks in front of Eli's house.

The uneven surface is the only reminder of the chaos that was here just yesterday morning. Now, not even the field grass lining the road moves. The night is deathly still. It makes the image of Eli being arrested feel even more wrong.

Pale moonlight hangs on the metal shop, and a subtle blue light caresses the front porch railing. The blinds part just as I'm climbing out of my car. I hug myself against the chilly night air and reach the front door just as Eli opens it.

He looks rough. Like a boxer who's taken a beating and keeps bringing his gloves back up, ready for more. He's got bags under his eyes instead of black eyes, and I feel the wall he's put in front of himself instead of his gloves. The porch light's unnatural glow even makes him look pale and gassed. Like he doesn't have much left.

"Mara Racette." There's an edge to his voice, but that's hardly unusual, and he only opens the door wide enough to stand in the gap.

I came here wanting the story . . . wanting him to explain himself because I know he *can*. But seeing him standing here, there's only one question I can ask.

"Are you okay?"

His eyebrows twitch. The light glints on the scar above his brow, and I'm pretty sure that's the smallest one he carries, even if the rest aren't physical. I glance back at his dad's truck. Is he the reason why Eli will only open the door a crack?

I should've called first. Or asked if he wanted to meet somewhere. Of course I'm barging in where I don't belong . . .

But he opens the door and steps aside. "Been better."

I glance at the truck one last time and brush past Eli. I head toward the same spot I sat in on the couch, but Eli doesn't follow.

He locks the door and stands motionless in the entryway. "So why are you here?"

I shift on my feet in front of the couch. "You owe me pancakes."

Finally, a smile chisels its way into one of his cheeks. It falls quickly, but he ambles into the living room and drops onto the couch into his spot.

I sit and position myself so I can see Eli and the hallway behind him.

"Do your folks know you're here?"

Shame heats my cheeks. I've never been a liar, but there's no way they'd let me be alone with Eli right now. "I told them I'd be at Loren's."

"Ah. I'm surprised to see you. You're not afraid of me now?"

I grip my knee. "I didn't believe it was you."

"You saw me getting thrown into a cop car."

"Yeah. I saw your face, and I admit, you looked guilty of *something*. But I just knew you couldn't have hurt those girls."

His face is stone-still besides one blink. "You hardly know me."

"You pinkie promised."

His lips pull into another quick smile. "Mara Racette, I hate to tell you this, but in the real world, pinkie promises don't count for much."

I bite my smile back. "I just knew it in my bones. I even told my parents, who, of course, thought I was crazy. But seeing their faces tonight felt like sweet justice."

"You really told them that?"

"I did." I lower my voice and lean toward the center of the couch. "And I told my dad's lawyer it was awfully convenient that they found so-called evidence right after your dad got home." I glance behind him toward the hall.

He cocks his head. "We're alone. Nobody's back there."

"Your dad isn't home?"

He shakes his head.

"Did they arrest—" The words run through my head again. "Is Cherie back there?"

Red seeps into his cheeks.

He tells me about where Cherie is. And why.

He doesn't cry, but I wish he would. It looks more painful to hold it in. I guess he's used to keeping this wall up and acting like he has everything under control . . . shouldering it all himself. It makes my eyes burn, seeing him so desperate to prove to himself he doesn't need anyone. I scoot to the center of the couch, close enough to feel the heat radiating from him. His fists are clenched on his legs, and he won't look me in the eye.

"I'm sorry," I whisper. Because what else can I say? I rest my fingers on his forearm. His skin is hot over the tensed muscle.

"She should be here, with me, but somebody screwed us." He tilts his head back and looks at the ceiling. A muscle in his jaw pulses over and over.

He's been holding it together for her. Alone. This entire time he's been trying to be a parent instead of a kid.

I run my thumb over the twitching muscle in his jaw. It freezes under my touch. "She'll be okay."

He squeezes his eyes shut but doesn't shift away from my hand.

"But will *you* be okay?" I skim my thumb over the red blotches in his cheek. He's done everything he can to look after Cherie with nobody looking after him. Of course he's cold and closed off. Who wouldn't be?

He turns his head, trapping my hand between his cheek and the couch. "I always am." The distance between us feels a lot smaller when he's looking me in the eye. "Mara Racette. You believed me when I said I didn't do it?"

"Yeah."

"Why?" He shifts on the couch, catching my hand in his before it slips.

That is the question. He wraps his fingers around the back of my hand, like a paused bro-handshake, though I doubt his fingertips skirt over the skin there on his friends' hands. I'm glad my long sleeves hide the goose bumps rising underneath.

"Maybe because you didn't just *say* it. You wanted to show it."

He slides his hand out of mine in a slow-motion continuation of the bro-shake. His fingertips trace the length of my fingers, sending more chills up my arm, and then he hooks his fingers against mine before they break apart in a dull *snap*. "Thanks." His smile squints his eyes.

"Even though everything got screwed up, at least more people believe you now."

His eyes drop with the allusion to Cherie getting taken. "I almost told you, you know. I wanted to."

I shake my head. "It's okay."

"Back in April, when I started wondering if he was really gone, I hooked up with Samantha." He skims his fingertips over his knuckles. "It was just a dumb snag, but then she started asking where my dad was, and I—I plumb shut down. Everything hit, and I knew I couldn't ever let anyone find out he left. I shut everyone out."

I get it. He had to protect his sister the best way he knew how.

"But even with everything happening now—I almost told you." There's some kind of reverence in his dark eyes, like it's the most intimate thing he's ever said to anyone.

I chew my lip but freeze when he reaches across the space between us to roll a lock of my hair between his fingers. "I'm sorry you had to tell *anyone.*"

"It was only a matter of time anyway. What was I going to do in the new school year with parent-teacher conferences and stuff? I can only forge a signature for so long." His eyes are glued to the ends of my hair flipping back and forth between his fingers.

We look up at the same time, now only inches from each other.

"But you believed me even before I had to spill my secret." His gaze dips to my mouth.

I'm terrified he's going to kiss me but find myself sliding my hand up his arm to make sure he does.

He leans closer, holding that smile I always hated noticing. He drops the single lock of hair and combs his fingers against my scalp behind my ear. He only loses the smile when he presses his lips to my forehead.

He smells like soap and fresh-cut firewood. When he pulls back just enough to meet my gaze, there's a question in his look and still a quarter of a smile. I lean almost the rest of the way to him, leaving a breath between our lips, and he closes the gap.

The best first kisses are the ones that somehow feel familiar. Like your lips know exactly where they fit together. Like you've already done it a hundred times. His are warm against mine. When we finally break, he rests the side of his head against the couch, fingers still gliding through my hanging hair.

"You're something else, Mara Racette." His fingers graze my collarbone, and his smile fades. He pulls out his phone to check the time. "Any chance you told your folks you were sleeping at Loren's?"

I raise my eyebrows.

A laugh sputters out. "I don't mean it like that. I just mean, I really don't wanna be alone."

The empty hall looms behind him. No parents. No Cherie. The light fixture above us is missing a bulb and only lights up the mouth of the hall, making it look like a dreadful, lonely cave.

He runs his fingers through his hair and then rests them on the back of his neck, waiting for my answer. I trace his jawline with my thumb. Sometimes the people putting up the hardest exteriors are the ones struggling the most. I lean in and kiss him again. His exhale on my lips is soft, his fingers behind my neck gentle. He's afraid to spook me.

His rough exterior is cracking open. His gloves are off. It feels like he's never let himself be this exposed and it sends an ache running through me. I pull him into a deeper kiss. His lips move against mine slowly, like this whole thing is fragile and he has to savor every second.

I run my fingertips down his neck, and when my tongue finds his,

his grip finally tightens. He pulls me closer and catches my lip in his teeth. I melt into him and forget everything except the feel of his body against mine.

He finally pulls back with a grin. "That's a yes, then?"

I don't want him to be alone either. Not tonight. Not when saying bye to Cherie is still so fresh. "I'll text my parents." It feels bad lying, but I do it anyway.

We slump down on the couch, feet on the coffee table, Eli's arm around my shoulders, and talk about life. Favorite movies. Favorite music. All the sports we've tried. Most embarrassing moments. First crushes. Best days. Worst days. We kiss. A lot. But that's it.

"Why'd you quit dancing?" I ask. "I heard you were a crowd favorite."

I think he won't answer until finally, he clears his throat. "I sold my regalia. Turns out running a household isn't cheap." He laughs ruefully. "I thought I was fine with it, but when that Flag Song started and I felt the pull in my blood—instant regret."

"I wish I could've seen you."

He pulls his phone out of his pocket and opens SnapShare. "There's plenty to see under the North American Indian Days hashtag." And there is. It takes him some time to scroll past all the posts from this year.

There are plenty of pictures of people smiling at the parade, in the arbor bleachers, at the rodeo, donning their impressive regalia. He pauses at a clip of the Indian Relay races. "I'll have to watch that one later," he says, putting his tongue between his teeth. "See what all my fans are saying about me."

Finally, the posts date back to last year's Indian Days. He leans his head against mine and plays a video of the junior fancy dance.

He's front and center in the frame. Underneath the roach of porcupine hair and rocker feathers shooting up from the top of his head, a teal circle of beadwork rests on his forehead, with darts of yellow, dark blue, and red. Strings of the same colors of beads hang in stripes from the matching headband down his temples and explode into teal fringe swinging across his chest.

More beadwork and fringe in rainbow colors hang from the buckskin spilling over his shoulders, jerking in precise and rapid movements to the beat of the drum.

The deep gray of the feathers shooting out of the twin bustles attached to his upper back and waist blur with his movement, and the red and yellow fringe hanging from his teal, geometric apron swats around his knees with each dramatic bounce.

All the colors spinning and swaying around his body bring even more focus to the bronze tan of his skin in his flexing arms as he swings his feathered coup sticks and to his bare, muscled sides underneath all the regalia.

He moves like a powerhouse, and it's undeniably attractive.

When the video ends, he shoves the phone back into his pocket. "I shouldn't have sold it. My grandma made it all for my dad, and he passed it to me—but we were desperate. *I* was desperate."

"Sorry."

He tugs me closer to his side.

As time goes on, we slip farther and farther sideways until we're facing each other, heads on the armrest, bodies pressed together. His fingertips glide along my arm and back, and I grip a handful of his shirt.

"If someone would've told me a few weeks ago that I'd be kissing Eli First Kill, I would've said they were dead wrong."

He smiles against my forehead. "If someone would've said I'd be kissing Mara Racette, I would've said, who's that?"

I scoff.

He laughs into my hair and presses his palm into my back. "I wouldn't have been that surprised. You're a smoke show. Just a quiet one."

I rest my head on his chest, his heartbeat echoing through my head like a slow drum song. We fall into silence, but it's not panic inducing with him next to me.

I think he may be falling asleep, but when I shift to look at him, he's staring at the ceiling. I guess the thoughts don't leave just because we're not alone.

I trace the lettering on his cross-country T-shirt. "I still wonder if it was Jason."

He laces his fingers with mine and rests them on his chest. "Maybe. But he has a pretty convincing work alibi for Rayanne. And he couldn't have been gone from the emcee table for too long at the pow-wow. Doesn't make much sense to me."

"I also wonder if . . . if it could be your dad."

He lets out a slow breath and looks back to the ceiling. "He left right before. He wouldn't stay in the area and not see Cherie and me. He has issues, but he's not *that* heartless."

I grip his fingers tighter and lock my gaze on the scar over his eyebrow. "Maybe he has more issues than you know about."

"Of course he does. Doesn't every parent?"

I picture my dad sitting motionless at the kitchen table. Not eating. Not drinking. He must talk about finding Rayanne with Mom behind closed doors. There certainly could be more issues than I can guess. I know he feels guilty for almost assaulting a teenager and uprooting us. He's probably seen me struggling with the move even though I try my best to hide it.

Eli opens and closes his mouth. "If suspecting dads is on the table . . . what about yours?"

"What about mine?"

"He was questioned hard enough he got himself a lawyer."

"We both were." I pull my hand out of his.

He rests his on my hip. "You guys moved here right before Rayanne disappeared. Right around the same time my dad left."

"That doesn't mean anything . . ." What's he on about?

"When your dad threatened to mess up that douchebag, do you think he really would've?"

Cold waves churn through my stomach. "No. He was just blowing smoke."

His hand still rests on my hip, but it's not comforting anymore. It's digging in like a weight. "Did he know how mean we all were to you?"

"No." I never once complained about my social situation. I made sure to keep them out of it this time so they wouldn't feel the need to fix things. I didn't want them to make my problems their problems.

And maybe because I was afraid Dad would overreact again.

"I'm just saying . . . he lost his temper once to protect you. Maybe it got worse here. We treated you bad. Samantha especially."

I sit up, putting some distance between us. "My dad would *never* kill anyone." It's such a preposterous idea. So far from who he is. The fact that Eli thinks he could do such a thing when he doesn't even know him . . . when he's only heard about his worst moment. But I guess I did the same thing. "I only brought up your dad because he has a problem that . . . alters him."

301

"My dad would do *a lot* of questionable stuff, but he wouldn't kill anyone either. Not on purpose." His eyes are steady when they meet mine. He sits up and slides his hand into mine. "No use speculating. Let's stop talking about it."

If I want Eli to trust I know my dad, I should trust that he knows his dad just as well. "Fine." I meld against him, letting his warmth calm me. We lie down, and he draws swirls across my back until his breath gets heavier in my hair.

The problem is, I don't trust Eli's dad in the slightest. He left his own children. Left them with *nothing*.

I run my thumb across his eyebrows and over the scar. Sleep softens all his harsh angles, making him look like the teenager he's supposed to be. My thumb follows the curve of his lips, and then I kiss him one last time.

A ghost of a smile is on his lips while I stare at the ceiling with his words repeating through my head.

He lost his temper once to protect you.

Somebody must be trying like hell to pin this on any one of us.

I gently slide my phone out of my pocket and go to the Indian Days hashtag on SnapShare.

Chapter 37

LOREN ARNOUX

Saturday, July 20, 10:00 a.m.

Grandma has the day off, which should make me feel better, but it only puts me more on edge. I stare at the fogged-up bathroom mirror and rub my palm against its surface. My face sits in the clear circle, surrounded by the blur of condensation on all sides. It looks like I'm sinking into rough water. Like I'm barely holding my face above the surface before it sucks me under.

I slide the towel off my wet hair and hang it up next to Ray Bear's. Grandma probably doesn't even remember it's still in here. Or maybe she knows and can't bring herself to take it to the washing machine, just like me.

I don't know what's next. What I'm supposed to do. Unease creeps into my chest like itchy, twiney ropes are slowly tightening around my ribs. The only other thing I have to go off of is Ray Bear's internet searches, but there's no way to know for sure if those mean anything. She could've just been curious. Or maybe it was for a health assignment. Maybe she was worried about Eli and his dad—that sounds most like her. She probably knew he was getting worse.

But . . . if she was getting into drugs, it wouldn't have been the only thing she kept from me—just the worst thing.

I pull against my bathroom drawer, but it doesn't budge. I rattle it and tug again. Anger meshes with the panic and bubbles into my chest, snapping the twine.

I yank the drawer, shaking the contents inside, panting. I grip the pull with two hands, arms quaking, and rip it out. Makeup brushes and tubes fly across the bathroom as I let the pull slip from my fingers and send the whole drawer crashing into the wall.

The corner sinks into the drywall and topples to the floor. White specks of drywall powder fall out of the fresh dent as I suck in tight gasps of air, fists shaking.

Grandma pounds on the door. "What's going on in there?"

I brush my hair off my damp forehead, gaze flicking across the contents scattered all over the floor. "Nothing."

"Loren." She rattles the locked knob.

I'm silent until my chest deflates, anger seeping out like syrup. I turn the lock and let her swing the door open. She takes in the room and the gash in the wall. "You okay?"

I drop to the floor, avoiding her frown, and gather everything back into the loose drawer. "Fine."

"I'm worried about you. This is getting out of hand. You're acting like . . ."

She doesn't need to say it. I shove the wobbling drawer back into its place and brush past her. I don't want to hear Grandma compare me to *her*. To the moments of rage Mom felt after I came along.

That's what started it all, isn't it? Mom got postpartum depression and postpartum rage. She should've gotten help. Instead, she tried to help herself in the worst way and turned to drugs. She was in and out of it for years. Torn between that life and ours. It won out in the end.

I've heard enough about Mom's mental health problems to know all this trauma is doing something similar to me. Sometimes my fuse is so short I'm exploding before I even know why. It's pulling me apart. I think the only way to make it stop is finding out who killed Ray Bear. I'm terrified we'll never find him—and then I'll be stuck in this awful grief for good.

Grandma follows me down the hall, waiting for me to deny it.

I can't.

"It's getting worse. Let the Two Feather Project set up counseling for you."

"I just need more time." I don't know if that's true, but I need it to be. And I have nothing else to say about it.

Luckily, the doorbell rings.

I head straight for the front door and peer through the peephole. Somebody's standing too close to the door to see clearly, except for a huge hawk on the front of their shirt.

I open the door to find Mara Racette shifting on her feet, hands stuffed into her kangaroo pocket. Worry churns up my chest and sends drips of paranoia creeping down my arms like rainwater. I want to close the door. To tell her to stay away from me, for her own safety.

But the red hawk on her black sweatshirt stares at me. It's just her old Bozeman High School mascot, but it reminds me of Grandpa. Years ago, when he was looking to buy some horses, a hawk landed on the electric pole in front of the owner's house. It perched there for the whole showing.

He smiled up at the hawk and said that was good medicine. A sign of something good to come. He bought the horses, and he and Grandma made a lot of good money breeding and selling after that.

"Hey," Mara says. I pull my eyes from the hawk to her shifting eyes. "Can you talk?"

"Sure." I lead Mara to the living room couches, shoving down the

305

anxiety biting at my neck. I tell myself the hawk is good medicine, but her words from my dream still whisper through my mind. *Make it stop.*

Grandma glances over her shoulder at us before disappearing into the kitchen, shuffling the contents of our fridge and turning on the stove.

I sit across from Mara and tuck my hands under my thighs. "What's up?"

She knots her fingers together. "Don't you think Staccona should've figured it out by now?"

"He probably never will."

"It feels like they're just running around in circles, looking into the wrong people," she says. "I tell you, I don't feel right about Jason."

"Why?"

"He gave off a creepy vibe at the party, watching girls. He was the only one in the photo group who didn't seem to leave with anyone else. I saw you, Brody, and Eli walk off together. Your grandma was talking to the visitors. Where did Jason go? Did he and Samantha leave together?"

I wish I'd talked to Sam right then. Heard what she had to say. She asked, but I wasn't ready. I wish I'd told her what giving her the shawl really meant to me instead of waiting to see it in the intertribal dance first. I wish I didn't let her pull away from me when my grief about Ray Bear was ripping me to shreds. Maybe she would've told me if something was wrong with her too. Maybe she'd still be here.

Maybe I'd be the one killed. Sam could've lived on, and I could be with Ray Bear.

I hear Grandma cracking eggs in the kitchen. But if I were dead too, Grandma would be all alone, and who knows how long she'd survive that.

I swallow the thoughts away. "Jason's boss has a record of him starting work on a car not too long after eight o'clock on the morning Ray Bear was taken. It's possible, but it would've been really tight."

"That's what Staccona said?"

I nod.

She chews her lip, staring at me a beat too long. "You know much about Eli's dad? You really think he's been totally MIA?"

Meth. I can see the search box filled with the word. I used to see Eli's dad around more. Sometimes stumbling outside a bar. Sometimes picking up Eli from our house when things were mostly okay. Then I barely saw him anymore. Addiction took over. Ray Bear would've seen him while she was involved with Eli behind my back.

I've been staring at the space between us for too long, wondering if I should tell Mara what I saw on Ray Bear's phone. And in Sam's laptop messages. Wondering if there was any way in hell Ray Bear went down that path. I'm like Mom in one way. Maybe Ray Bear was like her in another.

That would've broken Grandma's heart. And mine.

Mara stands and walks to the buffalo robe hanging on the wall. "You think his dad could've done something? Maybe he didn't happen to leave around the same time Rayanne disappeared; maybe that's *the reason* he left. We both looked in Eli's truck at the party. There was no jacket in there. Maybe his dad's still around. Maybe he put it in there."

It's one of the maybes stitched into my thoughts. But it also feels unlikely. "It would be pretty hard to believe not a single person saw him secretly hanging around town." The rez is huge. He could hide out somewhere remote if he wanted. But if he were holed up somewhere, why would he go back and frame his own kid?

Mara blows the hair falling over her eyes. "We're missing something."

I sink into the couch, digging my nails into my arms. Maybe Eli's meth-head dad got those girls into drugs. Maybe Eli's still keeping secrets. Maybe the creepy visitor lied to everyone about his alibi. Maybe Youngbull has been hiding a violent side all this time.

The maybes are slowly killing me.

"What do you remember about that morning in April?" she asks.

"I already told the police everything about the last time I saw Ray Bear."

"I mean at school. What do you remember about Brody?"

I run my fingers up and down my arms. I hardly remember anything about Brody, which is the odd thing. Usually, he's the one cracking jokes and wasting our time with useless conversations.

I didn't think anything of it then. "He was quiet that day."

She runs her hand down the thick buffalo wool. "Brody quiet, huh?"

He's only halfway in my memories of that morning. Sam was distracted. She was talking about track and how she couldn't wait to get an athletic scholarship after senior year and leave Browning. I think her exact words were *get the hell outta here*. She was worried her grades would ruin her chances, though—she'd been falling behind. And there was no way she'd be able to afford leaving without a full ride. I was trying not to be hurt that she couldn't wait to leave when I knew I'd never want to. She wasn't talking to Brody. He actually buckled down and worked on the project. Sam was the unfocused one.

"Yeah. But that doesn't mean anything. It was early. He's not a morning person." Plus I forced him there. I left Ray Bear alone to ride the bus. It's silent for a few moments until Grandma starts whisking what must be scrambled eggs in the kitchen.

"I figured it doesn't mean anything, but look at this." Mara pulls her phone out and shuffles over to sit next to me. "I was looking through all this year's Indian Days posts." She scrolls through rainbow-colored squares on SnapShare. "I almost missed this."

She pulls up a picture of two freshmen girls in their regalia standing in front of white tents. Far off in the background, there are the two white horses from the giveaway.

Only Eli's arm is visible in the frame, Cherie somewhere at his side. My hand is on Storm Runner's neck. Next to me, Brody walks with his head turned almost completely backward. Like an owl.

I take the phone from Mara and pinch with two fingers to zoom as much as the post allows. In between the horse's head and the first row of horse trailers is Sam. The rest of her surroundings aren't visible. She appears to be staring down at her phone, and Brody appears to be staring right at her.

Every single one of us said we didn't see where Sam went after the photos, but Brody might have.

Maybe he's hiding something.

Chapter 38

BRODY CLARK
Saturday, July 20, 4:00 p.m.

Sweat drips down my back in the dry heat, and warmth radiates from Fox underneath me. From this side of the ranch, we're just high enough to see both the distant outline of the Sweet Grass Hills far off in the east and the jagged peaks of Glacier's Rockies to the west. I'm just a speck in the dry, windblown plains between them.

As miserable as it is baking in the sun out here, it was better than sitting inside, letting my guilt eat me alive.

I'd rather let the mosquitoes do that.

I grip the reins with one hand and swing a bucket of chokecherries in the other. Most of them weren't quite ripe yet, but I got a few. Enough to make a little syrup. My fingers are stained reddish maroon.

Like blood.

I ease into Fox's swaying walk, letting him take me along the wood of willows that lead the rest of the way home. Letting my regrets creep into my head.

I shouldn't have told First Kill what I did to the guest book, even if he was gonna hate me. Now he knows how desperate I felt.

It makes me look guilty, like I had something I was trying to hide. I never touched Samantha in any type of way—she made sure of that. And I sure as hell never hurt Rayanne.

But somebody's word can only go so far.

It's terrifying knowing that people can dig their fingers into our lives and twist things around. I just wanted things to go back to how they were before Rayanne went missing. It wasn't perfect. Not by a long shot. But I was happy. We all had a good thing going here.

I wanted to get the cops off all our backs and take one step toward normal.

I made a mess of things.

Seems like I always do that.

I don't want to think of my regrets when it comes to Loren either, but they're hard to forget. They burrow into my skin like a tick, sucking me dry.

That night when Loren was in my room, I may have been drunk, but I know I said more than I should've about the guilt I carry.

The thing is, I can't stop feeling like it's my fault. That it's on *me* Rayanne was even alone that morning. We were working on the project because of me. I can't ignore the fact that my choices could be the thing that started this whole situation and every jacked-up change that's come with it.

Fox takes me over a small crest and sidles up to the fence of the pasture, where Marshmallow and Lightning graze with Double Stride. The house looms in the distance, a splotch of dark brown in a sea of muted, dead green. I can already feel the claustrophobia pressing on me just looking at it.

It started after that night Loren tore into my bedroom. She has a way of making me act weak when I should be strong. Steady. I don't know why I let her have that power over me. I'd say it was because I was drunk, but it's always been that way with her.

Fox takes me all the way back to the horse barn, where Jason is waiting for me, a smile plastered to his shining face.

I hop off and shove the bucket of chokecherries into his chest. "What?"

"My lawyer, Dalton Gaudreau, is on his way here."

My stomach clenches. "Why are you happy about that?"

Now that First Kill's off the hook, I knew it was only a matter of time before Youngbull would turn his horns back on Jason. Isn't there anyone else he and Staccona can bother?

He slips Fox's halter off and shuts him into his stall. "He's coming because I finally found something to fully clear myself."

"What?"

"Remember how I said I was looking into things?" He winks. "Now they'll have to leave me alone."

"What is it?"

"Come in to see for yourself how people like me get things done." His tone is a clear dig at me for not being able to find anything useful myself, but he has to know I really tried.

I follow him out of the barn and across the parched yard. Dalton Gaudreau crunches into the driveway just as I'm washing my sullied hands at the kitchen sink. The screen door screeches, and Jason motions for Dalton to take a seat at the table, still sporting that stupid grin.

I slowly towel off my hands and sit across from Jason and Dalton. "So what've you got?" the lawyer asks, hands clasped on the table.

"I knew I got to work on time that day Rayanne went missing," Jason says. "I knew it. I'm never late."

Dalton nods.

"I just remembered I had to make a call to our parts dealer sometime around early April." He pauses, throws me a pleased glance, and continues. "Today, I called the guy and asked him to check through his caller ID history. I called him the morning Rayanne went missing at eight o'clock on the dot."

Dalton brings his hand to his chin, certainly running the numbers in his head.

Jason leans back and cracks his knuckles. "Staccona said Rayanne's bus stop was scheduled at 7:40. She couldn't have been out there waiting much earlier than that. It would've been physically impossible for me to pick her up and drive all the way to the location they found her and back to get to work by eight a.m."

The lawyer hums.

"I mean, it was already nearly impossible when they assumed I was fifteen minutes late that day. I'd have to have been gunning it to even get close to their timetable. Now they'll have to admit it's impossible." He thumps his fist against his palm with a huge smile. "I'm innocent."

"I'm with you," Dalton says. "Give me the guy's number, and I'll get a record of the call that will hold up in court." He taps his fingertips on the table, a slow smile spreading across his face. "This is huge, Jason. Nice work. Now, Agent Staccona may still try to prove something else. Like you could've kept her body in your truck during your whole work shift or stashed it somewhere close until you could get to it later, and so forth."

Jason glances between us, downright pleased with himself. "I went to the Oki bar right after work that day and stayed for a good while. Then picked up some stuff at the grocery store before heading to dinner. It's all on my bank transactions."

Dalton hoots. "Ays, that won't hurt either."

Jason smacks his palm on the table and points at me. "Finally free from Staccona's grip."

I smile, despite the nerves still sparking in my stomach. "Get outta here, ol' Kurt Stick-in-his-butt."

Jason laughs. I haven't heard that in too many days. "Finally they'll have to believe me."

Dalton pats his shoulder, relief easing out of both of them. "They sure will."

I retreat back to my room while Jason and Dalton work out the logistics of submitting the evidence to the feds. Maybe they really will back off now. Maybe things will finally start going back to normal for us.

I should've trusted he'd figure his way through this, like he told me he would, instead of driving myself up the wall.

My phone buzzes violently on my desk. A text from Loren lights up the screen.

Loren: Can we talk?

Guilt bites at my throat like a coyote clamping down on my windpipe. Things will never go back to normal for Loren. Or Samantha's family. It's selfish of me to be happy we won't be bothered anymore.

My thumb hovers over the message, ready to delete it, but I freeze up. She has that way with me.

She probably shouldn't be around Jason because of the investigation, especially when his lawyer's here.

Me: Where?

Loren: Not my place.

Me: Not mine either.

Her typing dots appear and disappear.

Me: How about our storage barn at the very back of the property?

It's a mile or so from the house. Only accessible by dirt road.

Private. We had a party there once, so she knows where I mean, even if it was years ago.

Loren: See you there.

I pass Jason and the lawyer on my way out, still deep in conversation. "There's one more thing," Jason says. "I found it strange that MJ Racette hired that young hotshot lawyer when he really wasn't a person of interest. So I did some digging."

I don't stick around to hear what he found.

I climb into my truck and take the long way around our property. Once I open the gate and turn onto the back road, I bounce and bob over the rough dirt. Long grass sways in the middle between the lines of dirt the tires drive over. Low tree branches scrape my roof as I move through wooded patches. Gophers pop in and out of holes in the fields.

I pause as a group of cattle comes into view around the final bend. There aren't as many as we used to have, but I still have to watch where I walk on this side of the property if I don't want a fresh cow pie up my ankles.

I lay on the horn until they amble off the dirt into a grove of trees, and then I rumble the rest of the way to the small barn made of graying wood. It's not too hot in the shade of the building, but it smells like manure. I sit on the tailgate of my truck, swinging my feet until an engine sounds in the distance.

Loren's sedan rocks harder than a truck over the bumpy surface. Her face is scrunched in concentration when she turns around the bend and descends the slight hill. Her eyes peel open wider as she's picking up speed, and the tires skid in the dry dirt.

The cows erupt in moos.

So much dust billows behind her car as she barrels down the hill that I barely notice a cottontail rabbit shoot across the road. It disappears under her tire as she skids to a halt a few yards past me.

The dust floats over, sending me into a coughing fit. Loren slams the car door shut, "Sorry," she says, waving the dust out of her face.

The cattle finally fall back into mostly silence, and that's when I hear it. Loren freezes, staring at me as she tries to figure out the sound.

It's a grating, repetitive squeal. Quiet but disturbing. It's one I should know well. Coyote hunters use a call with the mournful cry of a rabbit to lure in their quarry, but right now, it sends crackles up my spine.

Loren scans the field. "What is that?"

I hop off the back of the truck and walk a few feet up the road, Loren on my tail. "You ran over a rabbit."

"What—" Her mouth gapes when she sees it.

Partially hidden in the field grass is the jacked-up rabbit. Close to meeting his maker.

Loren groans. She squats and then stands back up with a fist over her mouth.

His eyes are half-open, and his squeal keeps the crackles shooting down my limbs. I force myself to walk away.

"Can't we help him?" Loren asks my back.

I fumble the combination into the lock on the barn's door and shove it open.

"Brody?" Loren calls, still staring at the suffering animal. She can't take her eyes off it, but who does that help?

I scan the barn walls, find what I need, and stride out into the sunshine. The squeal meshes with the scream that's burned into my memories.

Loren's eyes are almost as panicked as they were while she screamed that night in front of Samantha's dead body. "What are you—"

I swing my arms up and heave the axe down, shutting the rabbit up for good.

Loren stares at me in shock. "What the—"

I retreat back into the barn and toss the axe into an empty corner of the room. The metal clanks against the concrete until it settles, the half-sullied blade glinting in the window's light. I lean onto a shelf of tools, chest heaving.

The room is dead quiet, like it's filled with warm water, tugging me where I don't want to go.

"Brody!"

I readjust my hat and compose myself before walking out the door. I force my shoulders to relax as I face her.

She's looking at me like I'm a monster. "What'd you—why?"

"Why? What else were we gonna do, Loren?" It's clear how this paints me to her. Heartless. Cold-blooded. Cruel. But still, I don't regret ending his agony.

She stares at me, gaze flicking between my eyes.

I can't handle how she's looking at me. Like I'm . . . Like I *enjoyed* that. I throw my hands out to hide a shudder. "Were you just gonna keep standing there watching him scream?"

Her mouth opens and closes. "We could've—"

"What? Taken him to the vet? He'd have died before we got there." My gut twists in its own agony, begging for her to understand. "He'd have suffered the whole time."

She paces, cutting a line in the field grass.

"I put him out of his misery. That's the most humane thing we could've done for him."

"But you just . . . You did it so fast . . ."

I can't help but laugh in disbelief. "Did you want to call Father Nielson to give him his last rites? C'mon."

She stammers. "I— No."

I cross my arms, steadying myself. "I had to end his torture as soon as I could. Please tell me you understand that."

She rubs her forehead and retreats from the scene. "I just don't know how you could stomach doing that."

I follow her to my truck and sit next to her on the back. "Did you never go hunting with your grandpa?"

She shakes her head.

"That's what you do. You dispatch the animal. You make it as quick and painless as you can. I have the stomach for that. What I *don't* have the stomach for is sitting there watching them die in slow motion. *That's* sick."

She leans onto her knees. "Yeah. You're right. I just can't believe you did it right in front of me."

"Sorry I forgot to ask you to *please step away for a moment*."

"You should've. I didn't know you were gonna kill him."

My arms tense. I need her to know there's a huge difference. "*I* helped him. *You're* the one who ran him over."

She rolls her eyes, but I can tell she finally understands I did the right thing, or at least the best thing in a crappy situation.

"I mean, talk about a hit 'n' run, enit."

Her mouth drops open, but the corners perk into a smile. "Shut your stupid face. You're terrible, you know?"

I bump her shoulder with mine. It almost feels normal. Almost. But her smile drops too fast.

"So then what did you want to talk about?"

She stares at the cattle in the distance until one unloads. "I have a question." She pulls her phone out and unlocks it. "You said you didn't see Sam after the photos, but this makes it look like you're lying."

I take the phone and find all of us, including the two gifted horses, in the background of a powwow photo. When I zoom in, it does look like I'm watching Samantha, and it hits me that if this picture were taken a few beats later, maybe it could've actually caught something. I play back the moments from that day the best I can remember them.

"I wasn't looking at her. I was looking at Youngbull outside the break in the bleachers. He was watching you walk by and I was wondering if he felt guilty for never finding your sister."

"He was?" She's slow to grab her phone when I hand it back.

"Yeah. I bet *he's* the one who's lying. He has all kinds of claims about what he saw that day; you'd think he saw where Samantha went too."

She stares at the rippling of the breeze in the wild, dull grass and slips her phone back in her pocket.

"Samantha was eyeing him after the giveaway, like maybe they were snags."

She considers it for a beat. "Ehh, Sam was wild but not *that* wild."

"Just sayin'." I wouldn't put it past either of them. Not for a second.

The silence oozes between us as she picks at a loose thread in her frayed jean shorts. There's something else on her mind. The real reason she asked me here.

"Spit it out."

The thread tears off the denim and she lets it flutter to the dirt. "Something's been bothering me."

Isn't that the understatement of the year . . . "Yeah? Just one thing?"

She fights another smile. "I'm serious."

"What is it?"

She scratches at some dirt caked on the edge of my truck. "That night at the party . . ."

I knew this was coming.

"I was telling you how guilty I felt about leaving Ray Bear that morning."

I nod. "After you slapped me, yeah? And not in that good way."

She ignores that. "You said you felt more guilt than you knew what to do with. I thought you were just talking about how we had to do the project in the morning because of you. You were pretty wasted, so I didn't think much of it. But then . . ."

"I cried."

"You cried. And now I can't stop wondering if there was more to that . . ."

Loren's gold-flecked brown eyes make it hard to think. The guilt worming into my head makes it almost impossible.

I force out a laugh. "You know, you cried first. Would you believe me if I said I was just a total empath?"

"Everyone who knows you would never believe that."

"Would you believe me if I said I'm just a weepy drunk? My dad used to get on crying jags when he drank too much. Maybe it's in my genes—"

"I've seen you drunk plenty of times." Is it just me, or is her voice getting sharper the longer she sits next to me?

A cow moos, filling the tense air between us. I hop off the truck and pace, ready to give some voice to the guilt following me everywhere I go. She might think differently of me after this. She'll definitely resent me for being a liar.

Her eyes track me back and forth until I stop dead in front of her.

"It's my fault Rayanne was taken."

Chapter 39

MARA RACETTE
Saturday, July 20, 5:00 p.m.

I pause the workout video and check my texts for the thousandth time. I shouldn't be nervous . . . Loren has been alone with Brody loads of times. They're close friends. She sounded pretty certain that what he said to her the night of the party probably didn't mean anything, that he just felt the same guilt she did about leaving Rayanne to take the bus because of their project. But when you pair that with the picture of him possibly looking at Samantha . . . it might.

She shouldn't have met up with him alone. Just in case. But I've learned there's no stopping her when she thinks there's any chance of finding a hint about her sister's murder.

I prop the phone on my dresser, push play, and copy the instructor, looping a resistance band above my knees. Now that my last moving box is empty and broken down, there's even more space in here. My legs burn as I count out the squat holds, trying to distract myself from wondering why it's taking Loren so long. She said she wanted to get it over with while her grandma was visiting a cousin, so she should've been done by now. Hopefully she'll be wrapping it up any second.

My phone pings and a message banner covers the instructor's face, but it's just Eli. I smile. *Just* Eli.

Did you watch the relay video yet?

I did. About twenty times. He's got some serious athleticism. I'm about to grab the phone and text back when a violent pounding on the front door booms through the whole house. My band falls to my ankles.

There's only a couple seconds of silence before the pounding starts again. It's urgent and each one makes me flinch. I kick the band off as I peer out the blinds and see a police cruiser the same time I hear the front door open.

No.

I tear out of my room and jog into the living room.

"You can come to the station voluntarily, or we can cuff you and put you in the back of our rig," Youngbull says. "And we have a warrant to search your vehicle."

Dad's face is drained of most of his color. "I'm not talking without my lawyer present."

"That's your right," Agent Staccona says. "You better call him now."

"What's this about?" Mom asks, voice strained. "You already asked him your questions."

Staccona trains his gaze on Dad, who's fumbling to unlock his phone. "We looked into your digital work calendar. On April 9, you were out in the field. You never went to the office."

Dad doesn't say a word as he brings his phone to his ear, waiting for his lawyer to answer his call.

"He's in the field all the time," Mom says. "He works for Blackfeet Fish and Wildlife!"

Dad raises his palm, shutting her up. He tells his lawyer he's being taken in for questioning.

Mom paces between us. "That doesn't mean anything."

Staccona focuses his gaze on Mom now. He cocks his head just slightly and pulls out his phone. "We've already established MJ has a history of threatening his daughter's friends when they treat her poorly." He turns his gaze on me.

I can feel Mom's eyes on me, waiting for me to say nobody here treated me poorly. I can't.

"We also got a tip." Staccona taps his phone a few times and turns it to face my mom. "Nobody mentioned MJ *did* leave the bleachers after the giveaway."

I lean over Mom to see a screenshot of a SnapShare post. Somehow I missed it in my own scrolling.

It's a photo of the back of the bleachers basked in golden light. The sun is getting lower over the powwow grounds, and dancers are grouped, preparing themselves for their competition dances. Dad's face is barely visible at the edge of the arbor opening. His long hair is swinging as he peers around a group of dancers, looking somewhere past the person snapping the picture—toward the area we disappeared through to take the photos. His arm is outstretched and his leg's in stride, either because he's stretching to see us as he tries to stay in place or because he's in a hurry to get somewhere.

Youngbull is in the photo too, his back turned to Dad as it was taken.

It almost looks like he's sneaking around Youngbull.

But the picture doesn't mean anything. He's still basically in the arbor anyway.

Dad runs a hand through his hair, but it falls back over his face as he leans in to see the picture. "That's nothing. I—" He stops short, knowing he's supposed to wait for the lawyer.

"Come on," Staccona says. His voice is sticky with arrogance. "Don't make this difficult."

Dad hugs Mom. "You know how often I had to go out for the chronic wasting disease research," he says quietly. He glances at me over her shoulder. "And I just wanted to catch a quick glimpse of you with your friends after the giveaway . . . I didn't know you had any." His lips flatten into a tight smile.

And then he's gone.

He disappears out the door and into the police car.

Chapter 40

LOREN ARNOUX

Saturday, July 20, 5:00 p.m.

Brody's face pales, and his eyes shift between mine. It takes everything in me not to dig my fingers into his throat. "What do you mean it's your fault she was taken?"

He slides his tongue along his lip. "I lied to you, Loren."

The muscles in my hand seize as I squeeze my nails into my palm instead of his face.

"The night before Rayanne was . . . taken, I wasn't busy."

What does that have to do with anything?

"You and me and Samantha were supposed to finish the project that night. . . ."

It clicks. "You said you couldn't because your cattle got loose and Jason needed help rounding them back onto your property."

He glances at the cows grazing nearby. "I *was* with Jason, but it wasn't anything important."

"What were you doing?"

"It's stupid." He runs his hands down his pant legs. "He was playing video games with me, and he never does that anymore. It was like things were back to normal for a minute. I didn't want to go do homework and ruin that."

I can't sit anymore. I slide off the truck and pace through the dirt.

"So because you wanted to play *video games* . . ."

". . . we had to go in early the next morning to finish the project. And you had to leave Rayanne alone." At least he has the decency to look humiliated. Ashamed.

Anger brings sweat to my forehead. My arms ache to swing, to push him, to twist my fingers into his shirt and shake him.

"See, it *is* my fault," he whispers. "None of this would've happened if I didn't change our plans on purpose. And for what?" He shakes his head, cheeks pulled back. "I didn't hurt her, but I played a part."

I sink into a squat, rubbing my eyes. Sam and I could've finished the project without him that night . . . but I made us wait for Brody. I was immature and didn't want him getting off easy again. This whole time I've blamed myself for leaving Ray Bear alone that morning, but now . . . violent shades of red blossom and clash under my eyelids. I hate him right now. I hate him so much it's pulling my chest apart. I look up at him, seething. Tears spill over his cheeks.

Inappropriate, witty Brody, crying. Again.

He hates himself too. Probably even more than I do.

I'm halfway home, and Mara *still* won't answer her phone. She was so adamant I call her as soon as I got the story from Brody, and now she can't even pick up? Maybe that's for the best.

The nightmare still haunts me, and that's not any kind of medicine I want to mess with. Getting mixed up with Mara Racette is foolish. After a warning like that, I'd be making my own medicine—of the worst kind.

I pass the bus stop and hold my breath as I turn onto our street.

If Brody's telling the truth, the pictures don't mean anything. But he's spit lies at me before.

I don't know who to believe. Who to trust.

When I reach our driveway, Mara is parked on the street, sitting on her hood. The lowering sun casts shadows across her body, making her look harsh and scared.

This can't be good.

After I park in the driveway and climb out, I get a good look at her. "What happened?"

Her eyes are swollen from crying and she's restless. "I swear on my life, Loren, my dad is innocent."

I step backward and repeat myself. "What happened?"

"Staccona took him in for questioning again. You didn't know?"

"I've been with Brody the last hour."

"*Somebody* found a picture of him watching the giveaway group from the entrance to the arbor." She folds her arms. "I figured that was you."

"It wasn't. But didn't he say he never left?"

"He left his seat. But he didn't leave the actual arbor. He just stopped at the back of the bleachers." She doesn't leave her car, and I don't walk any closer.

"That's what he said?"

She nods. "What did Brody say?"

I give her the quick summary of Brody's lie that led to Ray Bear waiting alone on an empty road.

"I swear . . ." Mara says again. "My dad would never hurt anyone. He's a good person."

A horse whinnies into the still air. I scan the distant houses along my curving street. How well do you really know anyone? Every killer is somebody's kid. Somebody's friend. Sometimes you might see it coming, but most of the time, you probably don't.

Mara hugs herself so tight she's nearly collapsing in on herself. "I was thinking about it . . . we keep finding pictures that tell snapshots of the story at the powwow. Tiny moments leading up to Samantha's murder are captured. Maybe they don't mean anything, but at least they're there. Rayanne doesn't have any moments we can search through. Nobody captured any photos of *that* day."

She makes a good point. It sends those familiar feelings of hopelessness crawling through my veins. "It sure would've helped."

Mara rests her hands on the hood of her car, watching me. I'd think she was looking at me with pity if it weren't for the fresh tears welling in her eyes. I can't find it in me to feel sorry for her though.

"Wait." She pulls her phone out of her pocket. "There *is* one."

I walk the rest of the way to her car and lean over her phone. She's opening *my* SnapShare page. My last post is from that morning. Sam, another friend, and I are huddled together outside the school in front of the parking lot, jacket hoods up.

We took that picture between classes. I think we were a little late for second period because of it. Even though it was chilly, we were enjoying the sun, thinking we were getting a taste of an early spring. We didn't know it was going to dump snow the next day, and of course, we didn't know something was happening to Ray Bear.

Mara and I look at each other at the same time, eyes wide.

Something in the picture's background makes my stomach drop like a sinking rock.

Chapter 41

ELI FIRST KILL

Saturday, July 20, 8:00 p.m.

I carefully empty a jug of oil into my truck's engine, thinking about Cherie while I wait for it to settle. Her foster family wants me to wait a week before visiting. They think it'll help her settle in better. It's too long. I bet the real reason is they don't trust me yet. I guess it doesn't look too good when a girl gets sucked into the foster care system because her brother is arrested for murder.

You'd think being released would've helped things.

I pull the dipstick out to check the oil level but freeze when headlights coming up the driveway glint on the shop's metal framing.

I slide the dipstick back in and snatch a rag from my truck's open hood. I don't know who could be out here. Mara Racette's been radio silent for hours. Little Bro's been acting weird ever since he admitted to forging that signature.

My mouth dries. The cops might not be done with me.

The engine rumbles closer. There's no way it could be Dad. But if it was, would Cherie get to come back? Or would he be the next target of the investigation?

I force myself to the open garage door, greasy fingers digging into the rag.

The headlights shut off as Mara Racette slams her car door and jogs toward me. There's a joke on the tip of my tongue until the overhead light illuminates her splotchy face. She storms past me.

"Holy. What's going on?"

She paces alongside my truck as I finish wiping my hands. "They've got my dad at the police station again."

"Oh." I swallow when no more words come. I feel bad I'm not more surprised.

"And they're searching his car right now."

I lean against the worktable in the back of the shop and wave her over to the stool.

She almost sits, then resumes her pacing. "They don't even have anything. *We* do."

"Who's we? What are you talking about?" I toss the rag into a box of tools.

Finally, she stops pacing and perches on the edge of the stool next to me. "Look what me and Loren found." She opens SnapShare and shoves the phone into my hands.

It's a picture of Loren, Samantha, and Kat. I don't notice anything strange. They're outside school, probably in between classes, with other kids milling around in the background.

"Look at the date."

April 9. "The day Rayanne—"

"Zoom into the background."

I pinch the image to see who's in the background and immediately recognize a sweatshirt. It's gray and black with a bright yellow Guns N' Roses cross down the entire front. Even though the person is looking down and his flat-billed hat is covering most of his face, I know who it is. Anyone would.

Little Bro.

He was always wearing that sweatshirt. In the picture, he's walking toward the school from the parking lot, head down, lanyard of keys hanging from his hand. But that's all it shows.

I hand the phone back.

Her eyebrows shoot up. "So?"

I run my hand through my hair. "It doesn't tell us anything."

"He left during the school day! He's coming back from his car."

"Maybe he forgot something in there and just got it out. Maybe he couldn't remember if he locked it that morning. He was there early for the project—maybe he went to have a quick bite in the car between classes."

She's staring at me like I've grown another nose.

"Or he left." She taps something into her phone and scrolls for a moment, then hands it to me again. "And look at this."

It's a picture from the powwow. In the background, I see the horses Geraldine gave us and Little Bro looking backward. At Samantha.

"Doesn't that look strange?"

I grip the phone. "They're just pictures. You can make them tell any story you want."

"Seriously? You don't think they mean anything?"

"Honestly? No. I think you're reaching. Big time."

She sighs through her teeth. "They have to mean something."

"I'm sorry about your dad, but—"

She shoves off the stool. "But what?"

"Maybe he found out we were all jerks to you. You said it yourself: he's overprotective."

"He didn't know. I never told him anything about school. The most he's ever said was today when he said he thought I didn't have any friends."

I lower my chin, letting her hear her own words. "Rayanne and Samantha were the most outgoing girls at school. They should've been your friends. Maybe he was taking something out on them." She has to see how it looks.

"Stop saying stupid crap. He's innocent."

"Then you've got nothing to worry about. If he's innocent, they'll let him go. Just like me."

She snatches her phone back. "They need to talk to Brody."

I rest my hand on the edge of the table, trying to keep my temper in check. "I already told you, Little Bro wouldn't hurt anyone."

"Would you bet my life on it? Loren's life?" She hugs herself. "Cherie's life?"

I grip the worn wood. "I'd bet *mine* on it. Nobody else's."

She paces again.

It sets me on edge. "You're acting all desperate."

She laughs without smiling. "Aren't we all? Two girls have been murdered, and the cops don't have a thing to show for it. Shouldn't we all be bending over backward to find this sicko?"

"Take your feelings out of it for a minute." I ease onto the table and lean my elbows on my knees. "Are you positive your dad couldn't have done it?"

She rolls her eyes. "Same question, for Brody."

I think about it. For her sake, I *really* think about it. "I'm positive he didn't kill Samantha. I was with him until I had to take Cherie to the bathroom for *one* minute. And then he was already in the bleachers when we got there."

She stops pacing. "And?"

"I guess I can't say with one hundred percent certainty he didn't kill Rayanne. I usually never saw him at school until third period. But I'd say 99.9 percent sure. I mean—he was with Loren all morning. . . ."

"But if he left after first period . . . What if—"

"Stop." I rake a hand down my face. "One passing period between classes isn't enough time to do *anything*. Now can you say with one hundred percent certainty your dad didn't do it?"

She growls. "When you asked me to believe you, I did. Even when they threw you in the back of the police car, I did. Now I'm asking you to believe that my dad is innocent." A strange calm passes through her face. "Can you?"

I clasp my hands and stare at her. I don't know what to believe. All I know is that dads aren't perfect, no matter how much you wish they were. She purses her lips and nods as the seconds stretch on.

She strides to the door. I should stop her. I want to. But something else I know is that she's better off without me anyway.

Chapter 42

LOREN ARNOUX

Saturday, July 20, 9:30 p.m.

After Mara left, I sat on the porch until the golden light of the sinking sun turned into a cool blue. Goose bumps rose on my skin when the blue turned into a haunting gray. Now, as the night's complete darkness settles around the house, only pale moonlight winking against the low roofs of the far-off houses down my road, I still can't move.

The picture of Brody possibly leaving school probably means nothing. But if it doesn't . . .

I want to believe Mara about her dad, but it's impossible to know. Just like Eli's. Is he really gone?

Above all else, I want to believe I really knew my sister.

But did I?

I twist my fingers into my hair, pulling until pain radiates across my scalp. I'm going in circles. Round and round. If only the dead could speak. Then Ray Bear and Sam could tell us what we're missing. Who's fooling us.

An eerie hoot echoes through the quiet night. I stand and scan the electric poles, paranoia rooting into my shoulders—like someone's watching me. The owl hoots again, long and raspy.

I step off the porch, heart pounding. I spin at the next hoot and nearly lose my footing. Eyes glow above me like orange moons. The owl stares down from my own roof, sucking away my breath.

His call becomes more like a wail. I scramble back up the steps and fumble the door open. I slam it behind me and sink to the floor, fingers plugging my ears.

That ugly omen is following me. He's tracing my life, bringing death wherever I go. Or it's me . . . Is that beast drawn to me?

I'm the harbinger of death.

Thick fear falls over me so heavy I can't move. My breath comes in tight spurts, sending the room into blurry lines around me.

Either he's here to warn about my death or because he knows I'm about to bring death to somebody else.

My body's all locked up like twisted wires. Tears leak down my cheeks, and suddenly Grandma takes my face in her hands.

"Breathe." She turns my face to hers, only inches apart. "In . . ." She inhales with me, a force of calm. "Out."

My chest seizes as I force the air in and out in time with hers.

"Again." She releases my face and wraps her arms around me. "You're having a panic attack."

I don't know if seconds pass or minutes, but she squeezes me the entire time.

"What happened?" she finally asks when my limbs release the tension and I slump on the floor.

I speak the words that have been burrowing into my bones. "I think everyone is dying because of me."

"Shh. No."

"Then I think I'm next."

She stares at me for a long while, and then I tell her almost everything. I tell her how I should've talked to Sam right after the giveaway, how I've blamed myself for leaving Ray Bear alone that morning. I tell her about the SnapShare photos of Brody and Mara's dad. I tell her about the guest book Brody refuses to turn in and how the guy was cheating on his wife. I tell her about the night Brody cried and how he lied to get out of working on our project, hanging with his brother instead. I tell her how much it hurts to doubt my own friends. I tell her that I don't trust the tribal police or the FBI to solve any of this. How I still feel small from Youngbull towering over me in that shoebox-size bedroom.

I tell her because I can't go in circles anymore.

Anger sharpens her gaze on me. I think she'll tell me I need mental help. That I've been foolish, careless, that I've made a mess of things. But all she says is, "Show me."

"Jeremy Youngbull is a useless crook," Grandma says. "I've never respected him much. You know, he used to give some leeway to his buddies. Let 'em get off easy with things."

I hug my legs, pressing closer to Grandma's side on the couch. "Like who?"

"His cousin was running with the wrong crowd a few years ago and got caught up in a drug bust, but he squeaked out without any charges on him. And I know he got Jason out of a DUI once."

"How can he do that?"

"That's just how it is." She shakes her head. "I'll be honest; I suspected him for a bit."

"Really?" I can still feel him posturing over me, clenching Sam's laptop. I thought it was just me.

"It seemed like he was *trying* to delay looking for Ray Bear. Dragging his feet. Not taking it seriously." Her gaze gets lost somewhere on the carpet. "I don't know why. I don't think he could've done it, though. I think he's too inexperienced of a detective and has no idea what to do and won't admit it. Too cocky. He probably didn't want you looking into things and finding something he missed. I had hope for Kurt Staccona, but I'm losing it, especially after that mess with Eli First Kill. He doesn't care enough to raise hell for our girls." She digs her fist into the couch cushion, rings grinding against the fabric. "I was right all along. They're not solving this."

Somebody has to. I'd give up anything to make sure of it. *Anything*.

And for once, it seems like Grandma feels as desperate as I do.

There's one thing I didn't tell her earlier. "Grandma . . . do you think Ray Bear got into drugs?"

"Not a chance in hell."

I wish I still had her confidence in that answer. I hate myself for even wondering. The silence and the doubt hover between us like a cloud of dust.

She runs her fingers over the pillow seam until she breaks our silence. "Jeremy Youngbull called this morning before you woke up."

I sit up straighter. "What did he say?"

"They got some more results from the autopsy." She runs her hand back and forth across her collarbones, sadness meshing with the anger radiating from her. "They found some gray and black fibers inside what was left of Ray Bear's throat."

I force myself to swallow, my own throat tight like it's stuffed with ratty fabric. "Why didn't you tell me?"

Her eyes squeeze shut with misery. "Like it's going to help anything. Gray and black are the most common colors of clothes or blankets or . . ." The motion of her hand halts. "No. The only way Youngbull or Staccona is solving this thing is with some help."

"I've been *trying*."

"You know what, I have a picture too." She pulls her phone out of her deep scrubs pocket and brings up the picture of the giveaway group. It turns my chest inside out seeing Sam right next to me. Our shoulders are almost touching. Somehow, we're hiding the mile-wide gap in our friendship. Her knee is popped out to make room for the backpack between her moccasins, and the end of her dress is barely brushing mine.

If only I knew what was about to happen.

Grandma zooms in on Sam and me, staring, looking for clues that aren't there. The longer I look, the worse it feels. I was a bad friend too. I should've talked to her. Something was definitely wrong and I brushed her off.

Finally Grandma zooms out enough to see Brody standing behind us. He's got an open-mouthed smile and his face shines with sweat. She zooms in on Sam again.

My fingers curl against the temptation to chuck the phone at the wall. "What are you looking at?"

"That backpack," she whispers. The one sitting between Sam's feet. "Did you see it in the trailer . . . where you found her?"

I fight against remembering that scene. Seeing the life drained out of her face and the shawl spewing around her. The trailer was as empty as her eyes. "No. The police bagged her phone. There wasn't anything else there."

She nods slowly.

The realization hits with a chill. "Whoever killed her stole it." Nobody ever found Ray Bear's purple schoolbag either. "We should tell Staccona—"

"Listen," she says, voice suddenly low and serious. "We're on our own. Nobody is looking out for us but ourselves. Nobody will fight for Ray Bear like *we* will. If you want to know for sure your friend Brody had nothing to do with this, you need to go to his house and get into his phone."

I dig my nails into my palms, memorizing the colors in the beadwork on the backpack's looped handle and the shape of the red zipper. "And look for that stolen backpack."

So we make a plan.

Chapter 43
MARA RACETTE
Sunday, July 21, 10:45 a.m.

I pound on the door until my knuckles ache. I know Eli is inside. He knows I know. Where else would he be? Both trucks are parked in front of the house: the running one and the broken-down one.

He doesn't open the door. I don't know why I'm even here. He thinks my dad actually could've killed those girls. He called me desperate. And *of course* I am. It's like he forgot he lied to everyone for months because *he* was desperate to keep Cherie safe. I guess he's drawing his line in the sand.

He'll fight for his family and his *own*. He'll defend his deadbeat dad and douchebag friend Brody.

Not me and my family.

I'm on the other side of the line . . . with the ones he'll let drown when it comes down to it.

I guess it's better to learn now than later. I hit the door one last time, sending shock waves up my forearm. He was glad to have my trust—so glad he kissed me. But when it comes to giving it, he's out.

"Fine," I yell. "I guess I'm on my own."

I stomp off the step, crunching into the gravel. I don't need anybody anyway.

"What's that supposed to mean?" He sticks his head out of the cracked door.

I don't know if I'm glad or even more pissed off that he finally shows his face. "Loren went to confront Brody."

"Why?" He steps out from behind the door, barefoot and shirtless. "And what's it have to do with you?"

"Because the picture might mean something." I look at the time on my phone: 10:50 a.m. "And it might not. But she hasn't replied in ten minutes and I'm worried."

He leans onto the porch railing, shaking his head. "You guys are chasing smoke."

"At least we're chasing *something*."

He throws his arms out. "What do you want from me?"

"I thought you'd go with me to make sure nothing happened to Loren, but I should've known better."

His fingers flex against the railing.

"You'll defend Brody to the grave even though he didn't doubt for a second *you* killed them."

"That's not true."

I stalk through the gravel to my car and yank the door open. "Go ahead and bet my life on it." I flip him off and duck into the car, skidding as I turn around and speed back down his driveway.

In the rearview mirror, he leans his elbows on the railing and rests his forehead on his fists. I guess I wasn't wrong about Eli First Kill after all. He's selfish and stubborn and closed-minded. And he trusts the worst possible people in his life.

Screw him.

Chapter 44

LOREN ARNOUX
Sunday, July 21, 10:45 a.m.

I'll never have enough time. Brody finally left his room to check the horse barn out back—just like I wanted. I had set my purse on top of his phone on the desk earlier to make sure he'd leave it. It took him longer than it should've to get out.

He could come rushing back any minute.

I open his messages and pull down the top menu to search April 9. The only texts from that day are from a couple of friends in the afternoon and a few from his mom about her birthday dinner. Nothing incriminating.

I open his call history and scroll down to April. It doesn't take long because he hardly calls anyone. There are two calls with the same number on the morning of April 9. I take a picture with my own phone, nearly dropping it, and send it in a message to Grandma.

A creak sounds down the hall.

I exit the apps and put Brody's phone back on the cluttered desk. I fumble a dresser drawer open and see his Guns N' Roses sweatshirt on top of a pile of T-shirts. The acid-washed gray-and-black material makes the yellow cross look striking—just like in the picture of him in the school parking lot.

Gray and black.

I pull it out and set it on top of the dresser to take a picture of it, hands trembling. Another creak sends panic itching across my skin, but I stride to Brody's closet and carefully slide the door open, searching for Sam's black backpack with the beadwork carry loop.

There are hunting rifles standing in the back corner behind hampers of dirty clothes. Boxes marked *Dad's Stuff* sit on the very top shelf, along with messy piles of blankets and junk.

And something purple.

It dangles out from between cardboard and fabric. I yank it, sending an avalanche of crap cascading to the floor. The bedroom door behind me bursts open as Ray Bear's purple schoolbag sways from my fist.

Chapter 45

MARA RACETTE

Sunday, July 21, 11:11 a.m.

I should've driven to Brody's as soon as Loren told me what she was doing. If there's any chance he could really be a killer . . . she never should've gone alone to snoop through his stuff. She should've taken me with her. I wasted precious time trying to recruit Eli. I should've already been there.

I hope that mistake doesn't haunt me.

I check my phone again just as I park at the end of Brody's long driveway. Still nothing from Loren, but her car is parked next to Brody's. My stomach flops like a fish out of water.

This can't be good.

I slip out of the car and jog through the grass instead of the rocky driveway. No shadows loom in the windows. No sounds come from the property. I squat behind Loren's car, making sure she's not inside, and shoot off a final text to Eli. As if he cares.

Still no word. I'm going in.

I don't need him. I never did. I can fight my own battles. My fingers curl around air, but I imagine them gripping that shovel. I could've protected myself from Sterling. I could've stood up for myself with that jerk Reid. And I can do it now too if I need to.

I duck and run to the side of the house and peer around the backside to the property. Nobody is outside and I still don't hear any voices. I creep back to the front of the house and up the porch steps.

I test the doorknob, which clicks open. I peek through the crack before I slide through it and quietly shut the door behind me. I'm in the entryway with a view straight through the dining area and living room to the house's back door. I can see half of the kitchen beside it, with a sink full of dishes and an overflowing trash can. To the other side is a long, dark hallway.

I slide along the wall into the darkness and freeze when I finally hear something.

A spring mattress creaks once. Could they be . . . No. Loren wouldn't have forgotten to update me. And she sure as hell wouldn't get with Brody after all the questionable things we found.

Please no.

I sidestep farther down the hallway, silence weighing me down again. I pass an open door to a bathroom. Drips of water are splattered all over the counter, and the soap pump is on its side.

I creep to the next doorway, which is cracked open a few inches. I freeze as my eyes meet Brody's. He's sitting on the end of the bed but stands immediately.

I suddenly feel so small. My hands so empty. All I have is my lanyard of keys and my phone. No weapon. I should've stopped in the kitchen first and found a knife.

He stares at me through the five-inch crack between us, face pale, eyes wet. I can see enough already but can't stop myself from shoving the door. It swings open with a whining creak, revealing the entire scene between us.

Time slows to a withered crawl, and I take in all the details in one shallow breath.

He stands still as a fossil, turquoise phone in hand, a crack splintering across its screen. There's blood on his shirt. There's blood on the carpet between us, splotchy stains of it. A handprint of it clings to the doorframe. There are huge smudges up his dresser where his Guns N' Roses sweatshirt is perched. Bile burns the back of my throat.

"It's not what it looks like." His voice rasps out like he's the one who lost all this blood. Like he's the one drained of life.

His face is so pale, I could almost believe it. But on the floor beside the dresser is one of Loren's beaded earrings. The circle one with red, yellow, turquoise, and a black feather in the center. Her signature pair. And *her* phone is in his hand, the screen lit up to a photo of the sweatshirt folded on his dresser.

This is Loren's blood. And there's way too much of it.

Rage and fear collide in my chest, screaming at me to move. Now. I twist my keys into my palm, letting their pointy ends stick out. Red surges into my vision, thick and dark like the blood between us.

I lunge at him, driving the pointy keys toward his face. He ducks his head like a linebacker, arms outstretched, and the keys only graze his scalp.

His arms are around me as we both fall into the hallway. His forehead collides with the wall, stunning him for an instant. An instant just long enough for me to slide the lanyard in front of his neck and swap ends behind it. I pull it taut around his throat, body aching from his weight pressing down on me.

My fingers burn as I yank the ends harder. He coughs against the pressure and pushes himself off the floor. I'm clinging to the lanyard so tightly that I get jerked up with him.

He wraps his hands around my arms and shoves me into the wall. My head thunks against the drywall, and stars prick the edges of my vision, but still, I tug the lanyard hard enough that the keys cut deep into my skin.

He twists his fingers into my hair with one hand and fumbles with the lanyard digging into his neck with the other. He claws at it desperately, drawing blood from his own skin. His cheeks pull back against the red blotching into his face. Panic sharpens his focus on me.

He yanks my head, pulling hair out, and shoves me harder into the wall. I suck in air, glimpsing the splotches of blood over Brody's shoulder. Stars still prick at my vision, but so does my own sea of red. Hot rage is burning through me, telling me to fight or die.

He can't have me too.

I throw my body weight against the lanyard and drive a knee between his legs. He buckles, but the lanyard tears away from the metal ring of keys. It flings away from my hand, sending me flailing sideways, and soars behind Brody. Freeing him.

He steps over me, coughing and gasping, his eyes greasy black in the dark hall, and I scramble backward into his room. My hands slide on the still wet carpet; my mouth waters against the acrid scent of metal. He stalks after me, eyes wild.

His face is completely unhinged, like he's ready to fight to the death. It's sickly primal, like he's a cornered animal, even though I'm the one literally cornered between his desk and his bed frame.

Brody sucks in a breath, the veins underneath his red, marred neck jolting. I pull myself up on the chair, fumbling to get a grip on anything from the desk behind me. I chuck a pen cup at his face, but he swipes it away, sending the pens scattering across the floor.

"Stop!" His voice is thick and grating. "Listen."

My fingers wrap around something else as he grips my shirt like he's going to throttle me. I bash him on the side of his head with a

PlayStation controller, but it only makes him flinch. He heaves me sideways while I claw at his eyes, his face, anything I can reach.

He slams me into the floor like a doll, knocking the air out of my lungs and making white sparks fry my peripherals from the impact on my head. He's straddling me, letting his weight trap me here while he tries to catch my swinging arms. "Stop," he yells again.

I gasp for air as he easily lifts my upper body and shoves me back against the floor.

Shocks of pain soar through my pounding head. I dig my nails into his arms and reach for his eyes, trying to tear past him one scratch at a time. Fighting for my life. Blood smears across his skin, both his and Loren's. He pins down one of my arms and leans his other forearm into my throat, choking me. It digs in like it's crushing my bones and squeezing until it feels like my head will pop like a balloon. My chest seizes, desperate for air.

I punch his ribs with my free hand, but the white, burning edges of my vision turn to black smoke. It fills my surroundings until all I see is Brody's panicked face hovering above me.

And then even his face turns to smoke.

He was here all along, the smoke we've been looking for. The trail of ash we've been chasing.

Chapter 46

ELI FIRST KILL
Sunday, July 21, 11:11 a.m.

I didn't want to get involved, Mara Racette. The investigation already crumbled what was left of my home. After everything we'd already been through with our family members dying one by one, Dad abandoned us. Cherie was all I had left. The only thing keeping that house from turning into my own hell.

Now Cherie got ripped away.

And while Little Bro has been like a brother my whole life, I wouldn't bet his life against Mara Racette's. Especially not after I realized something.

I speed down the road, gripping the wheel, telling myself it doesn't mean anything. Hoping it doesn't.

The nausea churning in my gut tells me the alternative is too serious to ignore. I finally remembered Brody stopped by my house the same night I rolled out the beater truck. I thought he was just getting out of his rig when I got home, saying he needed to talk, but he was getting back in. He's gotta be the one who hid Rayanne's jacket inside. He didn't fake the guest book signature for Jason—he faked it for himself.

If he really is guilty, and Loren is in trouble . . .

My phone buzzes with a text from Mara Racette.

Still no word. I'm going in.

I press against the gas pedal even harder, making the truck roar. The tires screech as I make the final turn toward Brody's property.

It's probably nothing.

I pass by Mara's car on the side of the road and slash through the rocks as I whip onto Brody's driveway. I fishtail through the gravel, sending rocks flying into the grass in my wake. The violent static of the gravel beneath my spinning tires makes my ears ring until I skid to a halt in front of the house.

Mara's car was empty, so is Loren's.

I sprint through the brown clouds of dust hovering over the entire driveway and throw open the front door, willing my eyes to adjust to the sudden dimness inside. There's commotion down the hall. I rush toward it.

At the end of the hall, Brody's door is wide-open, sending streams of sunlight into the shadowy hallway. There's a fresh dent in the drywall across from it, with white dust on the carpet beneath it.

I veer to a stop at the doorway, and my heart freezes.

It's like a gust of wind has surged out of the room and lifted me into the air. I'm suspended, frozen in time, staring at the horror below me.

Red.

It's smeared all over the carpet.

It has to be blood. But it can't be real, because that would mean—

Mara Racette's hair flops onto the stain in the carpet as Brody smashes her body against the floor.

Her eyes close, and she's almost motionless, but her arm fumbles under the bed beside her.

Finally, I fall back into my burning-hot body and tear into the room. Brody glances up, eyes peeled back in shock, just as Mara's eyes open and she slams a dumbbell into the side of his jaw.

The impact is a sick crack and sends him toppling to the side. Mara gasps for air with a horrible screech, dumbbell falling out of her hand as she jerkily scoots away from him. Brody struggles to get his feet underneath him, and I charge at him.

I pin him against the desk, shaking the contents of the drawers. I hammer my fists into his face, bone cracking against bone, until another grating, gasping inhale comes from Mara's corner of the room.

There's so much blood, I don't know how much of it is hers. Or where Loren is. They need help.

I hurl him onto the bed, trapping him beneath me, and wrench the string of the blinds straight off the window.

He's still dazed from all the hits to his face, so I easily roll him over and wrap the white strings around his wrists. I wrap them round and round and tie them into tight knots. His skin pulls white against the layers of string.

His sluggish muscles tense against the knots, but they're secure.

Mara hugs her knees to her chest, back against the closet door. Her neck is flaming red. I step lightly over the smeared floor and scoop her into my arms. She clings to my shirt, sucking in air through her teeth.

I stride down the hall and kick open the front door. "Where's Loren?" I ask into her hair as I trudge into the lifeless grass.

A wretched sob scratches out of her throat.

"Oh, Mara."

I sink to my knees in the dusty grass, facing the house I've been inside a thousand times. Mara buries her face into my chest, shaking with rattling sobs. I slip my phone out of my pocket, knuckles cracked and bleeding, and call 911.

Only moments after Youngbull and several other cops bust into the house, paramedics swarm us. They lift Mara onto a stretcher and bend over her. Red and white lights flash behind her. Shining metal medical tools glint above her.

I hold the only thing I can reach in the chaos: her bloodstained shin. Her gaze meets mine, and I see the weight of reality fully hit. She blinks once, and her eyes change. "He killed her," she screams. Her voice is raw and breaking, like sandpaper against rocks. She sits up and pushes a woman with a stethoscope aside to get a view of the house.

A view of the walls Brody hides behind.

Her chest heaves, and she steadies herself on the woman's shoulder. She tries to yell again. "He killed Loren." It only comes out in a hoarse whisper.

The woman pushes her back down to the stretcher, and tears stream out of her eyes, soaking her hair.

He killed Loren.

They roll Mara into the ambulance. As soon as the door closes, a paramedic from a second ambulance runs over and rests his hand on my shoulder. "Let me take a look." He pulls my hand into his and examines my bloody knuckles.

"Is she gonna be okay?"

He digs into his shoulder bag and glances at the house. "She's stable." He pulls out a small packet and rips it open. My skin burns as he rubs something over my knuckles, but I focus on a cop approaching with his hand on his belt holster. "Nothing looks broken," the paramedic says, more to his colleague than to me.

The cop stops in front of us, watching the paramedic wrap bandages around my wounds as he instructs me on how to clean them. I couldn't care less about what happened to my hands. I'm more concerned with what's on Brody's.

"Where's the body?" the officer asks once the paramedic is back at the ambulance.

I shake my head. "I don't know."

"You're sure that blood is Loren Arnoux's?"

I tell him what Mara said at my house. He steps a few feet away and speaks into his radio. "We're going to need to do a full sweep of the area." He turns his attention back to me and asks for the full story.

My story isn't long enough. Mara's is longer.

I should've been there. I should've gone with her right away. Maybe we would've gotten here in time to save Loren.

My eyes burn. Loren. First Rayanne, and now her little sister.

The girls who made me feel like I wasn't the only kid whose world was torn up. Whose parent didn't love him enough to *stop*. The girls who were there for me without making me feel like it was a big deal.

And Samantha. The girl I shut out when all she was doing was worrying about me.

They didn't deserve any of this.

I squat down, digging my fingers into the earth, grounding myself in our land. I thought Brody would never surprise me.

I was wrong.

Brody's front door swings open, and I see his puffy face. One of his eyes is swollen shut. I stand up and spit on the ground. He looks bad, but I wish he looked worse. If Mara wasn't injured in the background, I probably would've punched him dead.

Youngbull leads him down the steps, and it takes a second, but finally, he sees me standing here. The half of his face that isn't swollen out of recognition pulls into fear. Or sadness. I can't tell.

"You sick dog," I yell. "Why?"

Youngbull shoves him toward the patrol car, but he's still rubber-necking at me, head shaking frantically.

"Where is she?" My voice cracks mid-yell.

He ducks into the car, and the slam of the door shakes my chest. Once the car disappears onto the main road, Youngbull heads back into the house, speaking into his radio. "Get Staccona down there. And try to get ahold of Brody Clark's brother and mom."

The officer next to me beckons me with his hand. "Come on, we have to get to the station."

"What?"

"You're not in trouble. We just need to get your official statement."

"Can't I go to the hospital to see Mara first?"

He glances at my bandaged hands. "Yeah. C'mon."

Chapter 47

BRODY CLARK
Sunday, July 21, 12:00 p.m.

This entire day has been on fast-forward. Seconds have been sliding past me like raindrops in a violent downpour. I didn't have a second to think. Not one. I still don't know how everything ended up off the rails.

Now the rain halts. Time inches by like a fat worm in parched dirt. Anger pricks at my fingertips as I wait. My whole face throbs in time with the ticking clock above the interrogation room door.

I rest my cuffed hands on the cold table. Blood is still sunken into the lines across my palms and buried in the cracks around my fingernails.

When the door finally opens, I shove them under the table. Out of sight.

Kurt Staccona comes in and pulls the chair out across from me with a harsh scrape.

He folds his clean hands on top of the table and stares at me for a solid fifteen seconds. It takes everything in me not to squirm.

"Where's Loren Arnoux?"

No words come. All I can do is shrug.

"We've got units out looking for her as we speak. You could save yourself a lot of trouble if you tell us where to find her right now. Time is of the essence."

"I didn't do it."

He squints. "Didn't do what, exactly?"

"Any of it."

He taps his fingers on the table in a jarring rhythm. "I'm sorry to say you haven't made too good a case for yourself, kid."

"It was all Jason."

"You're going to need to be more specific."

"Jason killed Samantha and Rayanne. And—and I think Loren."

"That's an awfully convenient story." He folds his hands onto his crossed knee. "Listen. Rayanne's purple schoolbag is in your room. We have gray and black fibers from Rayanne's throat that we just matched to a sweatshirt from your room."

"That's not—"

"You told us you didn't see Samantha after the photos were taken, but we have an image from that evening where you are looking right at her. And she's alone."

"I wasn't."

"Loren Arnoux's car is parked in your driveway. She told Mara Racette she was going to talk to you. And now she's nowhere to be found, but her phone and purse are in your room. And there are bloodstains in your room too."

I close my eyes, trying to ignore the bile sending acid into my mouth.

"Where is she, Brody? Is she dead?"

The handcuffs clank as I slam my fists onto the table. "I didn't kill Loren. I've loved her for as long as I can remember. If she—if she's

357

dead, Jason did it." My one good eye burns.

Staccona slides a hand along his jaw. "Let's say for a minute I believe you. Did you see it happen?"

I blink away the blurriness building in my eye. "No. I found my room like that."

"So why didn't you call 911?"

"I *just* saw it . . . I didn't . . ." The clock above the door ticks on. I've never felt so helpless. So out of control.

"And if you're innocent, why attack Mara Racette?"

"She attacked *me*. She was choking *me* out." I point to the tender skin across my neck. There was a second there I really thought she'd kill me.

He focuses on my neck for a few beats. "Again . . . let's say I believe you. Why keep quiet about the murders of Samantha and Rayanne all this time? Why accuse Jason now?"

"Jason's my brother . . . I didn't . . . I shouldn't have . . ."

"He went after Loren—the girl you like. That made you mad?"

"Yes!" The word echoes through my aching head.

"So why didn't you call 911?"

"When Mara came in, I was still figuring out what happened. I didn't know what to do. I wasn't thinking straight yet." A tear slips down my burning cheek. "I hate him for it."

"So you say he killed Rayanne and Samantha, but when he killed Loren, *now* you think he went too far? *Now* you hate him?"

"Yes."

"Is that why you killed him?"

Chapter 48

MARA RACETTE

Sunday, July 21, 12:00 p.m.

The officer leaves the hospital room with his pad of paper covered in a hurried scrawl. A nurse with a long, black braid swinging down her back slips into the room as soon as he's gone. "Sorry about that. He insisted we had to let him question you."

"It's fine." My voice is painfully hoarse, and I automatically bring my hand up to my neck but stop when it tugs against my IV line. They can ask me any question they want if they think it'll help find Loren.

"At least they waited until after the CT scan," Dad grumbles.

The nurse smiles politely. "And great news that the scan looks clear. It could've been a lot worse than a mild concussion. Push the call button if you need me. I'll be back soon." She updates some info on the whiteboard across the room before hurrying into the hall.

Mom scoots her chair closer to the bed and wraps her hand around mine.

"On the bright side, at least they'll leave you alone now, Dad." My strained voice is hardly more than a whisper.

He can barely look at me. "I'd rather have them digging through all my stuff than having you"—he glances at me and waves his arm in my general direction—"going through this." He folds his arms and looks up at the ceiling.

"I'm sorry I didn't tell you where I was going."

Finally, he looks at me and puts his hand over Mom's and mine. "I wish you would've, but I know why you didn't. I'm sorry I made you feel like you couldn't."

I get it now, more than I did before. When I looked at Brody in that room . . . my instincts took over. Just like Dad's did before and how they do when he feels the need to protect his family. I know he'd do anything to prevent my pain.

His eyes shine. "I can't believe he did this to you."

"It could be worse."

"You're right." We fall into silence, thinking about Loren. And Rayanne. And Samantha.

It could've been so much worse. And it almost was.

I don't know how long I could've kept fighting or how far I could've run if Eli didn't show up when he did.

On cue, he appears in the doorway. He's still tense and guarded. His hands are bandaged, and his clothes are smeared with old blood. But when he meets my gaze, his face slips into relief. He rests a hand on the doorframe and glances at my parents.

Mom elbows Dad, and they both stand up. "We'll give you a minute," she says. Dad squeezes Eli's shoulder as he walks past, and Mom pulls him into an unexpected hug. His eyes find mine over her shoulder and get glassy. She releases him and slips out the door.

He shuffles over and perches on the bed right against my legs, scooping my hand into another frozen bro-handshake.

"I'm so sorry, Mara."

I search his eyes. The same guilt darkens them, just like the day he lost Cherie. As if any of this is his fault.

"I should've believed you sooner." He brushes his fingertips against the back of my hand. "It's my fault all this happened." His gaze lingers on my blotchy neck and travels to the IV in my arm.

"You showed up." My throat feels like it has gashes across its insides.

He drops my hand and grazes the backs of his fingers along my cheek. "I showed up too late."

"Me too."

I pull myself into his chest. He wraps his arm across my back, and we cry for Loren.

That monster fooled us all.

Soon, Eli's shirt is soaked with my tears. He only pulls away when the nurse returns to check my vitals again. He stays perched on the bed, one hand around mine. He stands when my parents file back into the room, followed by the tribal police officer. "Can we have a few minutes?" the officer asks the nurse.

She looks at each of the adults in turn. "Just a few. Mara needs her rest."

My parents drop back into their chairs and Eli stays at my side, one hand on my shoulder. The officer stands at the foot of my bed, hands resting on his gigantic belt.

Over his shoulder, Geraldine appears, face wet and splotchy. She paces back and forth outside the doorway like she isn't sure what to do with herself. I think the officer asks how I'm doing, but seeing Geraldine's panic makes my ribs wither into rotten sticks. One by one, they collapse inward.

"We still haven't located Loren," the officer says. "But when we searched the property, we found Jason in an old supply barn." He pauses, too long. "He had a gunshot wound to the chest and was already deceased."

I gasp, sending jolts of pain into my throat.

"What?" Eli whispers.

Geraldine rubs her trembling hand across her collarbones, wrinkling her nurse scrubs.

"We don't have the full story yet. Brody is claiming Jason killed all three of the girls."

Geraldine whimpers from the hall.

"The two working theories are that Brody is telling the truth and was so mad Jason went after Loren that he killed him, or that Brody killed all of them and had to go after Jason once Jason found out about it. Based on what we've found so far, and what he did to Mara, it's most likely the second one. Either way, it's pretty clear Brody shot Jason."

Eli leans against the bed railing, squeezing my shoulder harder.

Geraldine approaches the doorway, wiping her face. "You said Brody shot Jason?"

The officer half turns, sympathy twisting his face. "That's how it looks."

Geraldine takes another step forward. "What else did you find?"

The officer looks so small in the middle of the room, all of us staring at him for more. "Nothing yet."

"I mean at the place you found Jason's body. Was there anything . . . suspicious, any hint at why this whole thing started?" Her quivering fingers skirt across her forehead.

The officer shakes his head. "No. Nothing."

Geraldine steadies herself on the doorframe, slowly shaking her head. "There had to be something. Why was he there? What else was in the barn?"

"All we saw was a broken window and an old axe with a possible blood mark." He grips his leather belt. "No sign of Loren at all."

Dad glances at me. He's barely holding it together, probably imagining himself in Geraldine's shoes. He almost was.

"You searched the whole thing?" Geraldine is breaking open in front of us. Hung up on the details of the barn instead of what the plan is to find Loren.

Impatience slips into the officer's tone. "Yes."

"There has to be something there. Why . . . why would he do this?" Her voice cracks, but with anger. Not sadness. She pushes off the doorframe with a frantic energy in her posture. "What else was in there?"

Her repeated questions are ripping me up. What else does she think they'll find next to Jason's body in an old supply barn? A written confession detailing what really happened? Shelves full of ranch tools and a hand-drawn map to find Loren? She's desperate for answers. My eyes burn watching her try to fight for them.

The officer's voice comes out with a new edge. "We're sending out more search parties now. We'll find your granddaughter. Just give us a little time."

They've said that before.

It's a slap in the face, and even I can feel its heat. I can't blame her for being ready to tear into him.

Her gaze darts between all of us in the room, though she's not really seeing us, then settles back on the officer. "Can you at least tell me who was the first to arrive at the scene? Who found Jason?"

"Detective Youngbull found him and radioed it in."

Geraldine wrings her hands so tightly they might bruise.

The officer turns toward me, getting back to why he came in here in the first place. "We'll keep you in the loop. In the meantime, if you think of anything else that might tell us where Loren could be, call right away."

I nod.

He rushes out the door, beckoning Geraldine to follow him. Her face is tight with every emotion, but it settles into a raging fury before she disappears down the hall. I can't imagine what that poor woman is going through.

Again.

Maybe Loren is still alive out there. We won't know until they find her. But the fact that somehow, Jason is dead over this . . . tells me chances aren't great.

Just like the moment I got a glimpse of Brody's room.

It was obvious something horrible had happened there, and Brody was absolutely terrified I saw it.

Chapter 49

BRODY CLARK
Sunday, July 21, 12:20 p.m.

"I'll tell you everything. The honest truth."

Staccona doesn't move a muscle. He's as still as the interrogation room walls. "First, tell us where Loren is."

"I told you I don't know where Loren is. And I don't know who killed Jason." Each breath makes my chest squeeze tighter, like the pressure to find the best way out of this is crushing me.

Loren is dead. Or close to it.

The thought makes my aching head pound harder.

I should stop talking, but my back is pressed against the wall, and it isn't even my fault. He needs to see that.

"Fine," Staccona says. "Tell me."

"The night before Jason took Rayanne, I was supposed to be working on a project with her little sister and Samantha. I blew them off, told them I needed to help Jason with a cattle emergency." That was my first mistake. The lie that set us on this messed-up path.

Staccona leans back in his chair, a picture of control.

"They wouldn't do it without me. So I told Jason I was meeting them at school early the next morning instead. He *knew* Rayanne would have to take the bus. That morning, he even asked me if Loren had her own car or shared with Rayanne. I was leaving an hour earlier than he had to, but he was already dressed and ready when I left. He was all antsy-like."

Staccona stares at me, unconvinced.

"He knew. I figure that's why he drove past the car shop and all the way up Duck Lake Road to that bus stop. He knew Rayanne would be waiting alone."

"You *figure* that's why?"

"I figure an opportunity presented itself to Jason, and he couldn't stop himself. He grabbed Rayanne before work that morning. Strangled her and stowed her in the back of his truck."

"But he showed up to work at eight a.m. That's not enough time to drive to the place her body was left. You're saying he just left her in the truck in the parking lot, customers walking past her all day?"

I force myself to swallow. It tastes like blood. "He called me from the work phone. Begged me to leave school and trade cars with him. Said he'd explain later."

Staccona shifts in his chair, subtly creaking.

"So I did. I left right after first period, and we swapped. He told me not to look in the back. Said he'd call again soon."

"Did you look in the back?"

"No. I was trying not to be too late back to class."

"What then?"

I can barely push the ugly words out. "He called again in my next passing period. Told me he accidentally ran over Rayanne and put her body in the back of the truck. Said I was already involved now and had to get rid of her body."

"You could've called the police right then."

I'm gonna be sick. "I should've." But he needed me. I've needed him all these years, and then he needed *me*. "But he convinced me I'd be in trouble too."

"So he told you to get rid of the body."

"Right after school, I drove her out of town. Chucked her phone out the window. I was heading to my mom's in Saint Mary anyway. I just took some back property roads and found an out-of-the way spot."

His eyes squint just slightly.

"Then I looked at her." I've tried to shut out the image for months. "He sure as hell didn't hit her with his truck. She had bruising all around her neck."

I try to force it back, but tears leak out of my good eye. I open and close my mouth, trying to find the right words. "So I dumped her there, cursing Jason's name."

"So you knew he killed her on purpose."

"That's how it looked."

"And still, you didn't call."

"I knew I should've, but he pressured me, and by the time I had a clear head about it, he said I was already an accessory."

He stares at me, a hundred scenarios scrolling through his eyes. "What about Samantha?"

"I think he saw her standing alone after the giveaway photos."

"So you think he just grabbed her when the rest of you cleared out? Why?"

"Maybe he got a thrill from it."

Staccona grips his knee. "That's a pretty big assumption. This isn't like the movies. In real life, there's usually some kind of motive."

I stare at the table, muddy thoughts churning.

367

"What real reason would Jason even have for killing Rayanne and Samantha?"

I squeeze my eyes shut, forcing myself to add up everything I've avoided looking into. Putting it all together. "Jason started getting moody and withdrawn sometimes. He stopped wanting to be around me much the last couple years. Something about him changed." I've felt it for a while, but I didn't know how to fix it. "I thought maybe it was drugs."

"Huh."

"I looked up symptoms of meth addiction, but he didn't have any of those. But then he'd disappear sometimes and wouldn't tell me where he'd been."

Staccona's expression doesn't change in the slightest.

"When my dad worked the ranch, we were dirt poor . . . but Jason started throwing around money like it was no problem. I convinced myself that maybe he was just better at the business side of things. Plus his part-time gig at the car shop. But sometimes I wondered if he was dealing or something . . . I just never asked. I didn't want to know."

"I gotta say, you're not convincing me here. We haven't found anything in the house or in the structures on your ranch to suggest he was dealing drugs. Nothing on his phone either." He folds his arms.

"You even checked the supply barns?"

"Yes. Officers have searched all the buildings on your property. Anywhere else you think he'd hide things?"

I shake my head. I explained away all the money we seemed to have lately. Told myself there was a logical reason. Maybe he was just shoveling himself into debt, desperate to have a different life than Dad did. To prove to Mom that she was a selfish pig for leaving all of us and not sticking it out.

"So even after your brother roped you into getting rid of Rayanne's body, like you claim, you really never asked why he killed her?"

I grind my teeth, sending bursts of pain through my jaw. "When I asked him why she looked strangled . . . he told me to stay out of it. That knowing would only get me in more trouble. I thought she must've stolen his drugs or ratted someone out . . . but I convinced myself I was better off not knowing. Just like with the money situation. And I never asked him about Samantha. I just . . . guessed. I didn't want any reasons to be in more trouble."

Drugs are the only thing that made sense. Why else would he have thrown us into this mess?

He nods slightly. He doesn't believe any of it. Not a word. He sees blood on my hands. Literally. And that's all that matters. "And why Loren?"

"She was snooping in my room . . . she found some things that pointed to Jason. I think he overheard us talking."

"Loren was looking for evidence in your room? Is that why you hurt her?"

I wipe my wet cheek with my sleeve. "I never hurt her. I never hurt anyone."

"Sorry, kid. None of it adds up to me. The way I see it, *you're* the one getting the thrill from it and Jason found out, just like Mara did when you tried to kill her."

"No."

"The evidence says otherwise."

My vision tunnels onto my stained hands. Everything has already fallen apart. The floor beneath me is long gone. I don't have a single thing left to lose. Not one.

Any way I play this, I lose.

Because of Jason.

Maybe my old man was right after all. Maybe I should've seen this coming. Jason was acting different. He resented me for the life he gave up . . . I should've seen the warning signs that he was changing. I should've known he'd screw me. But I was too stubborn, hanging on too tight to the way things should've been.

"Fine," I say, meeting his gaze. "I left one part out."

He clasps his fingers over his bobbing knee.

"When I got into the back of the truck to pull Rayanne out . . . one of her eyes opened."

His knee freezes. Everything in the room freezes. I have to force my lips to move. "She wasn't dead yet, but . . . something wasn't right. She wasn't moving. And when her other eye opened, they didn't look the same. Only one of them was tracking my movement."

"What did you do?"

The screams of the run-over rabbit blare inside my head. His broken body blinks into my vision. "She was suffering, bad."

"You could've called an ambulance."

I almost did. "They couldn't have helped her."

"How could you know that?"

"I've seen enough animals at death's door. I swear, I never hurt Rayanne. I helped her."

For the first time in any interrogation, Staccona's cheeks pull into a snarl. "If she got to the emergency room, you could've been the hero."

"She was past help."

He tries to force his face back into a neutral expression, but his lip still curls. "So what did you do instead?"

"I pulled off my sweatshirt and smothered her."

"So you are admitting you killed Rayanne Arnoux."

"Jason hurt her. He hurt her so bad she should've died. I put her out of her misery. *I* never hurt her."

He folds his arms, the tendons in his hands taut. "That's bull. I know you don't actually believe that."

I didn't hurt her. It's the lie I've been telling myself for months. The lie that let me keep looking Loren in the eye. Fire pumps through my veins. It was all Jason's fault. All of it. He dragged me into this mess. Used me. He's been manipulating me this whole time. I didn't see it at first. I wanted to help him.

I was afraid of losing him.

When I saw Rayanne was still alive, my gut twisted like it always does. I knew in that moment, if I called anyone, Jason would be screwed. And I'd be screwed for helping him. Our lives would've exploded. I'd have lost *everything* and nothing would ever be the same.

I was a coward.

And the truth is—that's the moment everything changed for good. I'm the one who destroyed any chance at walking back from this the second I took off my sweatshirt.

It hurts, but I force the words out. "I made a rash decision out of fear. I didn't want her to get Jason in trouble. And . . . *I* didn't want to get in trouble. So I made sure we wouldn't."

He nods, disgust wrinkling his forehead.

"And that's why I was quiet about all of it. Jason was holding that over my head. He said if he went down, I went down too. Because I was with Rayanne at the very end, not him."

"So you killed Jason so he'd stop holding it over your head?"

"No."

"You killed him because he went after the one girl you actually, truly cared about?"

I swallow fire. "No."

"Then why?"

"I didn't kill Jason." They can think what they want. I'll swear that up and down until I meet Creator.

Chapter 50

MARA RACETTE
Sunday, July 21, 3:00 p.m.

I grip the edges of the sink as pain cinches around my throat at my own gasp. Red blotches mar most of my neck. Some spots almost look like blood, and I can imagine the placement of Brody's elbow across my neck. My eyelids are swollen, and there are bursts of red in the whites of my eyes. Abrasions run up and down my arm from where he dug his fingernails into my skin.

I turn on the faucet and frantically splash water onto my wounds. The nurses already cleaned all my cuts, but suddenly I feel dirty. Brody's sick hands were on me, breaking my skin. I'm desperate to get the feel of him off me. I slather soap over my neck and up my arms and scrub at it until the pain is biting.

I thought *I* was an outsider. I was struggling against myself, trying my best to prove I belong here. Trying to prove I was one of them.

All along, Brody was the one who didn't belong.

He isn't one of us. *He's* the outsider.

Water drips down my chest and back, soaking my gown, when I finally shut off the faucet and rip paper towels out of the dispenser. The corners of the bathroom fade to gray as the flurry of activity leaves me light-headed.

I stumble back into my hospital room as the gray in my vision creeps farther around me. I collapse into a chair, blinking rapidly to clear my eyes.

When the gray fizzles back to the edges, I know I must've passed out.

Because Loren is sitting in front of me.

I heave in shallow breaths, trying to go easy on my throat. I blink once, twice. Ten times. Even when the shapes around the room sharpen back to their normal states, Loren still sits in front of me.

"I'm sorry." Her voice is clear, though a little weak. She's sitting in a wheelchair, an IV bag dangling on a pole behind her.

I close my eyes and rub them. She's still here. "You're okay?"

She smiles.

Eli appears in the doorway behind her, making her look over her shoulder.

And then I know it's real.

His mouth pops open. "Holy!"

She laughs quietly and stands as Eli wraps himself around her.

"We thought you were . . ." He can't even finish the words. He buries his face in her shoulder and cries.

When he finally releases her, I pull her into a hug until both our legs are trembling. She sinks back into the wheelchair, and Eli guides me back to my chair. He sits next to me and assesses Loren, just like I do.

She looks whole.

"What happened?" I ask.

Her eyes fill with tears. "I'm sorry, Mara. I shouldn't have told you anything. . . ." Her gaze drops to my neck. "I should've known you'd follow me there."

"I'm fine." My scratchy voice betrays me, but compared to what I could be . . . I really *am* fine. "We were worried about you."

"What happened?" Eli asks.

She gingerly combs her fingers through her hair. "I'm fine." She leans forward as she pulls a section of her hair back, showcasing a swollen line of stitches curving up the side of her head. "A little banged up and concussed but fine."

My entire neck pulses at the sight of it. "What did he do to you?"

"After we talked last night, I told my grandma everything. I thought maybe Brody was involved. She said I had to secretly look at his phone to really be sure."

Eli cusses under his breath. "She told you to go to his house? Knowing full well you suspected him?"

"We were desperate." Loren's knee bounces, gently wobbling the wheelchair. "I was supposed to take you with me, Mara. My grandma told me to, so we could have each other's backs . . . but I couldn't. I had this feeling that you'd get hurt if you were with me. I've felt in my bones that *I'm* the reason Ray Bear and Sam were killed. I couldn't do that to you too. I wanted to protect you." She rakes her hand down her face. "So much for that."

"Don't you dare put that on yourself." Eli's voice is somehow gentle and demanding at the same time.

She should've brought me from the start, but I get it. "Nothing is your fault, Loren. And I'm okay. Really."

She smooths the wrinkled fabric of her gown, nodding. "So Grandma thought you were with me when I went and broke a window to their supply barn at the very back of the property. And when I drove to their house. I told Brody I went to meet him at the supply barn to talk, but it looked like somebody broke into it. When Jason heard that, he was really upset and jumped on his four-wheeler to go check it out, just like I planned. That's the last time I saw him." Her gaze falls to her hands. "I told Brody he better go check out the horse barn behind the house, just in case it had been vandalized too. While he was doing that, I got into his phone."

"He just left it unlocked?" I ask.

Eli and Loren answer in unison. "1111."

Right. Bet he's regretting that code now.

"I found out he got two calls the morning Ray Bear disappeared. I sent the number to my grandma at work, who was ready to look into anything I found. They came from Jason's car shop."

Eli rubs his chin. "Not from his cell phone . . . which they searched."

Loren swipes at her cheeks as she tells us about the gray-and-black sweatshirt matching the fibers in Rayanne's throat. Then about finding Rayanne's purple messenger bag in his closet. "I was holding it when Brody walked in."

My stomach churns.

"He froze, like he'd never seen it in his life. Like my dead sister's schoolbag had materialized from *nowhere*. I screamed at him and he got real agitated, his arms trembling. Then he had the mind to say it was all *Jason*. He begged me to believe him. Tried to convince me I *knew* him."

"We don't know him at all." Eli grimaces like he wants to spit.

Loren nods. "That's what I said. Then he backed up into his desk, knocking things around. I could see it in his face then . . . fight or flight. He was out of his mind and terrified, and he was going to do something about it.

"So I did before he could. I smashed a dumbbell into the side of his head just as he was shoving off the desk to come at me."

"Good for you," Eli says.

She perks an eyebrow. "Knocked him out cold—but he fell right into me. I couldn't catch my balance in time after swinging that weight, and he sent me falling right into the corner of his dresser." She gestures at her long line of stitches again. "Gave me a huge gash that was spewing like a geyser."

The memory of the acrid smell pricks at my nose. "Believe me, we saw the spew."

"I was all dizzy, tripping over his legs and stumbling out of there in a panic. I took off across his property like he was chasing me. My phone was still in his room, so I couldn't call for help. I just ran until I passed out."

Eli is tense next to me.

The scene I walked into looked a lot worse than what she's describing, but it makes sense with how much head wounds bleed. "Who found you?"

"My grandma. She was helping the police look. Then they brought me here and fixed me up. And here we are." Her throat bobs. "I didn't plan on you coming after me, Mara. I'm sorry he hurt you." Her voice cracks. "I never expected him to hurt Jason over it either."

We're silent for a moment.

"Why?" There's so much pain in Eli's single word. Why would Brody or Jason do this? Why would they turn on Rayanne and Samantha? Maybe we'll never know.

Whatever Brody's story is, he's a murderer. Either he thought Loren died, just like the rest of us, and killed his own brother because of it, or Jason walked into that scene with the blood and the schoolbag and saw all of Brody's sins splayed out like a filleted fish. And died for it.

"It's over now." Loren squeezes my hand. "We stopped him."

I find Eli's tight fist with my free hand. "We all did."

LOREN ARNOUX
Sunday, July 21, 9:00 p.m.

"We don't normally allow this," Youngbull says.

Maybe he's grateful for what I did. Maybe he thinks he owes it to me after everything we've been through. Doesn't matter much what the reason is, as long as I can look Brody in the eye one last time. Now that I know what he's capable of, after all the things he's admitted, I wonder if he'll look different. If his demons will be slipping through the cracks in his face.

Youngbull leads me through the back of the police offices, past the interrogation rooms. We go through a locked door into an echoey hallway. Goose bumps rise on my skin as the cold air hits us and the door snaps shut behind us.

It's too clean in here for what it holds. The walls are so white, it's like they've been scrubbed with bleach. The floor is white with gray specks, hiding any scuffs. We pass two empty cells, blankets folded in neat squares on top of flat pillows.

Youngbull stops in front of the next cell, hands clasped unassumingly in front of his belt buckle. "You got a visitor." A faint creak echoes into the empty hall. Youngbull nods at me and heads back toward the locked door.

I still feel weak from the blood loss, but I straighten up and fake my strength back.

I step in front of the bars, facing the person who ripped my world apart.

His bloodshot eye meets mine. His hand shoots to his mouth, fingers digging into the side of his swollen jaw. His other hand clings to the bar of the door, skin squeaking against metal.

He looks awful. Good for Eli First Kill.

He rakes his hand down his face and steadies himself against the door. Even his legs shake. "You're not . . ."

I clench my fists at my sides. "Dead? I bet you feel real stupid now."

His uneven gaze looks me up and down. "What did he do to you?"

"Nothing. You shot your beloved brother for *nothing*."

His shoulders shudder. "What?" Even though his face is smashed into a puffy mass and one of his eyes is swollen shut, he still looks like Brody. The mask was supposed to be off.

"You're a sick and twisted monster. I hope you rot in hell for what you did to my sister."

"Did Staccona—"

"Yeah. He told us everything. Whether you're lying or telling the truth—"

"Then you know I *helped* Rayanne."

Mad laughter bursts out of my mouth, shaking my insides. White ash flutters at the edges of my vision. My body is losing the little energy I've built back up. The room is already starting to sway. "The only person you helped was Jason. And you killed him too. You're a coward and a monster."

He rests his forehead on the metal and takes a shaky breath. "Listen. It's just like the cottontail rabbit, Loren. Remember? There was nothing else I could do for her." His one good eye pleads with mine.

I could kill him. I could tear him apart with my bare hands. "Keep telling yourself that."

"Please," he whispers. "You're right, I screwed up. But Jason manipulated me, dragged me into his mess. He put Rayanne's bag in my closet."

"And you were jumping up to attack me when I found it."

His puffy face flinches. "No, I was going after Ja—" He closes his good eye. "He was trying to frame me. Set me up to take the fall for everything. I was going to confront him about it."

"Right."

He slowly shakes his head. "I'd never hurt you, but *he* would. I really thought he killed you because he *would*. *He's* the killer, Loren."

"Maybe he was *one*." I grip the bars, leaning in only inches from his disgusting face.

He takes a sudden step back. Something clicks in his gaze . . . like he's realizing just how tight the corner he's backed himself into is.

"But *you* killed my sister. *You* almost killed Mara. *You* killed your own blood. Look in the frickin' mirror, Brody. *You're* a killer too."

Chapter 51

UNKNOWN
Friday, July 26, 7:00 a.m.

Everyone had secrets. Some weighed heavier than others. This was one that took effort to keep. It would be held to the grave, but it was better this way. No matter what kind of regret bloomed . . . *he got what he deserved*.

Those were the words on repeat, looping in and out of all other thoughts.

For the final time, the podcast streamed.

INTO THE AIR
EPISODE 123

[INTO THE AIR *THEME*]

TEDDY HOLLAND: Good morning, listeners. First and foremost, I just want to thank you all. In the last two weeks, our subscriber number has more than tripled. You've been sharing this podcast far and wide, and from the bottom of our hearts, thank you. When we started this Missing and Murdered Indigenous Women feature, we hoped we'd be able to use our platform to spread awareness, and thanks to you, I think we have.

We were planning on giving away a few admission wristbands to the Bozeman Sweet Pea Festival, but to say thank you, we'll be giving away fifty. Stick around to the end of the episode and be one of the first fifty to claim yours.

This is Teddy Holland and Tara Foster, and you're listening to *Into the Air*.

TARA FOSTER: We have a special guest here in the studio with us today. She's a member of the Montana State Missing and Murdered Indigenous Persons Task Force. She's going to answer a lot of the questions you've emailed in for us, but first . . . we have even more updates on the Rayanne Arnoux and Samantha White Tail cases.

TEDDY HOLLAND: That's right, Tara. The tribal police and the FBI made an arrest in Browning earlier this week. They arrested a seventeen-year-old boy named Brody Clark. He was close friends with Samantha and Rayanne's younger sister.

DETECTIVE YOUNGBULL [PHONE]: Yes, we have a suspect in custody. I can't discuss all the details, but he has admitted to killing Rayanne Arnoux, and he assaulted another girl, who survived.

TEDDY HOLLAND [PHONE]: What about Samantha White Tail?

DETECTIVE YOUNGBULL [PHONE]: We're still reviewing evidence and will present it in court.

TEDDY HOLLAND [PHONE]: Is it true Brody Clark killed his own brother?

DETECTIVE YOUNGBULL [PHONE]: His brother's cause of death was a homicide, but we don't have any evidence to determine with certainty who killed him yet, only theories at the moment.

[DISTANT SIREN]

TARA FOSTER: What we do know is that emergency services were dispatched to Brody's ranch home earlier this week. A teenage girl was taken by ambulance after being assaulted by Brody, and a search was conducted for Rayanne's sister, who at one point was presumed to be dead. The police arrested Brody and found his brother's body somewhere else on the property.

TEDDY HOLLAND: We reached out to Rayanne's grandmother for comment, but she was unavailable. I think she's finally getting some much-needed rest after the mystery of one granddaughter's murder was brought to a close and the other granddaughter was found injured but alive.

TARA FOSTER: The Arnouxs and White Tails have been through un unspeakable tragedy. Their families will always be missing a piece. Their hearts will always be broken, but at the very least, they can have the closure of knowing who did this. They will get to see the trial through to the end. They'll see justice. So many other families who go through this don't get that far. So many other families are forced to wonder for years, never getting any answers.

TEDDY HOLLAND: That's where we come in. So many other cases don't get the attention they need. We need to put these cases on the mainstream news. We need the public to be aware of the missing persons clearinghouses and the avenues to donate to families impacted by these issues. We need to fix this huge disproportion of missing Indigenous people. We can all do our part to spread awareness and stop the silence on this issue.

TARA FOSTER: We can all stand for the Missing and Murdered. We have Beth Picard here, ready to discuss ways we can do just that.

ELI FIRST KILL
Saturday, August 3, 10:00 a.m.

The cemetery is still. Like the days I used to go hunting with *them*. With Brody and Jason. We'd hike into the snowy mountains through blankets of fresh powder, orange hunting beanies on our heads, rifles strapped to our backs.

Sound wouldn't carry. It was like the snow sucked all the sound waves into itself, letting us creep up on elk. We became silent predators.

I kill myself thinking about how I should've known.

They were the true predators.

Jason was nice to me. And Cherie. It couldn't have been real, though, not if Brody is telling the truth about Jason starting all this. Not when that other side of him was so vile. Maybe Jason had more poison than anyone and, worse, was better than anyone at hiding it.

I wish I knew why. What changed? Where did that sickness come from?

I thought I knew him—them.

I told Mara that Brody was my best friend because he'd never surprise me. I couldn't have been more wrong.

The cemetery isn't blanketed in snow, but the same stillness hovers here. Something else seems to mute our footsteps through the grass. It's an uncomfortable peace.

Mara slides her fingers into mine, and we trek between rows of headstones of our people. Feathery clouds rest over the distant mountain range in front of us and I have to believe that ancestors are looking down. Loren walks toward us, a long ribbon skirt swinging around her ankles. A crowd is already gathering behind her for Rayanne's burial service, and a drum group murmurs around their drum.

An old man wearing a cowboy hat with an eagle feather and a white vest with black, red, and teal geometrical designs down its front follows close behind Loren. Fringe from the edges of white buckskin gloves with matching designs swings as he walks.

His wrinkled jowls hang almost as long as his dimpled chin as he smiles politely. "This is Eli First Kill and Mara Racette," Loren says. "The ones we told you about."

"I'm Earl Big Crow, Loren's uncle. Geraldine is my youngest niece."

I stick out my hand.

He shakes it with more gusto than his feeble frame would show. "*Oki.*"

"*Oki.* Nice to meet you."

"*I'ksimato'taatsiyiop.* I knew your Grandpa First Kill. I taught him all my old Indian tricks." His lips pull into a crooked smile. "Ay, he would've been proud of you. He always was."

"Thanks." I chew the inside of my cheek, letting the pain overpower the emotions.

He shakes Mara's outstretched hand. "I've heard quite a story, and I'm very grateful for what you and Loren were able to do here." He clasps his other hand over hers. "Can I honor you with an Indian name?"

Mara's throat bobs in the gentle silence as the small crowd pauses their conversations. "Of course."

He leans in closer, speaking as if she's the only one here with him. "*A'pissupiitsiitsii*. Looking For Smoke. You could've stood in the background. Kept to yourself. But you helped Loren. You helped her search for what seemed to dissipate like smoke in wind. You used your knowing gut to help her see enough to expose the evil those boys were bringing. Most important—you had her back. We'll always be grateful for you, relative. You're one of us in every way."

She is. She's always known it, but there's no way she can ever doubt that now.

Earl gestures to Geraldine. "Bring me that sweetgrass." He takes the dry braid of sweetgrass and pulls a lighter from his pocket. "Stand here, Mara."

Mara takes her place in front of Earl, her back to him, and exchanges a smile with Loren.

The old man lights one end of the sweetgrass, sending thin wisps of smoke across Mara's shoulders and over her head. He places his other hand on her shoulder and says a prayer in Blackfeet, the sweetgrass carrying it over us and up to Creator. When he finishes, he pushes Mara forward, into her first steps as *A'pissupiitsiitsii*, and another of Loren's uncles sings a prayer holler song. Warmth eases through me.

"Thank you." Mara's eyes shine with suppressed tears as Earl pulls her into a hug. "You'll have to write the name down for me."

Earl laughs heartily and releases her. "Thank *you*." He puts an arm around Loren. "And now we honor another stolen sister."

We follow them back to the open grave. A dark wood coffin shines in the morning sunlight. Loren takes her place next to Geraldine and other relatives, and Mara and I slide into the back row.

The drumming starts. It pounds vibrating life into my bones. My blood thrums with it. The men circling the drum wail with the beat, and I feel connected to them. To the people around us. To the land beneath our feet. To Rayanne's bones in front of us.

These are my people. And even if it has chewed me up and spit me out, this reservation will always be my home. I squeeze Mara's hand in mine.

We're a resilient people. We always have been. We'll get through this. Loren will get through this. I'll get Cherie back. Mara will find her place. And we'll all be stronger for it.

That's the way of the Blackfeet.

Chapter 52

MARA RACETTE
Saturday, August 3, 9:00 p.m.

I wave a mosquito away from my face and pull my hood up. The full moon casts cold light across the dry field. There's a heaviness here . . . maybe it's the lack of wind, or maybe the land knows what Loren is doing.

Eli's truck sinks to a stop in the dirt next to my car. His face is shadowed, but when he steps into the moonlight, his eyes are bright. He takes my hand and leads me to the rest of the group already huddled under the night sky.

Loren's at the center of the group, adjusting her beaded headband. A handprint is painted across her mouth. The darkness mutes all of the surrounding colors, but I know the handprint is red. The color of the MMIW movement. The symbol that she will not be silenced. The cone-shaped tins lining her jingle dress twinkle softly as she picks up her fan of feathers.

"Ready?" Geraldine asks. Loren nods. The circle parts and everyone touches her shoulder as she walks alone past her grandma's truck to the open field, jingling with each step.

Eli takes my hand, and someone taps my other shoulder. Sterling is only inches from me, sending waves of nerves into my stomach, but his eyes are steady. "Hey. I'm sorry for that one night."

I tighten my grip on Eli's hand. "Oh?"

He glances past me to Eli and lowers his voice. "I was so wasted I really thought you wanted me to follow you into the barn, but that punch from First Kill showed me the great error of my ways." His smile is too big for his face.

Eli runs his thumb over mine. I didn't know he hit Sterling.

"Anyway. With all this going on . . . I just—sorry." He gives me an upward nod, then heads to his place around the drum, leaving me sorting through my memories of that night as I hurry back to my position behind my open car door.

Eli stands behind his truck door, and several more cars form a crescent in line with ours in front of Loren.

She's only a shadowed figure in the distance. When her jingling stops, she almost disappears into the night. Then the drumming starts. The thumps vibrate into my chest. Into the dirt under my feet.

The first car in line flicks on its headlights, then with each beat, the next car adds its light. I twist my headlights on, and in a matter of seconds, Loren is completely bathed in harsh light. She bounces to the beat, spinning and kicking up swirling dust. It hovers in the light around her moccasins like someone set up a fog machine.

With all the headlights on, I get a good look at the group watching the jingle dress dance. Samantha's mom stands next to her car, the back seat filled with Samantha's younger siblings. I don't recognize the handful of other people working their headlights and watching with reverence.

The group of drummers is made up of Samantha's cousin, Sterling, and a few boys from school. At least a couple of them did track with Samantha and Rayanne. There are some older men in the circle, probably their dads or uncles. Their voices melt together as they sing over their drum, sending prickling chills across my skin.

Geraldine stands in the center of the crescent of cars, filming Loren, smiling through her tears.

Loren's making this video for SnapShare. I know she'll go viral, at least on Native SnapShare. Hopefully, it will reach even farther. Hopefully, awareness will spread.

She waves her fan of eagle feathers in the air to the drumbeat, her braids bouncing against her chest in the same rhythm. The jingle dress dance brings healing. She's dancing for Samantha's family and for her own. She's dancing for our community. For our tribe. For all the other tribes battling the epidemic of Missing and Murdered Indigenous Women.

She's dancing for all the stolen sisters out there.

My eyes burn until tears pour out. Warmth fills my chest. I catch Eli's gaze. His jaw is clenched, holding in the emotion, but he feels it too.

Burning pride.

Chapter 53

UNKNOWN

Sunday, July 21, 11:11 a.m.

She pressed her back against the tree. The rough bark dug into her skin as she shifted on her already tired feet. She'd made a plan, and she was steeling herself to put it in motion.

Jason made sense. Brody didn't. But when she thought about how the little brother always followed along with the older one, maybe he knew something. There was a reason everyone close to him called him Little Bro.

The thought of Jason's hands around those girls' throats . . . it sent heat lashing into her limbs.

She had a theory, one based on circumstantial evidence, personal insight, and a good old-fashioned hunch. She just had to wait now to find out for herself.

Like she knew Brody let his older brother influence him too much, she also knew Jason was used to getting away with things. She'd heard about the time shortly after their dad died, leaving them no money, just a ranch to work. Jason was out driving drunk. Drowning his sorrows as too many young men do.

Highway patrol pulled him over just off tribal lands. They were getting ready to arrest him, slap him with a DUI, but then tribal police rolled up. His old best buddy Jeremy Youngbull pulled up and said he'd take over.

Fresh, green Youngbull did his buddy a favor. He drove him back into Browning and dropped him at home to sleep it off.

She thought that must have been the first taste he got of being invincible. Using people close to him for an advantage. He was well-liked enough—it wouldn't be that hard. He'd cleaned himself up after that incident, though; she'd assumed it was a wake-up call, but maybe it was just a pivot.

She wondered if Youngbull was *still* looking out for his old buddy. That's what sat heaviest in her mind—that Jason might have Youngbull in his back pocket.

She wasn't willing to risk it.

Her phone vibrated with a text. She plugged the information into an internet search, and the results confirmed her hunch.

She slipped her phone in her pocket and picked up the antique rifle. She wove between the trees, staying on the long grass instead of the two tire-size dirt strips, and perched behind a four-wheeler. The small storage barn sat in silence at the end of the rough, dirt road. Shards of glass were scattered in the pale green grass below a broken window. As she crept closer, sounds of shuffling floated out of the open door.

She stepped in front of the doorway, rifle raised. The butt rested comfortably against her shoulder. Her arms didn't shake. She flipped the safety off with a click. "Don't move," she said. Her tone was strong. Commanding.

Jason turned, fists raised. "The hell?"

Her pointer finger rested alongside the trigger, just like her daddy taught her, ready to swing down to the trigger should the moment change.

"I know what you did," she said.

"You don't know anything." He lowered his fists, feigning casualness. He didn't want to take her too seriously.

He'd regret that.

"I know you picked up Rayanne. I know you used the car shop's phone to call Brody at school."

His face stayed in its frozen scowl, but he didn't have anything ready to say to that.

"I know he switched cars with you. There's a picture of him in the parking lot that day, and *your* truck is in the background. Not his."

"You don't know what you're talking about." But his scowl fell.

"I looked at the giveaway pictures you took. I almost missed it, but Samantha had a backpack with her. It had turquoise and red beadwork stitched on the carry loop. I knew I'd seen that before. On you. That was *your* backpack."

He stood still as rock.

"Why'd she have your backpack? Did she steal it from you? Or did you get yourself involved with a teenager?"

"You're full of it. I don't know what you're talking about."

She was sure he knew exactly what she was talking about. "I know you killed them. Brody has been protecting you, but we both know when it comes down to it, he won't take the fall for you."

"You're out of your mind." He shifted on his feet, glancing at the line of cupboards on the barn wall. "None of that proves anything."

"Maybe not, but Brody's going to sing when he's looking at murder charges."

Jason dramatically ran a hand through his greased, black hair, then laughed. The son of a gun actually laughed. "I'm gonna let you in on a secret. Brody worships me. Even if I *was* guilty, he'd never rat me out."

She steadied her finger above the trigger, hot against the cool metal. She doubted he'd bet everything on that.

His eyes shone as he watched her. "Maybe *he's* guilty. Think about it. Everything making you point a finger at me points at Brody just as easily. Maybe I was calling him that morning because I was pissed he took my truck that day. Maybe whatever backpack you think you recognized on Samantha got handed down to him just like all my other old stuff. He's the one who knew those two. Not me."

She could see through the act. He was spouting lies like a busted pipe. She just had to think of a way to shut it off.

Before she could, he lunged toward the wall of cupboards in a burst of motion and clawed one open.

"Back up," she yelled as she strode forward, finger finding the trigger. She was a hair away from pulling it, electric adrenaline soaring through her limbs, but he jumped back before the cupboard door was even done swinging open.

He stepped backward into the corner. There were only eight feet between the barrel of the gun and Jason's open palms.

She kept her finger on the trigger, chest heaving, and glanced in the open cupboard. She saw the black backpack with a red zipper, but the carry loop was cut off, the beadwork nowhere to be seen. Bits of frayed thread spewed at its old edges. She knew he must've ripped it off.

Next to it, metal objects glinted in the dull light. Pill presses. A scale. Stacked on the shelf above them were fat bags of white powder. There were smaller baggies of gel tablets and a crystal substance like broken glass. Her sweaty fingers squeaked against the rifle. Meth. And probably fentanyl. She should've known.

And barely visible on the top shelf was a flip phone and the black grip of a pistol.

He was going to shoot her.

As he stood in the corner of the barn, some of the smugness melted off his face, but his eyes held steady on hers. She could see the thoughts racing. He'd kill her in a second. Just like Rayanne and Samantha. "Easy," he whispered.

She forced her voice to sound calmer than she felt. "That's the backpack Samantha had."

He shook his head, ready to spit another lie.

She raised the rifle higher; the fury heating her blood begged for her to shoot. He was a murderer. She knew it. She nodded toward the bags of drugs. "Why?"

He looked at his feet and dug his fingers into his hair. She could see the panic curling his muscles until all of a sudden, that cocky slant to his face returned. "Have you ever had everything you wanted?"

She kept her mouth shut. A bird screeched outside, high and sharp.

"My dad couldn't give us anything. He worked himself to death on this ranch, and what did he have to show for it? *Nothing.* We barely got by. He left me with nothing but problems." He laughed breathlessly, sweat beading on his forehead.

She kept her aim trained on his chest but positioned her finger above the trigger again.

"I found my own way to provide. I found a way to have everything. *I* did that." He jutted a finger to his chest.

She should've guessed he was desperate enough to fall into that trap, but she knew those girls weren't anywhere near that life. She shook her head. "What's any of this got to do with those girls?"

"I never wanted to do it, you know. I'm not a killer." The words tumbled out of his mouth. "But Rayanne stuck her nose where it didn't belong. She thought she could pull one over on me."

"What are you talking about?"

He cocked his head. "She saw a . . . transaction. A massive one. When all was said and done, I turned my back for a second, and then my bag and the product inside it were gone."

He wasn't making any sense.

"Rayanne swiped it. She almost got away with it too, but I saw her car turning the corner a minute later."

That wasn't the Rayanne she knew. "She wouldn't do that."

"She did." He laughed bitterly. "She stole a hundred thousand dollars' worth of drugs from me. That little piss probably didn't even know it."

She'd never understand that kind of sick greed. "And you killed her for it?"

"I was gonna get the stuff back from her." Anger flared in his voice. "But she told me she flushed it all." He raked a hand down his face. "Flushed a hundred grand."

"You killed her because of money?" It took everything in her to keep her finger frozen in place.

His words squeezed out quicker. "She crossed me. And even if I let good-girl Rayanne get away with it, she would've ratted me out. And my supplier. He'd rather I *die* than be arrested. He told me to take care of it. He hates loose ends. I'm lucky he didn't blow out my brains himself for her stupid stunt." He paced a tight line in the corner, as her aim tracked him the whole time.

She knew better than anyone how much Rayanne hated drugs. She hated that they took her mom away and stole part of her childhood. Hated how they changed people. She hated them so much she did something stupid and put her own life in danger. But this wasn't on her. "You're a selfish pig."

"She should've stayed out of it." His voice was cold.

"And what did Samantha do to deserve your hands on her?"

"That's the funny thing." To his credit, there wasn't a lick of humor in his tone. "Turns out Rayanne didn't flush anything. Somehow Samantha got all of it . . . because there she was at the powwow, right in front of my table, carrying my own backpack. The one Rayanne stole."

The way his cheeks pulled back in disdain brought her finger closer to the trigger.

"I saw her eyeing Youngbull like she was nervous he'd search that bag. She'd been helping herself to it for three months. Or maybe she'd been selling *my* product. Nobody gets away with that. If my guy found out those bags and those pills were on the streets after all that . . . after I said I took care of the loose ends . . . I'd be dead. I was already walking on thin ice." He stopped pacing and stood eerily still. "I couldn't plan that one, but I managed. You squeeze hard enough . . . it doesn't take long."

Her own throat seized at his words. She could hardly stand to look at him. "You killed her for that without a second thought?" Her voice fried with hatred. "How'd you even know anything was in there?" He was even more sick and twisted than she'd thought. The money and power had completely soured his head. Any good had long bled out of him.

"It's—it's what had to be done!" He threw his hands out. "It's not

397

like I enjoyed it. You don't just take a hundred grand from someone. Not in this world."

She'd heard enough to know there was no talking any sense into him. He believed in the rules of his sick, backward world.

"She didn't know it was mine until I grabbed her. She admitted she almost sold it a few times because she needed the money so bad, but she brought it to the powwow to turn it in. She said that's why she was looking at Youngbull; she was on her way to give him the bag when she got called for the giveaway, then before she could hand it to him afterward, I pulled everyone over. She was going to tell him she found the bag there and nobody would ever know she had it for so long. But I knew. She begged me to take it back and let her go and she'd keep her mouth shut. I didn't believe any of that, though. Desperate users will say anything."

Unease thrummed through her. She couldn't help but wonder if Samantha had come forward sooner, maybe they could've traced the drugs and Rayanne's disappearance to Jason. Maybe they'd have found her body sooner. And Samantha could've saved her own life.

"But I assumed wrong. Not a single ounce was missing." The lack of remorse in his words said more than anything else.

She shifted her weight, creaking the old wood floor. Neither girl used any. A bit of relief trickled into her head, but she knew it didn't matter one bit either way. That piece of garbage killed them anyway. And he thought he could get away with it. "You'd really let Brody take the fall for you? Does he even know about your *business*?"

"He'd be an idiot if he didn't have some idea, but he was smart enough to keep his nose out of it. He'd only make things messier for me." His fists clenched at his sides.

"Brody's not going to keep his mouth shut for you." He was a fool if he really believed that. She knew Brody had been protecting him all this time, but she'd always thought that kid was weak-minded. There was no way he wouldn't give up everything when it was him in the corner. She'd bet anything that he'd fold at the drop of a hat. "You're not getting away with any of this."

She'd make sure of that.

"I will." Jason stared at the barrel of the rifle, but there was no fear in his eyes. "That morning in April, I took Rayanne's jacket and messenger bag. I hid the bag in Brody's room and let him plant the jacket in Eli's dad's truck. Or so he thought." Pride dripped out of his mouth. It was all an elaborate game, one he thought he was winning. "Brody was always meant to take the fall if things got screwed up. He can sing all he likes. He'll never turn it on me."

"That's your baby brother . . . the kid you came home to take care of. You'd let Brody be framed for murder . . . over drugs?"

"You still don't get it. I—I have to." Somewhere deep down he knew it was wrong. Part of him had to remember why he wanted to raise Brody instead of his mom. Maybe that's what started this all. He was desperate enough for money, for a solution. Maybe at first he had Brody's best interests in mind. Maybe he loved him.

His gaze hardened, and his body stilled. "I can't just back out. It's him or me. Call it self-preservation."

If he did break into this dark world for Brody, it wasn't the case anymore. The only person who mattered to him now was himself.

It was exactly what her gut told her. Jason would find a way out of this. Real justice wouldn't be served. And it was all for *drugs*. For the poison he was bringing to her tribe. And the most sickening part was, he thought it was worth it. Even with a gun aimed at his heart, he still thought it was worth it.

"You'd kill innocent girls and betray your own brother over money." She could taste acid in her mouth, begging to be spat at his face. "Your mom left your family for money. You *destroyed* yours for it. Your dad would be disgusted with you. I won't let Brody take all the blame."

Jason's lips twisted into something ugly.

She steadied the rifle with one hand and pulled out her phone, ready to dial 911.

"Brody deserves just as much blame."

Her finger hovered over the numbers.

"After I slammed Rayanne's head into my truck and strangled her, she still held on."

She froze, chest tight with dread at the violent image.

"She should've been dead, but apparently, she was a fighter. *Brody's* the one who smothered her to death. That was all him."

Her grip slackened. Loren was still in Brody's house, looking through his things. Brody—a killer. She hadn't prepared for that—she didn't know he was capable of that. She assumed it was all Jason; she just needed Loren to find any bit of evidence from Brody's phone or room to make her certain. And she needed her to get Jason alone. Loren wasn't supposed to be in danger. She was supposed to be safe. That was the plan—the plan she was desperate enough to believe would work.

What would Brody do if he caught Loren?

In the half second her focus drifted, Jason snatched an axe from the concrete floor. In a single beat of her heart, he was swinging the blade toward her, dried blood marring its sharp edge.

She dropped her phone and pulled the trigger.

The butt rammed into her shoulder as Jason stumbled backward.

The axe slipped from his fingers in his shock, clanging at her feet. The blast made her ears ring. Red bloomed on Jason's chest. He collapsed into the corner, limbs trembling.

Her whole body went numb, frozen in place, panic clogging her thoughts. What had she done? What had he made her do? The rifle's weight bore down on her. This was not part of her plan, but she reminded herself it's what he deserved. He had brought it on himself.

She forced herself to step over the axe and walk through the heavy, metallic scent of the gunshot toward Jason. "You're a disgrace."

He stared at her, wide-eyed, as his chest jerked up and down in undefined breaths. Blood seeped from his mouth. She pulled the bolt up and back, ejecting the spent casing, and shoved it back into place, pushing another round into the chamber. Gun raised, she watched him for another moment. Then he was still. His eyes still stared, but they drained of focus. His chest stopped jerking.

Hers buzzed with adrenaline.

She believed every selfish, sick word he said. After Brody ruined his life for his brother, Jason would repay him by washing his hands of it all. Brody killed for him, and he'd planned a way to get off scot-free from the very beginning. All for his precious money and pathetic drug business. His fool of a brother made it easy.

Not anymore.

She lowered the rifle and picked up the spent casing, still warm to her touch. She rolled the brass in her fingers, thoughts racing, then shoved it into her pocket. She'd make sure Brody would pay for his part in it. He'd be paying his whole life.

But Jason got the ultimate punishment. He deserved it. If she didn't shoot him, he was going to kill her, without a doubt, but even so . . . she had to admit she wanted to. Her anger and hate burned so hot it felt good to release it. And maybe she'd go to hell for that. She'd just killed a man, but at least she knew Loren and other girls would be free of him. He wouldn't hurt anyone else.

After all, she did tell her granddaughter Loren she'd go to hell and back defending her. She just didn't know she'd be taking somebody else there with her.

A Note from the Author

When the characters in *Looking for Smoke* slipped into my head fully formed, begging me to tell their story, I was scared I wouldn't be able to do it justice. Their journey would tackle the very real issue of Missing and Murdered Indigenous Women, the toll of which is devastating. The numbers speak for themselves: 84 percent of Native women have experienced violence and 56 percent have experienced sexual violence. The murder rate of Native women is three times more than that of white women, and in some locations, the rate is more than ten times the national average.

In writing the story of a group of teenagers grappling with the disappearance and murder of their classmates, I hoped to bring readers' attention to these startling statistics and, more importantly, to the emotional reality of the families and community members impacted by this epidemic. It's a sensitive issue that needs a careful hand when weaving it into a fictional story. I didn't want to write anything that would trivialize the real cases or sensationalize the heavy pain so many Natives are enduring. I wanted to shed a light on the issue while creating characters that would stick with readers long after the book ends.

I wanted to send a message that is not easily forgotten.

But I was afraid I wasn't qualified enough to pull it off. Or talented enough. Or Blackfeet enough. I worried that because I'm bicultural and grew up off the reservation, my words wouldn't be as valid. The significance of this story, and the question of whether I was the right person to tell it, weighed on me. It brought out my doubts, much like Mara's move to the Blackfeet reservation brings out hers. Still, I knew this was a story that needed to be told, so I discussed it with my dad. He listened patiently to all my concerns, then shut down my doubts and said something I'll always remember: "You're Blackfeet, my girl. Nobody can take that from you."

So I wrote it. I dug into my own experiences and my family's lives, bringing as much authenticity to these pages as I could. I filled them with childhood memories and family stories. I borrowed wisdom and expertise from loved ones. I honored my family by using many of their names throughout, including First Kill, Big Crow, and the very title of this book, Looking For Smoke, which is the name of my fifth great-grandfather. I even put my dad's guiding reassurance to me into a scene with Eli and Mara.

While I tried my hardest to create an authentic cast and setting, I did take creative license for the sake of the story. I do not attempt to claim this is an accurate representation of every Blackfeet's experience, and it is certainly not intended to be a representation of the hundreds of other tribes across the US, but I do hope each reader can see a piece of themselves somewhere in this book.

These characters may be fictional, but their emotions are real. Their desire for belonging, commitment to family, and respect for community are things we all feel. The joy and pride they have for each other and for their culture is powerfully accurate. Their heartache is real too. The profound sense of loss, anger, sadness, and thirst for justice is true of countless Natives who want their voices heard. They want awareness, support, and outrage.

I wanted to write a book about Native teens because I wanted to bring more Native representation into popular media. We see too many stories of Natives in past tense, but we're still here, and we deserve to see ourselves in characters in the contemporary lens. But as I wrote this book, it became equally important to me to lift these particular voices, to draw attention to the epidemic of Missing and Murdered Indigenous Women. These Native women deserve better, and my heart is with them.

Throughout this story, I drew inspiration from the powerful women in my own life who have carried themselves and their families through pain, betrayal, and loss, and come out stronger on the other side.

Like Loren's grandmother Geraldine says, we are a resilient people. I have seen that despite all odds, we can thrive.

And we deserve to.

Learn more about the Missing and Murdered Indigenous Women issue by visiting the hashtags #MMIW, #MMIWG, #MMIWG2S, and #NoMoreStolenSisters, or visit my author website, kacobell.com, to find information, resources, and ways to donate to the cause.

Acknowledgments

There are so many people who helped make *Looking for Smoke* a reality. I could fill another novel detailing the support I've been given on this journey, but I'll try to keep it short. A million thank-yous:

To my husband, who always believes in me and my abilities, even when I don't. I love you.

To my mom, who will read anything I write. You helped me brainstorm my way out of many fictional binds, and it was you who inspired me to start writing in the first place.

To my dad, who continually teaches me. I got my creativity and cultural pride from you. Thank you for walking with me through this whole process.

To my agent, Pete Knapp. I'm now officially an author, and still I can't find enough words to explain just how thankful I am to have you in my corner. The care you take with your clients and our books is unmatched. You have been *Looking for Smoke*'s biggest champion, and I couldn't have done this without you. And thanks to Stuti Telidevara, Kat Toolan, Danielle Barthel, and the rest of the team at Park & Fine for all the time and hard work you've put in on my behalf.

To my editor, Rosemary Brosnan, for believing in this story and making the perfect home for it at Heartdrum. Thank you to the many other team members at HarperCollins who made this possible, including Cynthia Leitch Smith, Liate Stehlik, Suzanne Murphy, Kerry Moynagh and the sales team, Sean Cavanagh, Vanessa Nuttry, Mikayla Lawrence, Gweneth Morton, Shannon Cox, Audrey Diestelkamp, Lauren Levite, Kelly Haberstroh, and Patty Rosati and her team.

To Leah Rose Kolakowski, Molly Fehr, and Joel Tippie, for creating such a gorgeous cover and design.

To my UK agent, Claire Wilson, and to Safae El-Ouahabi at RCW, along with my PRH UK editors, India Chambers and Naomi Colthurst, for finding a place for *Looking for Smoke* in the UK. And thanks to the rest of the team at PRH UK, including Shreeta Shah, Jannine Saunders, and Harriet Venn.

To my film agents, Michelle Kroes and Berni Vann at CAA, for seeing the cinematic potential in this story and this setting.

To my Pitch Wars mentor, Fiona McLaren, for helping me sharpen my vision for this story. Your advice and guidance brought it to another level and set me on an incredible path.

To Jared and Jesse, my expert sources who I harassed with questions far more often than I should have. I couldn't have made this work without you.

To my critique partner Karen. You were my first real writing friend. Thank you for suffering through the very first draft of this book and supporting me all the way.

To Emily and Lisa, my earliest readers. Your excitement gave me the confidence to keep writing.

To Charlie Crow Chief, Elliot Fox, and Robert Hall, for helping me include a few special words from the beautiful Blackfoot language.

To Isi Hendrix. I joke that you basically became my life coach, but that is the honest truth. You have been a wealth of wisdom, help, support, and laughs. I am so grateful to know you and honored to watch you shine.

To Gabi Burton, Paula Gleeson, and Dante Medema, for giving me very good advice at very pivotal moments. You steered me in the direction I needed to go.

To my There or Squares. I am so lucky to know each of you: Sana Z. Ahmed, Emily Charlotte, and S. Hati, whose thoughts were vital during edits; Megan Davidhizar, who has been a friend and sounding board through each step of this long process; and Christine L. Arnold, Aimee Davis, Channelle Desamours, Lally Hi, Laurie Lascos, P. H. Low, and Valo Wing, whose endless support means the world to me. I love you all and would be lost without this group.

And thank you, reader, for picking up my book. I'm honored you chose to read this story, and I hope it stays with you.

—K. A.

A Note from Cynthia Leitich Smith, Author-Curator of Heartdrum

Dear reader,

Looking for Smoke is an intimate, intense, and layered mystery. The story asks us to consider who, among the suspects, could murder two teenage Native girls. With respect and sensitivity, author K. A. Cobell calls on us to reflect on the complexities of the heart and the characters' connections to one another.

To those of you who are Native readers, I send love, courage, and healing as we combat the crisis of Missing and Murdered Indigenous Women, Girls, and Two-Spirit Relatives. As you read about this fictional case, I hope that it offered an opportunity to process what's happening, to achieve a sense of catharsis, and to remember that, even amid tragedy and loss, there are everyday heroes in our communities. We are so much more than the worst of what can happen to us. We deserve to live full and fulfilling lives unburdened by vulnerability and violence. Given the steady rise in Indigenous advocacy and political power, I'm prayerful that, together, we can end the #MMIWG2S crisis. We will see a day when stolen sisters are a memory.

To those who are non-Native readers, I hope that you have gained a heightened awareness and understanding of our strength, humanity, and the challenges faced by our young people. Only about 7 percent of the population within the United States and Canada is Indigenous.

The solidarity of friends like you is key to building a better, safer future for us all.

Have you read many stories by and about Blackfeet people or other Native people? Hopefully, *Looking for Smoke* will inspire you to read more. The novel is published by Heartdrum, a Native-focused imprint of HarperCollins, which offers books about young Native heroes by Indigenous authors and illustrators.

Mvto,
Cynthia Leitich Smith

K. A. COBELL, *Staa'tssipisstaakii*, is an enrolled member of the Blackfeet Nation. She currently lives in the Pacific Northwest, where she spends her time writing books, chasing her kids through the never-ending rain, and scouring the inlet beaches for sand dollars and hermit crabs. *Looking for Smoke* is her debut novel.

CYNTHIA LEITICH SMITH is the bestselling, acclaimed author of books for all ages, including *Sisters of the Neversea*, *Rain Is Not My Indian Name*, *Indian Shoes*, *Jingle Dancer*, *Harvest House*, and *Hearts Unbroken*, which won the American Indian Youth Literature Award; she is also the anthologist of *Ancestor Approved: Intertribal Stories for Kids*. She has been an NSK Neustadt Laureate. Cynthia is the author-curator of Heartdrum, a Native-focused imprint at Harper-Collins Children's Books, and has served as the Katherine Paterson Endowed Chair on the faculty of the MFA program in writing for children and young adults at Vermont College of Fine Arts. She is a citizen of the Muscogee Nation and lives in Austin, Texas. You can visit Cynthia online at cynthialeitichsmith.com.

In 2014, We Need Diverse Books (WNDB) began as a simple hashtag on Twitter. The social media campaign soon grew into a 501(c)(3) nonprofit with a team that spans the globe. WNDB is supported by a network of writers, illustrators, agents, editors, teachers, librarians, and book lovers, all united under the same goal—to create a world where every child can see themselves in the pages of a book. You can learn more about WNDB programs at www.diversebooks.org.